To my Yeh-Yeh.
1913-2006

Marjorie M. Liu

The Red Heart *of* Jade

A DIRK & STEELE NOVEL

AVON

An Imprint of HarperCollinsPublishers

This is a work of fiction. Names, characters, places, and incidents are products of the author's imagination or are used fictitiously and are not to be construed as real. Any resemblance to actual events, locales, organizations, or persons, living or dead, is entirely coincidental.

AVON BOOKS
An Imprint of HarperCollins*Publishers*
10 East 53rd Street
New York, New York 10022-5299

Copyright © 2006 by Marjorie M. Liu
ISBN 978-0-06-201988-2
www.avonromance.com

First Avon Books paperback printing: March 2011

Avon Trademark Reg. U.S. Pat. Off. and in Other Countries, Marca Registrada, Hecho en U.S.A.
HarperCollins® is a registered trademark of HarperCollins Publishers.

Printed in the U.S.A.

10 9 8 7 6 5 4 3 2 1

ACKNOWLEDGMENTS

Many thanks to Christopher Keeslar, for his infinite patience, compassion, and sheer talent as an editor; Lucienne Diver, who is sharp, funny, and wonderfully supportive; Brianna Yamashita, for all her creativity and hard work at Dorchester; Nikki, for her insights; and my parents, who are the kind of best friends most kids can only dream of having.

I would also like to thank my fantastic readers, who don't seem to mind joining me on these wild rides inside my head. Thank you for the company.

Because of you, my flowerlike fair,
The swift years like waters flow—

I have sought you everywhere,
And at last I find you here,
In a dark room full of woe—

—Tang Xianzu (1550–1616)

Chapter One

In the moments before Dean Campbell opened his eyes to the fire burning him alive, he found himself lost within a dream of stone and light, where bones crunched underfoot and a chain pressed hard around his ankle, binding him tight within the center of a raggedy sand circle. A deep dream, an old dream, the kind he rarely had anymore, and it was only the scent of roasting meats that pulled him from the mystery of shadows inside his mind. Pulled him free and floating, consciousness returning with a hard peeling light that became, after a moment's confusion, an inferno, a sheet of pure heat washing over his naked body.

Fire. He was on fire.

Dean screamed. He screamed until his eyes bulged, but he made no sound. His throat was hostage. And like his voice, his body refused him. He could not move. Paralyzed, or maybe he was already dead and this was hell: forced to watch himself burn to ash, his life given up like a paper doll to a matchstick, some human sacrifice to the white-hot beast licking his eyes, melting his mouth, pushing deep inside his ears to roar like thunder; a sound to ride his terror upon as he silently screamed, screamed and screamed until something broke inside his head and shattered.

He felt hands on his body. Real hands, the kind he had not felt in years. Small and female, delicate. Moving against his chest, sinking into his splitting flesh. Scratching. Cutting. Carving an incision above his heart. He felt no pain, no—*nerve endings melting, sloughing away like old skin*—but he sensed those fingers—*oh God, oh God*—slide into his body past bone to wrap tight around his hammering heart, and he thought, *This is it, I'm gonna die, I'm already dead, what a loser, what a goddamn way to end it.* But as the hand squeezed inside his chest, fingers unforgiving, another voice intruded on Dean's mind, a voice loud and clear and unfamiliar, and he heard a man say, *No, not yet, not again.*

And just like that, the fire boomed, puffed, the pressure eased. The world collapsed into darkness.

Screams. Dean heard terrible screams. He thought someone else must be hurt, dying—*get up, get up, get your gun and fight*—but after a moment of dazed horrified wonder he realized that it was him—his voice, finally working—and what a beautiful, awful sound. He could not shut his mouth. He could not stop his body from writhing as the paralysis eased. Yet still, blindness; a darkness absolute … until Dean raised a shaking hand and touched his face.

He opened his eyes. The world came into softly lit focus: a white ceiling, creamy walls, a darkened window covered in ivory sheers. Hotel finery at its best. Clean and perfect and not on fire.

Not on fire.

He sucked in his breath and closed his eyes. Gripped the rumpled sheets between his fists to steady himself before slowly, carefully, touching his body. He was naked, covered in sweat, but his skin was smooth and he felt no pain. He was whole. Intact. Still had a penis and all the other bits that went with it. No bad smells, like meat or smoke. Just the light, sweet scent of orchids.

So. Just a dream, then. A goddamn dream.

Dean sat up. Cold metal spilled from the hollow of his throat; a woman's locket, hanging from a thin chain around his neck. He gripped the necklace hard, savoring the rounded edge that cut into his palm. Gulped down long cold breaths that did nothing to slow his heart. He felt woozy, nauseated. Tried to imagine the fire as a dream and could not. The heat was still too real.

His knuckles brushed against his chest, the skin above his heart. He felt a scar, but that was familiar, old news. Except, just below it he touched something else, a ridge that should not be, and Dean opened his eyes.

There was a mark. A curving red line, like a welt or bloody tattoo, the afterthought of a sharp knife. Dean pressed his fingers against it, tracing the edges. He felt pain. The first pain since opening his eyes to the fire, the dream.

Or maybe not a dream at all. Dean remembered those small hands, the sensation of fingers pushing, pushing so damn hard into his chest, wrapping around his heart. Squeezing. He remembered that voice in his head. He remembered fire.

All of it, so real. Real enough to kill. Real enough to almost make sense, considering what he had been chasing for the past three days. Which, given his luck, meant one thing only.

He was in some very deep shit.

Night in Taipei. It brought out a different crowd. Dean rode the hotel elevator down to the main lobby, surrounded on all sides by the sleek and dazzling, men and women glittering at a high sheen like polished dia-

3

monds, airbrushed and ready for an evening of pretend fun and deadly earnest networking. Little games of the rich, with a wineglass in hand. Do a little dance, sing a little song. Get down tonight.

Dean felt like the odd duck in a cage of swans. Unshaved, unpressed, almost unhinged; just jeans and dirty sneakers, with highbrow brownie points deducted for his threadbare *Transformers* T-shirt and scuffed denim jacket. High fashion, Wal-Mart style. Not even a shower, and God, he figured he needed one by now. Three days into his current assignment, running the streets like a hound on the hunt, and in Taiwan's summer heat. Like doing the Iron Man in a sauna, with no time to stop, no time to rest. At least, not until day— and Dean thought he would have been better off staying awake.

Nausea swarmed his throat. He pushed it down.

Smile, he told himself grimly. *Not now, because it'll freak out the pretty people, but smile. Get a fucking smile in your motherfucking heart, you son of a bitch.*

Because that was the only way he was going to have the strength to get out of this elevator, walk out of this hotel, and face the rest of this night. No other option. If a man did not smile he just might cry—or lie down and die—and that was just no way to carry on. Dean had things to do. He had to keep on trucking. People were depending on him, lives had to be saved, and if that meant being the most cheerful son of a bitch on this planet, then goddammit, he was going to be that man even if it killed him.

Which it might. His chest still throbbed. Dean curled his hand against his thigh; he wanted to keep prodding the mysterious injury, had spent the past thirty minutes in front of a mirror, naked, doing just that. Staring at the curling incision, staring and staring until it was all he could see. No way to shrug it off, either. Might be he had witnessed enough shit over the past three days to qualify for nightmares, but this was physical, real, not self-inflicted. Dean's nails were clean, and there was nothing around his bed that could have made that incision. Nothing to cut, nothing to scratch, not unless his mind was playing tricks. Riding high on insane.

The elevator doors opened. Dean entered an octagon-shaped alcove framed by dark marble and golden globe lights made of glass. He smelled orchids, lilies; the air tinkled with the fine murmur of quiet voices, the low melody of piano, the click of high heels, and the chime of fine china. The ceiling floated more than one hundred feet above his head, emanating a sheer warm glow from tiny lights set like baubles in speckled white. Beyond the elevators, in a wide hall leading directly into the main lobby, men and women mingled in suits and evening gowns, casual chic; dressed for nights on the town, for the tropical heat, for the elegance demanded by wealth and good breeding and lives far from the street, the universal gutter with which Dean was so familiar: violence and poverty and good old-fashioned dirt.

Some of the people looked at Dean like he was dirt. Which was fine. He knew the score. Expected nothing less. He did not look like a nice man. He did not look rich. Of course, that was the entire point.

The guns strapped to his ankles chafed. The rig beneath his T-shirt was not much better. Three illegal weapons, smuggled into the country, loaded and ready to go. Dean could already feel them in his hands—natural and perfect extensions. Practically the best parts of him. Right up there with his mind.

He let go of his control as he walked through the lobby, taking a circular path that led him directly through the crowd. His shields dropped, the world shifting as flesh melted into light, bodies quivering into comet trails, pillars of energy, leaving wakes in the air like strings and threads. Footprints, fingerprints, soul prints—echoes of the living, lingering vibrations quivering to some quantum jazz, making him feel like a musician as he moved through the light—tasting the world, trying to find the right color and note, the perfect combination of identity and murder.

But it was a waste of time. He found no fire as he stared through the eyes of the people around him. He found no death as he pulled himself along the fading trails of energy crisscrossing the lobby, nothing at all as he tracked the actions of every man and woman who had walked this floor in the past day. Picture shows flickered through his head—incontrovertible testimonies—remote views not barred by distance or time. Hard sex, fights, parties and national monuments and designer shops. Interiors of limousines and dance clubs, cigarette smoke and crying babies. Nothing incriminating. Perfectly boring. Not one person to use a bullet on.

And you were expecting what? A break in the case? A miracle? When everything else about this assignment has been shit in the drain?

Yeah, well. There was nothing wrong with being an optimist. Especially now, given that he was so totally and irrevocably screwed.

No traces in my room, nothing recent in the hall. I burned like there was a flamethrower up my ass, got sliced in the chest, and the bastard didn't even leave a trail. Fucking uncivilized.

And unnatural. Just like everything else he had encountered over the past three days. Dean had been stymied before on particularly tough cases, but nothing like this. Taipei had a killer on the loose, an arsonist and psychopath—a cruel vindictive son of a bitch—but tracking the man was like trying to find a ghost; a creature with no energy left to share, someone who did not exist. Dean had found nothing of him at any of the crime scenes, just impressions from the lingering vibrations of the dead—their last visions, the world around them as they burned. The sensation of a man watching. Dark eyes.

Not much of a description. Nothing else to go on, though. Nothing about the energies crisscrossing the lobby that tickled Dean's brain as he soaked in the light; nothing familiar, not even some gut instinct crying, *There, you might just have him there.*

He shut off his inner sight, and the world snapped back into place. People had bodies again; the material had form, substance. All those bits and pieces of energy, invisible. He almost wished that was not the case. He liked seeing people as nothing but light. It put life into perspective, calmed him down, all Zen-like. He needed some calm right now. Really badly.

His wandering had brought him close to the massive flower display arranged near the hotel entrance: a tanglewood, sprouting orchids and wild lilies, misted ferns and curling vines; other, more delicate blossoms tucked away like pixies. Dean heard laughter. Women, voices low, husky, warm like whiskey with the rough burn. He peered around the flowers and saw short skirts, long golden legs, fake breasts, perfect hair. Some of the faces were nice, too. Six high-maintenance women, glossy mouths shining, clinging to the arms of a tall man in white—white linen pants, loose white linen shirt, long white hair framing a pale chiseled face sporting mirrored sunglasses. Definite dye-job. A diamond glinted from one ear. The women looked ready to tear open his fly and take him down like a fat, juicy deer. Dean thought it must be nice to be that wanted.

The man in white smiled at the ladies, but not with his teeth; his mouth simply curved and curved, curved so much it was like looking at the rock star version of an albino clown. Very disturbing. Very familiar. Dean recognized him, had seen that pale mug on a billboard at the airport, on the covers of local magazines, on Tai-wanese television, in a music video playing on monitors in a night market. He was the new hot tamale, the best man around town. Always in white, always with those glasses, with that same damn smile cutting his face like an upside-down frown.

Bai Shen. White God. Singer, model, playboy. Not in any immediate danger of spending an evening alone. Bastard.

Dean backed away toward the glass doors. He studied Bai Shen, the spectacle surrounding him, and thought for a moment he was being watched through those mir-rored sunglasses. Watched with the kind of intensity that could explain the sudden shift of that curving smile into nothing more than a crooked line.

Odd. Dean did not like it.

You're being paranoid. He's a pansy-ass pretty boy, who at the worst thinks you're white trash. He's not some mother-fucking psycho with pyromaniac tendencies. That's just kooky.

Maybe. But it still rubbed Dean the wrong way, and he had no trouble matching that mirrored gaze. Pure stubbornness, defiance, a childhood spent dealing with Philadelphia steel men, gruff sons of bitches who worked hard, drank harder, and who could probably turn this rock star albino-wannabe into toilet paper with noth-ing but spit and a glare. All kinds of good times.

Bai Shen looked away first. He turned his head and said something to one of the women hanging on to his arm. A cheap save. Dean smiled and left the hotel.

The night air hit him hard; heat stuffed itself down his lungs, along with the scents of exhaust, smog, a sin-gularly wet odor of humid cement, fresh with grease and some distant open sewage line. Cabdrivers leaned out their windows, alternately spitting beetlenut juice on the sidewalk and whistling.

Dean ignored them. The latest crime scene was ten

minutes away, easy at a fast walk. He had made the trip earlier that day, but at nine in the morning the area was too crowded: cops swarming, family mourning, nosy neighbors, journalists with their microphones swinging. Better to go back to the hotel, catch up on some food and sleep. Try again when things got quiet.

Yeah, right. What a joke.

Skyscrapers ranged tall and sharp, framed against a nighttime backdrop of light-reflected yellow clouds. At street level the roads narrowed and the shops transformed, high-end polished gems of austere beauty giving way to colorful crammed alcoves full of plastic jewelry, trendy cast-offs, and blasting music. Beetlenut girls, dressed in glittering shreds of almost nothing, tottered down the street in six-inch wedge heels, calling out to cabdrivers with their baskets in hand, giving Dean wary looks as he passed, ready to kick his ass if he tried anything. He wanted to tell them not to worry, that he knew they weren't prostitutes, but he settled for not looking. Hard, given the amount of skin showing, but he was not a complete sleaze.

He was not alone, either. A crow cawed, swooping down low, skimming the top of his head with a wing. Dean caught the flash of a golden eye, winking light like a tiny sun, and then it blinked and disappeared into the hot night; a ghost, a shadow flying. Dean bit down a shout, wished he could call the bird back, give him a sign, tell him it was time for words and human flesh instead of just glimpses and wings. He needed to talk to someone about what had just happened. He needed to give a warning. His backup needed backup, because if the killer had pegged Dean … well, bad times. But it would be worse timing now to make an ass of himself trying to get that bird's attention. It would bring attention to the bird. And Dean was not going to let that happen. Besides, Koni would find him again when he had something useful. Until then, the more distance the better.

Sweat rolled down his body. His jacket was too hot, but he needed the cover to hide the rig strapped beneath his shirt. The leather rubbed the edge of the cut, which continued to throb. He tried to ignore it. Tried not to think of fire, ash … but after a minute of wrestling with himself, gave up. He forced himself to embrace the memory, to turn it over and over in his head, examining every detail and sensation, the lick of fire that had rippled over his naked body. And as he thought of himself, he thought of the dead, the recent dead, moments of death and dying. Quiet murders, without struggle. Other men bursting into flame. Dean forced himself to relive the clips and fragments of those lives he had soaked into himself during his brief stays at the crime scenes.

It was good that his stomach was empty—good, too, that he was better at seeing the present than the past. He did not know how many times he had seen those deaths—too many, for sure—but someone had to watch, someone, anyone—because those people had died alone with a murderer, with no avenue of escape, no rhyme or reason or warning, and at least now there was another pair of eyes, another witness who could say, *I see. I see and I will make it stop. I promise.*

"I promise," Dean murmured, sinking deeper into himself, rubbing his mind against memory, all that remained of flesh and blood and dream. Fifteen people lost, with nothing to show for their lives but the remains of fires that had burned bodies to black dust while leaving homes untouched.

Impossible, said the local authorities. No accelerants, no sources of heat, no witnesses reporting explosions or screams or voices through the walls. The only clue, the only observation in a week of death, was from an old woman, a neighbor to one of the early victims, who had reported hearing a roaring sound while standing on her balcony. The kind of soft roar one might hear when striking a match; the hiss before the flame. Except, louder. Much louder.

Ignition. Fire. Burning alive in silence, at heats matching those of a crematorium. Not just sparks or a dropped cigarette. Not just a well-placed match. And not, as some had speculated back home in the office of Dirk & Steele, some weird case of mass spontaneous human combustion, which, if it did exist, was still an extremely rare phenomenon that did not descend in bursts of fiery fury to strike down helpless individuals like fat marshmallows on sticks. There was simply too much fire in this case. Too many occurrences in one city, and within just a week. Which meant that something else was involved. *Someone* else.

And that someone has got me pegged.

Bad. Not part of the plan. Good thing Dean had orders to wrap things up fast, tight. Shoot to kill, even if the boss did want him to ask questions, find out why the murderer was burning people—make sure all that death was not some kind of big mistake.

Right. Tea and crumpets, a nice little heart-to-heart. Get all touchy-feely, just before the bullets and *the fuckin' fire.* Jesus Christ. Dean did not take much stock in his own intelligence, but he wasn't that dumb. He didn't care, either, if he was supposed to play by the rules, be all noble. Bullets were better. Bullets were safer. They were more … just.

You're not an executioner. You're not judge and jury.

No, but he had a duty to protect others, himself, and Dean preferred life over death. He could make himself forget things like guilt and heroism and honor if it meant keeping people safe, if it meant another day with a beating heart, a whole body. Dean did not mess around. He had made that mistake once before—tried to do the right thing, been weak—and it had cost him everything. Made him dead in places, put holes in his spirit.

Not again. Not ever. Dean had enough scars. A charm hanging around his neck.

Dean turned down a darkened street, skirting bicycles, badly parked cars, fluttering laundry and plants too large for their cracked pots; old men sitting on plastic chairs with cigarettes in hand, T-shirts rolled up over their sweaty chests, shooting the breeze over battered mahjong tables lit by fluorescent lamps, with the click and clack tapping the night—and past them, old women gossiping on stoops, watching children kick balls in the darkness, screaming and laughing, voices ringing off the walls. Televisions sputtered through windows, pots and pans clanging; Dean smelled roasted meat. Packs of dogs scuffed through garbage, watching him with high whines in their throats.

The street twisted, curved. Dean did not get lost, though he imagined doing so on purpose: misplacing himself in the maze, putting off another night, becoming nothing more than a memory, a thread, his own energy just lifting off and dissipating like a cloud into the smog, into the heat, melting away like one big drop of nothing in the world.

But he ran out of time. Darkness fell away. Light entered, bright and artificial, and Dean left the quiet residential street for a world that blasted him with color, with crowds and whistles and battling scents; rolling neon and billboards that covered buildings, crowding for attention with American imports like a three-story McDonald's and a high-class Kentucky Fried Chicken, Colonel Sanders presiding like a fat white ghost. Young people pushed and shoved in their sexy finest, spilling out of booming clubs and stores, cell phones hanging from necks like silver bullets, laughing and smiling, unbothered by the heat, the crush, because it was night in Taipei and it was time for the wild to come out, the good times. Dean felt like an old man compared to the kids around him; thirty-six on his way to forty, with his first white hairs right around the corner. Pretty soon he'd be like some lonely cat lady, except with guns and *Playboy*s and comic books.

God. What an image.

The crowds thinned, the people changed. The high-class entertainment zone was an island surrounded by run-down cozy residential neighborhoods; pathways and backstreets cutting across the area like dark veins. The apartment complex, the crime scene, was a dull gray building that rose on the edge of an alley, away from the glitz. Thick wires hung in tangled masses down its walls—electrical, telephone, television—swinging free and dandy around balconies and windows and satellite dishes.

He was just about ready to get down to business when something hard and small hit the side of his head. Dean clapped a hand over his scalp and whirled, staring. His sight shifted, but only partially; flesh mixed with energy, thrumming, and directly across from him, deep inside a narrow space cutting between two buildings like a dark vein, Dean found a golden humming thread cutting through shadow like an electric current. He stepped close, wading through bouncing teenagers, and reached out with his senses. Found someone familiar.

Dean's vision shifted again, this time back to the real world. He blinked hard, but darkness perfectly concealed the hiding man. Dean hesitated. Another rock flew out of the alley. A small one. It hit him hard, just above his groin.

"Son of a bitch," Dean growled, and left the sidewalk for the shadows, ignoring the strong scent of piss in the gutters. The light did not reach; for a moment Dean went blind, and then … movement, into the dim light. Dean saw a lean male face framed by loose black hair. Sharp jaw, high cheekbones, narrow nose. Eyes golden and bright and utterly inhuman. Rippling flesh, following a line of soft black pushing through deeply tanned skin to course down neck and arm.

Feathers. Soft feathers. Disappearing in a heartbeat like a dream. Extraordinary, creepy, and out of this world. Kind of like everything in Dean's life.

Something sharp jabbed his ribs.

"Honey," Dean said. "Not in public. You know I'm shy."

The knife dug deeper. "You're a real bastard, Dean. You know that?"

"My mother put it on my birth certificate." Dean pushed the knife away from his side. "Hello, personal space. No sharp objects allowed beyond the periphery of my toes. It makes my bladder nervous."

"Then get ready to pee." Koni shifted his weight and flicked his wrist; the knife disappeared into the loose pocket of his black linen pants. His white tank was riddled with holes; tattoos covered his arms. Dean wondered where he had gotten the duds. Last he checked, Koni was not much for packing or stashing clothes. Like, not even underwear. Which made sense, in a twisted sort of way. But still, more than he wanted to know.

Dean said, "You dive-bombed me earlier. What is it?"

"Change in plans. Behind you, on the street. There are some men watching, and I don't think they're armed with daisies. They've been with you since the Far Eastern."

A sucker punch. Dean's stomach hurt. "I was followed?"

"Like a big dumb blonde joke. But if it makes you

feel better, they're good. I might have missed them if I hadn't been in the air."

Small comfort. Dean glanced out at the street, scanning faces, the rumbling, roving crowd. After a moment, he singled out two men standing just outside the slanted doorway of a chic rice soup bar. They were definitely not members of the youth movement; the men dressed like twins in tacky uniform: checkered short-sleeve shirts, black pants with the waists hauled up high; dark leather man-purses clutched tight in their hands. They watched Dean. Stared at him. No mistaking that look, either. They knew exactly who he was, and were not bothering to hide it.

Yeah. This was turning out to be a great night. Dean thought about shooting himself just to get it over with.

"Over there," he said. "The odd couple."

"Yes." Koni leaned away from the wall. Water dripped on his head from the old air conditioner rattling mercilessly above him. "At first I thought they were cops, that someone had seen you breaking into those other crime scenes." Dean began to disagree, but Koni held up his hand. "I know. The setup isn't right. Cops wouldn't just stand there like that. They would have made contact by now. Busted your ass. There wouldn't be a reason not to."

"I don't like where this is going," Dean said.

"Neither do I. I almost wish they were the police."

Dean could not bring himself to disagree, even though he had promised, sworn on his life, made a blood oath that he and Koni would stay under the official government radar—and not only because what they were doing was slightly illegal. Drawing the attention of local authorities would mean something worse than jail time. Like, questions. Maybe even media attention. Bad, because there were quite a few people who might not understand why an internationally respected detective agency like Dirk & Steele would be interested in investigating the murderous efforts of a serial arsonist halfway around the globe, no matter how heinous the crimes. After all, no Americans had died, and this was a country where gun ownership was illegal and fire was just another weapon—as were household chemicals, knives, rat poison, rope, or whatever else a person with premeditation could wrangle.

Nor did it matter that Dirk & Steele had an understanding with certain key members of the Taiwanese government; the Taipei police would *not* appreciate the implication that they needed help in capturing their murderer, even if they did. Local law enforcement argued the lack of evidence was due to a genius perp or just dumb luck. Dean could not rule out either one of those possibilities. But after tonight, after the past few days, he was quite certain that intellect or luck had nothing to do with the murders themselves. Just power. Cruelty. If there was another reason to set people on fire, he wanted to hear it.

"So," Koni said. "What's the plan?"

"No plan," Dean replied. "We finish what we started. Stop the fires. Stay alive. Anything else we play by ear."

"Sounds dangerous. As usual."

"You want fuzzy bunnies and happy endings, you better take to the air right now, buddy, and never look back. This is gonna be a rough night. It's *already* been a rough night." He hesitated, and lifted up his shirt.

Koni blinked. "You're flashing me, Dean. Stop. Please."

Dean rolled his eyes. "Look. I've got an injury. I got it tonight. Someone cut my chest. Set me on fire. *While I was in my hotel room.*"

"Dean—"

"No. I'm not kidding."

Koni stared. "That's impossible. You're fucking with

me. You have to be. There's no way he could have pegged you."

No way at all, Dean argued silently. But expecting the unexpected was part of the game, and that fire and cut in his chest were signs. Signs that he had messed up, signs that the killer was just too good, signs that they were in over their heads. Signs and portents, a future that was too hot to handle. Literally.

Maybe I shouldn't have said anything, Dean thought, but struck the idea down, fast. No doubt it would have been easier to keep his mouth shut, but that would be a lie—a lie by omission—and it was not just his own life at stake. If the killer knew about Dean, then Koni might not be far behind. And if those men out on the street were following them …

He had to know the risks. *All* the risks.

Dean waited, quiet. Koni studied his face, also silent, and then slowly, carefully, leaned close, studying the curving scar. He did not touch it.

Dean said, "I'm not lying."

"I know," Koni replied. "But it's still impossible. I don't see any evidence of fire. No burns. And you're still alive. Our killer doesn't leave anyone alive, Dean."

"No one we know of, anyway."

"And you're sure it's him?"

"I'm not sure about anything but, hello, fire? Us chasing a serial murderer who just might be a pyro-kinetic? Tell me that's not too much of a coincidence."

"I don't believe in coincidence. But I had to ask."

"Trust me, if I could have blamed the fire on a nightmare I would have. But there's nothing imaginary about that cut."

"It's deep. You should be bleeding. You need stitches."

"It was a clean wound. No blood. Just the incision."

"God. You're screwed."

Dean scowled. "If the murderer knows who I am, and now I'm being followed by those jokers out there—"

"Like I said. Screwed. Both of us." Koni pressed back against the concrete wall and closed his eyes. "I need a drink. A goddamn cigarette. I'm too tired for this shit."

"How do you think I feel?" Dean dropped his shirt. "You think those guys out there work for our killer?"

"If they do, then we've got a bigger problem on our hands than simple murder."

"We've got an operation," Dean said. "Organization. Not just a psycho who likes to play with fire."

The two men stared at each other.

"Dean," Koni said slowly. "We need a better plan."

"Koni," Dean replied. "I need to get to that crime scene. Right now."

"You'll be bait. You won't be able to shake those guys."

"I got no choice. We're not going to find answers anywhere else." Dean glanced over his shoulder. The men were still watching. Bold, confident. A bad sign. He felt like giving them the finger or waving them over for a thumb-wrestling contest to the death. Anything to end the mystery, the possibilities of who those men might be working for.

Don't think about it. Don't you dare. Not now.

Koni said, "Fine. Okay, then. Let's go."

"You're coming with me? On the ground?"

"Don't look so surprised. My legs work as well as my wings." And Koni pushed past him and headed out of the alley, turning right, moving quick and sparing only one hard look at the men standing on the other side of the street. The trackers did not blink, showed no reaction at all. Dean turned around to watch them, walking backward, throwing in a moonwalk for good measure, because hell, acting serious and moody wasn't going to make much of a difference at this point. He smiled at the men. Made the sign of a shooting gun. Pointed, and mouthed, *Bang, bang. You're dead.*

Koni, glancing at him, said, "Every time I begin to have respect for your intelligence, you do something like that."

"It's a gift," Dean replied. "My powers of survival and intuition are endless."

"Ha." Koni sidestepped a pile of broken glass with a curious mincing motion. He was not wearing shoes. Around them, the ground glittered with yet more glass, odd bits of trash, some dark puddles fed by trickles of water streaming out of hoses where women were washing vegetables and small children. Koni did not complain, but Dean felt the debris crunch beneath his sneakers.

"You should have given me a pack to carry for you," Dean said quietly. "It wouldn't have been any trouble."

"I don't like depending on anyone," Koni replied. "No offense. I'm just used to taking care of myself."

"You've been with the agency for more than a year," Dean reminded him. "You can rely on us, you know."

Koni said nothing. Dean did not push. There was no formula for making a man feel at home among a crowd that clung together like family. For Dean, it was easy. Always had been. First meeting and he'd curled up like a little kitten in a warm towel. Wasn't like that for everyone, but he had been alone too long, and recognized a good thing when he saw it. The agents at Dirk & Steele were the only people he had; the secrets they shared formed a bond no one on the outside would ever understand. Or believe.

Us against them, he thought. Minorities, hiding in plain sight against the rest of the world. Dirk & Steele might operate in a very public setting, with clients rang-ing from governments to the poor, but its entire image was a bald-faced lie: that all of its agents, men and women spread across Dirk & Steele's worldwide offices, were normal ordinary human beings.

Flesh and blood, yes. Human, yes. But not ordinary. Call it genetics, odd wiring, twists of magic and fate— but the agents of Dirk & Steele had abilities beyond the normal ken of man. And even among them, some were more extraordinary than others. Like Koni and the rest of his kind: shape-shifters, men and women who changed into animals at will. Tigers, crows, cheetahs, dolphins— dragons, too—and God only knew what else. Magic and science, coming together to form miracles embodied by flesh, blood.

Little more than a year ago, Dean would have thought shape-shifters nothing more than fairy tales, figments of some overactive and highly drugged imagination. Hell, it was hard enough for him to believe some of the shit *he* could pull off. Anything else belonged in the *Twilight Zone.* Which was … totally right on.

Dean stopped at a small booth where an old man hawked cheap clothing. He glanced over his shoulder; the men following them had fallen back, but they were still islands in the surging crowd, staring, eyes cold and hard.

Gritting his teeth, Dean turned away and grabbed a pair of large foam flip-flops from a bin. He pushed cash into the seller's hand. No time for bargaining. He dropped the shoes beside Koni, who looked at them, and then Dean.

"They're covered in flowers," he said.

"Weenie," Dean said, and then turned away, walking fast. No time to waste—none at all—not with those men following them, and a trail fading fast. He felt Koni move up close behind him, and that was reassurance enough, to have someone watching his back as he approached the apartment building where the last murder had occurred.

He split his vision, extending his fingers as he glided through the shadows, translating energies as his mind sorted and pressed and peeled, searching for anything familiar—anything at all that was reminiscent of the areas around the fourteen other crime scenes he had spent the past three days scouring. It was not enough to search inside the buildings; sometimes trails could be found outside as well, glimpses into lives that had intersected with the victims'. Sometimes he saw the victims themselves; the trails they had left before dying, not yet faded from the air. People had to go places, after all. Killers used legs. They could not fly.

Well, maybe some people could fly. But ... he hoped not in this case.

The world inside Dean's head filled with light: a tapestry, a quilt of intersecting threads, people leaving behind bits of themselves with every step, layering emanations upon emanation, trails of energy and vibration until it almost seemed the air was heavy enough to walk on; a stairway to heaven, to hell, to secrets and lies.

Dean waded through soul prints. He took measure of the adding echoes, opening himself to remote glimpses of lives that were ordinary, full of television and playing children and families at tables—a man singing karaoke like a wounded dog—a woman sitting naked in front of a computer—dishwashing and arguing and sexy ups and downs—lives that were quiet—wild—lonely—

—violent—

—deadly—

Dean froze. Just a glimpse, an awful premonition. He had walked through the thread so quickly that was all he had time for.

No, he thought. *I can't be that lucky. There's no way.*

No way, not a chance, not a flaming turd in hell. Not

21

after three days and a personal apocalypse. Dean turned, looking hard. Light tangled; it was impossible to know which thread he had touched—just that it was there, somewhere, in the mess.

He took a deep breath and cleared his mind, trying to steady his heart and hands. His chest throbbed, but he pushed down the pain, the memories attached with it, the uncertainty. No fear, no doubts. Not now. Dean swallowed hard and took a step. Looking for a victim.

The reaction was instantaneous; a punch to the gut. Images overwhelmed him. Dean forced himself to remain still, but the rush was hard, harder than anything he had ever felt, and he wanted to run, to turn away, to shut off his mind. Instead, he let himself taste ash on his tongue, and gazed upon a vision of a dark room, a body on the floor with duct tape wound all around like a mummy's skin, bandages sticky, gray. The floor was black and wet around the body, which was mostly torso; like a potato with stumps.

Movement. A hulking body silhouetted by a window. In one fat hand, a sheaf of papers; a photograph, the face too blurred to see. In the other hand, a bulging plastic sack from a local bookstore. The mouth of the sack was open. Dean got a good look inside. He saw blood. Other stuff.

And then, light. Fire.

Dean moved. He left the thread at a run, but the echo remained with him as an imprint, a stamp upon his mind, a screaming line pulling and pulling like a rope. Koni called out, and then suddenly was at his side, racing with him down a narrow unlit walkway between a clothing shop and a DVD parlor. Instinct guided Dean, the trail inside his head tugging like a rope. The air smelled rank; it was difficult to see, but ahead of them a fluorescent bulb flickered over a wide metal door. Bingo.

Dean reached beneath his shirt and unclipped his gun. He held it out to Koni, but the shape-shifter did not take the weapon.

"I don't do guns," he said, breathing hard.

Dean stumbled. "You shitting me? When did that happen?"

"I thought you knew. I told Roland when he hired me on. It's why he usually puts me on surveillance."

"Fuck." Dean clicked off the safety. "No one told me. I just assumed."

Koni flicked his wrist; the knife appeared like a bright spot in his palm. Dean did not know how he had hidden it without sleeves.

"Hypocrite," he said.

"Differences in philosophy," Koni replied, glancing over his shoulder. "Those men stopped following us."

Bad. No way those men would just drop off. Not unless they had a good reason. And any reason good for them could not possibly be good for Dean and Koni.

The apartment building's door was unlocked and they barreled through, racing up the stairs. Dean tried to catch that familiar thread, reaching out across the space between himself and the victim's present: a remote view. He managed a glimpse, and saw their target was no longer in the apartment. Above them came a scuffing sound, large and loud.

Dean grabbed Koni's shoulder. Both men stopped, breathing hard, listening. The person above hesitated on the stairs. But instead of coming down, he began to go up. Fast.

"Shit," Dean hissed. His legs and chest hurt. Breathing was damn hard in this heat; running worse. Koni passed him and leaped up the narrow metal stairs four and five at a time, nimble, light-limbed. Gold threaded through his rippling tattoos, black feathers shimmering down his arms. Dean gritted his teeth and pushed harder. He did not know exactly what to do once he reached the roof, but those were the breaks. He would just play it by ear. Like always. Plans were for sissies.

Koni reached the roof access door before Dean. He waited there, crouched before the heavy metal. Sweat rolled down his skin; he tore off his tank and discarded it. His drawstring pants hung low over his hips, loose and ready to strip off in case he needed to make a quick shift.

"He knows we're here, doesn't he?" he whispered. His eyes glowed.

"We're not on fire yet," Dean replied, though that was small comfort. The both of them were going to be dead fast or find themselves very surprised.

Koni opened the door, crouching low while Dean swung past with both arms out, guns aimed high. A hot breeze clipped his face, carrying a scent: ash, bitter and metallic with blood—and there, directly in front of him, framed against fluttering laundry and a sky penned in by glittering skyscrapers and rusting clouds, was a large man, one of the largest Dean had ever seen. A white gelatin belly hung over tight shorts, propped up on legs thick with muscle, and higher, broad shoulders brushed silver hair, heaving into a rolling face wide and flat and hard with fat. A mean face, a meaner body, and for a moment Dean was once again a little kid facing up to one of the glue-sniffing, crack-smoking, steel mill bullies who used to hang out on his street back in Philly. His sight shifted; the man rippled into a thread. Quivering fast, almost double, like there were two of him at extremes, wrapped up tight, coiled, with one side dark, thicker than the other. Quantum vines tangled, maybe fighting. No harmony. Just a big damn mess of hard times.

But he had no trail. His energy was completely self-contained.

And he carried a blood-spattered plastic sack in one hand.

Dean opened his mouth, ready to make the obligatory statement of "Surrender, you asshole," but Koni made a strange choking sound that kicked his gut into high alarm. His finger tightened on the trigger. Forget words. The white flag of peace could go to hell.

"No," Koni gasped, standing and stepping in front of him. Dean tried to move, to see around his taller body, but Koni pressed his chest against the gun and said, "No, you can't."

"Fuck you doing?" Dean said in a low voice.

"Look at him," Koni said, all cool grace and calm gone from his face. He sounded like he was begging, which was unnatural, bizarre, because Koni was a man who asked for nothing. "Look at his eyes, Dean."

Dean looked. For a moment, it did not register—it was too strange, too unexpected. But then, the glow. Two pinpricks of light in shadow. Golden. Hot.

"Oh, shit," Dean said. The man in front of them was a shape-shifter. A fire-starting, got-a-bag-of-bloody-bones, shape-shifter. Dean wanted to pull out his hair. These were the guys the agency was supposed to find and protect—like Koni, like Hari back home. But if a shape-shifter turned murderer?

Nothing has changed. He kills, he pays. He tries to hurt you, hurt back. Those are the rules of the game. Live first, ask questions later.

Dean tried to keep his thoughts black, to go Yoda and push away the fear, the confusion, but the murderer smiled and that was almost enough to stop Dean in his tracks and contemplate jumping off the side of the building. Sharp teeth poked over his thick bottom lip, sharp and long and white, and though his eyes glowed brighter, Dean imagined the light was cut with black, a ghost darkness, bleeding and bleeding like ink against his eye. Dean's gun grew hot. The man's smile widened, stretching his mouth wide, stretching and stretching, until the sides of his face bulged with some horrific grimace.

Fuck this. Dean raised his weapon and pulled the trigger. Nothing happened. Just clicks. Quiet, deadly, clicks. The metal burned his skin, and though he tried to hold the gun, it seared and reflex took over. He let go. Watched the weapon clatter to the ground. Thought, *I'm so dead.*

"Dead and gone," said the man softly, speaking for the first time. His voice was thick with teeth, surprisingly gentle. "Ash. Quickened flesh. You should have left me alone. Please. You should have let me be."

"Stop," Koni said. "As a brother—"

"Your brotherhood means nothing to me." Golden light spilled over the man's eyes, gold running into darkness down his skin … and in its path, an even brighter whiteness, ridged and hard and gleaming like mother-of-pearl. Scales. Scales were pouring from his fat belly button and pushing outward across his gelatinous body while that hard-lined forehead receded and the meaty jaw jutted far and farther, until Dean felt like Conan the Barbarian in the temple of the Snake King, watching James Earl Jones go *cobra de capello* on his ass, and it was bad—real bad—worse than the creepiest creep-show horror of his childhood nightmares. He could not believe this was happening. He smelled smoke and his skin felt hot, like he was beginning to glow and glow, and he thought of his dream, the fire, and he felt paralyzed with the memory—the first time in his life, unable to move, to think, except to remember what it felt like to burn—

And then Koni was there in front of him, shoving hard, and before he knew it they were both falling backward through the door behind them, tumbling down the stairs. Dean hit the landing hard, but had no time to recover; Koni grabbed the back of his shirt, dragging him down another flight. He could not get his feet under him; his ass got a beating and the air was knocked out of his lungs, along with bits and pieces of skin and maybe some rattled portions of his brain. He held his guns loosely, fingers off the triggers.

"Stop," he croaked.

"No fucking way," Koni said, still dragging him. "I'm not going to end up a crispy crow."

"We need to stop him."

"Then we need another plan. I'm no kamikaze runner."

Dean struggled to his feet and leaned against the wall. He gazed up through the stairwell, peering through the narrow space between the railing to the roof. He did not hear anyone coming after them, and glanced at Koni, whose eyes were pinpoints of wild light.

"He's not following," Koni said.

"There's not another way off that roof," Dean replied, but Koni gave him such a hard look that he felt obligated to once again revise everything he thought he knew about this case.

"Don't say it," Dean said. "For God's sake, man. My brain is going to explode."

Koni shut his eyes. "He's a dragon, Dean. That means he can fly."

Dean, still holding his gun, pressed the edge of his palm against his forehead. His brain felt like it was leaking through his eyes.

"A dragon," he muttered. "Fuck. Do you know him?"

"I have a friend in California named Susie. You know her?"

"Don't give me that. You guys are supposed to be almost extinct."

"Which means we don't exactly get around to throwing block parties for each other," Koni snapped. "The only reason I know that man up there is a dragon is because of the kind of shift he was going through."

Dean fought down a shudder. "Please don't tell me this is typical behavior."

"It's not. And I would never have imagined it if I hadn't see it with my own eyes. The murders are bad enough, but I smelled the blood on him, Dean. I could smell it from that bag. He's let the beast take over. He's gone into the animal. Forgotten his humanity."

"Or maybe it's the opposite," Dean said grimly. "Maybe he's more human than animal. Or maybe I don't give a shit. Either way, he's fucked up."

"And he'll take all of us down with him. He didn't care who saw him shift on that rooftop. A *dragon,* and he didn't care. Shit. They're supposed to be the level-headed ones. And if he did fly off this building …" Koni stopped, raking his hands through his hair. "Do you know how serious that is?"

"Yeah." Dean knew all too well. All of them survived on secrets. Staying out of the public eye, never drawing attention: There was safety in that.

But now one of the shifters was a mass murderer, and Dean had discovered why he burned his victims down to ash: to hide the signs of feeding.

And some of those people were alive when he started chewing.

"The latest victim is just a few floors down," he said, swallowing hard, trying not to puke. "Practically a neighbor to that other guy I came to investigate. The scene will be fresh. I need to be there."

"And if he comes back?"

"We fight," Dean said. "Or run. Whichever comes first."

They moved quickly down the stairs, listening hard for the tread of pursuit, and on the fourth floor entered a narrow hall. Flickering fluorescent lights hurt Dean's eyes, and the air was hot, sticky. He heard television sets, loud voices, children crying, and smelled grease, smoke. For a moment the smell turned his stomach; it reminded him too much of his cooking chest, the cooking body in his vision, the bag of blood and parts. Vegetarianism was definitely in his future.

The victim lived at the end of the hall. His door stood ajar. Koni pushed it open.

The room was dark inside. The ceilings were low. There were no bars over the windows, but the glass was dirty. Plants covered the sill. The ceiling fan turned. Dean smelled garlic. He shifted his vision, revealing a network of energy as he walked through the lines, turning and turning. He felt the echoes of a hard death, the presence of darkness, hunger, fire. A great black stain covered the floor of the living room. Ash. Dean almost opened himself to more vibrations, more of the victim's story, but he thought about fire—and truly, at the moment, he had no stomach for it.

Nothing of the murderer came to him, though. He even stood by the window, step for step where the shape-shifter had lingered, and found nothing.

Doesn't make sense, he thought, reaching under his shirt to holster his gun. *It's like the man is dead.*

Or self-contained. He had certainly seen energy when looking at the shape-shifter face-to-face. Twisted, fucked-up energy. But was it possible that some people did not leave traces, or that they could throw up walls around themselves, holding in everything that was part of them? What would that take? How was it possible?

Dean shook off his questions. He was not ready for them, and most certainly did not want to contemplate any fatal flaws in his abilities. His clairvoyance, his occasional ability to see the present and fragments of the past, all depended on the leavings of the living. Without that, he was as mind-blind as any regular person. Which was not a happy prospect.

Some of the trails inside the apartment belonged to people other than the victim. Dean followed them briefly, and found himself in two different locations: a grassy area outside a building that looked like a concrete strainer, followed by a golden cascade of light and marble, leather chairs, and a large statue of Buddha, set inside a wall that was remarkably familiar.

"Yo," he said to Koni. "You said I was followed from the hotel? Think those guys could be any relation to the dead fellow here?"

"What makes you ask?"

"Because someone came through here a day or two ago, and now that same person is sitting all fat and pretty in the lobby of my hotel."

"That doesn't make sense."

"Unless there's more going on here than we realize. The media said the murder victims weren't related, right? Maybe they were wrong." He turned off his inner sight, and the world reasserted itself; light poured through the window, outlining a sofa and television, a small table. A single chair sat in the center of the room. Dean caught the faint scent of something metallic. He walked out of the living room into the bedroom, checking out the messy covers, the tossed remote control, all the books lining the mantel behind the bed. There was a closet, and inside, Dean rummaged around. His knuckles hit a metal box. He lowered his shields and saw—

—*a figure wrapped in shadows and a hard mouth whispering, "You know what you have to do, you know the risks if you do not, because if the Book is revealed, if the Book comes to flesh and he finds it now"*—

The voice broke off, as did the connection. Dean tried to reestablish the link, but he got nothing, and found himself wishing he was a better retro-cog, a stronger psychometrist instead of just a clairvoyant. So much was lost in his visions, so much left incomplete.

From the other room, Koni said his name. Dean picked up the metal box, carrying it under his arm. The shape-shifter stood by the chair. He held up a small notebook thick with words, the white pages splashed with blood. Very familiar. The murderer had been reading it.

"Names of the other victims," Koni said. "And a few extras, maybe people who haven't died yet. It's all there, along with some pictures."

Dean set down the metal box. It was locked, but he hammered the bolt with the butt of his gun. It fell off. He opened the lid. Inside lay a gun.

"Huh," Dean said, and took the paperwork. It was true—all the names on the list were those who had been murdered. Names, addresses, phone numbers. Written in English, not Chinese.

Beneath it all, he felt something glossy. A photograph. He pulled it out for a look and saw a candid moment of a woman, sitting at a chair in a coffee shop.

Dean's knees buckled. He hit the floor hard, barely noticing Koni's low shout, the pain radiating up his legs. All he could do was stare at the picture, stare and stare at the woman gazing somewhere distant with serious dark eyes. Lovely familiar eyes.

Dean shook his head, tearing away his gaze, staring at the floor. It could not be. It was impossible. He thought, quite seriously, that he might be having a stroke.

"Dean." Koni crouched beside him. "Man, what is it?"

He shook his head, unable to speak. Hands shaking, he turned the photograph over. There was a piece of paper attached, and on it was a name and location.

Mirabelle Lee. Far Eastern Hotel. Room 2850. 9 p.m., lobby.

Dean closed his eyes, shutting out the world. He felt

the locket against his skin, his burning skin, and he tasted the name written on the paper, rolling it in his mouth. Mirabelle Lee. Mirabelle. Miri.

No, he thought. *No, don't do this to yourself.*

Because it was probably just another woman with the same name. It happened. It also happened that complete strangers sometimes resembled each other; as in, were perfect twins, right down to a beauty spot on the edge of the chin, the shape of the mouth, the turn of the head. Twins in spirit, like the one shining from those eyes in the picture—eyes that Dean saw every night in his dreams.

Right. Typical. Just coincidence.

Dean ran. He heard Koni shout his name, heard him try to follow, but Dean did not wait. He barreled from the apartment, down the stairs, out the building into the slick night. He did not look for dragons, or the men who had been following him; he did not look for anything at all as he sprinted through moving traffic, battling crowds and heat and his own raging heart, relying only on instinct to guide him back to the hotel— *my hotel*—as his mind fought with the photograph in his back pocket, the name on the paper clipped to the glossy picture.

Impossible, Dean told himself. It had to be. That girl was dead. Her heart had stopped beneath his hands. No energy, no trail, no connection—and God, he had looked. Twenty years he had spent searching for a thread, even though it was crazy, because all he wanted was a ghost, some line up to heaven. One more word, another glance, that sweet, sweet, smile.

But nothing. Not ever. No moments of *I see dead people.* The only girl he had ever loved was gone from the world, gone forever. His mind never lied.

And if you were wrong? If she has been alive all this time? You weren't able to track one fucking murderer, and even

*when he was standing in front of you he didn't leave a trail.
What if she was the same?*

Dean pushed himself faster. Somewhere above he
heard Koni caw, but he did not know if it was because
his friend was worried, or if he was still being tailed. He
did not care, either way. Let the whole damn city chase
on his heels.

He entered the hotel at a dead run, risking security,
outraged guests in all their glitter and finery—but just
before he hit the elevator alcove, his skin tingled and
he skidded to a stop. His mind glanced out, vision shifting, and he found a thread. A familiar line, a connection.

Dean, breathing hard, stepped close behind one of
the fat marble pillars and leaned against the cool stone.
He threw out his mind, pulling himself along the energy trail, and found a man sitting in the lobby behind
him. The same man who had been in the victim's apartment. Dean did not peer around the pillar to look. He
shut his eyes and used a different sight, studying and
searching.

The man was not alone. There were others nearby,
dressed like him, all in dark suits. They almost looked
like religious types, out to save the world, one conver-
sion at a time. Dean bet they were armed. They held
open newspapers in their laps; worthless accessories,
given that the men were doing a shitty job of pretending to read them. Their eyes did nothing but sweep the
lobby, moving, moving, moving. Like wolves in black,
jaws ready to snap.

Holy shit. This is a setup. This is an operation.

But for what? The woman in the picture? There was
a time attached. Nine o'clock, but it was a quarter until
ten and these men were still sitting here. Was she supposed to meet them, or were they planning to intercept
her? And if all those other murder victims, the men who
had burned, were connected to some conspiracy—if

the dead individual Dean had just visited had intended to be here tonight, waiting for the lady in the photo—

Life just got more complicated. You don't know who the bad guys are anymore.

Unless they were all bad. But that still did not explain why he was being tailed, nor did it explain the woman or the name associated with her. And frankly, Dean cared way more about that. Shallow, maybe, but he could live with his shifting priorities. Forget shape-shifting murderers and flames shooting up his ass. Nothing else mattered but the woman. He had to find her, and fast, because if the men were waiting, their target had not yet been acquired. She was still out there.

He fretted all the way up to the twenty-eighth floor—*twenty-eight, my room is on twenty-seven, oh God, I can't believe this*—and his head felt funny. Light, dizzy. His chest hurt. That mark, burning and burning. Dean pulled away his collar and looked down.

His wound was glowing. Golden light seeped from the cut.

He stared at himself. The elevator dinged. A man stepped on, took one look at him—Dean apparently appeared just as disturbed as he actually felt—and stepped right back off, smiling weakly. It was the kind of smile that made Dean feel like he was the rich man's version of a wild dog. Call the pound, get the gun, wear thick gloves.

Dean didn't mind. He felt rabid. He touched his mouth, but did not find any foam. All the crazy was in his head, then. He was glowing. He had a goddamn lightbulb beneath his skin. Jesus Christ.

The elevator stopped again, but this time it was for him. Dean slapped his hand against the sliding door, holding it open for a moment while he leaned against the shiny metal wall. There were cameras everywhere; someone was probably watching him even now, but he did not care. He could not take his eyes off himself. He waited too long; the doors tried to close on his arm.

The woman, whispered a voice inside his mind. *Remember her.*

Dean closed his eyes and looked away. He patted his collar tight against his throat and stepped off the elevator. Took a moment for one more deep breath, trying to ignore the burning, the pain, the memory of light.

And then he began to run again.

The halls were quiet. Too quiet, it seemed, and the trails of energy crisscrossing the carpet were old, as though no one had been on that floor for more than a day. Odd. The higher levels in the hotel were usually more popular—more prestige, better views—but as Dean moved he found only one new trail, a path weaving away from the emergency stairwell.

He got a bad feeling when he stepped into that energy stream—felt a shiver run through him, like he was walking through a cloud of electricity. It was the kind of sensation he had felt only a time or two before.

Age and power, he thought, remembering his one postmortem encounter with a very dangerous man. An immortal, a magician, an old disgusting fart who had tried to screw over Dean's best friends. The Magi's energy, even with him dead, had felt like this, only much stronger—like it could strip the hair off Dean's body if he lingered too long within it.

Dean reached the room number written on the paper. The energy signature ended there and he flung his mind into the trail, letting it carry him past the door into the room, into dim light—riding like a cowboy on a bucking bronco made of nightmares—and he opened his eyes and saw movement, he saw skin, he saw—

A naked body, pinned and fighting. And attached to that body, a face.

Dean grabbed his chest—grabbed it because it hurt so bad—and for the first time in twenty years remembered there was a line inside his heart; a mark, a place never to cross. He had forgotten—but in that moment, filled with the image of the woman, he glimpsed and touched it, felt himself hug the edge of crazy, and it was a good place to be. The only place. Because *she* was there, and he finally let himself believe. He let himself speak her name—breathed it, again and again, until it was the only sound he made, the only sound in his head as he threw himself against the door, raging wild on the tail of another man's soul, watching through his mind's eye the fight, the bloody struggle only yards away.

He saw it all, and got out his gun.

Chapter Two

On the morning of that very same day, Professor Mirabelle Lee's Monday began, as it usually did, with death. Death, and the leavings of, everywhere like charms and omens. Had she known the evening would bring more of the same—though in a much more colorful way—she might have stayed in her hotel room, savoring her one day off from what had been a grueling week of guest lectures and tiresome dinner parties, taken her day to sleep and dream, descend once again into a world where spirits were made flesh and the past breathed, keeping alive memories that deserved to die.

Instead she took a shower, threw down an early lunch in the hotel's posh atrium buffet, and then took a cab to National Taiwan University, where, after a brief walk to a building that bore more resemblance to a concrete strainer than a center of deep thought and learning, she found herself welcomed by the dark brittle faces of mummified bodies. Two men and one woman, all of whom were curled in poses of ceremonial burial, foreheads touching knees, arms crossed over their chests.

Beautiful people. Less than two weeks out of the ground, thanks to Miri's mentor, Owen Wills. A rare find, deep within Taiwan's Yushan National Park, a mountainous region at the center of the island, and one of the few preserves of its kind in a country ravaged by industry and a population unmindful of the dangers concurrent with environmental degradation.

The air smelled like chemicals, which Miri did not mind. Labs of this kind were home, no matter where in the world she found herself. The examining tables were wide and clean and made of stainless steel. They sat on wheels, so that when the professors and assistants and technicians were done poking (very gently) and prodding (even gentler) the ancient dead, the bodies could be easily returned to the pressurized chambers connected to the lab. The men and women were old—several thousand years more ancient than Miri, at any rate—and every time they were examined in the lab it was a detriment to the continued well-being of their corpses.

So, it was with some surprise that Miri found all three bodies exposed and unattended. Only the woman had a light over her. She was still new enough not to have been christened with an official name, which Miri thought was a shame. But the only name that would have been appropriate—and respectful—was a native name of her time, which was so far removed, so distant, that Miri could not begin to imagine what would have been considered feminine and appropriate for the woman while she had lived.

It mattered to Miri. She knew the assistants had their own pet names for the mummies, but she could not bring herself to use them. It did not seem respectful, and it was bad enough tearing a person from her grave, from the land of her birth and death, and only for the purposes of cold, hard science.

It's more than that, Miri reminded herself, staring

down at the shriveled face, so remarkably and impossibly preserved. *She is teaching us about her world.*

And when she was done teaching, this woman and the others would rest anew—not in the earth, but in the Royal Palace Museum in Taipei, as part of a growing exhibit on Taiwan's ancient history. The country's native aborigines were already up in arms, but the government was good at throwing money at people when it wanted silence. It made Miri uncomfortable to be part of the controversy—by virtue of her deep ties to Owen—but that was part of the job when you studied someone else's past. When what you found was not yours by culture to claim, you were bound to step on toes.

Miri bent over the preserved woman and peered down at the corpse's chest, half hidden by its spindly arms. There was a spot that bothered Miri, that was different from her memory of the last examination she had participated in; a section of delicately woven cloth that appeared to have been lifted and then replaced. A skilled job, and only one person currently at the university had the guts—and the authority—to do so much to the body. Miri's frown deepened.

"Owen?" she called, leaving the body and walking deeper into the lab, on loan to her mentor for the duration of his stay. He had been in Taiwan two months already as the lead excavator on the Yushan site—a position obtained, much to the chagrin of some, by personal invitation from the Taiwanese government, which had granted Owen all kinds of oversight powers. That was not the standard way of doing things, but Owen Wills was the world's foremost expert in Chinese artifacts—with Miri close on his heels—and there were some who cared more about having the right name attached than proper procedure.

Not that Owen was complaining; or Miri. She had spent a month in Yushan before heading back to

Stanford—back to writing yet more grants, dealing with recalcitrant students and colleagues—but with these new mummies found, it was the perfect excuse for Owen to request her presence once again. And to get the Taiwanese government to pay for it.

Miri pushed open the narrow swinging door and entered a small cavern, dark and musty with books and bones and the various relics her mentor had collected over the past eight weeks. He had more in America, all locked up in storage, a product of being a pack rat—everywhere he went, he collected and stored and accumulated. She loved Owen's office, here and elsewhere. It might not have windows, but the warm glow of his lamps, the scent of the air, and the crinkle of his papers always instilled in her a sense of home.

She found him hunched over his desk, gray hair tufted and wild as he gazed through a large stationary magnifying glass. A light shone down past his head, illuminating something small and red in his hands. As Miri neared she heard him humming "Rhinestone Cowboy" under his breath. A good find, then. Glen Campbell rated nothing less.

"You've been busy," she said.

"You have no idea," he replied, without looking up from the magnifying lens. "The results came back on the X-rays early this morning. The men were relatively normal—some badly healed bones, missing teeth—but the woman was different. She had something … strange inside her."

"Strange?" Miri echoed, peering over his shoulder. Owen turned his head. His blue eyes were bright, his cheeks flushed.

"Strange," he said again. "She had something embedded in her chest. Really, truly, embedded. Her flesh had grown over the edges of the thing. It was the devil to pry out."

"Is that it?" Miri asked, gesturing at the object cradled in his hands. It had a waxy sheen; nephrite, by the looks of it. Red jade. From this vantage point it appeared to be a beautiful specimen; high quality, most definitely chosen with care.

"Remarkable," Miri murmured. "Almost as remarkable as your terrible manners."

Owen flinched. "Miri—"

"Did you bother telling *anyone* that you were going to perform an invasive procedure on that body? Did you, Owen? Or did you just go gung ho?"

Owen said nothing. Miri had another terrible thought, a horrible premonition, and she said, "Oh. Oh, Owen. Tell me you contacted Kevin first. *Please.* If you didn't get permission—"

"Kevin Liao is a nincompoop. Of course I didn't contact him. He would have ripped into that woman like a lumberjack with a chain saw. Destroyed her body just like he ruined that child we found in Alishan. I could not let that happen. Besides "—and Owen looked away, voice dropping to a mutter—"he's out of town."

"Out of town looking for more grave sites."

"Of course. He can't stand that I found those mummies."

"His ego is mighty," Miri agreed, "but he's also the head of this department, and like it or not, you are a guest. Back home you might rule the roost, but the rules are different here. I don't care how much of a celebrity you are."

"You used to be such a rebel," Owen said. "You never played it safe. What happened?"

"You became an even bigger rebel than me. Which means you're totally out of control."

"Ah. My golden years. Well, regardless, you needn't fret, my dear. I *did* find those mummies, and that gives me some claim to first examination, regardless of the gnashing of teeth that might cause."

"Oh, there's going to be gnashing, all right," Miri muttered.

Owen patted her hand. "It's been hours since I extracted the artifact. The man has probably already found out what I did. His little spies, as you can guess, have been in and out of the lab all morning. I haven't yet heard a single complaint."

The assistants. Kevin's eyes and ears. The man wanted to make sure Owen did not try and steal his research during his brief forays away from the excavation site. Like Owen needed to. Although, this latest action would most definitely fall under the category of stealing Kevin's thunder.

Actually, Miri was okay with that. What the hell.

"You should have called me." She plopped down on the stool beside Owen and peered at the artifact, its red surface almost glowing beneath the light. She wanted to touch it.

Owen leaned back in his chair. "You're upset."

"Yes. If you wanted to be the one to do the procedure, that's fine, but I thought—"

"No," he interrupted gently. "No, my dear. Only, I did not want you involved when I removed the stone. I may act flip about the consequences of today's action, but truth is, not much can be done to me at this point in my career. You, on the other hand, are still young. I had to protect you."

"Owen."

"I know. Chivalry and paternalism stopped being fashionable long ago. But allow an old man his eccentricities. I only meant you well, Miri. You are like a daughter to me. My *only* daughter, and I know that Emily … Emily felt the same. She would never forgive me if I got you into trouble. In fact, she's probably already quite vexed."

"Emily was an angel," Miri muttered, staring at her hands, trying very hard not to think of Owen's wife, now two years in the grave. "She never got angry with you."

Owen smiled ruefully. "My dear girl, you did not live with her for thirty years. She was pure fire, in both temperament and passion." He held the red jade fragment out to her. "Truce?"

"Oh, stop that," Miri said, but she took the artifact and shouldered Owen aside as she stole his seat and placed the jade beneath the lens. The stone was larger than her palm, sharp on three ends and shaped like a rough triangle. One edge was softer than the others; she noted odd scratches, quite deep.

"There's been a cut or break," she said, running her fingers down the opposing sides, sheer and smooth. "This is part of something bigger."

"Yes," Owen said. "Tell me more."

Miri turned the artifact over in her hands. It felt warm. She blamed it on the light, on her own body heat, but holding it felt good, sweet on her palm. She made a closer examination of its waxy red surface, the scratches she had noted earlier.

Only, the marks no longer looked so random. Lines, yes—but curving, delicate. Ordered.

Miri sat back, blinking hard. Owen chuckled. She stared at him, then looked back at the jade "That's writing. Those are words."

"I'm glad you think so. I wasn't sure at first, but after three hours of staring at the thing, I have become more than a little convinced."

Miri traced the lines with her fingers, trying to stay calm. As she considered the possibilities, though, a chill stole through her, a weight that settled hard in her chest.

"Owen," she said quietly, "those men and women are almost four thousand years old. The earliest examples we have of Chinese pictograms don't show up until twelve hundred BC, and those are only on oracle bones."

"Go on," he said. Miri narrowed her eyes.

"The Chinese written language is based on a logographic system. Symbols, with each one representing an idea. The inscriptions discovered on the oracle bones show that more than two thousand years ago there was already a highly developed writing system in China, one that is similar to modern day classical Chinese. It takes time to develop those kinds of systems, Owen. Even if the writing on this stone is almost a thousand years older than those other inscriptions, there should be some resemblance between the two. Some kind of kinship." She turned the jade in her hands and pressed her fingernail against the swirling ordered lines. "Look at this. Nothing of these inscriptions resembles a logographic system. In fact, it looks almost like modern day Arabic."

"That would certainly be impossible," he said. "Nor is this a derivative of cuneiform. But yes, there is a certain … melody … in them, isn't there?"

"Are you *sure* it's writing? It could be art." Which in itself was a kind of language.

"Miri, you know as well as I do that without more evidence, it is impossible to say for certain. But"—and here he placed a fist against his heart—"I feel it. All my instincts say it is so. And so do yours, if I'm not mistaken."

"You're not. But what, then? The ancient people who migrated from China to Taiwan had their own writing system? If that's the case, wouldn't it show at least *some* relation to the system that later developed on the mainland?"

"Yes. One *would* expect certain similarities. Which is why I believe this is something completely different. Different enough that I am not convinced that its origins are Asian."

Miri stared. "What are you saying? These people migrated from somewhere out of the region and died on the island?"

"The preliminary genetic tests haven't yet come back, but perhaps the stone was inscribed somewhere distant and brought there—either by these individuals, or by others."

"Nephrite is typically found in the southwest part of Xinjiang, part of the Silk Road."

"And we already know, based on the Urumchi mummies, that humans traveled far greater distances than was ever previously imagined."

Miri chewed her bottom lip. Just outside Urumchi, the capital of Xinjiang, exceptionally well preserved mummies with European features had been found. They dated back as far as four thousand years, and still had archaeologists and anthropologists scratching their heads. The timing was perfect. No less inexplicable, but every theory had to start somewhere.

"Miri," Owen said.

"This is big," she said. "This is … really big."

"Oh yes." He leaned against the table, folding his arms over his round belly. "This is the kind of thing that rewrites history."

"The kind of thing traditionalists will hate."

"Making us the harbingers of the best bad news of the last decade."

Miri shook her head. "We need more evidence before we can publish anything. Before we can even apply for a grant. Right now this is less than speculation."

"Of course, of course." Owen pushed himself away from the table and spun on his heel, pacing. "We know, based on the breaking point in the stone, that this is just one segment of a larger artifact. We need to go back to Yushan, see if there are similar men or women buried with pieces of jade—perhaps other fragments of the larger stone. There might be pottery that survived, inscriptions on bones, other jade artifacts—anything to support the theory that there was cross-cultural contact or migration into Southeast Asia during this time period."

"Or evidence that refutes it," Miri reminded him. "This jade might not be what we think it is."

Owen's mouth quirked. "I think our bigger problem is Kevin. I might be the government-appointed leader on this dig, but he can still make trouble for us."

"*Us* now?" Miri swiveled around on her stool. "Why, that is very kind of you, Dr. Wills."

"Not at all, Dr. Lee. Your expertise will be most valued."

My trust, too. Owen was going to need someone to watch his back once word spread—and it would, that was inevitable. People talked, especially in this part of the world, where it was not just intellectual politics that got nasty, but other elements of the illegal, black market kind. This red jade, and anything associated with it, was going to become a very hot piece of property.

"I suppose you've already recorded evidence of your initial findings with the folks back home, right? Sent some pictures to sit on the Stanford server?"

"Of course." Owen gave her an affronted look. "Kevin will not be able to claim we stole any ideas from him. Everything is documented."

"Well, good. But you realize, don't you, that he's got every right to be on the team?" And once that happened, the games would begin. Kevin cared more about politics than good science, cared more about making himself look good instead of getting the job done.

"I could always arrange to break his kneecaps," Owen said, with the mock gruffness of a man who had never ever attempted to take a crowbar to another person's legs.

Miri had. It was not something she thought Owen would have the stomach for. Nor would it really solve any of their problems. Although, hearing Kevin scream might be very satisfying.

She picked up the red jade. The color was soft, but rich. She could not stop staring at it, those words in the stone curling light in her eyes. It poured such heat into her palm, moving up her arm …

She put it down. "You said this was in the woman's chest?"

"Embedded. Rather gruesome, I suppose. Part of her breastbone was removed to make room for it. The stone was partially cradled in the bone."

"That should have killed her."

"It clearly didn't. The flesh had time to grow around the artifact."

Then it hurt like hell, Miri thought, wondering what it would take, with only primitive tools, to remove enough bone to embed this flat piece of jade inside someone's chest. Unable to help herself, she pressed the red stone between her breasts and tried to imagine it hanging there, in her body, as part of her skeleton. Flesh and blood.

She shivered. Owen touched her shoulder.

"I know," he said quietly.

Miri placed the stone on the table. She did not want to touch it, not anymore, though as soon as the thought passed through her, she felt the urge to press skin to stone, and soak up its warmth.

"What could be so important that a person would go

through that kind of torture?" She looked at Owen. "What would be the point?"

"Why do cultures ever practice mutilation? Beauty, rites of passage—"

"Protection," Miri interrupted, thinking of the tiny scar just above her own heart.

"Yes," Owen said. "Sacrifice is easier when done for the good of others or oneself."

Something Miri understood all too well, even if it was a hard knowledge, and bitter. "Anything else you need to tell me? If we're heading down to Yushan for an extended period of time, I need to go back to the hotel and make some calls."

"Just clear your schedule for this evening. Wendy Long wants to meet with us tonight. When I told her about the find—"

Miri made a small sound of protest. "You called Wendy before me?"

A deep scarlet flush stained his neck, rising high into his cheeks. He opened his mouth to speak, but Miri—resigned—cut him off with a curt wave of her hand. "Just ask the woman out on a date. It's not that hard, Owen."

His expression grew pained. "I can't."

"Owen."

He held up his hand. He still wore his wedding ring.

"But you like her," Miri said softly. "There's no crime in that."

"I know, my dear. I know. But ... I was with my wife so very long, and to think that I could possibly love another ..." He stopped, shaking his head. "Other men do it all the time. I don't know why I find it so difficult."

"Because you've got a heart of gold," Miri said. "Because you're the kind of man who believes in loving one person and no other. But hey, you don't have to marry Wendy. Just because you go out with her one time doesn't mean you have to pledge the rest of your life to her. Just … be friends. Have coffee. Or tea. Tea is better. Take her to that ritzy dim sum place over by the hotel where I'm staying. You can talk dead people. It'll be the start of something beautiful."

"It's not that easy."

Miri said nothing. She was not going to beg Owen to ask Wendy Long out on a date. Not when she knew exactly what he was going through. Of course, the alternatives to being alone had not exactly been all that attractive over the years.

Because when was the last time you met someone who kept you interested for more than ten minutes?

Long enough that she could not remember his name. Which was pretty damn long. Not that she was all that surprised or bothered. It seemed to Miri that all the relationships of her adult life could be summed up by boring, boring, shallow, self-absorbed, boring, and boring. And while not all of those relationships had been terrible—even the lawyer had made her laugh—Miri was not the kind of woman to waste her time with people who, ultimately, did not understand her. She liked herself too much. That, and she knew what it was to be in love—to find love in only one moment, eye to eye; to have love stay in that moment, in that person, and never fail her. Anything less paled, was not worth her heart. Better to have loved like that only once, than to try again and again, and tarnish the memory.

Which, really, when she thought about it, was so sickening sweet she wanted to vomit.

Not to mention the itty-bitty problem of being alone for the rest of your life. You really want that for yourself?

No, but there were worse things in life, so thanks but no, thanks. Single women unite. Books and cats and all that crap.

But then a memory came to her, sudden, like always,

the image hot and fierce; a face familiar as her own, blue eyes smiling beneath a crown of short blond hair, one strong hand giving her a rock in the shape of a heart, and that voice, that low, sweet voice, saying, *"Here, I know you like these."*

She gritted her teeth. Owen, sounding worried, said, "My dear, I'm sorry about contacting her first. Truly. I just … got carried away."

At first she did not understand what he was saying, but then she blinked, hard, and said, "Oh no, Owen. Don't worry about it. I was just thinking about … about something else. The artifact. The dead woman carrying that stone in her chest."

Carrying a stone like she carried one, though Miri suspected her own might be the heavier burden. Which was just great. She was a total melodramatic sap. What a time for a reminder. She was definitely the wrong person to give Owen advice about moving on.

"I'm heading back to the hotel." Miri stood. Ignoring Owen's concern, she gave him a smile that probably looked as cheap and fake as she felt, and then left his office. One of the assistants had put away the bodies. Probably listened at the office door, too.

Miri was glad the mummies were gone, out of sight. She did not want to look into the face of a woman four thousand years dead and wonder at mystery and pain, at how that could remind her of a childhood friend who had given her both and more, and then disappeared and died.

She did not want to think about why she still dreamed of that boy.

Miri took a cab back to the hotel, but made the driver drop her off several blocks away from the Far Eastern. She did not have a particularly good reason for doing so; the man at the wheel simply talked too much, drove too fast. Miri could only take so much car sickness, in addition to questions about her marital status, and whether she, as a *huaqiao,* a foreign Chinese, had come to Taiwan to look for a good man. Apparently (according to the driver), America did not have any decent catches for a girl who wanted her kids to belong to the motherland. Blood mattered, he said.

Yes, Miri thought, but only because she was imagining quite a bit of it streaming from the broken nose she was going to give him if he said one more word. Which he did. He acted like it was cute.

She paid her fare and got out to walk the last few blocks to the hotel. The heat was terrible, and though the sun hid behind a sullen sheet of clouds, the daylight felt too bright, like the inside of a steel oven. She shrugged off her tweed jacket, carrying it over her purse as she moved on light feet. Miri remembered other walks, other kinds of heat, nights spent running through steaming back alleys with the smells of grease and exhaust in the air, firecrackers spitting somewhere distant—and at her side a boy with his hand wrapped tight around her own, laughing hard. Wild times. She could feel him even now, like a shadow rubbing her shoulder, glued to her side.

Stop, she told herself. *Don't go there.*

But she still found herself fumbling at the throat of her blouse to touch the light scar above her heart. A tiny ridge, a puckered hole. A kiss in the shape of a bullet wound.

The old memory made her feel tired, homesick. She wanted her little apartment, her office at Stanford with its walls covered in books—books and bones, mementos of her travels through the world. She wanted to surround herself in the cocoon of her work, where she was safe from prying eyes and people who talked too much, who did not understand her. Owen was different; Miri could be herself around him. But he was the only one, and sometimes, she held back even with him.

You don't know what it's like to be totally free around anyone. Not anymore. You've been on your own for almost twenty years.

On her own, but surrounded. Alone in a crowd. Which was not always so terrible, except on days like this, when she wished for older things, when she remembered times that had been, when she'd had a friend.

She reached the Far Eastern Hotel—made a detour through the glittering mall built alongside it—riding escalators, going high and higher, trying not to think of herself as irredeemably dowdy as she passed window upon window of beautiful lovely things. Eventually, though, her stomach growled and her feet ached. Worse, she began to feel uneasy. An odd sensation. Like she was being watched.

Big brother, she told herself. *You're picking up security cameras. They're giving you the willies.*

Maybe. But the sensation felt stronger than that, more primitive. Ignoring the prickling sensation between her shoulders, Miri made her way to the narrow glass corridor linking the mall and hotel. She had things to do before her meeting with Owen and Wendy. Knowing her mentor, she might end up in Yushan by morning. With finds like this, time was of the essence. Four thousand-year-old mummies had been significant enough to draw worldwide scrutiny, but when word of the red jade leaked out, especially given its placement in the body …

Well. Dangerous times. Big money from big artifacts could make people do terrible things. By tomorrow—perhaps even tonight—extra security would be needed down at the Yushan site. At the university, too. Owen, undoubtedly, would put the red jade artifact in the de-

partment vault, but that still left the bodies exposed.
The locks on the basement doors could not be trusted
to keep anything safe.

Miri's uneasiness did not fade as she walked through
the hotel lobby, but she watched the faces around her,
memorized and analyzed. No one seemed all that interesting. No bad vibes. Just a florist tweaking the vines
on an enormous flower display covered in orchids,
workers hurriedly mopping and polishing while bell-
hops scattered, most of them struggling with fat luggage. She passed the bakery set just off the lobby and
saw, behind the glass counter, a shelf full of elaborate
chocolate statues: animals, mostly, representations of
Chinese astrology. Horses, tigers, roosters, dragons—

*Wendy's last name is Long. Dragon. She might get a kick
out of that. And if I can catch Owen before Wendy arrives, so
he can be the one to give it to her ...*

It was a good plan. Owen needed all the help he
could get.

As Miri stood at the counter to buy the chocolate,
she felt a gentle tap on her shoulder and turned. A man
stood behind her. He smiled when she looked at him.
His eyes were a remarkable shade of pale green. Miri
did not know what to make of his gaze, which seemed
friendly enough, though with a cool undercurrent, a remoteness, that made her uneasy. He had dark red hair,
and wore a loose green linen shirt over tan pants. Very
relaxed. A small silver medallion hung around his neck.

"I'm sorry," he said. "I was wondering if you could
help me. I need to buy a gift for my mother."

He had a faint accent, the edge of something British.
Miri waited for more, and he said, "I was hoping you
could recommend something."

"Sorry," she said. "But I would say if you're traveling
somewhere, the chocolates are the best. They'll keep
better."

Obviously. There was no reason he needed to ask. He was just looking for an excuse to talk to her.

He thinks you're cute, she told herself, but was not consoled. The man made her uneasy. His eyes were odd.

"Are you here on business?" He moved closer to the counter. "You have a very American accent."

"Just wandering the city with some friends," she lied. "I'm meeting them here. You?"

"I'm a journalist," he said, and held out his hand. "My name is Robert."

Miri did not let herself hesitate. She shook his hand, testing his grip. Firm, but not painful. "My name is Maxine." Another lie, all kinds of lies. She did not want to tell this man the truth.

"Very pretty," he said, and Miri knew that was his own lie. His gaze never left her face. She did not blink. He smiled, and then made a great show of examining the chocolates in the glass counter.

Miri did not stick around to make a purchase, and Robert did not say a word or follow as she walked away. She glanced over her shoulder only once, and found him still engrossed by the bakery's offerings. She was not reassured. She did not trust him.

And yet, no one tried to ride the hotel elevators with her. She walked alone down her quiet hall, stood alone outside her dark door, with no one stalking, no hunter on the trail.

But she still had a bad feeling about *something*.

Premonitions aside, the afternoon passed quickly. Miri took a shower. Ordered room service. Made some calls. She was scheduled to return to Palo Alto the day after tomorrow. Like that was going to happen now. She was glad it was summer and that most of her graduate students were gone, or independent enough to handle her long absences. E-mail was a godsend.

Miri kept her eye on the clock, and when the hour grew late enough to be morning in California, she called her parents. It was good daughterly duty, nothing more. And luckily, they were out. Probably for a power walk, their united team effort to stay fit, because everyone—the ubiquitous, mysterious "everyone"—said that was the right way to live.

Miri left a message. Simple, to the point. "Hi. Hope all is well. I may have to stay in Taiwan for another week or two, maybe longer. If we don't get to talk, don't worry. Take care. Bye."

Easy. Anything else would be superfluous. Anything mushy or more affectionate, strange. Her parents, unlike her long-dead grandmother, believed themselves too intellectual for high emotion. All their passion, all the dreams that had led them to face an uncertain future in a foreign country were withered now and dead. It was the consequence of success, all those monetary and intellectual accomplishments that had demanded terrible sacrifice.

Like raising Miri. Severing the bond until she was more stranger than daughter. Reducing love to a concept, a fashionable exercise, and all in the name of making a better life—because college was difficult enough for a new immigrant, but saddled with a small child? Better to leave Miri behind in Philadelphia with her grandmother. Send for her later.

Miri supposed it made sense. Good intentions, and all that. Only, she had never lived with them again. It was always something: school, work, the neighborhood they were staying in. Not wanting to burden their professional lives with a child, a willful teenager, when things were going so well. Even the accident had not persuaded them. Nothing, nothing—not until it was too late and Miri was seventeen, almost full grown, mourning a heart twice broken. Her grandmother, dead. And the other, the boy …

Dean.

Miri closed her eyes. Past was past, nothing to change, nothing to do but let go, let go and move on. Twenty years and it was time to grow up, to leave behind those wicked lovely ghosts. Thirty-six years old, kicking the high road to forty. Not sixteen anymore. Not some kid with her heart full.

Still full, she thought. *Ni-Ni never left you. And neither did Dean.*

Small comfort. Maybe no comfort at all. Everywhere she went, there were reminders, like the world was a decoder ring unraveling fragments of her past, sending them straight to her heart—her quiet practical little heart. And while the ache of her grandmother's death had dulled, Dean's still cut. He was too much a part of her. He was still a mystery. Dead, while she lived. Dead as she had died, with a bullet in the chest.

The phone rang. It was Owen.

"I considered your suggestion," he said, without preamble. "I agree. Tea is good."

"Wonderful," Miri said, trying to sound more cheerful than she felt. "Are you still at the university?"

"Of course. I'll be leaving soon, though. It's already seven o'clock and I haven't yet … cleaned up."

"Wear the red tie," Miri said, and then, quieter, "Maybe I should sit this one out. You and Wendy could make a night of it. At the very least, have her all to yourself."

"Absolutely not. All feelings aside, this is still a business meeting."

"Business isn't everything, Owen."

"Then humor me. You need to be there. I insist. You are my partner in this, Miri. You are the only person I trust."

"You trust Wendy."

"Trust, maybe. But verify, always."

"Fine. I'll be there. Where are we meeting?"

"At your hotel. The walls are too thin in the lab, and I want no chance of spies."

"And the jade? Wendy will want to see it. The bodies, too."

Owen hesitated. "Let me worry about that. I have … special precautions in mind."

"Special precautions?"

"Intuition, my dear. Ever since you left me I have had the most uncomfortable feeling."

"Really?" Miri's shoulders prickled.

"Quite." His voice dropped to a whisper. "I am carrying the jade on my body at this very moment. The lab vault is not safe, Miri."

"Jesus, Owen. Someone could accuse you of stealing that thing."

"Then better I steal it than someone else. You know how artifacts disappear in this part of the world. People walk right in off the street and remove the most precious items imaginable, only to disappear without a trace. Inside jobs, Miri, all of them, and I *refuse* to see this new discovery follow its brethren to the black market and some idiot collector with more money than honor."

"Good intentions won't save you if Kevin finds out."

Owen said nothing. Miri let him have his silence. She did not trust the vault, either, but his alternative did not inspire much confidence. Forget the potential legal trouble. Carrying around a four-thousand-year-old artifact was not exactly high-tech protection—and Owen was no Bruce Lee.

No other option, though. And if you're both having bad feelings …

"I hope you're prepared to return to Yushan," he said.

"I assume that will be tomorrow?"

"Perhaps even tonight."

Which Miri had expected all along. "Kevin?"

"I don't know," Owen said. "Really. The man is a turd."

And with that, after a short reminder to meet in the lobby at nine, they said their good-byes. Miri put down the phone and lay back on the bed. She stared at the ceiling, trying not to think too hard, but the life of that woman in the lab continued to haunt her. Why would she inflict that kind of pain on herself? Ritual? Religion? Neither was comforting, but that was only because part of her thought it made sense. People could—and did—do incredibly mystifying things to themselves and others, all in the name of religion. Gods and legends.

Either way, it was just something more or less to prove, another shade to the theory; an equation missing parts, bricks and crumbles. And one day, Miri thought, one day in the far future, another woman would likely rest in another bed, also thinking about the past, with some enigmatic clue in her hand, dreaming questions, wondering. Maybe she would feel her own body weighed down with the monumental task of uncovering half-truths, conjecture, poor shadows of a past holding true meaning and significance only to the dead.

Nothing lasts forever, Miri reminded herself. *All this around you, already dead. You, Owen, gone. Ni-Ni and Dean and everyone you love, dead to nothing, except to you. Only to you.*

Miri closed her eyes. She did not want to think about mortality. Flesh was worthless. It was the mind that mattered. All those thoughts and dreams, every little hurt and triumph, the trivialities and epics of a single life, fading into nothing. Human hearts left no records.

Maybe the jade was a record, a book of a heart. It was there, ready to be read, perhaps in the afterlife, perhaps by those left behind.

A nice thought. Miri preferred it to the self-mutilating idolatry of mysterious gods—enjoyed the poetry, the idea of some woman, millennia dead, realizing the significance of her life and taking immortality into her own hands, into her body, replacing jade with bone.

Miri touched her chest, imagining once again stone instead of flesh. Warm and red. She traced the lines in her mind, feeling them on her fingertips. She tasted them on her tongue, heavier than air, sweet and close as song. In her heart, familiar as English, Chinese; a dead language resurrected. It did not make sense, but Miri was suddenly too tired to care. Overwhelmingly weary, with weight bearing on her body and mind. Holding her down with sleep.

Butterflies, she thought, drifting. *Open your mouth and let them out.*

She almost did, almost said the words floating on her tongue—because this was dreamtime, fantasy, all reason cast to wayside—but at the last moment her body jerked, flung down hard with the sensation of falling, and she snapped out of the hazy daze. Awake, awake. The sensation, the *knowing* in her mouth, disappeared. Butterflies, scattered.

Miri touched her lips. She remembered something alive, beating fierce inside her mouth. Ghost words.

Or just ghosts.

She sat up, uneasy, and forced herself from the bed. Standing was a mistake; she swayed, putting a hand to her head as pain struck; an ice pick through her temple. She was light-headed, too. Miri closed her eyes, but the sensation did not pass. She walked to the bathroom, stumbling as her bare feet hit the cold marble. The world spun; she steadied herself against the counter, fighting to stay upright, glancing at herself in the mirror. No treat, there—not with the hard set of her mouth, the crease between her eyes that refused to disappear. A low ache spread through her muscles, accompanied by a prickled flush, like the onset of fever. The crease deepened.

Miri stripped off her clothes and stepped into the shower. She did not wait for the water to warm, but turned it on, full-blast and cold. It felt good. She did not shiver. Her skin ate up the water, the unrelenting bitterness; she felt like she was on fire. Her heart hurt, too, the skin over her left breast tender to touch. She tried to ignore the burning, but the heat was too much. She could not breathe. She could not breathe enough to fill her lungs, and it was too much, too crazy. She never got sick. Never, and not like this. This was too fast.

She shut down the water and fled naked and dizzy from the bathroom. Cool air hit her wet skin; she collapsed on the bed, drawing her knees to her chest, fighting to slow her hammering heart. She wanted to vomit, she wanted to scream, she wanted to disappear into the covers like a ghost and never feel again—to give up the flesh, the body, this inexplicable misery with her skin hot to the touch, burning and burning. Darkness flickered in her vision. Shutting her eyes only made it worse; she wondered if she was dying. Wondered, too, why the hell she wasn't already calling the front desk and screaming for a doctor.

She flung out her hand toward the phone—got as far as dragging the receiver to her ear—when all that discomfort, the fire skimming her skin, cut away. Severed so sharply, at such contrast, that the air against her skin felt like pure ice, cold as the frigid water she had been standing under only minutes before. Miri sucked in her breath, holding it, holding everything inside so tight. She did not try to stand. She did not try to move. She did not take anything for granted. Her body felt too tender; the heat, the illness, might return. Miri lay very still with her eyes closed, sinking deep into the quiet. Exhausted, frightened. Breathless.

Her mind floated. She fell asleep. She dreamed of fire, and from the fire a shadow crawling from mind to heart, sucking on shades of red: pink for love, pink for death.

She dreamed she ate death.

The next time she opened her eyes, the room was dark. She thought that was strange; she remembered the lights being on. There was also a cover draped over her body, which was a little less odd, but also not something she recalled.

Miri rolled on her side. The clock blinked. It was almost nine thirty.

Nine thirty. Oh God. Owen is going to kill me.

The air was colder than she remembered; Miri dragged the cover with her as she scrambled off the bed, all twisted up, staggering. Her head felt fine—no pain, no dizziness, no unnatural fever, no words on her lips—but just as she regained her balance, still moving, still trying to run to her luggage for clothes, she heard an odd click. Sharp, loud, with a faintly metallic edge.

Miri froze, her body reacting before her mind, which was slow to catch up. But when it did, she knew that sound—an impossible, wrong, hallucinatory sound. There was no way …

She turned. At first she could not see—too many shadows, a subtle glare from the bright city lights beyond the large window—but then her vision sharpened on the darkest corner, on the chair by the table.

And in that chair, a body. Legs, torso, arms. A man. A big man.

There was a gun in his hand.

The world stopped. Everything in her life was gone except for this moment, that figure sitting so still. And then ...

"Dr. Lee," said the man. "What a pleasure to meet you again."

Chapter Three

It was only the second time Miri had ever found herself on the pointy end of a gun. The first was also unpleasant: sixteen, partially naked, and taken completely off guard. Twenty years later the pattern was repeating itself. Except Miri was not ready to die again.

She ran for the door, giving up the blanket when it slowed her down. Not that it helped. In seconds the man had her and the darkness of the room closed in thick until all that existed was the steel pressed to her throat, the body against her naked back, the heart hammering with fury in her chest.

He did not talk. He nudged her with his leg—a silent command to walk—and Miri did not refuse. But the moment the gun wavered she went completely limp, sliding like an eel through his arm. The man caught her halfway down, grabbed an armpit, a fistful of hair, but Miri thrashed and screamed, lashing out with her fists to punch his groin, break his kneecaps, bite his ankles—anything and everything to force him to let go.

He did not. He bent down and in the middle of a

scream, blocked a blow to his face and stuck the gun in her mouth. Miri's voice broke. She went very still.

"Thank you," said the man. "Now let's try this again."

He made her stand. The gun did not leave her mouth. The metal had an unpleasant taste, like something recently oiled. Miri's gaze did not waver; it was difficult to see his eyes, but not his mouth, which was a hard flat line.

He guided her backward. He did not touch her body, merely pushed with the gun. Miri did not bother trying to hide her nudity. Clothes would not make her less vulnerable. Not from this. Not from anything else. All she could do was fight her heart—stay calm, focused, clear and hard and ready to fight.

Just like old times, she told herself, breathing around the gun. The backs of her knees bumped up against the bed. Miri sat down hard and the gun left her mouth, but only just. Metal touched her cheek.

"You can scream if you like," said the man, in a voice that was suddenly familiar, "but there will be no one to hear you. This entire floor has been rented out by my employer, and the soundproofing beneath us, state-of-the-art. You may also fight me, if that is your wish, but I think you know what will happen if you do." And he ran the barrel of the gun across her lips. Miri briefly closed her eyes.

He stopped touching her and moved away, pausing over the cover on the floor. He picked it up and tossed it to her, waiting until she covered herself before turning on the lamp beside the bed. The sudden light made her blink, but she did not shield her face. She fought the glare and stared.

Pale eyes. That was the first thing she noticed. The palest she had ever seen, a green that was almost white. Eyes that were just as familiar as the voice, the red hair, the silver around his neck.

Robert. The man from the bakery.

You knew, she told herself, but it was too little, too late. Miri kept her mouth shut, and the man mirrored her silence, unblinking and calculating, judging and measuring like he was holding her up to some terrible light. And the silence lasted; it grew, until each passing second felt like another kind of weapon, a bullet in her head and heart. She needed sound. She needed engagement. She needed to be something more than just an object, and if she could not fight a gun, then at least she could talk.

Talk with the taste of metal still in her mouth.

Robert finally sighed—a long sound, almost a word, a statement—the corner of his mouth curving into something wry and bitter, and when he spoke it was a murmur, a slow, crisp extension of every syllable, giving it a color, a taste, as it rolled off his tongue.

"Dr. Lee," he said. "Dear and lovely Mirabelle Lee. Professor of archaeology, with numerous accolades attached to the title. One of the world's foremost experts on ancient China, second only to Dr. Owen Wills. Rumored to be having an affair with said colleague, though after meeting you, I believe that can be safely ruled out."

Miri's fingers dug into the cover, holding on, holding on so tight, and she bit her tongue until she tasted blood.

"You've done your research," she managed, stifling a very strong desire to scream. "You know who I am. I can't imagine why."

"Because I must," he said. "Because that is my job."

"Which is?"

"Whatever is necessary," he said. "And I am a great believer in the motivational power of necessity."

"How nice for you," Miri said, thinking wildly of escape, of any weapons close at hand. There was a lamp behind her, some heavy glasses above the minibar, perfume in the bathroom that she could spray in his eyes …

Robert smiled. "I appreciate your level head, despite how sudden this must be for you. I do apologize for the way we are being introduced. But circumstances, unfortunately, have taken a turn for the worse, and I find that a proactive stance usually serves everyone better in the long run."

"I have no idea what the hell you're talking about," Miri said, "but you've got a gun on me, I'm naked, and that's very uncomfortable. So if you have something actually important that you need to do or say, let's get it over with now, so you can get the fuck out of here before I take that gun and shove it up your ass."

"I am here for the jade," Robert said. "Or rather, I was. I was also sent to collect you. Is that clear enough?"

Of all the things she had expected him to say, that was not it. Robert tilted his head, the corner of his mouth curving, and like a switch, she felt a flush creep up her neck into her face. She could not pretend.

"That artifact was discovered only this morning." Miri tried to keep her voice steady, calm. "Nor do archaeologists form package deals with their findings."

"I don't ask why," he said. "I just ask how much."

Miri narrowed her eyes. "You're no grave robber."

"I am what I need to be. I am a professional."

"And the time frame? Who told you about the jade? Who hired you?"

"Those are incredibly naïve questions, Dr. Lee, and I know you are not a naïve woman. That is the fear talking. The confusion." Robert sidled sideways toward her suitcase, gun still trained on her head. He crouched, and began rummaging through her clothing.

"What are you doing?"

"Looking for underwear, of course." He pulled out a

lacy number and flung it toward her. Miri let the panties hit her chest and fall to the floor. Robert did not seem to notice, merely continued to remove more clothing from her bag. And then, in a voice so soft she could barely hear him, said, "I am here because Dr. Wills is already gone. He has been taken. While you slept, he was stolen away."

So easy—the words came out so easy—and it took her a moment to understand him. But when she did— when the words finally translated into something her mind would accept—her breath froze in her lungs, her heart crunched down and down, and she thought, *You should have anticipated this as soon as he mentioned the jade. The logic was there, you idiot, you selfish frightened—*

"Owen," she said. "Tell me."

"If only," he replied. "But I can tell you nothing. I have not even seen him. Dr. Wills is not in my possession, nor do I know where he is."

"Liar."

"Occasionally." He smiled thinly. "If you take a moment, however, you might conclude that the leverage I hold presupposes any need to lie. So, up. If you want to save yourself, you must stand and dress. It is time to leave this place."

Miri shook her head, steeling herself. "I don't know what's going on, but whatever you want, you had your chance when I was asleep. I don't know why you didn't take me then, why you're doing it like this, but you're too late. I'm not leaving with you."

"Really?" he said, in a voice that made Miri feel like a baby bird dangled on the edge of a snapping mouth. Crocodile size. Bounce, bounce, bite—and with a gun to boot. But his eyes made it worse. Not crazy, not angry. Simply detached; the color of seawater, cold and luminescent. Much older than his face. "I am afraid, Dr. Lee, that you do not entirely appreciate the situation you are in. Someone is coming here for you. The same someone who took Dr. Wills."

"Because of the jade?"

"Because of money. Or rather, that is *my* reason. I really cannot speak for those I do not know." Robert stood and stepped around the suitcase. He picked up a pile of clothes and tossed them at her feet. "The world, Dr. Lee, is full of very wealthy people who will do almost anything to keep their hands free of filthy things. This, I can assure you, is one of them."

He sat down on the edge of the table, his posture loose, easy. He tilted his head, analyzing and calculating like a tick-tock machine made of flesh and bone.

"They have Dr. Wills," Robert said, almost to himself. "And one must assume they have the artifact. Very unexpected. Oh well. Up, Dr. Lee. Dress."

"No," she said. "You know too much about me just to have been called in last minute. You could not have been hired just this morning to kidnap the both of us and steal the jade."

He smiled. "That is a conundrum, isn't it? It would imply someone knew when and where the artifact would be found."

"Impossible."

"Really." His smile faded. "Very little is actually impossible in this world, Dr. Lee. Now please, enough talking. We must be going."

"You're crazy to think I'll leave with you, even with your gun."

"A little crazy, perhaps, but you should hope not *too* crazy, especially now with competition knocking on your door, another player in the game. I can vouch for my own rules of honor, Dr. Lee, but that is all I can do. Consider, for a moment, that you might just be safer with me." He pulled something from his pocket and held it up for her to see. It was a very tiny syringe, no longer than her finger. The cap was still on, but he pulled it off with his teeth and spat it out onto the carpet. His gun hand never wavered.

"Please," he said, very quietly. "Hold still."

"Like hell." Miri backed away. "You'll have to shoot me first."

He sighed. "I had a plan, Dr. Lee. It was a very good plan, and not the circus this is turning out to be. But I am, if anything, adaptable. The serum won't kill you, but it will make you pliant, and very, very sleepy. Exactly what I need."

Miri edged back from him. "I thought you needed me to dress myself and walk out of here."

"You will still be able to do that," he said, and then lunged.

Miri managed a nice loud holler, but it was hard to put much force into it while scrambling backward, legs tangled in the cover wrapped around her body. She launched herself backward, rolling, bouncing over the mattress, grabbing for the table lamp on the other side of the bed. It was bolted to the nightstand, which lost her precious seconds, and she rolled sideways again, losing the blanket, trying to evade Robert as he leaped onto the bed. Too late, too late—he came down hard on her body, straddling her waist, pinning her sideways to the bed. She could not push him off and the awkward angle stole her leverage; she tried to pummel him, which amounted to little more than hitting his thigh and chest with all her strength.

Robert did not seem to mind. He holstered his gun, then used his free hand to wrestle her down. Miri swore at him, snapping her teeth, kicking and pushing with her feet against the mattress, trying to roll them both. No good. He did not budge or make a sound.

"It can't just be the money," she gasped, when he paused for a moment to study her face. He was always studying her, she realized. Those eyes, those pale wheels turning in his head. "Why is the jade so important? And why me?"

"I don't know," Robert said, lifting up the syringe. Liquid seeped from the needle tip. "But I am beginning to wish I did."

He leaned in close and Miri thought, *Now, this is it, you have to fight,* and just as he was about to press the needle into her skin, she twisted one last time, lunged up, and fastened her teeth around his nose.

She felt a crunch, tasted blood. Robert did not cry out, but reared backward, the syringe slipping from between his fingers to land in the bedcovers. Miri let go the moment he was off her, rolling naked and uncaring, almost doing a cartwheel in her mad dash to get away to the door.

And then, quite suddenly, Miri was no longer alone. Outside the room she heard another man shout, a wordless cry that was every bit as desperate as the scream in her heart, choking her throat. She felt Robert close behind, his harsh breath, and she let out a strangled shout, high and breathless, as she reached the door.

She managed to throw back the dead bolt before he wrapped his hand in her hair, yanking her down to the floor. Blood covered his face, the front of his clothes. There was a terrible fury in his pale eyes. He did not seem the slightest bit bothered by pain.

"You are such trouble," Robert whispered. "Such trouble, Dr. Lee."

"Yes," Miri whispered, giving it up, going for it all. "I guess that payday isn't looking so good, is it?"

He did not respond. On the other side of the door, Miri thought she heard her name. The voice was familiar, though she could not immediately place it. Only, it was breathless, a cut against her raging heart, and as the door shook on its hinges—great thundering booms that Miri felt in her chest—she heard her name again and this time she shouted back, not caring who was there, only that it was another human being sharing her suffering.

Robert kicked her. Miri rolled with it, still yelling. Again she heard her name. Again and again, and her would-be kidnapper gazed uneasily at the door.

And then, quite suddenly, the voice clicked. It was deeper, older, swimming up from dreamtime—and the tone was the same, the intonation, the edge. The sound rode high into her head, darkness flickering at the corners of her eyes.

No, Miri thought. *No.*

Impossible—so much impossible this night—but that voice—*that voice*—it could not be. That voice was twenty years dead. Twenty years dead, resurrected only in dreams. It was her imagination, delusion, a desire born of desperation and fear and—

"Get up," hissed Robert.

"Fuck you," Miri said, and over another slam, another shout, added, "That guy out there is not going away, you know. You're going to have to open that door."

"Yes," he said. "Which is why I want you out of the way when I do."

Miri moved. She wanted that door open. She wanted to see who was on the other side. Scrambling backward, pushing herself up against the wall, she watched Robert move into position beside the door. He held a gun in his left hand, tight against his thigh.

Do it, she thought, and he turned the handle, jumping back as the door slammed open with enough force to put a crack in the wall behind it. Another man stepped swiftly into the room. There was too much light behind

71

him; Miri could not clearly see his face, but she saw a giant robot on his shirt and a gun in his hand—a gun aimed at Robert, who held his ground, weapon also raised.

"Put it down," ordered the new arrival, though he looked at Miri when he said it. She stopped listening after the first word. Her soul, walking out of normal into a world where women died with stones in their chests, stones meant for the eyes of gods, a world where strangers pointed guns and kidnapped friends, and where friends who were dead, friends who stole hearts and then gave them, suddenly walked through open doors, alive and whole and warm after decades of death.

You're crazy, she told herself. *Don't do this to yourself. Please, don't.*

But her eyes adjusted to the shift in light, and she could not look away. Could not stop staring at the person whose face was almost as familiar as her own. Older now, with more lines, but those blue eyes, those cheeks, that mouth—just like in her dreams …

Too much. All in my head. All in my head and all in my heart and all twisted up like—

"Dean," she breathed.

His heart was burning again. The skin above it, the cut, reaching hot into his flesh, pumping fire like his heart pumped blood. No complaints, though. Dean welcomed the pain. He needed it to stay focused, conscious, because the sight in front of him, the sight in his head only moments before, was enough to lay him out, for him to see lights, to spin the world around his head—all because there was a woman looking into his eyes, a woman who should have been dead.

He was ready when the door opened. Ready for anything, to kill or be killed, but when he looked into that room, past the man with his gun raised—*danger, that guy is dangerous*—all he could see was the naked woman standing in shadow, staring at him with eyes like black diamonds, glittering and bright with some astonishingly hurt light. Dean forgot to breathe, looking into those eyes. The photograph, the visions in his head … all lies.

This was better. This was real. This was good enough to die for.

And then she said his name—*his* name, murmured like an old song—and everything fell together inside his mind. He stopped questioning. His heart gave up the fight. His heart gave up everything but love.

"Miri," he whispered. *"Bao bei."*

She closed her eyes, but that was all the reaction he saw; the man stepped in front of her, the man who Dean had all but forgotten in that one moment of shock. Stupid, so stupid—the kind of carelessness that deserved a bullet.

Dean raised his gun and sighted down the barrel, aiming at a pale eye that was the coldest he had ever seen. The man's face was a mess, covered in blood. Teeth marks scarred his nose. Dean glanced at Miri again; red stained her mouth, the memory still fresh witness to the nightmare, watching her play Hannibal Lector like a born fighter. Perfect and lovely. His sweet girl.

The man shifted again, blocking Dean's sight. Behind, Miri moved; a subtle dance, trying to slip around him. It did not work. He threw out his arm, blocking the narrow hall. Miri stopped, but only just; her posture was breathless, quick. Dean tried not to look anywhere but her face; her nudity scared the hell out of him, made him think all sorts of ugly things. Made him want to kill.

You can't. Miri's standing too close.

And there was also the uncomfortable sensation of

not knowing what the fuck was going on. Though frankly, all he had to do was look at Miri, at her naked body, and remember that vision of her on the bed, on the floor with a hand in her hair and a foot in her gut, to remind himself that he was a man who needed to take care of some nasty business, and that bullets might just be fine.

Maybe more than fine. He glanced at Miri—back from the dead, real and miraculously alive—and remembered another night, years past, another gun in his face, and then—*bang, bang*—her body, broken and bloody in the rain.

Bad memory. Dean's chest burned like a bitch. He wondered if the rest of him was glowing, because Miri was still staring like he was a ghost and the other man couldn't take his gaze away, either.

"Well," he said. "This is unfortunate."

"What's unfortunate is your life," Dean said. "But what's gonna get you killed is the way you treated that girl behind you."

"Really?" A grim smile touched his mouth. "You have no idea what is happening here. The importance of it."

Dean ignored him and glanced at Miri. "You hurt?"

"No," she said. "But I think I'm insane."

"Good enough, sweetheart." And then he flicked his gaze right, to the dimly lit interior of the room behind her, and wondered if she understood, if she could still read his mind with nothing but a look.

And she stared, lifted her chin, and he knew the answer.

Miri flung herself backward, deeper into the hotel room, out of range and out of sight. The man turned to follow. Dean fired his gun.

It was a point-blank shot. The bullet entered the man's shoulder. High impact, high velocity—he should have been blown off his feet, but instead he staggered, folding, gun still in hand. And then, careful, like an un-wrapped doll, he slowly, slowly, straightened. His shoulder looked like hamburger. Blood poured down his chest. He did not seem to care.

Dean fired another round, another wounding shot. The man ate the impact with a swing, a twist, another spurt of blood, all the while his eyes growing colder, paler, almost white. Dean remembered energy, power, and shifted his vision, seeking out the wounds. Sparks flew from the gaping holes. Not typical.

"You have made a terrible mistake," whispered the man, as he bled and dripped. "Simply terrible."

"The only mistake I made was not shooting you in the 'nads." Dean aimed low. "But I can fix that."

"No," the man said. "Not like that." And he fired first.

For a moment, the world slowed; Dean imagined the bullet racing toward him, cutting the air, and somewhere nearby he heard a scream. His, maybe, though it sounded exceptionally feminine. And then time sped up and his chest exploded into fire, burning—*burning*—and he looked down and saw the bullet press above his heart, suspended still and hot in the air. Dean imagined a glow through the cotton of his shirt, and thought, *Holy shit. Take that, you son of a bitch.*

The man stared, something dark passing through his face, a darkness mixed with wonder. He aimed his gun at Dean's head, but that was it, game over; he never got a chance to pull the trigger. Miri ran out from behind the wall, so fast she was a blur, and jammed a pillowcase down over the man's head, blinding him. She jabbed something small into his neck. A syringe.

Dean moved in, lunging for the gun while Miri grappled with the man's free arm, trying to wrench it back, to hold him down from behind. The scent of blood washed over Dean like heat. His hands were slippery with it. He punched the man's wounded shoulder, driving him to his knees.

He was finally able to take away the gun, and the moment he had it, he slammed the butt down hard on the other man's head, again and again until the man stopped struggling, collapsing limp on top of Miri. Dean grabbed the front of the man's shirt and hauled him off her. Miri scrambled away, heading immediately for her clothes, holding them to her body. Dean, face hot, heart burning, turned his back. He rummaged through the man's pockets but found nothing: no wallet or cell phone, not even another weapon. The man's chest rose and fell with even breaths.

Miri appeared at Dean's shoulder, dressed in jeans and a navy blue tank top. She held a very long telephone cord, and had a look on her face that gave Dean a serious case of memory lane as he watched her loop the plastic around her hands, gazing down.

"He's still breathing," she said, and her gaze slid sideways to Dean's chest. He looked down. Nothing. No magic. No wild rings of fire or leaping leprechauns. Just the shirt. Optimus Prime and the Autobot logo. "More Than Meets the Eye" was taking on a whole new meaning. Miri made a small sound and tore her gaze away, looking again at Robert.

"His bleeding stopped," she said grimly. "That's not natural. He's going to wake up, isn't he?"

"Maybe. Are you going to tie him?"

"Yes," she said. And after a moment's hesitation Miri moved in, looping the cord around the man's neck like a noose, pulling hard and turning him face first into the floor so that she could straddle his body. Miri held the plastic in her teeth as she yanked back his arms, and Dean helped her tie the man's wrists behind his back, binding them high in a choking knot. He remembered Miri at eight years old, practicing this move on a doll. He remembered her at fourteen, doing the same to a bully on the playground—and getting away with it, too, because she was a girl and the boy whose ass she kicked was too embarrassed to place blame.

She doesn't look any different, he thought to himself. *Twenty years, and her face is almost the same as the last day I saw her. Give or take a few lines around her eyes.*

Dean holstered his gun and slid the second weapon into the back of his jeans. He pulled his T-shirt and jacket over it, and left Miri for a moment to go into the bathroom for a wet rag. She was waiting for him when he came out, standing just beyond the door.

"I want to know what's going on," she said.

"Ditto," he replied, and handed her the rag. "Wash your face, babe. You have blood on you."

She grimaced and pushed past him into the bathroom. The light was better, and he could see the shine in her black hair, the gold in her skin. There was a crease between her eyes, and after a moment, he realized she was just standing there, staring at him in the mirror.

She did not say anything. Simply looked into his eyes with all that cool strength fading, melting away into the wild diamond glitter of their first locked gaze. In shock before, maybe. Just pretending to be in control.

And then she twitched, a sharp jolt, like a body startled from a dream. Dean held out his hands. Miri shook her head, putting more distance between them, moving until she hit the glass door of the shower. Her hand touched the marble wall and she swallowed hard.

He saw it coming, flipped the toilet seat up just as she turned, staggering, shoulders heaving. She fell to her knees and gagged.

She stayed down there for some time, and Dean soaked and wrung out another warm rag. At the last moment, though, he hesitated before touching her. He did not know what to do, how far to push. It had been twenty years. Twenty years and now this, with violence to boot. Jesus. What a fucked-up night.

Dean split his vision, opening his mind, reaching out to listen to her quantum song. Her thread was light and airy, a sweet energy thrumming against his soul. Perfect harmony, just as he remembered. He knew how Miri felt better than he knew himself. He had spent the past twenty years remembering, keeping her alive inside his head.

Alive. She was alive all this time. And you never knew it. Of all the people in the world you needed to find, it was her. And you couldn't.

He checked the area around her body. No trail. Her energies were self-contained. Just like the murderer he had been hunting.

No, Dean thought. *Miri could never do that before.*

Not Before that night. Before he'd lost her.

Dean could not wrap his mind around the idea. He did not want to. He moved close, dropping to the floor beside her. He touched her hair.

"Miri," he whispered. "Mirabelle."

She wiped her eyes, but did not look at him or say a word as she pushed away from the toilet. She took the rag he offered, but did not use it. She stared at her hands instead, small and golden, pressed flat to the floor.

Her silence hurt. It drowned the pounding of his heart, the roar in his ears. He wanted to lie down in that silence, press his forehead to her knees. Beg for a word.

And then, quite suddenly, her pinky reached toward him. Just one twitch, but Dean held his breath and edged close, brushing his finger against her finger. He almost expected fireworks; somewhere distant, angels singing. But no, just skin. Warm, lovely skin. Miri sighed, and then her hand turned over and her fingers trailed themselves into his open palm, closing gently like a warm wing; meeting, rubbing, twining.

"Miri," he breathed.

"No," she murmured. "I don't want to know. Not yet."

Dean understood. He couldn't take much more of this, either. He picked up the rag from the floor and wiped her face, smoothing away her tears, the blood still around her mouth. Miri touched his chest, the spot above his heart. Dean caught her hand.

"I didn't imagine that," she said.

"No," he said, feeling sick about it.

They both heard a groan. Miri jumped, gazing at the open bathroom door. A tremor ran through her body, but after a brief moment, her mouth tightened into a hard line, and it was old times again, seeing that stubborn light in her eyes. And then she turned that piercing gaze on him and it was like being pinned spread-eagled under a scalpel and a hot lamp.

"You're just like *him*," she said, her voice breaking on the words. The crease deepened in her forehead, her hands curling tight against her thighs. She looked at him and all he could see was pain, the bright heat of tears. "You can't be real. You can't be my Dean. This is a trick."

My Dean. He blew out his breath and said, "I'm not like that man out there, Miri. I'm not. But everything else? Maybe. And maybe *you* aren't real." Though, if this was an illusion, then good God he wasn't saying no.

"But you were dead," she whispered hoarsely.

"*You* were dead," he said, and touched his forehead. "Dead here, Miri. Dead everywhere."

She knew what he meant; he could see it in her eyes. Dean stood and helped her up. "If there's anything you need, grab it now."

"Where are we going?" Her eyes were wild but her voice was calm, steady, like her hands.

Dean said, "Out of this building. It's not safe here. There are more men waiting downstairs for you. I don't know what you're into, Miri—"

"I'm an archaeologist. I'm not *into* anything."

"Yeah? Well, someone wants you, and bad. There must be a reason for it, too. That kind of thing doesn't just happen for nothing."

Nor did he like the implication of having a shape-shifter serial murderer setting on fire and *eating* the very men who just so happened to have Miri's photograph and location. Men who might, at any moment, get tired of waiting downstairs in the lobby for a woman who was most certainly not going to show up.

Dean peered out the bathroom door, but Miri grabbed his arm and pulled him back in close, tight. He felt her warmth run over his body, pool low in his gut, and every coherent thought in his head went screaming out of his ears. Standing so close to her, feeling her hand through his jacket sleeve, was practically an invitation to some kind of explosion. His brain hurt.

"That man out there told me his name is Robert," Miri explained quietly. "He said he was hired to kidnap me and steal something. An artifact."

"What kind of artifact?"

"A four-thousand-year-old piece of red jade, ex-tracted *just this morning* from the body of a mummified woman. But, Dean, I don't have it. My friend does. And he may be in danger. He may already be ..." She did not finish. Dean tugged on her hand.

"Later," he said. "Tell me when we're out of here."

He left the bathroom. The man—Robert—was still

on the floor, the pillowcase over his head. There was blood everywhere, but it was not as fresh as it could have been. Dean imagined the man's shoulder was already beginning to heal. He saw metal inside the flesh; the bullet. He thought it moved, told himself it was his imagination, but after a moment he glimpsed a twitch, and realized with dull horror that the man's body was rejecting the bullet. In fast motion.

Gee, he thought, totally disgusted. *Where have I seen this before?*

Dean crouched beside Robert. He felt Miri behind him, staring.

"Dean," she said, and her voice was so low, so hard, he knew she could see the bullet, too. Robert made a sighing sound, and rolled his shoulder.

"Remarkable, isn't it?" he said, his words muffled, the white pillowcase puffing out around the area of his mouth. "I am like that dreadful television commercial, the one with the ugly rabbit. I just keep going and going."

"Isn't that special?" Dean drawled. "Of course, you're the only one in this room tied up like a pig, so I don't know if you eating a bullet is all that much to brag about."

"I noticed you had much the same ability."

"And I noticed you shot me in the heart, you son of a bitch. At least I didn't try to kill you."

"Oh, if only," said Robert, and then, more softly: "Dr. Lee? Are you there?"

"Don't you talk to her," Dean warned.

"I'm here," Miri said, ignoring him.

"You're in danger," Robert said. "You need to go now. You need to find that jade that is so cleverly not in your possession, and you must run."

"I think you lied to me, Robert. I think you know more about what's going on here than you said."

"No, my dear. But if you run, that's just another chance for me to find you again. But if you get caught by the others …"

"What others?" Dean asked, though he already had his suspicions. "What do you know?"

"Only that there are more things in heaven and earth, Mr. Campbell, than are dreamt of in your philosophy."

Dean's breath caught. "You know my name."

"I know who you work for," Robert said, his disembodied voice floating up from the pillowcase. "What a shame that you do not know as much."

Dean stood. His body hurt. His mind felt worse. This was not something he wanted to hear, not anything at all he felt capable of contemplating.

Why are you surprised? It was only a matter of time. You knew all the agents of Dirk & Steele had been exposed.

Knew it because his best friend and colleague, Artur Loginov, had recently been kidnapped and tortured by a group calling itself the Consortium—a corporate crime syndicate run by psychics, just like Dirk & Steele. Only ruthless, hungry for power, wealth. And, apparently, from what had happened to Artur, quite eager to recruit from the ranks of the agency, by any means necessary.

Real charmers. Dean felt warm and fuzzy just thinking about them. It didn't matter, either, that Artur and his new wife, Elena, had managed to ruin the Consortium's power base. Another, even more mysterious, organization remained—and its intentions toward Dirk & Steele were still as yet unknown. It couldn't be good, though. Dean did not feel that lucky.

And now this. He was painfully aware of Miri standing close behind him, and turned to look at her. She met his gaze, eyebrows raised, and he could see the question rolling across her face, a loud and singular *What the hell is going on?*

He wished he could tell her. He wished a lot of things were different.

"Who hired you?" Dean asked Robert. "It wasn't the Consortium, was it?"

"The Consortium?" He sounded genuinely surprised. "I would never work for them. I have some standards."

Dean grunted. Dirk & Steele's agents had been sheltered like babies. "Who, then?"

Robert did not answer. The bullet popped out of his shoulder and rolled onto the floor. Miri stifled a gasp and took a step back.

Priorities, Dean told himself, staring at that slug. *Forget questions. You need to get Miri out of here. Now.*

Dean crouched. "Fine. Don't tell me who's paying the bills. But you come after Miri again and I'll finish what we started. I don't care how many bullets it takes. I don't care what I have to do."

"You don't have enough bullets to get your way," Robert said. "You don't have enough life in your body to take her from me. I have a job to do. You have no idea what that means."

"I don't consider that a problem." Dean backed slowly away, guiding Miri to the door. She did not fight him, only paused to grab her purse. She opened the door just a crack, listening, and after a moment slipped from the room. Dean followed, flipping off the main light switch as he left. Robert disappeared into darkness. No protest, no movement. But there was a promise in his silence.

The hall was very quiet. Dean did not like it. "There should be more people. We were shooting guns, for Christ's sake."

"Robert told me this floor was empty," Miri said. "That his employer had rented it out. He said I could scream and no one would hear."

Dean wanted to do some screaming of his own, but

behind them, out of sight and down the curving hall, the elevators chimed. The air was silent enough to hear soft soles scuff marble. No echoing clicks of heels or flats; their footfalls hit the carpet, disappearing into a muffled ominous silence.

And then, voices. Men. Too soft to understand, but Dean heard a click, the ratchet of a gun chamber loaded, the sounds of locks sliding and a door opening—*a key, they got a fucking key*—and he grabbed Miri's hand and tugged her hard. She did not hesitate, did not argue or ask questions; her color was back, her gaze focused, strong.

They entered the stairwell at the end of the hall. Dean carefully shut the heavy door and pointed down. They went quietly at first, on light feet, but after two floors, gave it up, risking bones and twisted ankles and heart failure as they raced down the stairs. Only once did he catch Miri looking at him, and it was just like when they were kids, the two of them running with the wind in their blood, something bad on their tails. Bullies, thugs, his uncle.

Careful. You don't know her anymore. She doesn't know you. She has a whole other life you're not part of.

Maybe. Probably. Only, there was a miracle running beside him and he could afford to throw out a line, reel in the possibilities. Anything was possible now. All he had to do was hang on. Hang on tooth and nail. Fuck everything else. Figure out exactly what was going on and take care of the problem. Take care of Miri, even if it killed him.

Which, he hoped, it would not.

"How did you find me?" Miri asked, and he heard the rest of it, unspoken, a quiet *How did you find me after all this time?*

"Accident," he said. "It's complicated."

"Must be. I still don't believe this. I still don't know if I can trust you."

"You trust me. You wouldn't be here right now if you didn't."

"It's just survival. Don't let it go to your head."

"Too late, babe." He remembered that he had a hotel room in this building, though it was long gone above them. He could hide Miri there, keep her safe until he called the home office and found out what the hell to do next.

But that man up there knew your name. He knew Dirk & Steele. You think any place is safe?

Fat chance, and no way he was going to risk it. Out of the building—that was what his instincts were screaming. Get Miri far and away. He did have other options, after all. Just not ones he had used in a very long time.

"You said there are other men looking for me?" Miri asked, breathing hard.

"In the lobby. They're organized."

"Is there another way out of here?"

"Basement garage," Dean said. He wanted to say more, but words seemed cheap, inadequate. Instead he settled for stealing glances—and found Miri doing the same.

No one pursued them. They ran themselves all the way down to the garage, which was universal in its flickering perfect-for-a-murder lighting, painted concrete walls, and stuffy humid air. Security personnel, men in bright orange jackets, lounged in chairs at various intervals in the garage, giving Dean some worry, but all the old men did was smoke their cigarettes and drink from tall, thin cans of mango juice, watching Dean and Miri like disapproving parents seeing their kids off for a first date.

They were on the first level of the garage; it was easy to access the street, and they did so, breathless and sweaty, on the far side of the hotel away from the main glass doors and glittering lights of the Far Eastern Mall. An old man with a tiny white dog walked past them; Miri almost clobbered him trying to get to the road. She hailed a cab.

"Why do I get the feeling you already know where we're going?" Dean glanced up at the sky to see if Koni was anywhere nearby. Nothing, not unless he was hiding. A small yellow car swerved toward them.

"Because I do," Miri said, and there was a challenge in her voice, a dare. Dean did not take the bait. He did not need to. He trusted her.

They got into the cab and drove away.

Chapter Four

It was, by the clock on the cab's dashboard, almost midnight by the time they reached National Taiwan University. The driver took them down Palm Boulevard, a wide street lined with tall old-fashioned lamps and even taller royal palms, and made several turns down dark campus streets populated by groups of students walking and laughing in the road and on the sidewalk.

So ordinary. So normal. Miri wanted to scream at the young men and women, rage against the simplicity and safety of their lives.

Everything is relative, she thought, and then, *Owen. Owen, hold on. Wherever you are, I'm coming to help you.*

If she could even help herself, which seemed unlikely. There was an ache in her heart, a rumble beneath her skin, like she was on the edge of jumping out of her flesh; screaming, screaming. Delayed reaction, maybe. Gung-ho chick at the hotel, shriveling down to nothing but an old adrenaline stain, less than a leftover flake of deodorant.

In fact, the only thing holding her together was

Dean, and even that was rocky. Looking at him made her feel like the victim of an aneurysm or some odd exploding eyeball disease. Not the way she would have imagined a miraculous reunion—which she had, all those years ago when it was so difficult to believe he was dead. Dreaming of him holding her again, laughing in her ear, in the kitchen with her grandmother with his hands greasy from dumplings and pork, poking her with chopsticks, making her crazy and crazy with love.

Miri, pressed up against her side of the cab, stole a glance at Dean, studying his loose posture. His profile was older now but still her friend, still familiar. Strong cheeks, strong mouth, strong eyes. That soft blond hair, tousled. He sat with his hands resting on his thighs, drumming his fingers as he stared out the window. He looked good, almost better than she remembered, which was also unsettling.

He turned his head and caught her staring.

"Hey," he said softly.

"Hey," she replied, and then, because she had to say something, anything, added, "This is crazy."

"Yeah," he said, and seemed to fumble for a moment, mouth opening and closing, hesitating on his next words. But in the end he said nothing at all, and gave her only a weak smile that was unabashedly shy.

How did you survive? she asked him silently. *Was it magic that saved you? The same magic I saw tonight? All those things you used to do, turning into something new?*

Something that could stop a bullet? Miri closed her eyes. This was insanity, pure and simple. She had lost her mind, and even if she hadn't, the coincidence of him being here was too much. She almost asked him, almost opened her mouth to pin him down with questions, but she stopped herself at the last moment. She was afraid of what he would say. Or what he wouldn't tell her.

It's all a conspiracy: Men breaking into my room, men coming back from the dead, men who won't stay dead …

And yet, here she was—with a man she had not seen in twenty years. A man she might not be able to trust. This Dean was not the boy she had known and loved. Not this strange man who carried a gun and who appeared out of the blue to wave around that weapon and … save her. That was just weird. Weird and frightening.

Too late, she told herself. *You can't run now. Besides, if he can still do those tricks with his mind, you need him. You have to find Owen.*

And if Dean refused to help her? It had certainly taken him long enough to track her down.

He told you it was an accident; he thought you were dead.

Maybe. If only.

The cab stopped on one of the side streets near the archaeology building and Dean paid the fare. There was a breeze as Miri stepped out of the car, but it did not help her breathing. She saw some girls walking down the sidewalk, holding hands, surgical masks covering the lower portions of their faces. A good idea. The night air was too hot and sticky, filthy with smog. Terrible for the lungs.

Dean joined her; the girls walking toward them stared and put their heads together. Their eyes crinkled.

"Where are we going?" he asked. The girls continued past, still staring, and Miri heard one of them say *"Shuai ge."* Handsome brother.

Dean heard; he glanced at them, and said, *"Xie-xie."*

They giggled and pranced off, still hand in hand. Miri stared at him. He tried to look innocent.

"What? Girls tell a man he's hot and he has to say thank you."

Miri's eyes narrowed. "We're going to the archaeology department," she said. "If Robert was telling the truth, then Owen was taken from there. He might even still be close. We can find him."

"And you want me to ..." He stopped, wiggling his fingers around his head.

"You don't mind?"

Dean frowned. "When did I ever? It's what I do, *bao bei.*"

"And you still trust me?" she pressed. "Even after all this time?"

His frown faded, smoothing into the hint of a smile. "I always trusted you, babe. Even when we were kids, you were the only one I believed in. I never held anything back from you."

"Nothing," she murmured, remembering. "Not even when life got so weird."

"The headaches," he said quietly. "The blindness. I missed so much school, and then those social workers got involved. Assholes made my uncle take me to the doctor. What a load of crap. They just made it worse."

"Because there was nothing wrong with you."

"Yeah. Developing psychic powers aren't exactly on the list of physical ailments." He shook his head, scuffing the ground with his sneaker, and smiled grimly. "Everyone thought I was a liar, a lazy good-for-nothing piece of shit. Except you."

Miri shrugged, suddenly shy. "I knew the truth."

"It wasn't just that," Dean said. "I remember how those teachers tried to pressure you to stay away from me. They thought I was trash. Twelve years old, and they wrote me off. But you always took up for me. You fought for me. Jesus, Miri, you got in fucking screaming arguments with those old ladies when you thought I wasn't being treated right."

"You were my friend," she said simply. And despite her misgivings, suddenly recalled everything with heartbreaking clarity. For eight years she'd had two anchors in her life, two people—one young, one old—giving her a real family, keeping her from drifting away. She would have done anything to protect that.

And she wondered, looking into Dean's eyes, if she was in danger of feeling that way again.

They started walking, remaining silent until the first edge of the archaeology building came into sight. It was difficult to see—some of the streetlamps were not working properly—but even in the midnight darkness the square lines were very distinct. Dean made an odd sound, low in his throat.

"This could be dangerous," he said.

"Gee, no. Never would have guessed."

"You want a gun?"

Miri stopped walking. "Do I want a gun? What kind of question is that? You know I hate those things."

"No," he said, startled. "I don't know. You never hated them before."

But even as he said those last words, his eyes changed, and Miri knew he understood. They were standing under a streetlamp; she pulled aside the neck of her tank top. Dean leaned close, his breath warm on her skin. Goose bumps ran up her arms as he studied the puckered scar above her heart.

She watched his face, and saw the echo of some terrible pain pass through his eyes, an awful sorrow that made her breath catch, her heart pound just a little harder. His hand twitched. She covered herself before he could touch her.

Dean said nothing for a very long moment. And then, slowly, he pulled down his own collar. The T-shirt was old; the material stretched easily. There was a thin gold chain around his neck, but Miri peered past that at his skin and saw a scar that mirrored her own: a circle, the shadow of a hole. She thought of the bullet that had struck him that night, twenty years past, and remembered the bullet that had slammed into him tonight.

Bad memories. She touched his scar. Dean sucked in his breath, but did not move. He held very still as she explored it—her curiosity morbid, surreal. She glimpsed something else just below the mangled flesh, and tugged his collar a little lower.

"You're hurt," she said. The cut was ugly, fierce. Something about it, however, seemed familiar.

"It's nothing," he said, but she barely heard him. She was finally looking at the chain, following it down to something small and round, a pedant, a locket—

She leaned close, not touching, but peering at the familiar round lines, the shape and glitter of the gold. He still had it. After all these years, he still wore the damn thing around his neck.

"Dean," she said, and there were no words, nothing to explain what it meant to her to see that locket still with him.

Dean finally touched her, wrapping his warm hands around her wrists. His voice was low, rough; she looked up into his eyes and found them dark, and very, very, close.

She tried to step back, but Dean did not let her go.

"Do you remember?" he said quietly. "Do you remember that night? I was going to teach you how to drive, and then we got distracted in the big backseat of my uncle's car."

Miri remembered. It was supposed to be best night of her life. Their first time together, naked and ready to do something more than just hug and kiss. Something special. Mind-blowing, like all those books said it was meant to be.

And maybe it would have been … if you hadn't been interrupted by that asshole with the gun.

Bang, bang. Miri closed her eyes. "I don't want to talk about this, Dean."

He let go. "I'm sorry."

"Don't be. There's a lot to remember." She sucked in a deep breath and forced herself to look him in the eyes. Only for a second, though. Her gaze slid back down to her hands, clenched tight in his collar. She did not know why she was still holding his shirt, and forced herself back. Tiny lights danced in her vision; she felt sick to her stomach. Her heart burned.

"We're wasting time," she said. "I need to help my friend. If you're worried about it being dangerous, you don't have to come with me."

"Now you're being insulting. What kind of man do you think I am?"

"I don't know," she said.

"Oh," Dean said. "Oh well. Thanks a lot."

"What did you expect me to say?"

"A compliment wouldn't have hurt. My ego needs stroking."

"Stroke it on your own time," she muttered. "We need to go now."

A crow cawed. The bird was close, its voice so loud and unexpected, Miri jumped. Dean, scowling, grabbed her hand and tugged her out of the light.

"Fine," he said. "You sure you want to do this? I could go in by myself. I'm a bad man, after all. Totally off-the-wall dangerous."

"I didn't say that. Besides, I don't care about the danger. I have to do this, Dean. You know how it is." How it is, how it was, all to commit to one thing for the sake of another. Because if you had a friend in trouble, you went balls out, or else you had no balls at all.

"Rule numero uno," Dean said, just like he could read her mind. His mouth crooked into a smile. "The Lee and Campbell book of survival. Yeah, I remember.

I just don't recall bone diggers ever being quite this popular, except on television. You're not channeling Indiana Jones on me, are you?"

"If only. I'd feel better with a whip and fedora."

"Who wouldn't?" Dean asked, and they started walking again. He made them take a circuitous route, cutting behind bushes and trees, hugging the shadows. She understood why—might have done the same on her own—but the slow pace was monstrously annoying.

The area around the building was quiet, and the few late-night students walking nearby did so with the oblivious weariness of the hard-core studier. They saw no guards, no suspicious loiterers, no unusual activity. Only once, from the corner of Miri's eye, did she glimpse another kind of movement: swift, large. Her stride faltered. She looked.

The shadow was flesh and blood; a tall, powerfully built man dressed in black, standing only a stone's throw away. Ordinary, simple. Nothing to be afraid of. But seeing him sent a shock through Miri's stomach that she could not explain, and she tugged on Dean's hand.

"What?" he whispered, and she pointed.

The man was gone. Miri stared, turning around and around, but she saw no trace of him.

"Someone was here," she told Dean. He said nothing. He made her walk faster.

The large glass double doors of the archaeology building were still unlocked and, inside, the halls were empty and even more still and silent. Some of the lights had already been turned off, and Miri's chest tightened when she saw the darkness, the shadows. Danger, calling.

This is crazy. You should be running away, calling the cops.

And then what? Get taken in for questioning by a bureaucracy that would not help Owen quickly enough, or worse, would not believe her at all? Besides, the local police would be coming after her soon enough, what with all the blood in her hotel room and a man tied up on her floor. If, that is, Robert stayed there long enough to be found by hotel management. Somehow she doubted it, given the sounds of those men who had gotten off the elevators just after she and Dean left the room.

"How did you know there were other men waiting for me at the hotel?" Miri asked, as she led Dean down a long corridor to a narrow stairwell. Bathrooms were nearby; they smelled like the *ai-yi* hadn't cleaned the dirty toilet paper out of the wastebaskets for days.

Dean hesitated, then pulled a picture from his back pocket. It was an up-close shot of her face. There was a name and location clipped to the back. *Her* name. *Her* room number at the Far Eastern Hotel.

"Where did you get this?" She did not recognize the moment the picture documented, but she knew it was not here in Taiwan. Someone had been following her at home in Palo Alto.

"I was investigating a murder," Dean said, carefully watching her face. "I found that with the latest victim. Just tonight. I went to the hotel immediately. In fact, I was staying there, too. Only one floor below yours."

One floor. One floor separating them. What a terrible irony. What an awful implausible thought. If it was true.

But she looked at him, at the open sincerity and pain of his gaze, and she could not bring herself to call him a liar. She believed him. And maybe she was wrong to believe, but it was impossible not to. Like breathing, like eating; trusting him felt so natural it was either going to kill her again or keep her going for the rest of her life.

"You found me," she said.

"I found you," he echoed. "I wish I had found you sooner."

He began to say something else, and hesitated. Miri found herself reaching for his hand—did her own dance of hesitation—but Dean met her halfway and wrapped his fingers warm around her palm before she could pull away.

"If I wasn't afraid of losing you," he murmured quickly, "of letting you out of my sight, I would tell you that this is the stupidest, most fucked-up idea I've ever heard, and lock you in a hole while I go and look for this friend of yours."

"You always were a charmer," Miri said, and tugged him down the stairs.

They moved slowly. Dean reached under the back of his shirt and drew out Robert's gun, holding the weapon close against his side. There was no place to hide between the stairs and the lab, just open territory at the bottom of the stairwell, followed by a set of doors into the exam room, and from there, Owen's office. They encountered no one. The area was very quiet. Dean's eyes went distant—just a glaze, a remoteness that she remembered. Although, she also recalled him looking a lot more cross-eyed. She wondered if had been practicing the use of his second sight in front of a mirror.

"There's been a lot of activity," he said. "So much, I'm having trouble locking in on any one current event. All the people who have been in this space in the past two hours have scattered. I'm seeing everything from dumpling shops to a television to … sex. Oh, *wow*."

"Wow yourself later. Do you see Owen in any of those locations?"

Dean moved around the lab, arms outstretched. He looked like a wannabe, somewhat crazed, ballet dancer. "Give me a description."

"Older. White. Wears a lot of tweed."

"Older, huh? You two close?"

"Excuse me?"

"You and this Owen."

Miri stared at Dean's back. She did not know what to say, except for a somewhat exasperated *Are you crazy?* but she kept her mouth shut. Over her silence he said, "I don't see anyone that matches that description."

Giving Dean one long last look, she left his side and pushed her way into Owen's office. Or at least, she tried to. The door was blocked, but Miri shoved hard and Dean put his shoulder next to hers and they opened a large enough crack for Miri to slip through.

There was a lamp on that illuminated, in warm light, disaster. The floor was covered in spilled papers and broken glass, glittering like ice, while books and bone fragments and large stones lay in scattered piles, priceless objects broken under overturned tables and cut leather and torn floors. Nothing had been left in peace. Miri felt as though she stood before actual physical wounds, terrible holes and scars in what had been a place of temporary comfort.

"Dean," Miri said hoarsely. "Dean, get in here."

"I already am," he said, and she jumped, startled. He touched her shoulders, drawing her close against his side.

"I see darkness," he said. "He's in a container or a room. I feel movement around him, but I can't make out who's with him. I'm also picking up bits and pieces of what happened in here. Three men, all in suits." Dean pushed deeper into the room; glass crunched underfoot. "They rushed him. He fought. But that's all I see. The men aren't with him now. They're doing regular stuff. They went home to their families."

"I don't give a shit about their private lives. Where's Owen?"

"Still in Taipei, but moving fast to the east. He must be inside some kind of vehicle."

"We need to catch up." Miri moved to the door. Dean grabbed her arm.

"You said there was an artifact. That's what Robert wanted, right? That's what he said these guys were after?"

It took her a moment to remember; the jade was the last thing on her mind. As far as she was concerned, it did not matter.

Think, she told herself. *If people want the thing, then it's leverage.*

Miri took a deep breath. "The last time I spoke with Owen, he was carrying the damn thing on him. He probably still has it. It's too big to swallow, but I wouldn't put it past him to stick the thing in his underwear if it meant keeping it safe."

Dean grunted. "What's so special about the jade?"

"I wish I knew." Miri rubbed her face, leaning up hard against the wall. "If it were any other situation, I would say money. That its only value is cold hard cash. Private collectors pay ungodly amounts for things like that, and Robert admitted that he was hired to steal the stone and kidnap me. But the timing is all wrong, Dean. Owen only discovered the jade *this morning.* Do you understand? The timing is impossible."

"Lots of things are impossible. Think about what you've seen tonight."

"I'm talking logistics. There just hasn't been time to launch the kind of effort that's taking place here. Not to mention that Robert knew personal details about my life."

"And then there's that photograph of you," he said grimly.

"That kind of thing takes time, research."

"Planning." Dean briefly closed his eyes. "Fuck. Why you, babe?"

"I don't know, but if someone wanted an archaeologist to analyze the jade, Owen would be the better choice. He's one of the smartest men I know."

"Really?" he said, and it was funny how his focus could turn so fast. Good old Dean. Miri did not know whether to laugh or kick his ass.

"Just say it," she told him. "You're jealous."

"You bet," he said. "I'm so green I'm putrid."

"Wow. Sexy. You're such a caveman."

"You better believe it, sweetheart. If I wasn't supposed to be an enlightened, politically correct male of the twenty-first century, I'd have you by the hair right now."

"You couldn't catch me."

"And this Owen can?"

"Owen is almost seventy."

"That doesn't make me feel better."

"Jesus Christ." Miri covered her face. "I'm not sleeping with him, Dean. He's like a father to me. In fact, he's a better father than my own father. He's like … like Ni-Ni. So just … shut up."

Silence, and then she heard him move close, shuffling through the debris. His body felt warm. He touched her hands and pulled them from her face.

"I'm sorry," he said.

"It's a compliment," she said. "But poorly timed."

Dean grunted. "Is there something here that belongs to him? Something he handled a lot? We should take that with us so I can keep tracking him."

"Yes." Miri pushed past him. Her nose was runny and her eyes felt hot. She tried to ignore both as she searched the floor in front of Owen's desk. She dug around until she found, with great relief, a small brass object the length of her finger. She brushed it off and pressed her lips against it. Dean peered over her shoulder.

"Is that Glen Campbell?" he asked incredulously. "With a guitar?"

"Owen's a fan."

"So am I, but I don't run around with statues of him."

Miri looked at Dean's T-shirt. "And I suppose you're going to tell me you don't own your very own Optimus Prime. With accessories."

Dean frowned. "That's different. He's collectible."

Miri rolled her eyes and handed him the tiny statue. "Is there enough of him on there for you?"

"Yeah," he said, after a moment spent rubbing the smooth surface. "I'm totally channeling 'Gentle on My Mind.' "

He helped her stand, but Miri hesitated, still searching the floor. Just beneath some scattered papers, she glimpsed something that made her go very still. She bent down again and pushed aside the debris.

There was blood on the floor.

"No," she breathed. The stain in front of her was the size of her head, and that was more than enough to make her mouth go dry, her heart squeeze and squeeze.

"He's still alive," Dean said quietly, speaking in a rush. "He's still alive, Miri. I saw it. We'll find him. I promise."

She nodded, drawing in a shaky breath. She could not stop looking at the blood. She could not help but imagine the injury that could have caused it. She wondered if Dean could see that particular act of violence— if he had seen it, and simply kept the truth to himself.

Don't ask. You don't want to know.

Dean tugged her toward the office doors, but just as they reached them he stopped, cocking his head as though listening to something. He swung around to face the office.

"What?" she asked, alarmed.

"Owen didn't have the jade on him," Dean muttered. "Son of a bitch."

And then, as though the room had strings on him and were tugging, tugging, he lurched back through the chaos, swimming into a distant corner where there was a tiny bathroom for Owen's private use. Miri clambered after him, but Dean was faster. He switched on the light and lifted up the toilet seat.

Taped to the bottom, wrapped in plastic, was something small and flat and red.

"No," Miri said. "He hid it in the toilet?"

"I hide things in the toilet all the time," Dean said. "But usually in the watery part."

She scowled at him and bent close to strip off the tape. "I'm surprised they didn't look here."

"Old guy wears tweed, I wouldn't think about the toilet, either."

"But?"

"I passed through a trail—Owen's, I guess—that showed him walking to the bathroom with something in his hands. I deduced."

"Deduced," Miri echoed, peeling away the plastic to reveal the jade. "That used to be your favorite word when you were thirteen."

"Sherlock Holmes is a god," Dean said. "Right up there with Kermit the Frog."

"They would make beautiful babies," she replied. The jade felt smooth and warm in her hands and she held it out to Dean. He did not touch it, but peered close, his gaze roving over the lines. He rubbed his chest.

"Okay," he said after a moment. "Okay, put that away and let's get out of here."

Miri frowned, but did as he asked. And then, once

again, Dean went very still. He put a finger on her lips. His eyes were bright and hard.

She heard voices. Sharp, a mix of Mandarin and Tai-wanese. Very familiar. She pushed against Dean, but he did not let her go.

"Wait," he breathed.

The voices grew louder. It was difficult to hear every-thing going on inside the lab, but wheels rattled—one of the exam tables, pushed—and she heard the storage chamber open.

"Hurry," someone said, and Miri's focus slammed down upon that nasal voice, eating it up and spitting it out. She heard plastic rattle.

Kevin. Kevin Liao was on the other side of those doors.

"Hurry," he said again. "The instructions were ex-plicit, and we are running out of time. He could be here any minute."

"Dean," Miri breathed. "Do you have a fix? Have they been in here?"

"Yes," he whispered. "Recently, too. I'm standing right in the middle of their trails. They're handling dead people, Miri. Really old and shriveled dead people. Do-ing a shitty job of it, too. Three men and a woman. You can hear that guy giving orders. Slicked-back hair, glasses. Dirt stains on his—"

"—goddamn *son of a bitch*—"

"—pants. So. Bad guys."

Miri moved. Dean held her back.

"No, no, no," he said in her ear. "Breathe, little cricket."

"Cricket, my ass," she hissed. "It all makes sense. There's only a handful of people who would have known almost immediately that Owen extracted something from the bodies he uncovered in Yushan. And that man out there is one of them."

"You know him?"

"Kevin Liao. He's the head of this department.'

"Oh yeah," Dean said sarcastically. "That's pure evil."

"You have no idea." She rammed her elbow in his gut, but he did not release her. Just made a grunting sound and tightened his arms.

"Let me go," she said. "I'll get nasty."

"You know what I like."

"Dean."

"Have you forgotten what we just left behind at your hotel? We need to get out of here, all quietlike, and find your friend. We don't have time for a fuss."

"That man in there may have contributed to Owen's kidnapping and my assault. Black market thieves, Dean. An inside job. And now they're stealing those mummies. *Stealing them.*"

"No," he said, eyes going distant. "I don't think they're stealing them, Miri. I think they're destroying them."

Her mouth fell open. "You're not serious. Dean—oh my God. I have to stop them."

"Maybe you should be thinking about running instead. Whatever is going on here is bigger than just some black market buyout. You don't hire a guy like Robert for a simple snatch and grab, you don't kidnap archaeologists over old pieces of rock, and from looking at your face, you sure as hell *don't* destroy something like those mummies out there unless you got a hard-on for crazy." Dean hesitated. "And maybe my Chinese is rusty, but I could have sworn I heard that guy say the word *instruction.* They've got a time line. They're working for someone."

"What are they doing now, Dean?"

He hesitated. "We should go, Miri. The only one left in the other room is the woman."

"What aren't you telling me?"

But instead of answering, he shook his head and said, "You're not going to pull some shit on me, are you? I know you're angry about what they're doing."

"Kevin is a weenie. I can kick his ass on the way out and not even break stride."

"Good times. Resist the urge."

"Spoilsport."

"Miss Gung Ho. I thought you were an intellectual now."

"With you, I'm all crazy."

"Wooo," he said, and reached under his shirt, revealing a nice hard stomach that was far more muscular than she remembered. No longer sixteen and scrawny, that was for sure.

"Now is not the time to fondle yourself," she said.

"I might not get another chance," he said, unclipping a gun from the rig beneath his shirt. He stuck it in the back of his pants, alongside Robert's stolen weapon. Miri stared. So many firearms. It made her uncomfortable, and not just because she had once been shot. Getting caught with a gun in Taiwan was a crime almost equivalent to drug possession—which usually meant jail or the death penalty.

Worse, she couldn't imagine the kind of life Dean led that would make him need or want that much fire power within easy reach.

Not the boy you knew, she told herself again. And maybe her face showed her doubts, the question. Dean reached out and slid his hand, warm, against the nape of her neck. Miri stopped breathing, her entire focus narrowing to the feel of his skin, the strength in his fingers as they entwined, ever so gently, in her hair.

"I'm no criminal," he said in a low voice. "I grew up good, Miri."

"Yeah?" she breathed, finding it difficult to speak. "What happened to you, Dean?"

He hesitated. "A lot."

His hand lingered. Miri touched him, holding his hand, being held, trying not to shiver as his fingers transferred from her neck to her wrist, tracing a path over her palm.

"Dean," she whispered, unable to pull away, but afraid, so afraid of what would happen if she did not. His eyes were so pained that for an instant she believed he had missed her, that the past twenty years had been just as difficult on his own heart.

"I'm not going anywhere this time," he said quietly. "You're stuck with me, Miri. Call me psycho, a stalker, whatever you want. I'm here."

"I don't believe you," she said. "You left me before. You *died*."

"So did you."

"Then it's been too long. Twenty years, Dean."

"That's not long enough to forget your best friend, Miri. Some things don't fade."

"Maybe not," she said. "But they do change."

He let go and smiled, lopsided, which was enough to transform his face into something rueful and exquisitely boyish. "I can live with that," he said, and then leaned in quick and kissed her cheek. "Come on, babe. Let's get into trouble."

He opened the door, and pushed Miri through.

Chapter Five

Moving dead people was always a delicate business, especially if the deceased were four thousand years old. Bodies tended to disintegrate rather quickly at those ages, and at a rate that could be calculated with a certain degree of accuracy, especially if the handler of said body was a complete and utter boob. Or a coldhearted son of a bitch. It was a toss-up.

Miri smelled Kevin as soon as she entered the lab. He wore a particularly malodorous brand of cologne manufactured by an Italian company that, as Miri had recently discovered, lived by the motto that every woman should be able to know when her man was coming. So to speak. Kevin loved it.

He was not, however, anywhere to be seen. The lab was a mess; Miri saw flakes of the mummified remains all over the floor, which was enough to make her dig nails into her palms and contemplate the swift removal of Kevin's body parts. Maybe there were men with guns hunting her, men who would not die, and maybe it was stupid to be so angry with all of that behind her and more, but Miri had her limits, her principles, and this was one of them. The dead had to be treated with respect. And the very ancient dead, treated with a great deal more than that.

But the bodies were gone and there was only one other person in the lab. A woman. Miri recognized her.

It was one of the assistants, a graduate student who called herself Ku-Ku. She sat at a computer, typing fast, but she broke off as soon Dean and Miri entered. Her pigtails swung as she turned around, little plastic Hello Kitties clacking around her shining black hair. She wore street clothes, latex gloves. She did not look happy to see them. Miri saw a thin flashing bar on the computer screen. Deletion program. Already in progress.

Calm, calm, calm.

Ku-Ku pushed away from the desk and stood. She had a pink purse slung around her slender body and her purple tennis shoes had platform soles that made her taller than Miri. She held herself straight, with a tense line in her arm that suggested she was ready to move, fast. Good. Because if Miri got a hold of her, hell was gonna be paid like, whoa.

Miri said, "Hello, Ku-Ku. Late night?"

Ku-Ku said nothing, which was unusual. She was the bouncy member of the department, always cheerful, with a sly word, a smile. But now her eyes were wary, her mouth set in a hard line, and when she glanced down the hall toward the exit, Miri thought, *You are so in the shit, little girl.*

Dean touched Miri's elbow. He edged her with his hip in the direction of the hall. His fingers thrummed against her arm, three times in quick succession. Their old code.

Hurry, he said. Hurry, get out. Hurry, run. Hurry, stop talking.

Miri heard voices at the end of the hall. She met Ku-Ku's gaze for a brief instant, and it was as though all those lunches and long hours and occasional girl talk meant nothing, jack squat, just notches on a belt of betrayal. No one in Miri's life was safe. She was surrounded by liars and thieves.

Not Owen, she thought. *And not Dean. Not him. Not to you, ever.*

If only that were true. Or maybe it was. Maybe. She hoped. Once upon a time, most certainly. And now ...

She felt him, strong and warm beside her, a twenty-year miracle come to life, and for a moment she was young again, sixteen, full of a wild rush that came with knowing she could do anything, be anyone, and that at her side, always with her, would be her best friend, her right arm, the eyes in the back of her head. And feeling that—the old love, the old loyalty—she thought, *Yes.*

Ku-Ku made a noise low in her throat. Kevin appeared around the bend in the corridor, accompanied by two younger men Miri did not know. He looked like a different person than she remembered, which was some feat, considering she had seen him only days before. Short, yes. Overweight, yes. Shrewd and intelligent and petty, most certainly.

But his eyes, like Ku-Ku's, were now cold and hard and utterly unforgiving. Dead eyes. Eyes like the old Chinese gangsters who had lived on Miri's street back in Philly, men who watched over their flock like embittered kings.

He looked at Miri and in English said, "You should already have been taken." Simple, easy, quiet, and she thought, *This night cannot possibly get any weirder.* But that was a lie and she knew it—could only look into the faces of these people, two of whom were distant colleagues, and know that yes, weird had come, and come screaming. Danger, too. All kinds of wicked bad, all of which she could never have anticipated existing—at least not in the life she had now.

Dean grabbed Miri's hand; she felt his strength coil between them, warmth settling hard between her breasts. It was an odd sensation, like the simple act of holding Dean's hand was allowing him to sink a limb deep into her soul. Something edged her mind, like memory: déjà vu, maybe. Standing here, linked with Dean, two against the world.

"And who are you?" Kevin said to Dean.

"Her sex slave," Dean replied. "At least, that's my goal in life."

Kevin blinked. Dean pushed Miri toward the door, keeping her behind him. They did not get far. Ku-Ku pulled a pistol out of her purse and aimed it at Miri. Yes, déjà vu. Miri stared at the young woman, wondering why she was doing this, but Ku-Ku's gaze gave her nothing in return.

"The man is armed," said the girl in English. "Two guns at the small of his back. Two more around his ankles."

"What?" Dean asked. "You got X-ray vision or something?"

Kevin held out his hands. "Your weapons, please."

"Um, no. Really."

"Even at risk of death?"

Miri watched Dean hesitate, and edged sideways—barely a step, more of a sway. She knew he noticed. Dean's fingers twitched. But even as she got ready to run, an odd thing happened. Her vision narrowed and she felt a tremendous pressure all around her, a darkness that blocked out the lab and seeped into her vision until all she could see was Dean—and suddenly he was gone as well, and she found herself staring at brown skin, darker than her own, a body both familiar and strange. She smelled rain, the richness of a wet forest, old and layered and hanging dark with wildness, and felt between her breasts a haunting warmth that was an open flame, throbbing to the beat of her heart.

Remember, whispered a voice. *Remember who you are.*

But all she remembered was guns and Dean and the lab, and she pushed hard against the images inside her mind, writhed against them with all her strength, and suddenly she could blink again, move, and the pressure eased up like an iron vise unscrewed from her head.

But only for a moment. Something else touched her, cold and hard, pressing against the back of her skull. Dean swore. Miri drew in a very slow breath. In her most controlled voice, she said, "You call that a threat? I know you want me alive."

"Alive, yes," Ku-Ku said, behind her. *How did she get behind her?* "But brain function is optional. Your friend should keep that in mind."

Miri slowly turned. The barrel of the gun moved with her, dragging across her scalp until it rested between her eyes. Ku-Ku did not look like she felt particularly guilty. Her gaze was flat, empty. Miri smelled bubblegum.

"Get that gun off her," Dean said. "You get that gun off her face right fucking now."

"No," Miri bluffed, still trying to stare down her former assistant. "Shoot me. I dare you."

Dean took a step toward her. Ku-Ku's finger tightened on the trigger and Kevin said a sharp word. She didn't immediately respond, although her gaze slid sideways to look at the older man. Her finger did not relax.

"Your guns," Kevin said, and even Miri thought he seemed uneasy.

"Just leave her the fuck alone," Dean said, pulling out both his guns. He held the stocks between two fingers, and Kevin quickly took them while another man stepped forward to retrieve the weapons from Dean's ankle rigs. Only when he was completely disarmed did Ku-Ku remove the gun from Miri's head. Dean grabbed her hand and tugged her close; she felt a fine tremor race through his body, smelled the acrid scent of his fear. He tapped a message onto her arm, a simple *You're crazy.*

Yes, she thought. *Very much so.*

Kevin pushed his glasses up his nose; sweat covered his brow, the edge of his slick receding hairline. He stared at Miri and she matched his gaze, defiant, until he broke the silence with a simple, "Where is the artifact?"

"I don't know," Miri lied.

"But you came here looking for it." His voice was brittle, his eyes cold.

"I came here looking for Owen," she said.

"He's long gone. Tucked away some place safe. It was for his own good, Dr. Lee."

"Really? And how does that explain the blood in his office?"

"An accident." He smiled grimly. "Those happen, you know."

"You bet," she said sarcastically. "Accidents during a kidnapping are par for the course."

Kevin shrugged, his fingers lingering on his round waist. "Yours was supposed to go very smoothly. How terrible that it did not."

"So I guess you've planned this for some time," Miri said, feeling sick. "Though I don't know how you could have known the jade would be found when it was."

"We didn't know," Kevin said, voice eerie, flat, not at all slick and fake with the charm she remembered. "But we are always vigilant. We planned for this day longer than you think, longer than all of our lives put together. Dr. Wills unfortunately stumbled upon something that should have remained buried."

"Jealous?" she asked him. Dean pinched her wrist.

A grim smile touched Kevin's mouth. "I am not a perfect man, Dr. Lee. So yes, I have been jealous of your mentor. But not about this. His ... discovery has been, and will continue to be, the cause of much pain. Much death."

"Fifteen dead already," Dean said in a hard voice, and Miri was shocked to see Kevin's eyes narrow.

"The fires," he said quietly. "You know about them."

"You could say I had a personal encounter."

"And do you know who set them?"

Dean smiled. Kevin glanced at Ku-Ku, whose mask seemed just slightly cracked. Miri imagined fear in her eyes—that, or a deep wariness. Some sharp anticipation of danger.

It bothered Miri that Dean knew something that connected him to Kevin and Ku-Ku. It bothered her more that she had no idea what he was talking about.

"You said fifteen," Ku-Ku murmured. "Only fourteen have died."

"You haven't missed him yet. It only happened a couple of hours ago. I found him at the very end."

"Where?"

"He was number fourteen's neighbor."

"And was it a bad death?"

Dean hestitated. "I would say he suffered."

Ku-Ku rolled her left hand into a fist and cracked her knuckles along her thigh. Kevin, watching her, said, "He'll be coming here next."

"He's killing you off because of this jade," Dean said. "Tell me that's not true."

"It's not your concern."

"If you want Miri, then it most certainly is my concern."

"And I should listen to you?" Kevin's mouth curved into a sneer. "You are nothing to me."

"Then who *does* matter?" Miri shot back, throwing herself into the conversation, uncaring if she didn't understand, if she was in the middle of another mystery. "Who set you up to this? And why the jade? Why Owen and me? Is it money?"

"Money." Kevin managed to look even more disgusted. "Money means nothing when compared to faith, Dr. Lee. Money is an insult compared to our duty."

"And is that duty to an idea or a person?"

Kevin smiled. "Do you believe in something larger than yourself, Dr. Lee?"

Miri refused to answer. Kevin's smile widened, though it was not happy. Bitterness clouded his eyes, a deep discontent that did not enter his voice as he said, "I believe, Dr. Lee. I believe in so much. But more than anything, I believe that there are creatures on this earth that are not gods, but who are still worthy of worship, who work to change this world, to make it better. I believe, too, that we are nearing, as a race, a profound end to our current existence, and that no one will survive unscathed. Not even those who ally themselves with the unearthly. Something bad is coming. The jade is just one part of that. A sign."

"An apocalyptic omen? Are you telling me that's what this is all about?"

"And if it is," Dean added, "then how does it involve Miri and Owen? Because really, I can think of better harbingers of evil."

Kevin did not immediately reply, which surprised Miri, given his demonstrated willingness to wax poetic about his so-called mission. She glanced at Ku-Ku—who maintained a perfect polished empty mask—and then the young men, who did not, who fidgeted and sweated and stared at their hands and her face.

And Miri suddenly knew the answer to her question.

"You don't know why, do you?" she said. "You don't

even know that much about the jade, just that you've been given some spiel that you can recite every time you begin to doubt your actions. But that doesn't have anything to do with me. You were given orders, that's all. You don't know shit."

"I know enough," Kevin said. "Anything more would get in the way."

"You sound like a member of a cult."

"I prefer religion." He smiled. "And really, the irony of this situation is a better reward than the truth. I have been wanting to rid this department of you and Dr. Wills from the very first day, and now I have the perfect excuse."

"Wow," Dean said. "Great evildoer speech. You gave me chills, man. Totally sexy."

"But next time rub your hands and tack on a cackle," Miri added. "That's pure poetry."

A flush stained Kevin's neck. Ku-Ku leaned close to whisper in his ear; her Hello Kitty hairpieces sounded like bones as they clicked around her pigtails. She kept her gaze on Miri, who felt like she was being studied through the lashes of a pink and purple snake.

Miri smiled at her. Dean squeezed her hand.

"Don't," he breathed. "We already used up our smart-ass allowance, *bao bei*. Keep your mouth shut."

"She deserves some pain," Miri said through gritted teeth, still smiling. "I'm sure I'm the perfect person to give it to her."

"I'm also sure this is not the best time."

"Don't tell me what to do."

"Like I ever could," he muttered.

"We need to go," Kevin said. "Dr. Lee will come with us. You, sir, will stay behind."

"Like hell," Dean said. "You'll have to kill me first."

Kevin shook his head. "You cannot protect her. She is beyond your help."

"I don't think you know what I can and will do in the name of protecting this woman." Dean said, in a voice so hard, so mean, it made Miri flinch. "I don't think you can imagine it."

"And I think you are only one man, easily subdued."

Ku-Ku and the other two men lunged, throwing themselves on Dean. He let go of Miri immediately, going down under the weight of those bodies like a rock. But that only lasted a moment; his fists and legs began connecting with flesh. Miri tried to jump into the fray, but a strong hand grabbed the base of her neck and refused to let go. She immediately went limp, tucking her legs up and letting gravity do all the work. She hit the floor hard, the contents of her purse spilling on the floor.

She glimpsed red, one slender corner of the jade. Kevin saw it, too. He stared and stared, eyes wide, sucking in his breath with a shudder that made her skin crawl. A mewling sound escaped his throat—so unexpected, so incongruous, Miri wondered if she imagined it. But there, again, he made that noise and it was a mix of childlike awe and gut-wrenching fear.

Miri reached for the jade, but Kevin beat her to it and she grabbed his hands, digging her nails into his flesh, grappling for possession. She did not care at all about its spiritual importance to Kevin or his benefactor; only, she thought she might need it to get Owen back, and that was a good enough reason to fight tooth and nail for it.

And she would have won if Ku-Ku had not cried out, startling her. Kevin pried her fingers off the jade, clutching it to his chest as he rolled from her. Miri chased him, but only for a moment. She looked at Dean.

The two young men were holding him from behind, arms looped over his shoulders. Ku-Ku knelt in front, staring at his upper body, much of which was exposed.

His shirt and jacket had ridden up during the fight, and the scars above his chest were now plain to see.

And the cut, that curving welt, was glowing.

You're imagining it, she told herself, but Kevin made a choking sound, and Ku-Ku sat transfixed. Miri could not look away, either. It was like staring out a window directly into a world of fire. Beautiful and eerie. Miri crawled close. Dean's eyes were dark, unhappy.

"You have been marked," Kevin whispered, but that was all he said because she suddenly smelled smoke, ash. All the color drained from Kevin's face. He staggered, staring at the lab door, and said one sharp word to the men holding down Dean. They released him and Dean scrambled to his feet, going instantly to Miri. His face was terrible; he knew what that scent meant. She could see it in his eyes.

"We're too late," Kevin breathed, and the young men behind him pulled guns from the bags slung over their hips. Ku-Ku moved like a dancer, eyes narrow and bright and hard. Her gaze flickered to the long corridor beside them; another exit, the way out to the vehicle unloading area.

And then Miri heard a rasping sound beyond the doors of the lab, an odd hard ripping. Something was on the stairs and it was large, ponderous, an unending rolling rumble that got louder and louder, like a truck engine wrapped in snakeskin and chains.

Dean grabbed Miri and backed her up against the wall, pushing her down the corridor toward the exit. His jaw was hard, his eyes as cold as anything she had ever seen.

"Miri?" he said softly. "Run. Run now, and don't look back."

"Dean—"

But she did not finish. The door slammed open, black smoke pouring like water into the room. Heat washed over Miri's face; the air sucked out of her lungs and she staggered, horrified. She heard a shout and someone opened fire on the smoke in front of the door.

It was Ku-Ku. Miri glanced over her shoulder and saw the slender girl with a pistol in her hand and pigtails flying, like some Manga warrior princess going hard-core on the kick-ass overdrive, and by God she was pumping those bullets like a prize. The young men flanking her lurched forward, but they were clearly less experienced in the ways of the gun. Given everything Miri thought she had known about the girl, it was like watching Strawberry Shortcake on a killing spree.

And in the middle of it all, clouded by the smoke, she saw an odd misshapen form begin to emerge; white, as white as snow, and larger than the door. She imagined a neck, or an outstretched arm, hair so long it touched the floor. And then Dean moved in front of her, pushing, yelling, and she turned and ran.

She did not look back. Dean propelled her down the hall to the exit with terrifying speed. Heat washed over her back. A man screamed.

No, she thought. *No, this is not happening.* Too much crazy, too many impossible things. Something in the air, the water, the entire freaking island.

Something about that red jade.

The back exit's double doors were open; they raced into a small parking lot and loading bay. Miri heard footsteps pound the pavement behind them and glanced over her shoulder. It was Kevin. He moved surprisingly fast for a man of his size and age—or maybe it was just the fiery inferno blowing up his ass from down the hall they had just left. He did not quite slam into her, but almost; Dean wrapped his arm around Kevin's neck and hauled the older man off, throwing him to the ground. Kevin tried to take Miri with him. She went down on one knee …

… and saw exactly what they had done to the mummies. In fact, she was crouching in them. Or in what was left, which was little more than dust. Kevin and his men had stomped on the bodies until they were nothing but broken fragments, bits and pieces of three lives, turned into something less than fertilizer. It was more horrible than she had even realized.

"How could you?" she asked, as Dean stepped close and rummaged through Kevin's bag. He found one of the guns that had been taken from him and pointed it at the older man. Kevin did not appear to notice. He simply stared and stared at Dean and Miri, eyes wide, mouth moving in some silent chant.

"Give me the jade," Dean said, and much to Miri's shock, the older man obeyed without hesitation, pulling the artifact from his front pocket. Another scream erupted from the building. Fire alarms soared; she heard the babble of nearby voices. Late-night students, drawn by the sounds. Kevin kept his arms extended toward Dean after he gave up the jade. Supplication, prayer, mercy; it disturbed Miri.

"Stop," Dean said. "Why are you looking at me like that?"

"Because you don't know what you are holding," Kevin said. "Because you don't know what you are."

"What I am," Dean echoed, gazing past him into the building. "What the fuck does that mean?"

Kevin shook his head. "You must take the jade and go. Get out of here. Now, before he finds you. *You can't let him find you.*"

"I don't understand," Miri said, as Dean grabbed her elbow and hauled her up off the ground. "Why would you do that? Why change your mind and help us?"

He said nothing, pressing his lips together into a hard line. Dean began dragging her away, but she fought him, crying out, "Why Owen? Why me?"

"Because we had to," Kevin blurted, suddenly pitiful and small, nothing but a helpless old man. "Because she said it would be the end if we didn't."

"Who said that? Your boss is a woman?"

"She is no ordinary woman," Kevin said, with a conviction and a fervor that were just as astounding as every other twist and turn of his personality.

"She's letting you die," Dean said. "Whoever your unordinary woman is, she's let all her people burn to death at the hand of that thing in there. You want to follow that? All for what? A ... a book? A book and flesh?"

A book and flesh? Miri turned, incredulous, but Dean still looked at Kevin, who stared at him with such profound horror that she knew whatever he had just spoken was the absolute truth.

"You know," he whispered, and it was suddenly difficult for her to remember him as the troublemaker she had loved to hate. His face now belonged to a stranger, a monster, someone weak and pathetic. All those things, rolling in his eyes.

"No," Dean said. "But you could tell me."

Kevin reached with shaking hands into his pocket and pulled out a set of keys. He tossed them to Miri and gestured at the squat, dingy dark blue van parked nearby. Miri ran to the driver's side and opened the door. Dean did not follow.

"Come on," he said, holding out his hand to Kevin. "You don't want to stay here. Not with that thing."

"No," Kevin murmured, and then, "There is another piece of jade. You must find it."

"I don't have to find anything," Dean said, inching close. Miri heard a terrible screeching sound from inside the building. Elsewhere, sirens. Students running from the darkness.

Kevin scrambled to his feet. "You have no choice but

to find it now. You've been marked. Your life is no longer your own."

Miri caught movement on the periphery of her vision. She looked down the long corridor into the fire, into smoke, and saw a body coming toward them. Indistinct, but utterly inhuman.

"Dean," Miri snapped. "Dean, we need to go!"

"What does that mean?" he said to Kevin, ignoring her. "Yo, what does that mean?"

"It means you are a monster," Kevin said, and he turned and ran into the inferno.

Chapter Six

Miri stared, horrified, unable to summon the strength to chase after Kevin. She had no time to cry out before his body disappeared behind the smoke, and for a moment, as she stared after him, she imagined another set of eyes in the fire, eyes behind the veil, with a gaze like the sun. Miri felt something sharp inside her head, a prick, a great heat against her skin.

And then Dean was there, shoving her into the van, and Miri heard a roar, like an animal, and he raced around the front of the van as she jammed the key into the ignition, yelling, "Go! Go! Go!" as the engine put-putted into a weak rumble.

He jumped into the passenger seat and Miri went. Tires squealed. Rubber burned. Dean twisted in his seat, hanging out the window.

"What do you see?" she asked.

"Nothing," he replied, but his voice was flat, hard, and she tried to look through the side mirror at the chaos they were leaving behind. It was too late, and there were too many curves in the road.

"What the hell just happened back there?" Miri asked, though it took her a moment before her throat worked. Her voice sounded weak, broken.

"Fire, brimstone, hell on earth." Dean flashed her a humorless smile. "You want an entire list?"

"Dean." Miri took a hard turn; he hit his head on the ceiling as he slid back into his seat. He grimaced, rubbing his forehead.

"You remember what I said about that picture of you? That I found it during an investigation?"

"Yes." She had been wondering about that use of the word and its implications.

"There have been a series of murders over the past week. That's what I was referring to back in the lab. People set on fire."

"Fire," she echoed. "I think I've heard about it on the news. Grisly news. People burning to death made a great headline."

"Yeah. And I'll give you one guess who the culprit is."

"You're kidding." Miri glanced at him; the look he gave her was deadly serious and she said, "Dean, that thing back there *was not* human."

"Not human." He grimaced. "You got no idea, sweetheart. But that's the easy part, the part that isn't hard to explain. Where it gets complicated are the people that thing murdered. What they knew, what they were involved in. They all had a connection."

"The jade," she said.

"*You,*" he said softly. "Just you. The last victim I found had that picture, your location. An assignment with your name on it."

"But you linked it to Kevin."

"A guess, but only because I found something else at the crime scene. An energy trail from someone who was walking through this university. I saw the exterior of that archaeology building, Miri. I just didn't know what it mean until I got there and saw it with my own two eyes."

"You think you picked up the edge of Owen's kidnapping?"

"Maybe. That victim also had a manifest. Most of the people on it are dead, but I bet if I looked, there would be a Kevin Liao on the list."

"Hunted," she said. "They were also being hunted because of the jade."

"Or something else they know that's related to it."

Miri swayed forward in her seat, knuckles white around the wheel. She wanted to set her teeth in the plastic and gnaw on it like some oversized chew toy.

"Do you need me to drive?" Dean asked.

"I'll be fine," she lied. "But I need you to tell me more. Like how you're involved in this mess, what you've been doing with your life for the past twenty years that could possibly have you investigating murders committed by monsters."

"I work for a detective agency," he said.

"Detective agency." She laughed, and knew it sounded bitter. "Are you kidding me?"

"You sound so cheated."

"Considering everything that's happened, I expected something more flamboyant."

"No. It's boring. Just a bunch of paper pushers. With guns."

"Guns," she muttered. "What I've seen today is way more hard-core than midnight surveillances and photos of men cheating on their wives. Are you sure you're not part of the government? Some secret agent, covert operation thing?"

"Please. Do I look like a secret agent?"

"Secret agents aren't supposed to look secret. That's the whole point. Besides, what kind of detective agency gets involved in shit like this?"

"The very cool kind. I could be my own action figure."

"I hope you can bounce back like an action figure, because one more joke like that and I'm kicking you out of this van and running you over with the tires."

"So much anger. Whatever happened to living life with a smile?" And he began humming a Jimmy Durante tune.

Miri shook her head. "You haven't changed at all, have you? You're doing the same thing. Still trying to make me laugh."

"It's not only for you," he said. "I was also just called a monster, don't forget. And somehow, I don't think Kevin meant that as a metaphor."

"Kevin is crazy," Miri said. "But you got him in the end with that mention of a book and … and flesh."

"It's part of another vision I had at the victim's home tonight. I heard someone giving instructions, talking about how some book couldn't be allowed in the flesh, or some crap like that. I can't remember exactly. Just that it was weird."

"And connected with the jade, and apparently that mark on your chest, which was ever so popular with everyone in that lab."

"About that—" he said slowly.

"Yes," she interrupted. "I saw the glow. And no, I'm not going to ask."

"Thank God. Because I have no idea what it means."

"And the only person who does ran back into that burning building."

"Bummer," Dean said. "I was almost beginning to like the bastard."

"Yeah," she said quietly, thinking of Ku-Ku, as well. Trying to imagine her dead. Despite everything, it hurt. She had liked that girl. Or at least, the mask she had worn.

"So you're a detective," she said. "You're a detective who travels to Taiwan to hunt someone who is distinctly nonhuman, and who is flagrantly setting people on fire. I'm surprised I haven't heard more about this on the news."

"I hope to God you *never* hear about that murderer in the media. You can't imagine what would happen if someone like that went public."

"Murder is already public, Dean. You can't get much more public than burning people to death. And hello? What he just did at the university? There are bound to be witnesses. Security cameras, at the very least."

"I know," he said grimly. "It's bad for all of us."

"Us?" she echoed.

Dean hesitated. "I really do work for a detective agency, Miri. It's just that my employer hires a bunch of ... diverse people. Diverse like me."

"Oh," she said; and suddenly it all made sense. Not in any detailed way, but pieces fell on top of other pieces, which fell into place: Dean's acceptance of everything weird that had happened, his ease and confidence in using his gift, his navigation of the bizarre and illegal.

"You found others," she said.

"They found me," he replied. "No one really knows about the agency, of course. It's all secret and we do regular detective work—finding kidnap victims, solving murders. The title is just a cover so we can use our gifts to help people. You know, without being called freaks or being watched."

"Or studied," she said.

"Or studied," he repeated softly. "So yeah, that's why I was sent to Taiwan. We knew that the killer was also ... like us, and it was up to me to bring him under control. So he doesn't ruin it for everyone else."

"And by doing so, look at what you got caught up in."

"It brought me back to you. I can't complain."

He said it like he meant every word, and Miri looked at him, really stared, until he pointed at the road and grabbed the wheel. The van swerved, and Miri swore silently, wrestling back control before she veered into oncoming traffic. Dean let go, but only just; his fingers trailed over her hand and lingered on her wrist.

"You okay with this?" he asked.

"Fine," she snapped, heart hammering. "Just jittery, that's all."

"That's not what I meant. I meant this, us, me. The way you looked … it was like you didn't believe a word I said."

"Would it bother you if I didn't?"

"Yeah. I'm not your enemy, Miri."

"Good," she replied. "What a pleasure to hear."

Dean's fingers slipped away from her wrist. "I don't get it. One minute you act like we're friends again, and the next … Jesus. I feel like I should be in handcuffs or something."

"And what? You want me to feel sorry for making you feel bad?"

"Of course not. I just don't understand why you'd think I'd try and pull something on you. Hell, if I wanted to hurt you I would have done it already."

That, she believed. Miri steadied her grip on the wheel, trying to find the words, wanting so desperately for him to understand. Nothing came to her except an overwhelming feeling of helplessness.

Miri rolled down the window. The van's air conditioner could not keep up with the heat, and the humid breeze was better than anything stale and stuffy. Sweat rolled down her back and face. She felt sticky and greasy and smelly. Fear, running off her body. She savored the rush of air against her hot face. Tears wet her eyes.

A hand touched the back of her head, stayed there with a different kind of warmth; dry and comforting.

"Hard night," Dean murmured.

"We've had other hard nights," she whispered. "But this is worse."

"Yeah." He hesitated, then pulled something from his pocket. The statue of Glen Campbell. He held it in his hand and closed his eyes. Miri's gaze moved from the road to his face; she caught the slow change in his expression, the frown, a growing crease in his forehead. Dread hit her low, in the gut.

"Dean," she whispered, but he said nothing and pressed his head into his hands, pushing the statue against his skin with his eyes squeezed shut. He rocked in his seat. Miri hit the brakes and pulled the van to the side of the road, deep within the mouth of a long residential alley lined with bicycles and large potted trees; an old man sat on a concrete stoop some distance away, smoking a cigarette. Miri looked down at her hands, knuckles white around the wheel. The engine ticked and rumbled. The air inside the van was almost too hot to breathe.

"Keep moving," he muttered. "We need to keep driving."

"What the hell is wrong?"

"Nothing," he snapped. "Owen's alive. I just can't track him anymore. I can't fix his location."

Miri briefly closed her eyes. "This night is just getting worse and worse. I'm not going to live to see morning, am I?"

"Don't talk like that. I don't want to hear it from you, Miri. Please."

"Okay," she said, peering into his stricken face. "Okay, Dean."

He settled back in his seat and returned the statue to his pocket. "I don't know why this is happening. It's like there's a block in my head. I couldn't track the killer, I couldn't track you, and now Owen's been cut off. It's like … it's like someone's manipulating the energy, making it self-contained." He looked at her, and she felt the shift in his gaze, knew he was studying a whole other part of her body that she could only imagine.

"You're self-contained," he whispered. "You have no trail, Miri."

"What do you mean?"

"I mean that everyone leaves a trail. You remember that much, right? It's how I track people. It's how I would have tracked you." He pulled the locket out from beneath his shirt, and bounced it in hand. She still remembered giving it to him; hooking the chain around his neck on a whim.

"I looked for you," he said slowly. "I did. I thought, maybe, I could still be with you somehow. Like, if you were a ghost. I thought I could follow you. I used the necklace. I used it every damned day. I did everything I could. I just … never saw anything."

Miri gripped the wheel until her hands hurt and said, "You're telling me that for the past twenty years I had no trail for you to follow."

"I look at you now and it's obvious you're alive, but you travel like a ghost. I saw the same thing with the … the creature back at the university. It's why I had such a hard time finding him in the first place. Tonight, earlier, I got a lucky break. But if I wanted to track him? If I wanted to track you? I don't think I could."

"How does that happen to a person?" Miri asked him. "Why would … my body be doing that?"

"I don't know, *buo bei*. But it must have started that night you were shot, because I never had any trouble finding you before."

Miri closed her eyes, forcing herself to breathe. "And Owen?"

"I don't know. If I had to guess, I would say that someone is running interference, though how that's possible ..."

"Are there people capable of doing that?"

Dean shrugged, still gripping the statue. "I've seen some crazy shit over the past year, not including tonight. I'd say just about anything is possible. Hell, seeing you again qualifies as a goddamn miracle."

"Amen," she muttered, and Dean cracked a smile that faded fast. He rubbed Glen Campbell's brass head.

"Still nothing. I'm so sorry, Miri. I think I know what Owen means to you, if he really is like Ni-Ni."

"He is," she whispered, feeling a terrible pain inside her chest. "I was eighteen and miserable when I went to college. Still not over you, and Ni-Ni had been gone a year. The only thing I had was my fantasy of being some Indiana Jones archaeologist. Because hey, the past is done, dry, dead. It can't hurt you, right? You don't experience all the grit and suffering of the living. Just the facts, all those puzzle pieces. And Owen ... I guess he must have seen something in me. Maybe hunger. I don't know. Only, he and his wife took me in. Made sure I had something stable to lean on."

"Your parents?"

"Same as always. Owen was a better daddy. You'd like him."

"Then I plan on meeting him. Soon."

"Always the optimist."

"Because you have to smile though your heart is aching," he sang softly. "Smile though it's breaking, with those clouds in the sky."

And she managed a smile, and said, "I'm glad you're here."

"What a relief," he said. "You're so cruel to me, I was beginning to wonder."

"Cruel?" she said, trying not to laugh. She shoved him and he grabbed her hand, cradling it, kissing it.

Her breath caught, and over the thudding over her heart, she heard him say, "I'm here, Miri. I'm not leaving you. You're not doing this alone."

Her eyes felt hot. She looked at Dean's hand on her own, savoring the warmth of his skin, the miracle of simply being touched by this man and friend who she thought she had lost.

And she said, quietly, "Did you miss me? All these years?"

"That's a dumb question."

"And you really thought I was dead?"

"That's even dumber. How could you ask that?"

"How could I not?" She said it gently, trying to take the bite out of her words, but she could see it cut him. It hurt her, too. More than she wanted to admit. She stared out the windshield as she collected her thoughts, taking in the lights, the endless signs and city decorations, trinkets for the eyes, cheap and soulless.

"You could have gone to Ni-Ni," she finally said. "Especially if you thought I was dead. She would have needed you at a time like that. But you didn't. You never went back."

"Miri," he whispered.

"No, Dean. They never found your body. You know what that did to me? I couldn't let go. I kept hoping, telling myself that I imagined you dying and that you were out there. But when you didn't come back, I thought maybe you had another reason."

"Like what?"

"I don't know," she said helplessly. "That was the worst part. Trying to imagine all the reasons why you wouldn't come home. And finally … finally it was just easier to tell myself you were dead. It hurt less."

She felt him staring at her, silent, but when he spoke his voice was so rough, so broken, she jumped in her seat because it was a different man talking, a man with a cut throat, bleeding out and out and out, and he whispered, "Jesus Christ, Miri. I'm so sorry. I'm so sorry I hurt you like that. I would never have made the choice to leave if I had thought you were still alive. Never. But you died. You died and I watched."

"I died," Miri agreed, reaching up to touch her heart. "I died. But then I came back. In the ambulance. They called it a miracle. The EMTs were able to start my heart. I had to have a transfusion. It was touch-and-go. I was in a coma for a while."

"I didn't know," Dean whispered. "I swear to you, I didn't know."

I believe you, she wanted to say. *I believe you mean that.* But instead she told him, "I saw you die, too. You took a bullet."

"But you went before I did," he breathed. "Or maybe I passed out and you thought I was dead. All I know is that we were together in that car, and that man came. That jacked-up no-name son of a bitch. He wanted to steal our ride, and then he wanted to steal you, and I couldn't let that happen."

"So you took a bullet," she whispered. "And then he got scared and shot me, too."

She still remembered the sound of the blast, the feel of the rain coming down on her head while she stood half naked on the street, watching Dean go crazy trying to help her, screaming at him to stop, that it wasn't worth it, that she'd be okay—which was a lie, but worth it if it kept him alive—and she remembered the blood, she remembered the pain, she remembered falling and falling and falling, down into a darkness and a light, and feeling even there that her heart had been torn in half. No peace in death. Only regret.

"I was awake when you died," Dean said. "I felt your heart stop. Right beneath my hand. And then the ambulance came, and somehow I could stand, and I got out of there. I don't know how I was able to move, but I did it because you were dead and I wanted to die and I couldn't stand it and that man was still alive. That man had run, too. He had run."

And you found him, Miri thought, because she could hear what he was not saying, she could see it in his eyes, and she wanted to cry harder for that, for what she knew he must have done.

"You could have come home again," she said.

"No. Not after what happened."

"You thought Ni-Ni would blame you for my ... my death."

"I knew it."

They stared at each other, and there was a look in Dean's eyes she recognized from long ago, a compassion that had once been for her only; those first days, which had turned into weeks and months and years, until one day friendship had matured into something deeper, unspoken, when holding hands suddenly meant more than just arm-wrestling or play, and when looking into his eyes, whispering in his ear, spread a warmth through her body that had nothing to with the heat of the sun or the overworked stove in her grandmother's kitchen.

Her heart crawled up her throat. All those years wasted, spent dreaming of something she could never have, feeling the wistful pull of that old desire. Because even so young, just a kid, she had known it was forever.

Dean leaned in so close she thought he might kiss her. He brushed her cheek with his fingers. His skin was smooth, light; she found herself leaning into his touch and it was not too much, it was not enough. She did not speak. She could not. The old memories were too strong for words.

"I did miss you, Miri," he whispered. "God, did I miss you!"

Miri closed her eyes, unable to stand his gaze, which was open and wide and held no lies. *I missed you, I missed you,* she heard him say, again and again, and though she wanted to say the same, other words came to her, harder words, and she said, "It broke Ni-Ni's heart, Dean. She was never the same after you were gone."

Never the same at all, though her grandmother had tried to hide it, even if that meant pretending she had company coming to excuse the extra bowl on the counter, the extra rice in the cooker. Even if it meant leaving her door unlocked far later into the evening than was safe, or treading the floor at ungodly hours to peer out the window, as though somehow she would find Dean there, magically resurrected by the strength of her will. She had loved that boy. Loved him more than her own son.

"Miri," Dean whispered, and there was still that break in his voice, that break that was like the one in her heart, and it made her eyes hot with tears. Miri could not bear that pain, but she forced herself because it was Dean, and he was here, and she would not be weak in front of him. Not now. She refused.

"She grieved for you," Miri said, swallowing hard. "Looking back, I think, maybe, she knew you were alive, knew you were out there, and every day until she died she expected you to come swaggering through that back door, back from the dead or wherever you were hiding. She told me—"

Miri stopped. She had to stop because she finally tasted salt, tears, and there was a sob rising up her throat, that old burning sorrow. She squeezed her eyes shut and felt his hand on her shoulder, a warm palm at the back of her neck, and she was drawn, tentative and careful, across the seat into a hard chest that thrummed slow with breath, the steady beat of a quiet heart.

"I'm sorry," Dean breathed. For a moment it made her angry—a terrible fury that he had not gone back to her grandmother, back to where he could have found her—but then he said it again and again, and she felt something wet hit her ear, and she gazed up into his face and found him crying. She had never seen Dean cry—not ever, not even when he was ten years old with his hand slammed in a door and still young enough for tears without shame. She had cried for him that day. She had cried for him on other days, too, even when he did not realize what she was doing.

Miri pulled back just enough to smooth her thumbs over his wet cheeks, savoring the feel of his face, the rough lines of blond bristle, the curve of bone, and the hollow of his throat. His shoulders had filled out with muscle. Dean grabbed her hands, holding them warm, and said it again, "I'm sorry."

Miri leaned close, studying his haunted face that was the same, and yet changed, and pressed her mouth against his ear. "She told me every day that even if it took a day or a year or longer, you would come home to her, to us, even if it was just as a ghost, because there was love waiting for you, all kinds of sweetness, and that you were a boy with a sweet heart, and that sort of thing carried a bond."

Dean shuddered, rocking against Miri's shoulder. She clutched at him, digging her fingers into his lean back, and it was not enough to hug him like this, not nearly enough, because even though she was still hurt and bewildered, it was good to be near him again. She had forgotten how good, and she wanted more.

"I imagined this," she murmured.

Dean's fingers threaded through her hair. "If I could have, I would have. I promise you that. Hell, I moved to California because your parents were there and I thought it was another way to be close to your memory."

She closed her eyes, marveling. "I've lived in Palo Alto for the past sixteen years. I work at Stanford."

"Goddamn," he breathed. "You're shitting me. You were so close. You were so close I could have just walked up and said hello."

"Hello," Miri said. "Nice to meet you."

"Hello," Dean whispered. "Hello."

Miri smiled and touched his cheek. "This kind of sustained heavy emotion might just melt you into a puddle if you're not careful. Your face is all wet."

He wrapped his hand around her wrist. "I'm man enough not to care."

"Dean—"

"Are you married?"

"Excuse me?"

"Boyfriend?"

"Dean."

"Come on."

"No," she said. "I'm none of those things."

"Neither am I," he said. "So, yeah. Good."

"Good?"

"Yes," he said, more firmly this time. "Things are different now, Miri."

"We already covered this, Dean. I'm not the same person I was back then. Neither are you."

"Close enough. Don't get too technical on me."

She tried not to smile. Dean stroked her palm with his thumb, and then, watching her eyes, raised her hand to his mouth and kissed it.

"My lady," he whispered, and Miri touched her throat, the place above her heart, and imagined she could feel her scars, pressing up through her blouse.

She shivered. "It's been a long time since I heard that."

"I was a lousy knight. Always getting into too much trouble and dragging you along with me."

"I was a willing partner. More than willing."

"Maybe, but it doesn't make it right. Things are different now, though. I'll do whatever it takes to prove myself to you, Miri. You're right. Twenty years is a long time, and the way we separated was bad. You don't have any reason to trust me, not anymore, and I shouldn't expect you to. So we'll start over, okay? We're adults now. We should be able to do this."

Miri tried not to smile. "Did it ever occur to you that maybe you shouldn't trust me? That I have something to prove, too?"

"No," he said. "It really didn't."

Miri pulled away, though she did not insist he let go of her hand. She felt like the victim of a split personality: the woman she had become, shadowed by the echo of her sixteen-year-old self. Both sides tugging, both sides wanting. She heard the wail of sirens, the sounds of distant voices; the world, returning to her, piece by piece. She wiped at her face.

"Police," she said, listening. And then, an odder sound: fluttering, the beat of wings.

A large crow hopped from the sky to the passenger-side mirror of the van. Miri was too numb to feel any surprise; only, she noted, its eyes looked strange. Light, somehow. Almost ... golden.

The crow cawed—once, twice—and its rasping voice twisted in the air like words.

"About fucking time," Dean muttered, leaning his head out the window. "You bastard."

"Dean," Miri said, and he glanced at her with a slight expression of consternation on his face. Like he was doing something wrong—or maybe right, and he was not quite certain how to explain himself. Behind him, the crow stared into the van. Really stared, like it was memorizing her face, taking notes. She did not like it. It was intrusive, and Miri, feeling irrational, met that golden gaze, tore off the air freshener on the rearview mirror, and flung it out the window at the bird. She had good aim. The crow squawked and flew off.

Dean stared at her. "You just threw an air freshener at my partner."

"Your partner.... Right." Her gut twisted. "We'll save that explanation for later."

The sirens got louder. Police, accompanied by a tiny ambulance not much bigger than the van, zoomed past the alley behind them. Presumably heading to the university. Again, Miri thought of Ku-Ku and Kevin, and that creature in the blaze. God.

"You think anyone is going to come after us?"

"Got a hankering for a good old game of Dukes of Hazzard?"

"Oh yeah. The power of this van is a mighty thing."

Dean snorted, rubbing his face. "Don't worry about the police, Miri. They're not the ones trying to kidnap you."

"Yet."

"Everyone and their mama, right?"

"It's a conspiracy," she agreed, then added, "I'm serious. Both Kevin and Robert had instructions, possibly from two different people. And if your serial killer is involved ... Dean, that's bad enough, but with all the other weird stuff?"

"Robert," Dean said. "I'm still trying to figure him out. Someone found him. Found him or made him, either of which would take huge amounts of money. And power."

"Everything comes down to the jade," Miri said.

"The jade and you. Are you sure you don't have any idea what this is about?"

"Yes, Dean, I'm sure. I'm boring. I have students, I teach, I do research, I run excavations with Owen, and that's it. The jade, on the other hand, came straight out of a woman's chest, so it's already got a weird vibe about it."

"A chest?" Dean rubbed the space above his heart. She remembered his glowing scar and touched her chest. The skin felt hot.

"The jade was placed there while the woman still lived," she told him. "It remained long enough for her flesh to grow over its edges."

"That's some beauty mark. How much do you think she paid her plastic surgeon?"

"Not nearly enough. It would have been incredibly painful. I'm surprised the initial surgery didn't kill her."

"So why would someone go through that? Was it forced?"

"No idea. Owen and I were planning to go back to the dig site in Yushan to look for more clues. One thing we're certain of is that the jade—and the writing on it—originated outside the region. Finding the other fragments, though … it'll be almost impossible. Research can narrow the location, but discovering the first piece was a miracle. I doubt it can be repeated."

"Maybe someone disagrees with you."

"Then they know something I don't. Or they have someone like you around."

She meant it as a joke, but one look at Dean's face and her smile faded. He said, "Money and power, Miri. If they can hire someone like Robert, what makes you think they don't have a guy like me on standby?"

"Because the odds are—" She was going to say *impossible,* but stopped herself. "Men like you are rare, Dean. What you can do … it's not normal. Don't you think

I've kept my eyes and ears open over the years? Looking for ... for more?"

For *you,* she wanted to say, and maybe Dean heard it in her voice, in her hesitation, because he shifted in his seat and said, "Miri, we're not exactly a public spectacle. At least, not the really talented ones. I mean, hell, can you imagine?"

"I don't want to. I find it hard enough to believe everything that's happened tonight, and I've even had some experience with ... abnormal things. Thanks to you. But if the rest of the world knew? It would be a spectacle. A circus. Maybe even panic in some parts. People would get hurt."

"Probably people like me."

"Wuss. You're bulletproof, remember?"

"That's more of a problem than an asset, Miri. I'm also thinking it's a one-time deal."

"You were shot in the chest before tonight," she said quietly. "You lived through that, too."

Dean gave her a long, hard look. "That doesn't count. The bullet went in. I bled everywhere."

"But you still walked away. Did you even try to go to an emergency room or a doctor?"

"No. I was too scared." Easy, simple. Miri felt him watching her, waiting, but she did not ask why he had been scared. She remembered everything he had *not* said about the man who attacked them—about what happened afterward—and thought she knew why he would not want to go any place where someone might be obliged to report a gunshot wound to the police.

"So you treated yourself," she said slowly. "What about the bullet? How did you get it out?"

"I didn't have to. It passed right through me."

"You still should have died."

He blew out his breath. "Why are you focusing on this, Miri? You survived, too, don't forget."

"But I had medical attention. I can't imagine what you had to go through."

"It wasn't easy," he said. "I don't even know what made me think I could do it, except that I was desperate and I'd watched too many Westerns. Cowboys were always patching themselves up, right?"

She shook her head. "And now this. I don't like the timing."

"I don't like any of it." He rubbed his chest.

"Is that cut bothering you?"

"A little." He hesitated. "I know you saw it light up all pretty."

"Very pretty. Very strange. How did you get it?"

"I don't know. Not really. It happened this evening. I … was having a nightmare related to the case I'm working on, and when I woke up, voilà."

"Voilà? That must have been some nightmare, Dean."

"You've got no idea," he muttered. Miri rubbed her throat, fingers trailing down to her breastbone. Her skin felt warm, damp with sweat. She tried to imagine a cut, a glow. Instead she pictured jade.

"You said it happened this evening?" she asked softly. "And that you were staying in the same hotel?"

"One floor beneath you."

"Crazy," she murmured, and then louder, she said, "I became very ill tonight. I felt like my body was on fire. Especially here." She tapped the skin above her heart. "Strange, huh?"

She looked at Dean and found him staring at her with an awful uneasiness that made her skin crawl.

"What?" she asked, alarmed. "Does that mean something to you?"

"You might say that." His voice was hoarse, strangled. "What time did you get sick?"

"Around seven thirty or eight."

Dean closed his eyes. "Unbelievable."

Miri stared at him, putting the pieces together. She shook her head. "No. No, Dean. It can't be related."

"Then why did you bring it up?"

"Because it was a weird coincidence."

"I don't believe in coincidence, Miri."

"It's easier than accepting that I experienced … whatever it was you went through."

"Fire," he said. "My dream was about fire. Me, burning alive."

Burning alive. That's how you felt. All torn up on the inside, like you had a nuclear furnace getting hotter and hotter inside your chest. Ready to explode.

Dean took her hand and cradled it loosely in his palm. His touch felt good, but strange. Still new.

"What is going on?" she asked him quietly.

"Don't know," he murmured. "But it's got us all wrapped up."

"Who's the person doing the wrapping?"

"We gotta find that out, babe. Regroup, figure what to do next. Sitting in this van isn't doing us any good. If I had a direction, I'd say chase after Owen. That's a no-brainer. But I don't, and we can't. The only thing we do have going for us is that we've got the jade."

"Leverage."

"Maybe, maybe not. Problem is, we're outnumbered. I can call my agency for help, but most of the others are stuck in America and it'll take them a while to get here. For now the best plan of action is to evade and hunt."

"Hunt what?"

"Kevin said there's another piece of the jade. We might have an easier time finding that, given we already have one piece."

"It's old, Dean. I thought you didn't take good readings of old things."

141

"I don't, but it's the only clue we've got. I have to try."

"And if you do manage to track it, what then? Four thousand years is an incredibly long time. The jade could have been destroyed, or lost within some utterly unreachable spot. *And* let's say we do manage to retrieve it. How will that help us or Owen? More leverage? It's like you said: they can just overwhelm us and be done with it."

"Yeah," he said. "I know my logic kinda sucks. But I can't think of anything better to do, can you? I don't want to just sit around, or throw ourselves out there without any direction. Hell, if they want the jade that bad it must be important. Maybe it's not even something they should have. Like, for bigger reasons than just principle."

"Because it's magic?" she joked.

Dean smiled. "Might be. Besides, what's better than finding treasure?"

"Finding hope," she said. "Which I know must be painfully cheesy for you to hear."

"Not really. I watch *Oprah*."

"Wow. You are lonely."

"That's what my action figures keep telling me."

Miri laughed. Dean grinned, but his smile faded as he rubbed his chest. She watched him, sharing his uneasiness.

"Kevin recognized that scar," she said finally, to fill the silence. "He gave you the jade."

"He called me a monster."

"You must have scared him."

"He totally pissed his panties."

"Books and flesh and jade and scars," she mused. "What does it all mean?"

"Trouble. On the other hand, it brought us back together, so it can't be all bad."

"I'll save my response until I've been around you for more than a couple of hours."

"Ouch, babe. Be a little gentle. My heart's already hurting."

"It's doing a little more than that." She frowned. "I think that cut is glowing again."

"What? Shit." Dean slapped his hand over the light seeping through his T-shirt. He looked out the windshield and Miri followed his gaze. The old man was gone. Down the street, another body with a cigarette hung out in shadows. She heard wings flutter, saw beneath one of the distant streetlights, a crow sitting on a motorcycle seat. She wondered if it had golden eyes.

And then the person standing in shadows began to move. There was some light—a fluorescent bulb flickering cheaply against a slick concrete wall, its blue-tinted light half hidden by iron rails and hanging plants. The figure glided into the dim glow and she felt a jolt; it was the man in black. Dark skin perhaps, though it was hard to tell. She imagined a touch of green around his eyes, which was impossible, given the poor light.

"I saw that man earlier tonight," Miri said. "Remember? When we were walking to the archaeology building and I stopped you?"

Dean reached for his gun. "Let's get out of here, babe."

"If we were followed—"

"No time, and this is not a good place to engage. Too closed in."

Miri put the van in reverse and edged carefully back onto the road. Several motorcyclists veered at the last moment to avoid a collision.

She glanced back at the man in the alley; he had moved even closer, but something seemed wrong with his body, which flowed, shimmering and frayed and floating like smoke.

The crow turned its head, looked at Dean and Miri, and cawed.

"Go," Dean said, frowning at the bird. "Just … go, Miri. Fast."

"Crap," she muttered, and hit the accelerator.

Chapter Seven

Dean knew where to go. It had been a long time—his fault, given that it was his responsibility to check in as soon as landing in Taipei—but despite him taking for granted, once again, certain key issues of safety that had actually become important, he remembered the way, the map that everyone in the agency had been forced to memorize. Or in Dean's case, implanted into his mind. Telepaths rocked. Especially when you had the attention span of a lemming.

Miri drove fast. He expected questions, some kind of talk, but she kept her mouth shut after they left the alley. He gave her directions, she nodded her head, and that was all. Silence.

So he watched her. He leaned against the door and stared, without apology, drinking in her body and face and every movement like it was wonderful and sacred and necessary to his survival; some essential ingredient of the air he breathed.

And it was, though his heart still hurt, his head throbbed, his eyes played tricks. No, she was not here—

but yes, she was—and no—and yes—and still, though she was so near and he had touched her and smelled her and felt her breath against his breath, he could not believe.

Miri was alive. Miri was here.

And she's being hunted, he reminded himself. *You both are.*

Which seemed oddly appropriate, given that the highs and lows of his day had thus far been so violently extreme—so incredibly bizarre—that *of course* the only girl he had ever loved would find herself in danger from extremely fucked up voodoo *just* when he found her again. Because really, that was his kind of luck.

Not this time. Not matter what it takes, I'm not losing her again. Because even if having Miri at his side still felt more like a dream than reality, it was a dream worth dying for. Melodrama was not his usual shit, but this … this was different.

"Can you stop staring at me?" Miri asked suddenly. "You're making me nervous."

"Sorry." Dean rubbed his palms against his thighs. "I'm still trying to get used to you being alive. I can't believe how stupid I was."

"You had your reasons," Miri said. "And they probably felt right at the time."

"Yeah. Still wrong, though. That's not the way your grandma raised me."

Miri smiled. "Do you remember the first time you met her?"

"It was the first time I met you. I was eight years old, lost, and hungry. And Ni-Ni's shop had the best roast pork and dumplings in Chinatown. I smelled her cooking a mile away. I just followed my nose, that's all."

Followed it to Ni-Ni's little corner shop with its old-time stone facade, bordered by a grocer and a Chinese pharmacy. Wandering down the street, trying to act like he knew what he was doing, and all the while thinking that grand adventures in exotic locales were not all they were cracked up to be, and that he was going to spend the night on the street, that he'd be lost forever and ever, and while that was miserable it still might be better than the alternative: going home to his uncle Pete, who had a date with a Jack Daniel's and a Miller and God only knew what else. Maybe a hose jammed into a tank of gas. Couldn't be any less harmful than knocking back the contents of all those bottles and cans, nursing another day of trouble at the steel mill, which was nothing more than the cumulative effect of a life made up of bad choices and lost opportunities.

Dean had not, even at that age, wanted to be anything like his uncle. His parents, who had also worked at the mill, were better role models. Only problem was that they were dead. Which sucked.

"I was playing on the floor," Miri said softly, drawing his attention back to her. "I was building a fort out of boxes. And I looked up and saw you standing in the doorway, and you were so pathetic I couldn't help but like you."

"Thanks," he said dryly. "I guess Ni-Ni felt the same?"

"You know how she felt." Miri glanced at him, a smile haunting her mouth. "After all, you were the only other child she ever took in."

Dean leaned his head against the window. "I practically lived with you guys above that shop for eight years."

"Give or take. More so when you got older. Not as many people were on your uncle's case at that point."

"Hit puberty in that town and you're a man," Dean said. "Shit, you know that my uncle's friends used to give their baby vodka so he could hold his liquor when he got older? Kid was a total monkey. Way more hyper than me."

"Probably not by much," she muttered.

Dean grinned. "This is good, you know. Talking."

"You act like you don't do it much."

"Not with chicks. Not like this. I mean, I love the ladies and all, but this is personal stuff."

"And you don't get personal with your girlfriends? Shame on you, Dean."

"It's not like that, Miri. It's just different with us, that's all. We got history."

"With a big twenty-year blank spot."

Dean shrugged. "You can harp on that as long as you want, *bao bei,* but eventually I'm gonna wear you down. Twenty years? Nothing. Or hell, think of it as a positive. It'll keep the relationship fresh."

"You're the one who's fresh. What makes you think we're going to have a relationship?"

"I'm totally not going to dignify that with an answer."

A light mist speckled the windshield. Rain. Dean kept his window partially rolled down. He needed the air, even though it was wet and humid and smelled dirty. The rain covered the streets with a slick reflective sheen that captured light and color against the darkness of the roadway. So much glittering light, neon fireflies caught in transit. Despite the late hour, nothing had dimmed. Shops were still open. Little restaurants, with cooks in the window chopping and frying, steam rising high. Business as usual. In a few hours, with morning, it would be booming.

"Sure you know where you're going?" Miri asked.

"Got a map in my head."

"And I'm supposed to find that comforting?"

"Faith, darlin'. You need to get some."

"Oh, hallelujah."

"Amen," he said, and pointed. "You see that McDonald's over there? There's a side street on the other side. Go that way."

She did. Dean watched the mirrors, the narrow road ahead of them, empty except for a stray dog, rooting through spilled trash. He did not see anyone following. But then, he had not seen the man in the alley tailing their car, though he wondered if he hadn't had some warning. The skin above his heart, that cut, the burning. Burning until they put some distance between themselves and the alley, the man who Miri had seen at the university. Made him wonder if there wasn't a connection. Which was so not comforting.

Priorities, priorities. Miri, first. Voodoo mark, later.

Dean said, "You can stop the car. Just park it wherever."

Miri gave him a dirty look, which was a thrill—even when she was angry at him, it was a wonder; he loved it—and she said, "Do you want to tell me what we're doing here?"

"Going some place safe."

"Really?" she said, and he felt her questions, her suspicion, and did not know how to reassure her. How to answer, even, if she asked. But she did not, and they got out and started walking. Dean led Miri through parked motorcycles and bicycles to a small pathway tucked between two apartment buildings. The air was hot and still, and though the misting rain had stopped, Dean was wet enough from sweat to want nothing more than to strip down and take a cold shower. For other reasons, too.

The path curved, twisted and crossed, writhing inward, away from the bustle of the city, enclosing them in silence until Dean's only reminder that he was still in Taipei was the 101 Building, the tallest in the world, which he could see looming when he looked up into the darkness at the narrow cut of sky. Dean thought it resembled a bunch of stacked take-out boxes. Very funky. It made up for the air, which smelled like a bad sewer, or the garbage rotting off to the sides; buffets for the stray dogs: little things with ratty white hair and big hungry eyes, a couple of larger ones, mixed breeds, ribs jutting.

Near the dogs, Dean found the door in the wall. Narrow, metal, and unadorned. In front, on the ground, Dean crouched and located a rough engraving in the stone. A skull and crossbones, surrounded by a heart. He felt the curving lines with his fingers and smiled. Roland's mark. The boss man's tattoo.

"We're here," he said. There was a keypad set in the wall. Dean punched in the sequence and heard a click. Below the door handle he found another pad, more buttons requiring another code. This click was softer. He opened the door and held it open for Miri.

She hesitated before walking through. "What is this?"

"Safety," he said. "For now, anyway."

"I have some questions for you," she said.

He grunted, and gestured again for Miri to precede him. She did, still tentative, but after the first step she sighed, and Dean was glad for it. He locked the door behind them.

They stood inside a courtyard, a little touch of paradise in the middle of the city. Miri fingered a broad-leafed miniature palm, which leaned low over a tiny reflecting pool where water ran down a small series of stones around which grew sweet-scented bushes and climbing vines covered in tropical flowers. Even in the darkness, where the only light was an ambient glow from the overcast city sky, he could see the beauty of the place. Dean felt his muscles relax, his chest loosen. Even the air smelled cleaner.

"Dean," Miri said. "Is this yours?"

"No," he said. "Um, come on. There's more."

Miri followed him to another metal door, with yet another keypad. He typed in the sequence, aware that she was watching over his shoulder, probably memorizing all the numbers.

Inside, the air was so cool he wanted to cry. Lights came on immediately; the motion detectors were still working. Again, Miri gasped, and Dean let loose his own long sigh. He always forgot how good Dirk & Steele's safe houses looked. No crap for the agency.

The main room was small but lush, with old furniture made of rich dark woods that gleamed under the track lighting in the ceiling. Velvet, silk, golden brocade—everywhere, lush—and while the furnishings and decorations bordered the edge of gaudy, Dean preferred to see the luxury for what it was: the perks of a kick-ass job.

"There's a bedroom and bathroom down the hall," he said to Miri, who continued to stare. "Kitchen, too, if you're hungry. It should be stocked. Someone, uh, comes in every now and then to take care of things. Do you need a drink?"

She gave him a look like he was crazy, but said, "Juice. Something sweet. I feel like a wreck."

"You look beautiful," Dean said, and Miri blinked, all wide-eyed like an owl. A faint flush touched her cheeks. He smiled and said, "Come on. Let's go and sit down. I need to have a beer and a nervous breakdown."

"Talk first, then breakdown. I want answers, not drool."

"You used to love my drool."

"Ha. You funny."

The kitchen was small and modern, covered in blue tile with stainless steel appliances and a stone floor. It was very clean. Dean thought about his own kitchen, which smelled like a garbage dump and was a breeding ground for a new strain of mold that he was growing in a series of smiley faces. By the time he got home, he expected speech and actual movement.

The refrigerator was stocked with drinks. Not much in the way of food, except for some fruit. The freezer had steak, but Dean did not feel like cooking. He certainly wasn't going to ask Miri to lay out the skillet. In her mood, she'd take his gun and hit him over the head with it. He grabbed some mangoes instead, a bottle of orange juice and a beer, dug around for some knives, and perched on a stool beside Miri at the island counter.

He cracked open their drinks. Took a knife to the mango, dropping the peelings on the counter.

"Here," Miri said, laying down a paper towel in front of him. She said nothing more as he cut the fruit for her and set it on the dish. Slow, easy, thinking about nothing but the sharp edge and the mango, about Miri sitting beside him, alive and not a ghost, about fire and pain and bullets, red jade and mummies. He thought about his life and the past twenty years. Time lost, time gained, time spent apart.

Dean said, "Remember when we were little we would sit in Ni-Ni's shop, and she'd cut us down some of her hot roast pork? We'd eat it in strips and get all greasy, and then she'd come with her hot rags and wash our faces and hands. Scrubbed me raw."

"She loved you. Said you were her *re xiao erzi*. Her hot little son."

"That's me," he said, and then, quieter, "She taught me so much, Miri. Things about life that I would never have figured out on my own if it hadn't been for her stories. She drilled them into my head."

"You and me both. She made us her little survivors."

"No fear," he said, remembering. "Never show fear."

Never show fear. And that from a woman who probably experienced more of it than any human should have to endure.

Because Dean still remembered her harrowing stories of life in China during the Second World War— fleeing to Nanjing because she thought it would be safe, only to live through one of the worst massacres in human history. He could still hear her soft accent, her passionate recitation of facts and lists of horrors: boiled babies and rivers of blood, gang rapes that left women cut on the inside with knives, men forced to eat feces and their own testes. The Chinese Holocaust of the Second World War, which she had witnessed within the embassy grounds of a German Nazi, who eventually radioed home to the Mother Country to plead that Hitler ask Hirohito to order the Japanese army to stop the massacre.

The world is a cruel place, she had said, and compassion had to be tempered with a keen eye for safety, survival, because nothing was ever safe. Nothing ever sacred. Nothing, that is, except moments. Moments of joy, of love; peace and good food and warmth at a table surrounded by those you cared about. Moments like those could be counted on, each one precious. Beyond that, a mystery. Good or bad, lucky or not, cast in a shroud. But either way, you had to be prepared. Prepared to fight. Prepared to stay alive, to keep your friends and family safe, no matter the cost.

A hard woman. A good woman. Dean missed her. He had not thought he could possibly miss her any more than he had, but after hearing what Miri had to say about the matter—

Well. If a man could die from stupidity, he guessed his number would have been up around age sixteen.

"I should have gone back," he said. "I was a coward, Miri. I thought you were dead, and I didn't help her. I ran. She wouldn't have done that. She would have marched through hell to help us, and I was too weak to do the same for her."

"We covered this. Don't beat yourself up about it."

"But she held out hope. Just like you."

"She wasn't the type to do anything different."

True enough, though it didn't make it any easier to accept. "How did she die?"

"In her sleep. It happened almost a year after the whole thing with us went down. My parents took me back after that. They hardly knew what to do with me."

Dean grabbed Miri's hand. She did not pull away, not even when he pushed their stools close and held her tight against his side. She felt good, small and warm, and the heady scent of her hair brought back memories from his youth. Moments like this, sitting close, being close.

"I miss her," she said.

"Me, too," he replied. He had figured she must be getting old, that she might have passed on, but thinking and knowing were two different things.

Miri wiped at her eyes. "Tell me what happened that night, Dean. Tell me why you really stayed away."

"Because I killed a man." The words were easier to say than he thought they should be, given the gravity of their meaning. Sixteen years old and a murderer. It was a hell of a way to kick off his life. He peered down at Miri's face, searching for her reaction. She smiled sadly.

"I figured," she told him. "Maybe not back then, but in the car when you were talking."

His gut tightened. "How do you feel about it?"

"I wish you hadn't," she said.

Dean set down his mango and took a long drink from his beer. "I knew what he was when I first saw him, Miri. I knew what he was planning, that he was some fucking bad news. Can't explain how, but I just did. And I thought I could talk our way out of it. I thought, for just once, that I could be a good guy."

"It wasn't your fault."

"Fucker was psycho. If I had done what I had to, early on—"

Miri squeezed his hand. "You weren't a killer."

But I became one, he thought, and knew Miri felt the

same. He could see it in her eyes. He saw something else, too. Guilt.

"Hey," he said. "Hey, Miri. *Bao bei*. This is not your fault."

"You killed for me. Because of me. You went looking for him out of revenge."

"It was justice. The only kind of justice I could give you. Maybe it was wrong. I don't know. I'm no Super-man with superhuman morals. And I don't regret what I did, either. The only thing I'm sorry about is that I let it keep me away from Ni-Ni. And you."

Miri touched his face, running the backs of her fingers over his jaw, down his throat. It was hard to breathe when she touched him like that, when she was so close, her eyes so dark and large, filled with brood-ing knowledge.

"Tell me," she said. "Tell me what happened."

"I caught up to him," Dean whispered. "In the old lot by the market. I was bleeding like a son of a bitch, but for some reason it didn't bother me. Told you that al-ready. The bullet didn't hurt like it should. I tracked the man—he had a trail a mile wide—and by the time I caught up with him he was going under a fence. Didn't hear me coming. I grabbed him by the legs and pulled him back. He tried to shoot me but his aim was bad. I still had my knife, that one you gave me for my birth-day. I stabbed him in the kidney first, and then I got his gun and ... bang."

That grass lot, the knife tucked in the back waist-band of his jeans and then magically in his hand. Crazy, bleeding, but it had been now or never because the man had killed, the man had murdered, the man had taken away Miri and Dean did not care what happened to him tonight because the man was a monster and God help the son of a bitch because Dean was going to move heaven and earth to make sure he never hurt anyone ever again.

And he had made sure. For good. For Miri.

Miri said nothing for a long time. Finally, in a voice so soft he barely heard her, she said, "I would have gone with you. If I had known you were alive, and where you were, I would have gone to you. I would have followed you, Dean. I was ready."

"You were sixteen," he said.

"Same age as you."

"I thought you were dead," he said. "And I was too stupid to go to your grandmother. But even if things had been different, I wouldn't have done that to you. You were good in school. You had promise. You had big dreams."

"I had all kinds of dreams. We used to talk, remember? About what we would do with a car and some money."

He remembered. Just the two of them, hitting the road into the big bad world. Nothing would have hurt him with Miri there. Amigos, musketeers ... and best friends.

But then, she would not have turned into some genius archaeologist. And he might not have found Dirk & Steele. Although, in some sense, that seemed just as inevitable a fate as being with Miri.

She began eating her mango, and in a calm voice said, "About this detective agency. Spill."

Dean coughed. "What about the deep emotional moment we were having? Don't you want to ... keep talking about that? Like, get it out on the table?"

"I can't handle any more on this table, Dean. I'm tired, I'm dirty, and I need to lie down. But first, I want to know how you joined up with a group of ... of psychics, and why you seem to have more money than God."

"Where do you want me to start?"

"From the beginning. And no jokes."

"No jokes," he said. "How horribly stifling of you."

"Dean."

He held up his hands. "Okay, fine. I spent a lot of time in the South after I left Philly. Caught a bus down to Tennessee, and then from there worked my way through Louisiana and Texas."

"I noticed you talk differently. It's subtle. Just a bit of a drawl."

"Helped me fit in, and then it became natural. When I turned eighteen I walked into an army recruiter's office. I got my GED while in the service, and later on the military paid for college. I didn't finish, though. I figured I didn't need a piece of paper to tell me how smart I wasn't."

"Don't do that. I always hated it when you put down your intelligence."

"And I always knew what my limits were. Just like I knew you didn't have any. I'm glad you got out, Miri. Sounds like you're a professor, right? Archaeology? That's so fucking cool."

Her cheeks flushed. "Don't change the subject. What happened next?"

"I was trained as a sniper while in the army. I got hired by the police force after I got out. SWAT."

"Bizarre. You hated the cops when we were growing up."

"Times change. I needed a job and it paid well. I didn't like it much, though. Too much pressure, not enough patience. Didn't like picking guys off without looking them in the eye. And then, later on, the … detective agency found me. Hired me. I've been with them for more than ten years."

"Huh. What are they called?"

"Dirk & Steele."

Miri snorted. "Dirk & Steele?"

"Don't laugh."

"It sounds like a seventies cop show, Dean. It's cornier than springtime in Kansas."

"Ha." Dean finished his beer and gave up on the mango. He was too tired. "You can have the first shower, Miri."

"You're going to do all kinds of things behind my back while I'm in there. I can tell."

"I am a devil," Dean said. "I do not deny it."

"And you haven't answered all my questions."

"Miri." Dean leaned close, looking deep into her eyes. Those lovely beautiful eyes. "We've made it this far. Let's not do the inquisition all at once. I'm ready to drop dead."

"I want the truth."

"Miri, please."

"Fine. Don't tell me. I understand."

"I don't think you do."

She punched him in the gut. It was light, more play than fight, but he doubled over anyway and said, "Ow."

"Serves you right. You turn around and I'll kick your ass, too."

He turned around. Miri blew out her breath, grabbed his shoulders, and spun him back to face her. Dean did not give her time to talk. He cupped her face in his hands, smoothed back her hair, and kissed her mouth.

She tasted like warm mango. She tasted like home. She tasted like the past twenty years had never happened and they were sixteen again with the fire high and sweet in their blood.

He did not want to let her go, but when he did she leaned into him, sighing against his cheek, body soft and hot with sweat and the night.

"Go on," he whispered. "Go on, *bao bei.*"

And she did, and he watched her go, and he did not follow.

When the water began running in the bathroom, Dean went to the living room, made himself comfortable, and called Roland Dirk. His boss answered on the first ring, and with his customary clairvoyant charm. "You look like so much shit, Dean."

"That's because I'm chin deep and surrounded by elephants on laxatives. It's gonna take a bomb to dig me out."

"Pure poetry, you little squealer. The fail-safe rattled. You've been talking."

The fail-safe, Roland's telepathic invention. All the agents had walls inserted into their minds when they joined, a mental block hiding all of Dirk & Steele's most precious secrets. And should an agent share those secrets, or even edge the line of them, it would be like poking a stick into Roland's brain. He would know who and how much, and whether that deserved an ass-kicking or something worse. As far as Dean knew, no one had ever required the latter. He was not entirely sure what would happen—and he most definitely hoped he never had to find out.

And I hope I never will. No one has ever betrayed the agency on purpose, but accidents happen. And no one's a perfect judge of character.

"Miri's safe," Dean said. "I promise you. I've known her since I was eight."

"No woman is safe," Roland said. "Trust me."

"This one is." And Dean's voice dared his boss to argue. For once, Roland let it go.

"So what's all the fuss?" he asked instead. "Where's all the shit coming from?

Dean told him. He tried to make it concise, using flash words such as "fire" and "conspiracy" and "big freakin' shape-shifter," and told Roland, too, about Miri and Robert and Kevin. The red jade.

"You're both fucked," Roland said. "Seriously. I'll start arranging the funeral now."

"I want a happy boss. Where's the positive re-inforcement?"

"Buried with Pollyanna in my backyard. Which is where you'll be if you don't play your cards right."

"It all comes down to the jade." Dean glanced across the room at Miri's black purse. "I don't know why or how this mess started, and I don't know who the players are. Though, given what happened to Artur I've got some suspicions. Freaks me out, man. And this guy taking bullets? The one who was *hired* to go after the jade? I swear to God, just like Hari when he was cursed by the Magi. I mean, that's not supposed to be possible anymore, right? I thought Hari was the only one who couldn't be killed—and Dela, she broke that curse."

Roland did not say anything, which was about as unusual as the sky opening up to rain acid piss, and yodeling opera singers and praying dogs. Unnatural. It gave Dean a bad feeling. Very bad.

"Roland," he said slowly. "Do you know something I don't?"

"No," his boss said. "That's the problem."

Dean agreed. Dirk & Steele had contacts all over the world, sources that were supposed to report on even the slightest hint of paranormal activity. The offices in New York and California made the basement in the *X-Files* look like a child's playpen. But even with all those resources, all the money pouring into research, discovering shape-shifters had still been a shock—and Artur's kidnapping, worse.

"Could this be the Consortium?" Dean even hated saying the name. "I asked Robert and he said no. The fact he recognized the name, though? Total panty-twister."

"Artur and Elena took care of the Consortium's leadership."

"We think they did, but hell, man. How much do we really know? All they saw was the inside of a lab and some fancy house in Moscow. That's nothing for an organization that was supposed to be some kind of international fucking crime syndicate."

"I need to make some inquiries," Roland said. "Have you taken a reading of that jade yet?"

"Been kind of busy with the running and escaping part of the night, but it's next on my list."

"Do what you have to do. Your decision to go after the second piece seems like the smart choice. Just remember that if everyone else has a hard-on for this thing, you can bet they got similar means of tracking down that other missing piece. Means likes ours, maybe. No one goes to that much trouble for something that's just gonna gather dust."

"I guess that's it, then. We really are dealing with folks like us."

"You already knew it."

"But it's different, hearing you say it."

Roland sighed. "It's not like the good old days, Dean. We had it easy for a long time."

"Easy when we thought we were the only ones? Easy when we thought it was just science, and our brains were random mistakes and magic didn't exist? Maybe we should have known better."

"Maybe we should have," Roland grumbled, "but maybe it wouldn't have mattered. Maybe it was good to be babies for a while."

"You going soft?"

Roland grunted. "Whatever. Sorry I couldn't send Eddie with you. He could have handled the fire bit with flying colors."

"How's his appendix?"

"Like crap. They almost didn't catch it in time, and he's still doing the ass-plant in a hospital bed, being doted on by an army of hot nurses. Makes me sick."

"Maybe *you* should rupture something."

"Any more of these stories out of you and I just might." And he hung up the phone. Dean was not offended. Roland did not like good-byes, which only made him more of a rock, the anchor of the agency in ways that its founders, Nancy Dirk and William Steele, Dirk and Steele, were not.

Dean stood and walked to Miri's purse. He hesitated before unzipping it, but figured the need outweighed any politeness. Besides, it wasn't like he was going to paw through her stuff. Much.

He found her passport jutting from a pocket. That was good. Getting her new papers would take time. He found the jade near the bottom of her purse, lost amid cash and pens and paper, but as he removed it he noticed something small and gray at the bottom, something that made his gut hurt. He hesitated, and reached in.

It was a small flat rock in the shape of a heart.

She kept it. Jesus Christ. All these years, and she still carries it around with her.

The rock was smaller than he remembered, but the memory of giving it to her was still as clear as anything. Miri, as long as he had known her, had always loved rocks. Loved collecting them, digging them up, imagining fantastic stories about what she found. But only when she was alone, or around Dean and her grandmother. No one else made her feel safe enough to be herself. Teachers at school had expected her to be one way—same with her parents—and that was all she was supposed to be. One big expectation, a life lived on someone else's terms. Doctor or lawyer, that was all that mattered. Do that and go to heaven. Anything else meant failure.

It was good that Miri's parents didn't raise her.

Not that he would ever tell her that, even though he thought she might agree with him. Dean remembered her parents: a cold man and a cold woman visiting only at Chinese New Year and sometimes during the summer. Spending a week, maybe two at the most, with that time spent hovering over their daughter's shoulder, drilling her about schoolwork, her plans, how she needed to be more motivated, more engaged in the Chinese community. They talked to Miri about her friends, too. Or rather, just one friend. Because she had only one. And he was white and poor.

Trash. They called me trash to my face. Like that made them any better.

Dean took a deep breath and closed his hand around the rock. None of that mattered now. Only this. Miri and him. Despite everything that had happened in their lives, they were back together again, and all he could blame was fate. Destiny.

Rocks.

Dean slipped the little rock back into her purse and picked up the jade. He cradled it in his hands, running his fingers over the smooth waxy surface. The color was beautiful, red like in the pictures of stars or cosmic clouds, a deep red touched with orange and pink, shimmering underneath with a subtle glow. There were scratches in the rock, lines, but Dean did not look too closely at those. It was not the surface that interested him, but something deeper, etchings from the past, lines of energy that no doubt had once encased this piece of jade, wrapping it like the flesh that had held it tight, embracing it as part of something warm and soft and—

"—dark that is sweet, my friend, because even the days now

grow long and I count my life in moments, too many moments, and it is a madness to me because I know they will not end, not ever. Men have their deaths to use, but our kind must bear on like the mountains, the sea, and that is unnatural. If I could be as the wren, or some simple beast, and think every moment is fresh and new, then perhaps the burden would not be so, but I am a thinking mind, a feeling heart, and too much has been laid to waste before me while I go on."

"And so you will simply give up? You will turn your back on the rest of us? You cannot. Please. We need you. There is no returning from that place, you know that."

"No guilt. I will not wait. The Book is ready for me and if I do not act now, there will not be another time. I have seen that much. Please forgive me. I do not know what is yet to come, only that I will regret leaving you. But that is not enough to stay. Not anymore."

"And the power you will release? It cannot be predicted. There might be consequences you cannot yet foresee—"

"No. No, I am done here. Now. I am done—"

The words of the two men died. Pain flashed bright in Dean's chest and heart—his burning heart—and he could not see. Darkness, he was trapped in darkness, rolling and heaving, and he did not know how long he stayed in that terrible place, but when he opened his eyes, he found familiar faces: Miri, wrapped in a thick white robe, and beside her Koni, his shoulders bare, bare all the way down—his nose bleeding.

Dean saw the ceiling behind them. A moving ceiling, spinning and spinning.

"Oh," he said. "Bad."

And then he rolled over and vomited.

Chapter Eight

With some effort and much grunting, Koni and Miri managed to move Dean into the bedroom. They laid him down on top of the covers, and the entire time he kept his palms pressed against his eyes. His head—all the bits touching the inside of his skull—hurt like hell.

He felt someone sit beside him and hoped to God it was Miri.

"Dean," she said, and he sighed as she touched his face. Her fingers were cool.

"What happened?" It hurt to talk. His head was dying.

"You tell us," Koni said. The shape-shifter sounded distant, like he was on the other side of the room. Dean heard doors opening; the closet, maybe. The rustle of clothing. He thought about Koni naked. Koni naked in front of Miri.

In spite of the pain, he took away his hands and cracked open his eyes. The first thing he saw was Miri, looking down at him with such concern that he thought,

Fuck pain, I'm going to live forever. And then he glanced past her and saw Koni sorting through pants.

"God," Dean groaned. "Go away. I don't want to see your ass right now. I'm in enough pain."

"I don't feel sorry for you," Koni retorted. "You deserve worse. My feet will never be the same—they smell like your stomach."

"It was you or Miri. Have some class, man. And while you're at it, put on some damn clothes. You're in the presence of a lady."

"Your 'lady' has a mean right hook," Koni muttered, touching his nose.

"What did you expect?" Miri asked. "I come out of the shower, Dean's on the floor, and you're standing over him. Naked. You're lucky all I had was my fists."

"So what stopped you from breaking other body parts?" Dean muttered.

"I didn't fight back." Koni pulled on some slacks.

"And he was naked and gross," Miri added. "I have my limits."

Koni scowled, grabbing a T-shirt from the drawer. "I wouldn't have come in, but considering everything that's happened tonight, I thought a planning session might be helpful. If I wait any longer, you might be dead."

"So considerate," Dean said. "Such an optimist."

"Hey," Miri said. "How do you know what happened here tonight? I don't remember seeing you."

"I get around," Koni finally said. "I see things."

"So you were following us," Miri said in a flat voice. "Naked."

"I had clothes," Koni said, but it was a bad lie, and Dean thought it was a mark of desperation he even tried using it. Miri flashed the shape-shifter a thin smile: pure danger. Dean wanted to yell, *Run,* but frankly, he was on Miri's side.

"It's okay," she said, deceptively gentle. "Really. I seem to be a magnet for strange people tonight. Though yours is the first pair of eyes that glowed."

"My eyes don't glow," Koni said.

"They did when I hit you."

Game over. A vein pulsed in Koni's forehead. Dean, trying to break the tension in the room, blurted, "He wasn't completely naked. He probably still had that air freshener you threw at him dangling over his naughty bits."

"What?" Miri looked at Dean as if he was insane.

"This is my partner. Who I mentioned earlier? He's a shape-shifter, babe. Like, human and crow."

"I—" Miri stammered. "I thought you were kidding when you said that."

Koni stood very still, like a statue, breathless, and for a moment Dean felt some sympathy for him. Koni did not know Miri like he did. He did not know she could be trusted.

"Miss," Koni said quietly. "Can you give us a minute?"

She almost argued, but Dean looked at her, begged with his eyes, and she sucked in her breath. Stood up and walked out of the room. Her backside swished quite nicely beneath the robe.

When she was gone and the door closed behind her, Koni said, "I'm going to kill you."

"Get in line. And listen, stop with the brooding. That woman out there has seen hell today, but she's still truckin' like a trooper. Not only that, she knows all about my gifts. She was right there when I first started having visions. She was the one who helped me control them. And she never said a word. Not one. You can trust her."

"You know each other." Koni turned to stare at him. "Huh. I wondered why the two of you looked like you were making out in that alley. I chalked it up to sheer desperation."

"Just old times," Dean said, uncomfortable that Koni had watched something so personal. "We haven't seen each other in twenty years."

"But you still trust her."

"With my life," Dean vowed. "There's never been a person in this world I trusted more than Mirabelle Lee."

"Dean—"

"No, Koni. Miri is smart. She's a good person, too. Honest, brave, loyal, all those things for wonderful. So don't you ask me to lie to her. I won't do it. Roland can kick my ass from here to Timbuktu if he wants, but that's it. Too much has happened to Miri. She deserves whatever truth I can give her."

"You're in love with her."

"Well, yeah. For Christ's sake, who *wouldn't* love her?"

"Well ..." Koni began, but Dean shook his head.

"Don't answer that. Besides, she's mine."

"Really? Have you told her that?"

"All in good time, my man. All in good time."

"Well, good luck when you do." The shape-shifter touched his nose, wincing. "Jesus, Dean. I don't know why you have me around with her watching your back."

"You're just jealous. But don't worry. One day you too will have your very own little Amazon."

"I'll just settle for a woman."

"If you're lonely, you can have the inflatable sex doll Blue gave me for my birthday. I don't want the two of you to miss out on an opportunity for love."

"You didn't like her?"

"I wasn't man enough to satisfy her cravings. I'm sure you'll be different."

"Wow. Your thoughtfulness astounds me, Dean."

"I know. I'm all teary-eyed thinking about it."

They heard a knock at the door; Miri poked in her head.

"Um," Dean said. "Hey."

"Hey." A smile haunted her mouth. "I apologize for interrupting you. Really. That was one of the most fascinating eavesdropping sessions of my life. But I'm still in a bathrobe and I saw clothes in that closet. Do the math."

Koni sighed, and Miri took that as her invitation to walk in—utterly confident, and looking, in Dean's opinion, spectacularly hot. Long wet hair, delicate shoulders, and a profile to kill for. He wished Koni was gone.

But the shape-shifter did not leave the room. He did not stare at Miri, either, which was good—the gentlemanly thing to do—but there was some tension left in his voice when he said, "Earlier tonight, in that alley, there was a man there watching you. I think you saw him. I assume that's why you left, anyway." Koni paused, still watching Miri. "He's not human."

"What?" she asked, matching his stare. "You expect me to throw up my hands and scream? I give up, man. There is a whole other world running parallel to the one I've lived in for my entire life, and apparently, it's just as messed up as anywhere else. So thank you both."

"You're welcome," Dean said. "We live to destroy."

Koni sighed. Miri looked at him again and said, "What do you mean, not human?"

"He vanished in front of my eyes. And before that, he looked at me and knew what I was. Had the guts to say hello."

Miri shook her head. "Dean, I don't suppose you checked on Owen again, did you?"

"Who's Owen?" asked the shape-shifter.

"My colleague," Miri explained. "He was kidnapped tonight by some of the same people who are after the jade."

"I tried tracking him earlier, but lost his trail." Dean pulled the little brass statue from his pocket.

"That's been happening a lot lately." Koni leaned close, frowning. "Huh. I have one of those."

"You own a miniature Glen Campbell? That you paid money for? Holy shit."

"Every man has a hobby," Koni replied. "Even you."

"Dude, you got nothing on me."

Koni's answering smile was distinctly unpleasant. Dean frowned and turned away, hunching over the statue. He opened himself to the lingering vibrations, holding tight to the golden hum within the brass. Owen. *Owen.*

But nothing happened. All he got was a wall.

Dean opened his eyes and looked at Miri. He didn't need to say anything. She nodded, and stared at her hands.

Koni walked to the door. "I'm going to get something to eat. You two … talk." He closed the door behind him. Miri, chewing the inside of her cheek, went to the closet and began digging for clothes.

"Um," Dean said. "We can talk about this if you want."

"What's there to talk about?" She turned and walked to him, abandoning her search. "I'm surrounded by people who aren't human, I'm being hunted because of a mysterious artifact in my possession, my career has probably been blown to hell, and I'm standing half naked in front of you. This is what insanity feels like."

"Hey, now. Didn't Indiana Jones handle all sorts of crazy shit? You never saw him complain when people were turned to ash or had their hearts ripped out of their bodies."

Miri sat down on the bed beside him and Dean touched her hand. Her face was very solemn as he stroked her fingers, but slowly, slowly, a smile touched her mouth and much to his shock and pleasure, Miri lay very carefully down beside him, tucking herself close against his body. Dean kissed the top of her head.

"Things were easier when we were young," she murmured. "We'd go to school, come home, play. Run on the streets and sometimes get in fights. Easy trouble."

"You remember that time we snuck out and watched *Indiana Jones and the Temple of Doom?*"

"You stole money out of your uncle's wallet to pay for those tickets."

"It was worth it."

"I was fourteen years old." Miri leaned her head against his shoulder. "That movie changed my life."

"You became obsessed with Harrison Ford."

"And then you went out and found every single one of his movies for me. We played hooky from school to watch them."

"It was the only time my uncle was at the mill. And then the lousy VCR my cousin rented for us wouldn't work right. The audio and video kept playing at different speeds."

Miri laughed. "Good times, Dean."

He did not respond. It was hard to think. Miri smelled flowery, like shampoo. Warm and sweet and clean. He found his hand trailing down her back, following the line of her spine as his fingers danced lower and lower. Miri sighed. Dean asked, "Do you know how I feel about you? What it means to me that you're here? Alive?"

"Tell me again," she said. "Pretend it's old times."

Dean reached for Miri's hand. Her gaze was stubborn yet sweet, and he thought about the locket on his chest, all those years spent pouring his heart into the thing, into memories and metal, remembering Miri as a teenager, in a time warp of Forever Sixteen. Old times, when they had never held back their feelings, when the word *secret* did not exist between them, and together they were an army of two. Two against the world, playing in an old woman's kitchen, and later, older and wiser, running down greasy alleys in Chinatown, past those borders into the grittier, grayer, streets of Philly.

But that was all twenty years past, and they were grown now, with full lives between them. He was holding sacred something that he could never have again.

Not true. You're holding the memory sacred, but you've got the real deal, right here, right now. You have a second chance. You've been given a miracle. Don't waste it.

He touched her face, tracing the dips and curves of every bone and muscle; Miri's lips were soft beneath his fingers, her eyelids softer, and the line of her jaw arcing up behind her ear felt like magic. She murmured his name on a sigh, pushing closer. His headache faded as he relaxed into the curves of her body.

"Hush," he told her. "I'm talking to you. I'm telling you everything."

"You're not saying a word."

"Then you're not listening." He grazed her cheek with his lips. A wry smile touched her mouth. It was different than he remembered. Older, wiser. Sexy as hell.

"Are you trying to be a grown-up?" she asked, soft.

"No," he said, smiling. "But I am trying to be a man. How's it working for you?"

"It's working. It's working very well."

Dean pushed his fingers into her hair, skimming her scalp, twining warm. "I won't pretend it's old times, Miri. I don't want to do that anymore. You got me as I am now. You can *trust* me as I am now."

Her smile faded. "Do you promise?"

"Do my promises still mean something to you?"

She hesitated. "Yes. Yes, they do."

"Then I promise," he said. "I promise you can trust me."

Miri chewed on her bottom lip. He wanted to kiss that lip, but he reined himself in. *Trust,* he told himself. *It's all about trust now. Don't screw that up because you want her.*

Miri held up her hand. He stared at her, questioning, and then she turned down her fingers until only her pinky curled up. Her mouth twitched. Dean grinned. He linked his own pinky around hers.

"I swear it," he said.

"I swear it, too," she said.

And then, careful, they held each other and drifted off to sleep, a deep slumber that to Dean was full of darkness, bones, and sand, and somewhere nearby a woman weeping, moaning, and sobbing, and he could feel the pain of her heart in his heart, feel her suffering like his own, and he staggered across sand because now was the time, now and always, with her blood eternally on his hands—

Dean opened his eyes, dragging in a deep shuddering breath that felt like knives in his throat, a pain that made him imagine what it would be like to scream for days. But he did not think he had been screaming; Miri still lay beside him, eyes closed and her breathing steady. He gently tucked away her long black hair to better see her face, which was tucked and burrowed within the crook of his arm. He felt some drool on his skin, but it only made him smile.

He wanted to touch her. He wanted to bury his nose against the hollow of her throat and just rest there. Listen to her heartbeat. Drink in the fact that she was alive. Dean did not think he would ever take that for granted; every breath she took was precious.

For a moment, though, he heard the woman from his dream, her sobs, and a great uneasiness stole over him, a sense of déjà vu. Bones and sand were typical of his dreams, but the woman was new. He wondered if finding Miri again had anything to do with the new addition, although the possibility was disturbing. It was not a good dream, nor did it have a happy ending.

Miri stirred, making small noises. Dean waited, patient, and finally she cracked open her eyes.

"How long have you been waiting for me to wake up?" Her voice was soft and warm, making his stomach turn to fire. Sleepy talk. There was nothing sexier.

"Not long," he said, touching her hip, imagining what it would feel like to rest his hand on the warm skin there, so preciously close to such wonderful delicious spots. Miri pushed closer and Dean took it as an invitation to touch her some more, his hand exploring all those bits and pieces that were covered—until his fingers grazed actual skin and both he and Miri jumped. She laughed, low in her throat, which made the ache in his body even harder, stronger. Miri rubbed against him and he closed his eyes.

"This is torture," he said.

"It doesn't have to be," she whispered, hooking her leg around the back of his thigh, which exposed all kinds of sweet skin as the edge of her robe fell away. Dean, holding his breath, touched her leg.

"More," she breathed. "You can touch more."

The four best words he had ever heard. His hand trailed higher, moving slowly as he savored every inch of soft warm skin, fingers dancing as Miri squirmed even tighter, exposing herself so that he could feel the heat of her through his jeans. His hand grabbed her backside, fingers sliding into the crease, and she bit down on her lips as he pulled her tight against him, rolling her so that he was on top, her leg still wrapped around his hip. He ground himself against her body, using the friction of his jeans to rub and rub. She cried out, and her tiny hands found their way under his waistband, seeking skin, moving and moving until she managed to push them down the front of his pants, her fingers barely grazing him. Dean groaned and Miri began to laugh.

"That good, huh?"

He buried his face in her neck. "If you really touch me I think I might explode."

"Only if you explode inside me," she whispered, and that was enough to send him to the moon. And he was just about to go to the moon—to peel back the front of Miri's robe to see her breasts for the first time in twenty years—when the door to the bedroom slammed open and Koni burst in, breathless.

Miri, much to Dean's amazement, clamped her legs like a vise around his hips, preventing him from following his first inclination to leap up and do the dance of shame. Which put him in a very awkward, and yet manly, position when he looked Koni straight in the eye and said, "What the hell do you want?"

"We've got a guest," the shape-shifter said, and his eyes began to glow.

Chapter Nine

It was, Miri thought, a mystery that her brain had not yet exploded. She gave credit to her grandmother for that, a woman who had seen more horror, suffered more in one lifetime, than Miri could ever imagine—and yet, to her very end, remained unbowed, unbroken. Still smiling.

The very least Miri could do was act the same. That, or die trying.

Pretend. Pretend to accept everything that's happening to you and maybe it'll stop being crazy. Maybe it'll make sense.

Which might be just as disturbing, but such was life. Miri accepted it. She had to survive. She had to keep her mind strong and intact. She had to believe.

"When you say guest …" Dean began, as Miri ran to the closet. She found some women's clothes and yanked out a pair of khakis. She did not take time to look for underwear, just stuffed her legs into the pants and grabbed a T-shirt. She hesitated for only a moment before turning her back on the two men, throwing off her robe and pulling the shirt over her head in one smooth motion. She felt the break in their conversation, but ignored them, looking for a jacket.

"Not someone we know."

"But I didn't hear the alarms," Dean protested.

"He, uh, flew in."

Miri stopped what she was doing and stared at Koni. "Flew in?"

"Shit," Dean said. "Shape-shifter?"

"Yeah," he said uneasily. "You really ought to go out there now."

Dean scowled and reached for the handgun on the nightstand. He tucked it in the back of his jeans.

"I don't know if you really need that," Koni said. Dean gave him a look and even Miri knew better than to push. The man liked his firearms. Fine.

They left the bedroom single file, Miri bringing up the rear, which meant she was the last to see their "guest," though the sound Dean made as he entered the living room was warning enough.

And, indeed, she got a shock when she saw who was waiting for them: a tall man dressed entirely in white, a perfect complement to his white skin and long white hair. He wore sunglasses. His mouth was a pale line in his angular face. A big mouth, and very wide.

Miri recognized him. His face was the new hot thing; she had even read an article about him in one of the in-flight magazines on her plane ride from California. Bai Shen, egnimatic rock star, who still managed to maintain a playboy image despite reports—meant to be endearing, no doubt—that he really did like to keep to himself. Unless there was a girl in front of him who was very truly hot.

And he's not human, to boot. Now that *is interesting.*

"Well," Dean said slowly, still frowning. "I guess you

were staring at me for more than my pretty face when I saw you in the hotel lobby tonight."

One pale eyebrow arched over the sunglasses. "You took me off guard. I didn't expect to see you there."

"Which implies that you know who I am," Dean countered. "Care to explain?"

"No," Bai Shen said.

Koni coughed. "Maybe we should sit down. Anyone need a drink?"

"No drinks," Dean said. "Just answers. But first, take off your glasses, hot stuff. I want to see your eyes."

Bai Shen did as Dean asked. Miri was not sure what she was expecting, but was surprised to find a fairly ordinary gaze—unique only because his eyes were the color of gold. Not just light brown or hazel, but a polished rich gold that reminded Miri of the real thing, deep twenty-four karats set into his eyes.

Dean nodded. "Okay, then. Let's talk."

Everyone sat down. Miri stayed close to Dean, more for his comfort than hers. She did not feel threatened by Bai Shen—which, considering everything that had happened, seemed remarkable. Dean, on the other hand, was practically quivering with tension. Koni was harder to read—especially because she barely knew him—but he also seemed to display a bit more … deference than she expected, given their brief encounter.

"So you're a rock star," Dean said. "Tell me how a celebrity playboy shape-shifter knows who the hell I am and how to find this place."

"I'm rich and I hear things. What more do you want?"

"A lot. But somehow, I don't think we have time for twenty questions. You know us, you found us, and it must be for a reason, so just spit it out fast."

"The murderer you encountered tonight is my father."

"Okay, not *that* fast."

"Your father?" Koni asked.

"Your *father*?" Dean echoed. "God. My brain."

"Are we talking about the man who burned all those people to death, the one who showed up at the university?" Miri looked at all the men. "Is he?"

"Yes," Bai Shen said. "And the jade your friend found is the reason."

Miri briefly closed her eyes. "Is there a billboard in the sky, or something? Why does everyone and their mother seem to know about this thing?"

"It's not that many people," Bai Shen said. "Really. It's just … what you have is so important, so world-changing, there are men and women willing to give up their lives—or the lives of others—to possess it."

"It's a four-thousand-year-old rock," Miri argued. "Other than its historical value, I don't see anything about it that would incite this level of violence."

"Do you have it?"

She hesitated, but that was answer enough. Dean sighed. "Miri, you got your purse?"

"Um, no," she said, trying to remember the last time she had seen it. She recalled slipping the jade back into her purse after Dean's collapse, but after that …

Bai Shen cleared his throat and reached down by his feet. He held up her black leather bag. "I believe this is yours?"

Miri, face hot, leaned over and took it from him. He smelled like wood smoke up close, the edge of some winter fire, and his eyes glowed just a little brighter as she neared.

"I didn't look inside," the shape-shifter said, glancing sideways at Dean. "I'm a gentleman."

Dean frowned. Miri, stifling a smile, unzipped her bag and removed the jade. It was warm in her hand, and she felt a gentle weight in her chest, a presence in the bone between her breasts that was, in her imagination, full of light. The sensation was so strong she almost looked down her shirt. Instead, she held the jade out to Bai Shen. Her arm shook.

He did not take it from her. Instead he stared, frozen, his body growing ever more white until for a moment, Miri thought he might begin to glow. Glow like his eyes, which burned golden like the sun, heat to the winter snow of his skin. It hurt to look at him. He was not beautiful, but his presence was powerful, and it was almost too much.

And then, quite suddenly, her mouth filled with words—those butterflies returning to flutter their wings against her tongue—and there were so many things to say, and she lost herself in words, in language, in a vision that was full of impossible light, and she thought, *Let it go, let it go, let it go.*

But a hand touched her, and the light died, and the butterflies went away, withering to dust inside her mouth, and she wanted to fight, to rage against that loss, but even as she struck out another hand touched her, and another, and another, and she was buried in hands and in voices. And yet, only one voice cut through, cut right down to her heart, and she clung to that sound and let it draw her from the rage, draw her completely and utterly into another place of light; not otherworldly, but effortlessly human.

Miri opened her eyes and found Dean only a breath's distance from her face. She tried to move and found she could not; it took her a moment to realize that all three men were holding her down.

"What happened?" she whispered. Her voice was hoarse.

"You began speaking in tongues," Dean said, his voice as ragged as his breathing. Miri's gaze slid sideways; she found Koni pressing upon her right hand, and at her feet, Bai Shen.

"Not just tongues," she said. "What did I do?"

"I touched you," Bai Shen said. "Or rather, I touched the jade. It was a mistake."

"You pulled me away," she murmured, exhausted. "From something ... beautiful."

"You sure as hell didn't want to leave," Dean said. "What was it?"

"Light," she said. "So much light."

"Pretty lights," he said. "Okay, I got that. But if we let you up, are you still gonna try and get back to that happy place?"

Miri had enough energy to give him a dirty look. Dean smiled, mouth all crooked. "Right, *bao bei*."

The men released her slowly, as though uncertain of what she might do, and Miri herself did not move for one long minute. She did not feel as though she owned her body.

"Can I just ... stay down here while we talk about this?" Miri said to them. Dean's smile widened—relief, it was relief she saw in his eyes—and he lay back down beside her and ever so gently propped her head up on his arm, nestling close.

"Good?" he asked her, and when she nodded, he looked at Koni and Bai Shen and said, "What the hell just happened?"

"The jade is powerful," Bai Shen said. A light sheen of sweat covered his brow; some of his hair stuck to it. He looked more normal, less like an otherworldly rock star.

"I get the power thing now," Miri said. "Really, I do. But this is only one half of a larger piece. What happens if we put them together?"

"Danger," Bai Shen said. "That is exactly why I am here."

"Not because of your father?" Koni asked him.

Pain passed, fleeting, through his face. "Not just because of him, though if he wasn't involved, I might not be here right now."

"He wants the jade," Dean said. "He's killing to get to it. All those people he murdered? He must have thought they would know where it was."

"Still in a mummy," Miri muttered. "The timing of this is all wrong. All this planning and preparation for something that two weeks ago was buried in a Taiwanese jungle? That would only make sense if someone could … I don't know, see the future or something." The moment those words passed her lips, she stopped, closing her eyes. "Oh God."

"Yes," Dean said. "Welcome to my life."

"Don't be too surprised," Bai Shen said. "The jade is a large enough event that a psychic of nominal power would feel some premonition of its discovery, even if they didn't know quite what it is they're feeling or seeing."

Dean frowned. "But that means we've got at least two different pre-cogs with the power and resources to put themselves into play for this thing."

"There can't be that many people who fit the bill," Miri said. "Can't you track them down or something?"

"I wish," Dean muttered, closing his eyes. "But first, I want to know what the jade is."

"A book," Bai Shen said. "A very *powerful* book."

"I've heard it referred to like that," Dean said. "But a book of what?"

"I don't know. It's very ancient. All that's left are legends, conjecture. Dr. Lee, you've heard of the Three August Ones, correct?"

"The God Kings. Men who ruled during China's early history. They predated the Five Emperors and the Xia Dynasty."

"There is a legend, Dr. Lee. It tells of a red book, a book carved in jade. A book that will outlast time. The words of the book were supposedly written for the eyes of the gods, and as such, only the gods could read them."

"What are you saying? That the legend refers to the jade?"

"Maybe. It fits the description."

"I took a reading of the thing earlier tonight," Dean said. "All I could hear were voices. Male. Talking about a book. There was a guy who wanted to die. It didn't make sense what he was saying, only that he acted like he had been alive for a long time. Like, immortal long. And he wanted it to end."

"So, what? This thing kills people?" Miri shook her head. "I'm sorry, but I just don't believe it. When I was inside … wherever I was, I didn't feel anything evil about it."

"I'm not trying to imply it's evil," Bai Shen said. "Just … powerful."

Dean held up his head. "Wait. How do you know so much about this? And don't give me any cheap excuses."

"Those are the only kind I have," the shape-shifter said. "I can't tell you why or how I know these things."

"But you expect us to believe you?"

"I don't expect anything," he said. "But I hope."

Dean rolled his eyes. Koni said, "Tell us about your father. What's his interest?"

"And why is he psycho?" Dean added. Miri poked his ribs.

Bai Shen frowned at Dean; his mouth was remarkably suited to a frown, which curved and curved like some awful rainbow made of only one color: white.

"He's not himself," he said in a hard voice, and with his glasses off it was easy to see his youth, all the cool varnish, the high-end maintenance, stripped away with the pain in his face. "My father's been possessed."

"Possessed," Miri echoed.

"You have to believe me, Mr. Campbell. This is not him. Something is controlling him. Forcing him to kill those people."

Dean did not counter his words with disbelief or more argument. He said nothing at all for a long moment, and then glanced at Koni, who nodded slowly. "Okay. Tell me more. Tell me what could do that."

"They don't have names. I don't know what they are. But the more they touch you, the more they change you. Your eyes, your teeth, your entire body and mind. They transform your soul. You know what my father is now, Mr. Campbell. What you see is not the same man I knew less than a year ago."

"Let's say that's true. What the hell do you want us to do about it? Fix him? And what does this have to do with Miri and the artifact?"

"Miri, I still don't understand. I wish I did. But what I can be certain of is that the thing controlling my father wants the jade. It wants the Book. The whole Book, and if it gets it, if it can use the power—"

"No," Miri said, remembering butterflies, light. She wondered where the jade was, and glanced about until she found it on the sofa. "Whatever is in there, we can't let anyone have it who doesn't deserve it. We can't, Dean."

"How was your father possessed?" Koni asked.

Bai Shen shook his head. "I don't know. Just that I felt the change in him immediately. He was not the same man."

"And again I ask, what the hell do you want us to do about it?"

"I want you *not* to kill him, Mr. Campbell. Please."

Dean blew out his breath. "Do you know what your dad has done? Have you been to the crime scenes?"

"No," Bai Shen said.

"And have you witnessed the murders?"

"Absolutely not."

"Then don't ask me to hold myself back when I deal with good old Dad. I'm sorry if someone is controlling his actions. I can't tell you how sorry. But I refuse to handicap myself just because he's got a big bad spirit sucking on his brain cells. I won't do it. There's too much at stake."

Bai Shen closed his eyes. "If you knew him—"

"If I knew him like you know him? I bet I'd like him. But that's not the man I know."

"I understand."

No, Bai Shen did not understand, but Miri admired him for saying the words, no matter how bitter they might be on the tongue. She did not feel particularly bitter; she was on Dean's side. Moral ambiguity notwithstanding, there was a bottom line to consider, and that was how many more people would have to die if something was not done.

Bai Shen stood. He put his sunglasses on. "I need to go."

"Now?" Dean asked. "Don't get me wrong, man, but you haven't really helped us."

"I've given you all I can." The shape-shifter sounded weary.

"What should we do next?" Miri asked him. "You must have some idea."

"Find the second piece of jade. The Book is dangerous, but only in the wrong hands."

"And you think we're the right hands to have it? Why? You don't know us."

Bai Shen said nothing. Dean gave him a hard, cold smile. "You son of a bitch. You're holding back. You know more than what you're telling."

"I'm telling you more than I should."

"No such thing," Dean snapped. "You come here talking about hope, you want us to trust you, but that can't happen like this."

"Then ignore everything I've said," Bai Shen told him angrily. "Use it or don't use it, I don't care. All I want is my father back. *That's all I want,* Mr. Campbell, and you won't even try not to hurt him. You won't even give me a goddamn maybe."

"You want him that bad, *you* hunt him down! You love him, don't you? Or are you just too scared? Too scared of your old man to go that extra mile, but hey, all you gotta do is get us to walk it for you, right? Some plan. Will that help you sleep at night? No guilt, because you tried? Big dragon shape-shifter, my ass. You got no heart, man. You got no balls."

Bai Shen's eyes glowed so bright Miri felt certain something—or someone—was going to catch fire. Perhaps Dean thought so, too. He was on his feet in a second, gun pulled, aimed at the shape-shifter's head. Koni crouched beside Miri, helping her scoot backward.

"Don't you dare," Dean whispered. "I will shoot you if you try."

"All I needed was help," Bai Shen murmured. "All I wanted to *do* was help."

"And we appreciate it. But I think you should leave. Right now." Miri got chills listening to that voice come out of Dean. It belonged to a man who had seen hard times for years and years; a distinct voice, like a fingerprint of the soul, telling Miri exactly how much he had suffered in the past two decades.

Bai Shen, on the other hand, suddenly seemed like the opposite of everything that voice embodied. Maybe not a bad heart, but an immature one. A psyche that had not yet been tempered or cut or broken. She did not wish any of that on him; only, she could tell the difference, which was profound: It defined who was a man and who was still a boy.

"I'm sorry," Bai Shen said. "I'm so sorry."

And with that, he backed away to the door and left.

No one moved. Miri held her breath. Dean stared at the door, gun raised. And then, slowly, he turned his head and looked down at Miri and Koni, and said, "What the fuck was that?"

"Someone who didn't know any better," Miri told him. "A kid who was trying hard and doing some things wrong, and others right."

"Are we really not going to help his father?" Koni asked.

Dean lowered his gun. "I'll help him if I can."

"You could have mentioned that to Bai Shen," Miri said.

"And make promises I'm not sure I can keep?" Dean shook his head. "I won't do that. Besides, he irritated me. I don't mind helping, but if you love someone, if you've got family that needs you, you don't … turn your back. You don't get someone else to do the dirty work for you."

He said the last in a careful voice, filled with careful meaning. Miri understood. She held out her hand to him, and when he took it, she squeezed hard. Dean sat down beside her on the floor, and it was odd: all that nice furniture feeling less safe than a rug and wood.

"I don't feel any better now than I did twenty minutes ago," she said.

"Ditto," Dean replied. "We have more information now than we did before, but talk about depressing."

"And overwhelming," Koni said.

"Don't forget bizarre," Miri added.

"As long as we're all in agreement." Dean rubbed his

face. "So we find the second piece of jade, if we can. I think we had already figured that one out."

"But oh, the pressure." Miri patted his leg. "It's okay. We'll figure something. Everything will be fine."

Dean shook his head. "Either you think I'm about to lose it, or you're turning into an optimist."

"Scary?"

"Not as scary as when you wigged out. You scared the hell out of me, babe. I was afraid the jade was causing you to have a stroke. Brain damage, at the very least."

"Brain damage?"

"It was the way you talked," Koni said. "Complete gibberish."

"Accompanied by some foaming at the mouth," Dean added. "Very sexy."

Miri lay back down on the floor, resting her hands on her stomach. She tried to recall the exact sensations that had flooded her in those moments when she had been open to the jade—or maybe just the world—but she could not duplicate the feelings inside her heart. So she drifted from there to Bai Shen, and imagined what she would do if her own father was hurt, committing crimes against his will.

You would help him. You would do the same thing Bai Shen did, if you knew that someone was hurting him.

She frowned. "We never did get his father's name."

"Shit. I'm losing my edge, babe."

"It was already lost," Koni said. "But since we're on the subject, how did Bai Shen know you were investigating his father? And how, for that matter, did he know Miri was in possession of the jade?"

"I put that under the grand umbrella of questions he answered with the whole 'I'm rich and I hear shit' comment." Dean grimaced. "I can't believe I let that slide. You sure he's safe? One of the good guys?"

"No, but he's a dragon, and that usually counts for something. Usually."

"Dragon," Miri said.

"Dragon," Koni said. "Just like I fly as a crow."

"Oh," she said. "Never mind."

"Thank you," he said, and closed his eyes.

Chapter Ten

He needed sleep, he needed to lie down beside Miri and hold her in his arms, but instead she went to bed alone, and Dean stayed by the phone to make one last call. Koni settled down in the adjoining room.

Artur picked up on the third ring. He answered in Russian, which told Dean exactly how deep in sleep he had been.

"Yo," Dean said. "Sorry to bother you."

"No," Artur mumbled. "You are not."

Dean heard another voice on the other end of the line; a woman, talking quietly, and sounding far more alert than her companion. Bed springs squeaked.

"How's the missus?" Dean asked.

"Suffering from jet lag," Artur said. "Elena is still on California time and cannot sleep. She is thrilled you called because it gives her an excuse to get me up."

"She needs excuses now, huh? Dude, that's sad."

Artur sighed. "What is it you want?"

"I have some questions," Dean said. "I'm in the middle of a case right now, the one involving those murders in Taipei. Only, the guy causing all the trouble is a shape-shifter and he's whacked-out like crack, man. Totally shit-zoid. And there's, um, some other stuff, too."

"Other stuff." Artur sounded wary.

"Kidnappings, magic, long-lost love of my life. Nothing to rock the boat. All in a day's work."

"Of course," he said dryly. "Which is why you're calling me in the middle of the night while I'm on my honeymoon."

"Man, you've been married three months. The honeymoon is over."

"Not until we leave Russia," Artur said. "And never even after that."

Which was like hearing the Incredible Hulk start talking like Gandhi.

"So," Dean said. "About the Consortium. I need you to clarify something for me."

"The Consortium?" His voice was suddenly stronger, more awake. "Have you had dealings with them?"

"I don't think so, but I'm not ruling anything out yet. Actually, my question is less about them than the mind control you mentioned having to fight. You called it the black worm, and you said it … possessed people."

"Possession is an accurate label," Artur said carefully. "As are others. But that question makes me very uneasy, Dean. What have you encountered?"

"The murderer's son found us tonight. He said that his father had been taken over by a nameless spirit that can physically transform its host depending on the length of contact. He specifically mentioned eyes and teeth."

"You said the murderer is a shape-shifter, yes? It is my understanding, at least based on my experience in the lab, that the worm cannot infect shape-shifters. Or rather, Beatrix Weave was unable to take command of

Amiri and Rik's minds, and so we just assumed that was the case."

"What if you were wrong? What if there's a loophole?"

Artur made a clicking sound with his tongue. "This is very serious, Dean. Has your murderer tried to infect others?"

"Not to my knowledge, but I'm not really on close personal terms with him, either."

Again, Dean heard Elena speaking quietly. Artur sighed.

"Instructions?" Dean asked, only half teasing.

"Elena wants us to go to Taipei," Artur said. "She thinks we can help."

"No," Dean said. "I know how much this trip to Russia means to you, and once you leave the country, Roland will probably find some excuse to get you back on another case. After which your fine-tuned sense of duty will kick in and you'll never escape again."

"And you think I value my leisure time over the lives of my friends? No, Dean. You are very wrong."

"Artur—"

"I will hear no more of it. Who else is there with you?"

"Koni is in town, but the only other agent currently in the region is Ren, and he's stationed in Hong Kong."

"We need him there," Artur said. "Fine. Elena and I will come as soon as we can."

And that was the end of it. Dean returned to the bedroom and kicked off his shoes. Miri was asleep and snoring, her tiny hands clutching the blanket in a white-knuckled grip. Dean crawled in beside her. She did not wake up, which was fine. He watched her for as long as he could, until sleep crept close and he closed his eyes and fell into another place that was far, far away.

He dreamed of a circle made of sand, and within,

bones. Familiar bones, surrounding a familiar altar made of stone. There was no woman hanging there, just a bloody spot on the rock, and Dean felt his heart beat like a vile vicious creature that had no business being alive, no business—*when she is dead and you killed her, you animal, you beast, you betrayer*—

A sound intruded. He woke up to a terrible ringing sound. Miri was sitting up in the bed beside him, hollow-eyed and with her hands clapped over her ears.

"Is that an alarm?" she asked, wincing. Dean grunted, rolling from the bed just as Koni burst into the room, breathless.

"Don't know how many there are," the shape-shifter said. "Could just be one."

"Anyone we know who might have forgotten their codes?"

"No."

"Shit," Dean snarled. "Someone's tracking us."

"Or maybe you guys aren't as secret as you think," Miri said.

Dean ran to the closet, and Miri watched as he inexplicably began reaching deep past the clothes. Koni handed Miri her purse and went back to shut the bedroom door and lock it.

Dean's head disappeared behind dress shirts. Miri wanted to ask him what the hell he was doing, but she heard a click, the whir of gears, and he stepped into the closet, past the clothes, and disappeared.

"Oh my God," Miri said. "You guys are crazy."

"I know," Koni agreed. "These are definitely people with too much time and money on their hands." But then he smiled like he thought it was fun, and for a moment, Miri thought she might just like him.

From the other side of the closet, Miri heard Dean call her name. She pushed back the clothes, took a step forward, then walked through with her arms extended, because even though Dean was gone she still expected a wall, an end to the illusion, a call to wake up.

All she found on the other side was another room, very tiny, about twice the size of the closet itself. There was one light in the ceiling, and it illuminated a metal wall covered in weapons: guns, knives, and a few that looked unfamiliar.

On the opposite wall, which was also metal, Miri saw drawers. Several had been pulled out, and Dean sat on the floor with them, muttering. She saw cash, credit cards, passports.

Miri felt a hand on her back. She moved aside to let Koni in, then pressed against the wall as he maneuvered the door back in place. Miri saw wood on one side, the same color as the closet—which she could still see, clothes and all—but as the door slid shut she saw the inside was metal, with a wheel for a knob. Just like in a bank vault. Once the door closed, the outside alarm noise cut off. Soundproof.

"Oh my God," she said again, and looked at Koni. "This is weirder than you."

"Good to hear it." His eyes still glowed. Miri imagined the shadow of something soft against his neck. Like ... down.

"Here." Dean passed an American passport and two credit cards to Koni. Miri did not catch the name on them, but she crouched beside Dean and flipped through the other passports in front of him. She saw names like Max Reese, Artur Loginov, Agatha Durand—and more, more than she could count, and credit cards with the same. Cash, too. Miri thought there must be thousands of dollars in front of her.

"Dean," she said. "What the hell is this?"

"This here is lawbreaking at its best and most efficient. Papers, cash—a safe house isn't much good without all the trimmings."

"But those passports must be fakes, Dean."

"The best fakes money can buy. They fool customs every time."

Miri sat back on her heels, staring. "This is not just a detective agency. This is an *operation*. The kind of operation I don't think most governments have."

"Miri. Don't be naive. All governments have operations like this."

"Okay, fine, maybe. But a detective agency? If you believe that's normal, then you have your head so far up your ass you're never going to see daylight again. My God. Who needs this, Dean? What's so dangerous about your lives that you need something like this?"

Even as she said it, Miri felt stupid. What in Dean's life *hadn't* been that dangerous so far? And yet, she could not help but feel the vault went right over the edge of everything reasonable.

"It's coming in pretty handy now," Koni said.

"And before tonight? How regularly do you use places like this?"

Dean shrugged. "The whole point is preparation."

"For what? *War?* Because that is what I see, Dean. A group of people prepared for an actual war. I sure as hell didn't notice any windows out there, either. Is this a fallout shelter, too?"

Dean said nothing. It was not, she thought, that he wanted to lie to her. Only that he did not have an answer to give. It made her wonder just how much he knew about the people he worked for. Or, if the people running the show were all psychic, just how much they knew about the future.

Breathe, she told herself. *Just breathe your little heart out. You have bigger things to worry about.*

MAR...
w.
...ful and
...enty
...
cient control. Their ex...
increasingly complex—b...
years was a long time.
A furrow appeare...
the same, as well...
though he was...
ent, though...
of his thro...
change. ...
did no...
Sh...
to...

...ense. I'm not o...

...," Koni said, and his eyes glowed, light ...n his cheeks. "It's there and you saw. Did ...e trail?"

...t know what state the other body will be ...e he carried is somewhere around Hong

...g?" Miri echoed.

...prising?"

...t. It's just that not much is known abou... ...s prehistory, only that people have live... ...host five thousand years. There should ha... ...ng settlement by the time your man arrive... ...e anywhere on the islands. Or rather, t... ...e anywhere. I doubt the body is still intact... ...me in that area and I'll find out for su... ...another. The pull is still strong, Miri. Go...

...t, then." Koni stood. A steel knife glinte... ...d his mouth curved into a smile. "We h...

...as a collection of cell phones in one

198

She breathed. Sucked it in deep and said, "I'm sorry. Now is not the time."

"No," Dean said. "No, you're right."

But he said nothing more as he stood and repacked everything into its proper drawers. He gave Miri more cash, as well as his passport and credit cards, to carry in her purse. Koni faced the opposite wall, pulling down knives and examining them. Dean joined him.

"Miri," he said. "You still play with sharp objects?"

"I pick my teeth with them," she deadpanned. Dean grinned and passed her a six-inch Bowie encased in a hard plastic sheath. She wondered where, exactly, she was supposed to carry the thing, and tucked it in her purse.

"You're making like we're going to get out of here," Miri said. "I don't see how. There's only one door."

"There's another," Dean said, pulling down a gun and its ankle rig. "Behind you. It blends into the wall."

Miri looked, and sure enough, saw lines set in metal. Very high-tech. She did not like it. Dean put down his weapons and gestured for the artifact in Miri's purse. "I'm going to try again."

"It laid you flat the first time."

"No choice. I'll try to be more careful."

"What did you see?" Koni asked. "What hurt you?"

Dean did not answer him. Miri held the red jade in her hands, tracing the words, the lines in the stone as Dean sat back down on the floor. She kept expecting someone to bang through the wall, but the men did not appear concerned. She wondered if it was just good acting. She handed Dean the jade. He hesitated a moment, took a deep breath, and closed his eyes. Miri watched his face. He had tried to take a reading of Owen's statue in the car, but the light there was poor, and she was curious to see if anything had changed over the years, if he had learned new skills, more effi-

vault drawers. Three-band, able to make international calls. Dean tossed one to Koni.

"Call Roland. Tell him we need a private jet. Commercial is out of the question. We need to be ready to leave within the hour."

"Tall order," Miri said.

"If anyone can pull it off, it's Roland."

Miri had nothing to say to that. It still seemed like an awful lot of power to wield, but Dean appeared completely oblivious as he continued sorting through drawers, trying to find yet another little treasure to travel with when they left this place. Miri did not mind watching him; it gave her a chance to see the boyishness of his face in pure action.

She got an odd feeling in her gut, though, and turned to look at the door separating them from the rest of the safe house. Watched and watched, so that when it began to swing open, she was the only one who noticed.

She cried out; the men turned, swearing. And then they all fell silent when they saw who was on the other side.

A head poked through the clothing. A wide, long head, flared with sleek white feathers and hair twisting like vines; wide nostrils set in a snout with whiskers made of flesh curling from a thick bottom lip. And the eyes—those golden staring eyes—

A dragon, she thought. Just like in the pictures, the old Chinese renderings.

Bai Shen.

"Yes," whispered the creature, in a voice as low and strong as the roar of a river. "And if you do not come with me now, Dr. Lee, I very much regret that will have to kill your friends."

Miri spun around to look at Dean, staring into his horrified eyes. He reached for a gun—Koni had his knife—but as the two of them readied their weapons she saw a glow surround them, a heat wave that rippled the air above the men's heads. Sparks few from their hair. They stopped moving, standing still enough to be frozen, statues.

"Stop," Miri said, backing toward the door, still with her gaze locked on Dean. "Stop, please. I'll go with you."

Dean said nothing. His throat worked, his eyes rolling in his head, but not a sound came out. He was paralyzed. Not that she needed to hear him to know he was screaming.

"But he is not screaming so loud that he cannot hear me," Bai Shen whispered. "So to you, Mr. Campbell, I thank you. I am taking your advice. I am going to help my father."

A hand fastened itself around the back of her neck. She smelled ash, blood. Claws dug into her throat. And then she was pulled backward, away from Dean and his screaming eyes, and the door slammed shut behind her.

Chapter Eleven

Miri blacked out, which was something she had thought would never happen to her. Fainting just wasn't her style. But it was her first sight of the teeth that did it, large and sharp, a set to make a great white shark jealous, and she closed her eyes and fell away into a different place, a room of sand and bone, a platform made of stone upon which she lay. She felt cold and hungry, her heart crying out for another.

And then she opened her eyes, and the wind was so strong it stole her breath, and she heard a great throbbing beat that entered her chest like some old drum. She squirmed, and whatever was holding her tightened like a vise, and she opened her eyes wider and realized she was staring at a chest. A very broad chest that was extraordinarily soft, with a slightly raised pattern that reminded her of scales.

A snake. A dragon.

And then she squirmed some more and glimpsed lights floating below. Many lights. An entire city. Just as though she was flying above it.

Just as though she … was … flying.

Miri screamed.

"Quiet," said Bai Shen, but Miri was too terrified to listen. She felt herself gathered up even tighter, and then suddenly it was the worst roller-coaster ride of her life as the creature holding her careened downward—almost straight down—toward the city. Like a bomb, a bullet, and Miri squeezed her eyes shut as her heart and stomach and lungs crawled up into her throat, and just when she thought it was time to die, that her poor frail little body could handle no more, the descent leveled out, slowed, like the drop of a feather. Arms released her. Miri cried out again; her legs had no strength. She collapsed on a hard stone surface, tears seeping from her eyes, and clung to the ground like a baby.

"Here we are," Bai Shen murmured.

Miri thought he was talking to her—had words in her throat to use, to scream—when suddenly she heard another voice, deep and soft, and the cold hard pit of her stomach twisted even more.

"So weak," said that strange voice. "I cannot imagine what they see in you. I cannot imagine how you draw such interest, except in your relation to the Book."

Miri rolled over. It was a mistake.

The first thing she saw was the tail. It was impossible not to see it first; it was huge, thick, muscular; a searing white that reflected the ambient city light with pearly luminescence. Feathers fluttered along the beast's curving spine, rising up and up to a muscular torso cut with ridges, arms that were far too long and that ended in claws, and that head—that remarkable face towering over her.

"Yes," said the dragon. "Thank you."

He can read minds, she realized. And if he could, then perhaps Bai Shen could hear thoughts as well, which explained how he had broken into the safe house and the vault. Though given the alarms that had gone off, he obviously was not all that smooth.

Miri looked over her shoulder at Bai Shen, who was less dragon now and more man. He stood several feet away, and the expression on his face was uncertain. Afraid, too. She could almost taste it, and knew what a mistake that was for the young man. No fear: That was the only way to survive such things, even when fighting against a parent. Show no fear.

"Good," whispered the dragon. "My son, I hope you are listening to her mind. She gives valuable lessons."

"I'm not here for lessons," he snapped. "I brought this woman in the hopes that you would listen to me this time. You, the thing inside my father, you want the Book. Take it! She has the jade, she has herself, which is one half already! Take it and let my father go. Find another host. Please."

There was black light in the elder dragon's eyes, and Miri looked at it for what it was supposed to be. A parasite, a worm. Some force that stole away free will, that killed and killed for power. In other words: evil.

"Foolish," whispered the dragon to his son. "There is no offering on this earth, save one, that would convince me to leave this extraordinary body."

Bai Shen shook his head. "Take me instead. Let my father go and take me."

The creature undulated across the smooth stone surface toward Bai Shen. Miri tried to sit up, but her body still refused her. She heard a rattling sound; after a moment she realized it was coming from the dragon's throat. A purr, maybe. Laughter.

"What a stupid boy. How so very stupid. I would have expected better from the son of Lysander Drakul."

"And I would have expected my father to be stronger than some formless, faceless, opportunistic creature,"

Bai Shen said grimly. "What a shame that Lysander *Drakul* was too weak to take care of his own soul, that he was so pathetic that he would *invite you in.*"

Miri wanted to tell Bai Shen to rein in the anger. It was painfully obvious how much the thing inside Lysander enjoyed it. Unless, of course, Lysander was more a part of his own actions than anyone realized. Which would make him very bad indeed.

"Yes, very," he whispered, swiveling that massive head until he could look at her. Miri matched that golden stare, taking in the threads of black that seemed to send memory shivering down her spine. She fought those thoughts, though—buried them down, and began reciting multiplication tables in her head, dry facts. Lysander bared his teeth.

"Your job here is done, Bai Shen. You may leave."

Bai Shen did not move. He gazed down at Miri, and she could still see the fear, but this time it was mixed with guilt and deep raging sorrow that she could only guess had less to do with her, and everything to do with setting one's heart on a plan that had proven itself to be The Dumbest Move Alive. Especially for a man who had taken quite a long time espousing the need to protect the very object he was so easily handing over.

Or maybe he doesn't truly believe in the power of the jade. Maybe that was just a ploy to ask us about helping his father. He wanted to feel us out.

Lysander's body swelled in height. "I said to go. Now."

"I don't believe you would hurt me," Bai Shen said. "I don't think my father would let you."

"Really?" said the elder dragon, and right then, Miri knew it was over. All she had was instinct, but that was something she had been raised to trust, and she knew. Bai Shen was not going to walk out of this the same young man. If he walked out at all.

Maybe he heard her thoughts; the younger shape-shifter glanced in her direction, and Miri shook her head, mouthing the word *Run*.

But the time for that was gone. Lysander moved—a blur, a silver streak—his clawed fist ramming outward toward Bai Shen's face with enough force to put a hole in his skull. But at the last moment Miri caught the shift sideways—so fast, so fast—and Bai Shen screamed. She heard a tearing sound, and then the young man's white skin was suddenly red, and he bent down low over his stomach, clutching the side of his face, gagging.

Lysander turned to look at Miri. He held an ear and part of a scalp. Long white hair, some of which was stained pink and red, trailed down his scaled wrist. Miri breathed through her mouth—slow and steady, slow and steady. Her heart felt like it was exploding inside her chest.

And yet, for one fleeting moment she thought she saw something in Lysander's black-flecked eyes that was so pained, so sorrowful, she forgot her fear, and found herself leaning forward with words on her lips, a simple *I see you in there.*

But the moment died so quickly, so completely, she wondered at her imagination. Lysander smiled—a horrible, sharp-toothed smile—and placed the ear inside his mouth. He bit down once, pulled away the scalp with its hair, and dropped it on the ground like so much gristle. He started chewing; the sound was loud and wet. A low hoarse sob tore itself from Bai Shen's throat; his golden eyes were huge, terrified, filled with the kind of heartbreak that made Miri forget everything she thought she knew about anger and betrayal, and she thought, *I'm sorry. I'm so sorry you had to learn the lesson this way.* She couldn't even bring herself to be mad at him for dragging her here.

Or for leaving her. Which he did, without a single backward glance. One jump, a spread of wings that burst from his body like rays of leather and light. *That,* at least, irritated her.

"As well you should be irritated," Lysander said, staring up at the night sky where his son had disappeared. "He has terrible manners."

"I'm sure I can forgive him, given that his *ear was torn off* and *eaten* by his father."

A crooked smile touched Lysander's mouth. "Life is never fair."

The dragon neared, body coiling and heaving and pushing across the ground like a snake. Again, laughter, a perfume made of ash and blood.

"You think you can run," said the shape-shifter, and his voice was gentle, low as the deepest roll of thunder, wild like the distant roar of a powerful river.

"I think I can try," Miri said, knowing full well her legs were still too shaky to hold her weight. "I also think you want me alive."

"Alive for a time," said the dragon. "But there is also a time for death. *Especially* death."

Miri forced herself to remain very still. *Never run from immortals,* she remembered; her favorite line from a favorite movie. *Never run.*

"What sensible advice, though I can assure you that the body I possess is no immortal."

"But you are," Miri said, taking a wild guess. "You."

Again, Lysander smiled. "Yes, me. Me and no other. Now, you have the jade. Give it to me."

Miri still had her purse slung around her chest. Hands shaking, she reached inside for the artifact. It was not there.

She knew Lysander felt her alarm, but he did not act until Miri was truly panicked. He tore the purse from her body, upending its contents on the ground. Her passport fell out, along with cash and pens and paper—and a little stone heart that clattered to the hard surface.

But the jade was not there. Lysander stared at her through narrowed eyes, and she knew he was rummaging through her brain. She fought it; again, with math, with triva, with bits and pieces of the flotsam always on the surface of her thoughts. It was not enough.

"You lost consciousness," said the dragon slowly. "Plenty of time to have lost other things, as well. I suppose my son was not so naïve as I thought."

The dragon leaned close; her chest throbbed for one brief moment as golden light seeped from the creature, gold mixed with a shadow that curled like claws, darker than the night air. Miri instinctively shied away from that black light.

"Be still," whispered the dragon.

Miri did not feel like being still. She reached out on her hands and knees and grabbed her passport, the little heart-shaped rock. She shoved them both in her pockets and then tried again to stand. She managed it, and found herself—with some shock—on the edge of a parapet high above an expanse of very familiar park. Miri looked down and saw wide and carved stone steps trailing away into a large walkway. The stone all around her was pale, almost as white as the dragon.

Chiang Kai-shek Memorial Hall. She was sitting right on top of it.

The park below was nearly empty. It was not yet dawn; merely, the quiet time between too late and too early. Miri wondered if anyone had seen Bai Shen and his father land; she could not imagine something so large and white would be easy to miss. In fact, she could not imagine most of the night's events going unnoticed. The university fire would certainly make the news, as would the loss of the mummies and several key members of the archaeology department.

"You are right that the news will talk of such things," remarked the dragon, and Miri found herself pinned to the wall by one large hand. Claws punched through her jacket, grazing her skin. "But there will be no mention of magic, or of otherworldly things. Humans see what they wish, and this is no longer an age of wonder. Miracles pass and no one sees. Great wonders speak and no one listens. Minds and hearts grow small. They shrivel. They become consumed with matters more human than magic, which is dying, which hides. But that could change. And it will. And when it does, *oh*. What a wondrous thing."

His voice was hypnotic; his eyes lulled. As he spoke, Miri forgot claws, forgot fear, and the darkness, the shadow, did seem sweet. She felt herself drift, and for a moment she thought she would fade away into another place, but then her heart began to burn, the space between her breasts, and she reached out, unthinking, and touched the jade still in the dragon's hand.

A spark raced up her arm, a lightning bolt, and the dragon jerked away, whiskers flaring wild, like a cat. Miri crouched, rubbing her hand. Her body tingled. Her mind felt clear, sharp—sharp enough to cut.

"No," said the dragon. "What did you do?"

"Nothing," she stammered. "You know it's the truth."

"I know it is the truth as you understand it," he said. "But that is *not* always the same thing." The dragon swayed, rocking back and forth on its tail. "They want you so badly," he whispered. "What does my mate and her servants want from you? So many wily ways, they have. So many. You must be a part of it."

Miri fought the dragon's interrogation, determined not to give him anything. But how could she not answer a question already in her mind? She could refuse to speak, but there was no way to stop knowing an answer. Good thing she had no truth to reveal. She had no clue what he was talking about.

And then, before she could stop him, the dragon

lashed out with his claws and ripped open Miri's shirt. She grabbed at the cloth, but the dragon held her hands over her head, peering down at her breasts. Closer and closer; Miri squirmed, furious and horrified.

"Nothing," he breathed, and pushed his nose against her skin to sniff.

Miri closed her eyes. "What are you doing?"

"I am searching for the touch of another," replied the dragon, "but there is none. You are ... human."

"You sound disappointed."

"I thought I might find a pleasant surprise on your skin. It is the only reason I can think that your life would be so important. My mate is not one to waste resources."

"Your mate? Is that ... is that who has been ordering those men to come after me?"

"She represents only one-half of the puzzle, but the larger half. She understands the mystery, you see. The Book and the power and all those wonderful consequences. Though she does not understand me."

"That's because you're a killer," Miri said, bits and pieces falling together inside her head. "You killed the people who work for her, you burned them alive."

"And I ate them." The dragon smiled, teeth spreading like knives across his face. "Never fear, Mirabelle Lee. My mate is keen. She can find more servants. But you ... you are another matter. I think, perhaps, you are too much. I think that I will have to discard you. It is safer that way. If she wants you, then she cannot have you. I will find the jade some other way. Perhaps ... in Hong Kong? Your friends will go there and I will be waiting."

"Why?" Miri breathed. "Why is this so important to you? To everyone who is involved?"

"Dreams and wishes, Dr. Lee. We all have dreams and wishes of the world as it should be. Would you not remake your existence if you could? Change your parents, change that night when you lost your life? Make it so your love never left and you lived happy and happy and happy together? You would deny yourself that?"

"Yes," Miri breathed. "Oh yes, I would."

Doubt moved through Lysander's eyes—another shadow, fleeting, and for a moment she felt that second presence, a second soul wrapped up tight inside the dragon. The sensation was familiar to her in ways she could not explain—almost déjà vu, but not quite. As if she remembered looking out through eyes that were not her own, eyes that had been stolen from her.

The sensation faded; Lysander said, "Tell me why."

Tell me why, she heard inside her head. *Tell me why I am possessed, tell me why I am a possessor, tell me why and why and why. Why this world, why me, why now, why this life that I invited darkness into. Why did I make that decision?*

She shut her eyes, blocking out that voice that was hers or someone else's, a voice she could not bear to listen to, and said, "Because every life is given only one chance. You cannot—you *should* not—go back and change your mistakes. The point is to learn from them. The point is to make the very best life you can with what you've got, and love the person that makes. But if you give yourself an out, if you turn back time, all that you were and are becomes meaningless, and we are *not* broken records. We are *not* puppets to be used and re-made and then discarded. Every life means something, you son of a bitch, and if you don't like the world the way it is, find another way to change it that doesn't involve imposing yourself on the rest of us."

Lysander said nothing. He stared at her for a long time, and then slowly, carefully, raised his hand, palm out. Heat washed over Miri, a great warmth, and she had a very bad feeling about what was going to happen next.

But then the dragon twitched, whirling, and as it

moved Miri heard a voice say her name and she flattened herself against the ground. A gun went off. The dragon rolled sideways, tail lashing.

As he moved, Miri saw a lean, lithe figure, a familiar silhouette against the city skyline, and she thought, *Miracles pass and I see. Great wonders speak and I listen.*

She looked at Dean, and believed in magic.

Something happened to Dean when he watched the shape-shifter drag Miri away; he crossed another line inside his heart. He did not know what it meant, only that he felt something shift inside him, beneath his skin, like things were being rearranged, and if he had not been so certain that he was human, he might have imagined that he was becoming a shape-shifter himself, because he felt transformed.

Inside his head, inside his burning heart, all throughout and all within, and in his eyes the world fell down, curled loose and wild into energy and threads, and he reached out—stretched—and began to gather them in. He did not think or plan; all he thought of was Miri.

Koni ran to the closet door and opened it. All the clothes had been torn away; the room beyond was empty. The shape-shifter ran through, disappeared for a moment, and Dean heard a shout. A moment later Koni reappeared. He held the red jade in his hand. He started talking; Dean said nothing. Koni stepped close and began shaking him, which was useless because Dean's body was not working correctly. Or maybe it was working too well. He barely heard Koni, whose voice was nothing but an echo—unlike his body: a bright vein of gold.

Dean drew some of that light inside him, milking away stolen fibers, weaving it deeper inside his heart as he molded and wove and fumbled. All he had was instinct, but as he worked he felt as though he remembered, that this was time repeating itself, and that once

211

before he had done such things—more, even—and a great thrill battled his fear for Miri, a tremendous rush that came from remembering. Just fragments, bits and pieces cutting holes in his heart, draining and refilling him with times from another life.

And then, quite suddenly, he had something inside him, an object built, glistening and glowing, and he called it a bridge, and placed his soul upon it. He moved …

… and found himself within a dark place, suspended in the center of a roiling cloud, green with lightning.

"Hello," said a voice. "Welcome to my home."

Dean turned. A man stood before him, also floating in the air. He had dark skin and green eyes, as well a quiet face, which contained … nothing. No emotion. No expression at all. Dean found him very familiar—remembered him suddenly from the alley—and reached for his gun.

"Don't bother," said the man, his voice deep and rumbling. He held up the weapon. "I find it fascinating that a man who becomes evolved enough to rip the fabric of space with nothing but his mind should find himself relying on a gun in times of need." The man tossed the weapon back to Dean. "It's a tiny little thing. Frankly, I'm surprised. Given your reputation, I expected you to have rocket launchers tied to your arms. A bazooka strapped to your dick."

"Too much recoil," Dean said. "I love my nuts."

The man's expression never even twitched. "You committed this act, this … movement across space … because of Miri. You did this because being with her is waking you up."

"I was never asleep."

The stranger smiled; a chilling look. "We are *all* asleep, Mr. Campbell. It is what we dream that matters."

"Then tell me how to dream of Miri," Dean replied, desperate. "Tell me how to find her."

"You're already halfway there. The moment you leave this place you'll find her. You're crossing the bridge you built between your souls. All I did was make you stop. There's something you need to know—more at stake here than you realize."

"All I care about is Miri."

"And Mirabelle is the key," said the man. "As are you. Not the jade, though that is part of it, but you and her. You are the results. You are both the meaning and the mystery."

"Cut the crap," Dean said. "Who the hell are you?"

"A friend of a friend. My name is Rictor. Artur and Elena know me."

"I remember now. Artur said you can't be trusted."

"And Elena?"

"I don't talk to her as much."

"Smart woman." He tilted his head. "There are many players in this game, but the only one you need to be afraid of is the dragon. Not the son, but the father. He has Mirabelle even now."

"Then why the hell are we standing here?"

"Because I won't get another chance to speak to you, and I need you to understand certain things. This is important, Mr. Campbell. This is the most important thing you'll ever do with your life."

"What?" Dean asked, fed up.

"You have to kill her," Rictor said softly, floating close. "When the time comes, you have to kill Mirabelle. Because if you don't, the world is going to be a very terrible place."

And then Rictor touched Dean, and everything disappeared.

* * *

The world shifted, and when next he opened his eyes Dean felt like he was on top of the city, and there in front of him was a dragon. And near the dragon—

You have to kill her. When the time comes, you have to kill Mirabelle.

Dean shook off Rictor's voice. He could not contemplate such a possibility. Unthinkable, horrible. That son of a bitch was going to get his ass kicked the next time Dean saw him.

But first, the dragon. The serial killer. Dean saw the creature raise its hand toward Miri's face, watched her stare with the knowing in her eyes, and he fired his gun.

It was a perfect shot. Dean saw the bullet impact the shape-shifter's neck, but instead of dropping dead, the dragon moved with about as much injury as a bee sting.

Dean cursed, and fired again and again. Blood sprayed across white stone, white flesh, and finally a roar filled the air, undulating, rumbling like thunder rich and deep, until Dean's heart shook with that sound, pounding against his ribs in a sharp tattoo. His chest felt hot— burning—as if for a moment energy was collecting, but then it all faded away as the dragon's eyes glowed. The beast raised his hand again to Miri.

Dean ran, shouting for her to move, and she did, scrambling away from the dragon, racing toward him. Her shirt was torn, her eyes wild, and just as she neared, Dean saw sparks touch her hair, the fine edge of a flame. Dean grabbed her wrists, hauling her around the central pillar in the center of the stone roof. There was a door, locked. Dean shot at it, kicked, pushed, but it would not budge. It was made of a thick wood and even thicker metal. Made to last.

But someone had been up here the previous day, and there was a trail Dean could follow, a lovely golden thread winding down and down the stairs beyond that door, to the lawn below.

"Dean!" Miri gasped, and he acted without thinking, without any kind of plan. He grabbed her around the waist, her skin burning to the touch, a blistering heat. He felt the energies gather around him, the golden threads winding and winding through his burning chest, and he found another bridge and placed Miri upon it.

She disappeared, and for one moment Dean thought he must be the stupidest son of a bitch on the planet— *and oh, shit, what did I just do?*—but then he heard her scream—only, at the bottom of the Memorial Hall, and Dean ran to the edge and looked down. She stood in the grass with working legs and working arms, and she shouted his name.

Dean felt something behind him and turned. He barely managed to keep his mouth shut because the man was there—the dragon—and he was a giant, a monster, more animal than human.

He had no legs, just one long tail he balanced upon, a tail keen and shiny, rippling long with muscle and gleaming white as perfect snow, marred only by the blood pouring down his iridescent chest. Whiskers made of flesh curled from his bottom lip, thick and twisting like vines, while sleek feathers pushed out of his white hair. The fringes looked sharp.

But Miri was safe. It was just Dean now. And he could handle this. He was ready.

Ready like hell, you fucking liar. Your pickle just trickled.

Which no one ever needed to know but Dean.

"And me," whispered the dragon. Light streamed from the corners of his eyes, smoke curling out of his wide white nostrils. He snorted once, like a bull, and a roar filled the air, a rush of hot air that made Dean choke and hold his throat, fall to the ground and slam his other hand into the ground to steady himself. He tried to reach for his gun, but the dragon caught his hand and held him tight. Easy, effortless. A toying motion. Dean felt like a chicken waiting to have its wings torn off. Good eating, maybe. Finger-lickin' good. Oh God.

"I am never the hunted," whispered the shape-shifter; and up close, Dean saw bits of meat between the sharp teeth, the purple of the dragon's long split tongue. For just a moment, Dean's vision split—but this time not along vibration, but something else, something inexplicably like memory: bones, darkness, a rough voice whispering in shadow; and a light—a light as pure as snow and star and moon …

The shape-shifter stilled. His nostrils flared. He gave Dean a scrutinizing look, as though he was trying to remember something. Dean was too proud to glance away. He wondered if Miri would miss him, how she would feel about losing him so soon, whether his friends would be next in line, all of them, his family, dying while trying to take this shit-head down. The possibility, so clear in his head, choked him.

"Your whole life is a lie," murmured the shape-shifter, and there was something in his eyes that could have been surprise, wonder—only tainted, twisted into a darkness rich and strange.

"What the hell do you know about my life?" Dean asked, finally finding his voice. He tried to move his arms, but it was like drowning in concrete: sinking, sinking, gone.

The shape-shifter never answered. Instead, he let go of Dean's wrist and reached out quick, raking claws through his shirt, popping buttons and tearing cloth as he bared Dean's slick chest to the hot humid air.

For the briefest instant, Dean sensed disappointment roll off the shape-shifter—just a flash, in his eyes—and then the dragon's jutting jaw tightened and he touched Dean with one long silver claw. Scraped his chest, the glowing scar over his heart. Fingered the golden charm, the little locket, resting so warm on Dean's chest.

The dragon made a sound, low in his throat. Smoke puffed from his nostrils: bittersweet, rich, like smoked meat. His eyes glowed, gold shrouded by a floating darkness that was pitiless and cold.

And then Dean began to burn.

Chapter Twelve

He blacked out when the fire exploded around his feet—fell into sweet darkness, removed and floating, lost in a dream that swept him up like the fire. The world diminished; in his heart, in his head, his life narrowing to a series of memories, flashing, and he recalled a face, young and breathless and pale.

Miri, Dean thought. *Oh God. Miri.*

And suddenly he was awake again and the fire surrounding him did not burn, did not choke—like the nightmare that had started his ordeal, only this time, Dean was not afraid. He stared into the flames and thought they looked like threads, something to be followed and played with and examined, and beyond those threads, he saw a body, a body of light wrapped up in something wiggling and dark.

A worm. Dean reached out with his mind and touched it. Or at least, he tried. The moment he made that first effort, the fire boomed, puffed, went out. He felt a great lurching sensation in his body, and the sudden darkness against his eyes was as blinding as the light—another curtain, another weakness—and Dean hit the ground hard on his knees, biting his tongue so hard he tasted blood.

Hands touched him. Dean flinched, twisting sideways, hands scrabbling for a weapon he could not find. A familiar voice cut the air, and he stopped moving, panting weakly.

"Miri," he gasped, and then she was beside him, rolling him into her lap. He felt grass beneath his back and looked up and up at the smooth white walls of the Memorial Hall towering above his head, framed by a dark cloudy sky. And next to that, Miri. Her hair hung loose past her face, shrouding her features in darkness. There was no sign of the dragon, which made Dean feel very uneasy.

"You all right?" he asked.

"Yes," she breathed. "You?"

"I'm not hurting," he said. "Do I still have hair?"

Miri made a choking sound. "Yeah, you have hair. You're naked, though. What happened up there, Dean? I was too far down to see anything, but I thought there was a glow."

"Fire," he told her. "That asshole set me on fire."

Her breath caught. "How did you survive?"

"Hell if I know. I'm bullet man, remember?"

She didn't laugh. Instead, he heard that choking noise again, except deeper, throatier, and he realized it was a sob.

"Hey," he whispered. "Hey, now. I'm fine. You're fine. We're all fine, okay? No crying, *bao bei.*"

"Sorry," she breathed. "Sorry. I thought you were gone. Dead."

Dean reached up and touched her face, drawing her down for a long, slow kiss that loosened parts of his body he didn't even know were uptight. Miri smiled against his mouth.

"We need to get you out of here," she murmured. "It's going to be light soon and you don't have any clothes. I'm also afraid that someone might have called the police. I couldn't see the fire, but I was too close. Anyone else in the park would have had a real light show, and I don't think we want to answer any questions about that."

Dean propped himself up on his elbows and gazed down at his body. He really was naked. The only thing he still wore was Miri's locket, and thank God for that.

"How did I get down here?" he wondered out loud.

"Probably the same way you sent me down, or the way you appeared at the top of the hall." There was a note of wonder in her voice.

"I don't know how I did that," Dean protested. He shifted his sight, testing the waters. Nothing seemed out of the ordinary; all the power he had felt only minutes before was gone.

Miri staggered to her feet. "I want you to stay here. We're fairly well hidden among these bushes and trees. At least until more people show up in the park. I'm going to find you some clothes."

"You can't go out there. It's not safe. He might come back."

"His name is Lysander, Dean. Lysander Drakul. Bai Shen brought me here to make a deal, but it backfired. Lysander … punished him, and he was about to kill me for being either too important, or too useless, to live."

"Nice options. Did you learn anything else?"

Miri hesitated. "I think the real Lysander might be trying to fight back. I think he's also the reason that *thing* is in there in the first place. Lysander let it in, and now he can't get loose."

"But you said he's struggling."

"Maybe. I don't know. But he knows about Hong

Kong. He picked it up from my mind. He said he would be waiting."

"Good thing we don't know where the second piece of the jade is, then. He'll be in the same boat as us."

"But just a lot more dangerous. I assume you have the other jade?"

"Bai Shen left it."

Miri shook her head. "That young man is screwed up."

"He's more than screwed up. When I catch up with him again, he's dead. Really, truly, dead."

"He made a mistake."

"Fuck that. He almost killed you. Hell, he was okay with you dying, or else he wouldn't have handed you over like he did. That's a lethal offense in my book."

"We'll talk about it later," Miri said. "I still need to get you some clothes."

"You don't even have money."

"I'll figure something out."

"Miri—"

"What? You think walking around naked isn't going to draw some unwanted attention? It's going to be light soon. Give me a break. I lived for twenty years without you looking over my shoulder, and I did just fine. In fact, I did great. So you just stay here and hang tight. I won't be long."

Dean grabbed her wrist as she turned away. He pulled her back, hard, wrapping his arms around her body like a vise.

"You don't get it, do you?" he whispered. "You got no idea. Being able to take care of yourself is not the issue, Miri. You always could handle things. But not knowing? Not knowing where you are, not knowing if you're in trouble and need help? *That's* what bothers me."

"We can't stay glued together forever," she protested. "We have lives, you know. And despite all this, I hope we both have something to go back to."

"Sure," Dean said. "But I'm not losing you again."

"And if I say no?"

"Say no," he said. "Say anything. I don't care. I have to be with you. I have to live with you. I have to know you're going to be there in the morning and night and whenever I need to see you. Jesus, Miri. If I can't sleep in your bed, I'll be sleeping under your window."

"Which is covered in cacti."

"Love hurts," he said. "It'll just hurt a little more, that's all."

She closed her eyes. "If you were any other man, I would be scared right now. You are such a stalker."

"I don't want you scared," he said softly. "But I do want you safe."

Miri placed her hands on his chest and pushed hard until he let her go. "You can't keep me safe, Dean. You can't control the world. One day, something is going to happen, and it won't matter if you're ready, if you're standing in front of me to take the fall. When the time comes, the time comes. The obituary is already written."

You have to kill her. When the time comes, you have to kill Mirabelle.

Dean closed his eyes. He heard Miri say his name, but he waved her off, and the next time he looked, she was gone.

It did not take Miri long at all to acquire what she needed. No money and no cell phone meant either stealing, or the kindness of strangers, and because there were no open shops within the general vicinity, her options became quite limited, indeed.

But she lucked out; a group of elderly men and women had just gathered on the lawn several hundred yards away, ready for their morning exercises of dance and swordplay—and Miri, blouse torn, hair disheveled, made the perfect victim of a violent crime, which not only she, but her American friend, had fallen prey to, in a most embarrassing fashion.

Five minutes later, Dean had pants, a shirt, and about as many dinner invitations as he could handle. He borrowed a cell phone, too, and called the safe house. Koni picked up on the first ring.

He brought clothes. A cab. And then they left for the airport.

No one gave chase. Or if they did, they were impossible to see. Dean made the cabdriver go down odd streets, take bad turns, while Koni watched traffic through the rear window. Miri sat between them and tried not to feel useless. Tried not to have a nervous breakdown as she thought of Bai Shen and Lysander, or his talk about the jade. She thought of Owen, too, but after a moment's thought, realized that his little Glen Campbell statue had been in Dean's jeans when he was set on fire. It might still be on the rooftop of the Memorial Hall—or melted down into nothing—but either way, it was irretrievable. She had no other connection to the old man.

And you forgot him. Granted, you've had a good excuse, but you're free and he's not, and he's almost seventy years old. He can't handle stress the way he used to. If you don't find him—

She stopped herself from finishing that thought. No, no, no. She *would* find him again. Owen was not lost forever. She just hoped he would forgive her for taking so long to catch up with him.

It took more than forty minutes to drive to the Chiang Kai-shek International Airport, but only because of Dean's shenanigans with the cabdriver. Once they hit the freeway, the cruise was smooth. Miri looked out the window only once and saw that the sky had lightened.

Dean held her close. She could feel the tension in

his body, a hard stress. He let go only once to use the cell phone Koni had brought with him from the safe house. He left a message for an "Artur," and explained they were leaving town, but that—and here, he glanced at Miri—there was someone else who needed help: an old man named Owen Wills.

"No offense," Koni said, after Dean placed the call, "but do you really want to use Artur like that? He could read that jade without a problem—probably find out everything you need to know about it."

"Just not where it is," Dean said. "Although you're right. He's better at the infodump than I am."

"Excuse me?" Miri interrupted. "What are you guys talking about?"

"A colleague and friend," Dean said. "He's a psychometrist. He learns things by touching objects."

"And you think he can find Owen?"

"I know it. Artur reads energy, too, but in a different way. I don't think he'll be blocked like I've been."

Miri nodded. "I care more about finding Owen than the jade."

"I figured," he said, and kissed her cheek.

At the airport, Koni gave special instructions to the driver, speaking in a fluent Mandarin that had both Dean and Miri turning their heads.

"What?" Koni said, when they kept staring. "I'm good with languages. Is that a problem?"

"No," Dean said. "But it's a surprise. How many do you speak?"

"I don't know. A lot. Enough. Maybe twenty."

"Holy shit."

Koni shifted uncomfortably. "It's not a big deal. Even you speak some Chinese."

"My grandmother taught the both of us," Miri said.

"I've forgotten a lot," Dean added. "But *twenty*?"

"You are such a jealous man," Koni said.

The driver followed a curving path that led them to a chain-link fence and a guard station where two young soldiers in full uniform with machine guns looped over their chests stopped the cab and, in polite terms, asked what the hell they were doing there. Koni rolled down the window, and in a Very Important Voice explained that a private airliner expected them. And that they had better be let through. Right fucking now.

The men made a call. Nodded their heads. Within seconds the cab was shown on its way. The driver smiled.

The next half hour was equally easy. A customs official met them at the stairs to a small Lear jet. He asked no questions; simply looked at their passports, scanned them with a handheld device, and then *stamp! stamp! stamp!* Good-bye, Taiwan. Miri managed to keep her mouth shut until they were on the plane, belted down in luxurious leather seats, assisted by a tiny Thai woman who made apologies for the awful state of the interior while handing them sparkling champagne in tall flutes that tinkled merrily when Miri's nails hit the glass.

"Not just a detective agency," she said to Dean. "Do you guys own a small country? No one gets this kind of treatment."

"You do if you know who to talk to and you have a load of money," Dean said. "Which Dirk & Steele does. It's not a perk the agency uses all that often, though. We don't want to draw too much attention."

"Right," Miri said. "Because this has all been a study in subtlety."

Their captain was young and cheerful, with a ruddy face and a good look in his eye, and they were off the ground in no time at all. Up until the moment the wheels left the ground, Dean and Koni and Miri glanced frequently out the windows for any signs of approaching trouble. Miri, in particular, looked for a silver head, a tall man with a gun and a smile.

But nothing happened, and Miri watched the sun rise from twenty-five thousand feet.

And then she laid back her head and fell asleep.

She awakened less than half an hour before they were scheduled to land. Koni was asleep. Dean was not. He looked at her when she moved, and she wiped her eyes, her mouth. Drool. Lovely.

"Did you dream?" Dean asked.

Miri thought it was an interesting question, especially coming from him. His eyes were tired, the skin around them dark.

"I had a dream," she said. "But it was strange. I was in a dark place. It was cold. I felt like I was waiting for something, and you were there, too. We were both waiting."

"And?"

"And then you were taken away. I woke up."

Dean did not say anything. There was not a seat directly beside him, so Miri settled for reaching across the aisle to touch his hand. She wanted to do more. "Did you sleep?"

Dean shook his head and pulled up the edge of the blanket in his lap; Miri looked down and saw the red jade.

"You keeping it warm?" she asked.

"Funny. I've been trying to keep it close to my body. Like it'll help strengthen the connection."

"And has it?"

Dean shrugged. "Maybe. I haven't had any visions, but I do … feel something off the jade. I can't really explain it."

"At least you're not speaking in tongues."

He grimaced. "Again, bad scene. You sure you can't tell me more about what happened?"

"If I could, I would." Miri hesitated, and touched the

jade. One light tap. Nothing happened, and she picked it up and weighed the stone in her hand. Warmth traveled up her arm, resting heavy in her chest. She touched her breastbone with her other hand.

"Miri?" Dean asked quietly.

"I feel a connection with this thing," she told him. "I can't explain it."

"Try."

Miri hesitated. "It's like it's part of me, Dean. Like it should be hanging right where I found it in that mummy. Right here." She tapped herself.

"Yeah?" Dean touched his own chest. "There seems to be a lot of that going around."

"You feel the same when you touch the jade?"

"I don't know. Maybe. I think that anything I feel may have more to do with that cut above my heart."

Miri tugged gently at the collar of his shirt. Dean frowned, but instead of helping her, he leaned just far enough away to pull off his shirt. Miri swallowed hard, trying to remain clinical. She had already seen him naked at Memorial Park, but that was in darkness and under highly stressful circumstances. Intimacy had been the last thing on her mind—only survival.

But here, now …

His chest was smooth and pale, though his skin was marred by scars. And not all of them she recognized. Miri touched a spot on his ribs: one long line that cut down his side.

Dean shivered. "Army exercise that went awry."

"And this?" she asked, touching another healed cut on his stomach.

"Cornered kidnapper in Brazil. I took the guy off guard and he had no gun. So he went for the kitchen knife."

"Who had he kidnapped?"

"The teenage son of some local doctor he was trying

to get money from. We were in the area on another case and found out about the crime from a contact. It didn't take much effort to step in and do something."

"Not much effort, huh? That was a bad wound, Dean."

"Too bad I wasn't indestructible back then."

Miri shook her head. There were other scars, but she didn't ask. She wasn't sure she was ready for a laundry list of all the times he had been put in danger.

It won't end. He loves his job too much. This is who he is now, guns and all. You think you can live with that?

Not that anyone was asking her to. Though when she thought about being away from Dean, not having him in her life …

She swallowed hard and focused in on the curving wound above his heart. It was a clean cut, a fine incision. She could see the edges of his flesh, just ready to peel away.

"This was no dream, Dean."

"I'd like to pretend it was. The idea of really being set on fire—"

"You think Lysander did this to you?"

"At first I did. But now? I don't know, babe. It doesn't feel right. And besides, there was more of a … female presence at the time."

"Female," she said. "Huh."

Dean scowled. "Not like that. Just … shit, I don't know."

"No need to squirm," Miri said, hiding a smile. "But it's just weird, that's all."

The jade still felt warm. Miri glanced down, turning it in the light, studying the lines cut into the stone. She looked again at the cut in Dean's chest and frowned as something tickled her brain. An odd thought. She held the jade up to his chest.

"You're making me nervous," Dean said, peering at

her face and then looking down at the jade in her hand. "What are you thinking?"

"Something wild," she said. "Something impossible."

"Miri ..."

"That cut in your chest, Dean. It matches a mark in the jade." And she ran her fingernail against the carved red line and held it up for him. "Right here. See?"

"You're joking," he said, barely looking at the jade. "Babe, there's no way there's a connection."

Miri stared at him. "Are you kidding? After everything that's happened tonight? How can you possibly reject it outright?"

"Because it's easier than considering the alternative. Glowing like a light bulb? Burning like hell?"

"Is there a pattern to it?"

Dean hesitated. "Magic types. When they're around, things start to bark inside my chest."

"Woof," Miri said. "What an alarm system."

He scowled, but there was something else in his eyes that made her sit up and frown. "What?" she asked.

Dean closed his eyes. "I need to tell you something, Miri. You're not going to like it."

"With an opening like that, I can bet I won't."

He sighed. "Just before I reached the roof of that Memorial Hall where Bai Shen took you, I had a run-in with an ... associate of a friend. He said some things about us. He said that we're both 'the keys' to this mystery, that the jade was secondary to us."

"Okay," Miri said slowly. "That's some statement. Does this guy know what he's talking about?"

"I have no clue. Tonight was the first time I've ever met this guy, Rictor, and the things I've heard before haven't painted him in the best light. Bottom line? He's not that trustworthy."

"But you must think there's some merit to what he said, or else you wouldn't be telling me now."

Dean shook his head. "No, he's full of shit. In fact, I know he is."

But there was something pained in his eyes when he said it, and Miri chewed the inside of her cheek, wondering.

"You're holding back," she finally said. Dean's gaze flickered, but Miri shook her head before he could deny it. "You can run, but you can't hide. What else did he say?"

She thought he would hold back, that she would have to fight him for the truth, but after a short hesitation, Dean said, "He told me that I needed to kill you."

Miri stared. A chill raced through her and she quickly sat back, trying to put some imaginary distance between herself and the words she had just heard. But Dean followed her, reaching out across the aisle. He touched her hand, the back of her neck.

"I would never hurt you," he said. "Miri, are you listening to me?"

She shrugged him off, scowling. "Give me some credit. I don't think you're a complete moron."

Dean blew out his breath. "I'm sorry I told you, but I haven't been able to stop thinking about what he said. I was gonna bust a gut if I couldn't share. And no, he didn't give a reason."

"Then chalk him up to being crazy and forget about it," Miri told him, trying to suppress her uneasiness. "Unless you think …"

"No," he said firmly. "I don't."

Miri smiled. She wanted to kiss him, wanted nothing more than to wrap her body around that bare chest and sink down into his skin for one long hug, like the kind Dean used to give her for no reason at all. Just because he thought she needed one. Just because it was the right thing to do.

Miri unbuckled her seat belt and crossed the aisle

to Dean. He stared at her for a moment, uncertainty flashing through his eyes, but as she sank into his lap he seemed to understand and he folded her close. The flight attendant glanced up once from her seat near the front of the plane. A smile played on her lips.

Dean held her. His breath ruffled her hair. The rise and fall of his chest felt like some silent music only her body could hear, and Miri cradled the jade in her hands. Her legs dangled over the armrest.

"Why are we doing this?" she asked him softly, lulled by his warmth, the safety of his presence, which felt so much like home—the old forgotten home of her youth—that she felt a tear curl into her eyes and blinked hard.

"Why this treasure hunt?" Dean replied. His lips brushed her brow. "I've been asking myself the same question. Because even if we do find the other half, what then? People will still keep chasing us. When does it stop?"

"It doesn't. That's what bothers me, Dean. There's so much going on here, and I just … can't see the whole picture. If there is a picture. Robert. A man who can't be killed, who says he has been ordered to steal the jade and kidnap me. Package deal, two for one. Kevin Liao. Department head who destroys four-thousand-year-old mummies, also wants the jade, and has an assistant—a girl formally unremarkable—who makes Rambo look like a mama's boy. They appear to be working for a woman, Lysander's mate, in fact—"

"Whoa. His mate? Like, as in, wife? You didn't tell me that."

"Sorry. But yeah, that's what he said."

"Dude." Dean rubbed his face. "Okay, who else? Bai Shen?"

"I don't think he wants the jade. But think about it for a minute. If his dad is Lysander, and Lysander's wife is running the opposition …"

"Then that would explain how Bai Shen knew so much, and why he might be desperate to get Daddy-o under control. But why do they know so much about us?"

"Last night when you were questioning Robert, you asked him if he worked for something called the Consortium. I assume, given the circumstances in which you asked, that they aren't very nice. But could there be a connection there?"

"I hope not," Dean said. "They're worse than not nice. In fact, they're the reason why I wasn't so surprised to hear about this whole possession deal. The Consortium's former leader had the same thing in her head, but she was further gone than our dragon. And she could infect other people with it. Though that may have just been a personal talent, since Lysander doesn't seem to be going around spreading the love."

"You could still walk away," she said, fairly certain of Dean's response, but unable to hold in the words, the message, the sentiment—unable, as well, to control the sudden thread of fear in her gut, the fear that maybe she was wrong, that she would see in his eyes regret; or worse yet, resentment for getting him into this mess.

But Dean grabbed her hand, twined his fingers tight in her own, and in a deep voice, with iron resolve in his eyes, resolve and something more, something even stronger, said, "The only way I'm walking is with you, Miri, and the only *place* I'm walking is at your side. Nowhere else I'd rather be, no *way* else I'd rather be. And that's the truth."

There was permanence attached to his words—a determination that was startling and thrilling. Like the old days, the days when common sense had been a myth, fantasy—where the only reality was miracles and coincidence, guts and glory. The streets had been their playground once upon a time, their deep dark forest, their kingdom. Both of them swashbucklers, both of them knights, both of them royalty. Running, always running.

He's back, a voice whispered inside her heart. *Don't let go.*

Don't let go. Not ever again.

They landed without trouble, and customs in Hong Kong—as in Taiwan—was also private, quick, and extremely efficient. Miri felt like a head of state as she disembarked from the plane, greeted by a portly and greasy official who managed to fawn while maintaining an utterly professional air. A small bus waited for them, and after a quick ride, deposited Koni, Dean, and Miri in the main terminal.

Shops and restaurants filled the wide corridors. Miri gazed out the massive windows, staring at the ocean. Green mountains rose from the water, peaks covered in morning mist. Tall columns held up glass walkways and colorful billboards, several of which required double takes because the three of them recognized the pale visage plastered in all its gargantuan glory.

"He's never going to be a model again," Miri said, staring into that mysterious face. "Lysander ripped off his ear and ate it."

"God," Koni said. "You didn't need to tell me that."

"Just be glad you didn't have to see it," she muttered, which was enough to end the conversation.

They had no luggage, nothing but themselves. Down in the lower terminal they found the main platform into the city. As they waited for the train, Koni and Miri stood watch while Dean closed his eyes. He got some curious looks, but nothing menacing; just some old Chinese women who studied him, and then transferred their scrutiny on Miri. Their expressions darkened. Miri ignored them. She had a fairly good idea of what they were thinking, and it was nothing new. Lone Chinese woman traveling through Asia with two foreign men? She was automatic trash, an *er-nai*, little better than a whore.

The world is full of expectations and assumptions, she thought, *and few are rarely right.*

Dean rubbed his chest, the spot above his heart. "We need to get out of here."

"You sense something?" Miri asked.

"Don't know," he said. "But I don't want to hang around long enough to find out."

The train arrived: a modern rail, sleek and white. They climbed on fast. No one tried to follow them, and after a moment the doors swished shut. The train accelerated. Miri sat down hard. She did not move as they traveled into cloudy sunlight, skimming away from the airport past ocean and rock, with green mountains on one side, rising into mist.

They were the only ones in their car. Dean no longer rubbed his chest, but his hand lingered over his heart like it pained him. Koni watched, wary. "This train makes a couple stops. You want to ride all the way to the city center before you play hot and cold with the jade?"

"Better than nothing," Dean said, and sat back with his eyes closed. His hand curled in his lap, bouncing against his thigh. Miri could not help but think that he wanted it pressed against his chest.

The train deposited them in the business district, near the harbor. She smelled the sea, felt salt in the hot breeze. Humidity wrapped tight around her lungs, making her feel even more sluggish. She wanted to rest.

At first she thought she would be able to. They got in a red cab and drove to a sky-rise hotel on the edge of Victoria Harbor, with its ramshackle chaos of colorful houseboats covered in barking dogs, naked children, satellites, and metal chimney stacks. On their right, in contrast, clean modern lines of glass and steel. The sidewalks were packed with young people, most of whom had spiked dyed blond hair, perfectly lean bodies clad in the latest fashions, and enough attitude to set a nun on fire with speeches of penitence and humility. Miri felt like an old fogy compared to them.

"No safe house?" she asked, as they exited the cab. Large seabirds circled high overhead, floating effortlessly in a sky pearly with clouds that were luminously silver and sunlit from within.

"We don't have one in Hong Kong anymore," Dean said. "Too risky. The P.R.C. is unpredictable in ways that even grease money can't compensate for. At least in Taiwan we can own property."

"China's left Hong Kong alone since the handover from the British," Miri said. "For the most part anyway. And there are plenty of foreigners going into Mainland to buy up buildings and apartments and tracts of land. The upcoming Olympics make it good business sense."

"Maybe," Dean replied, peering up and down the street. "But like you said, Dirk & Steele runs an operation, which means different standards. You can't smuggle guns or build secret high-tech vaults in just any old place."

Miri expected to walk into the hotel beside them, but instead Dean grabbed her hand and cut across the street toward the waterfront. Koni followed close behind, mouth curved in what could have been a grimace or a smile.

There was a walkway that led off the street to the trash-strewn beach; another that led to a pier surrounded by a nicer set of houseboats. Miri guessed they had money to pay for the privilege. She felt very conspicuous; some women washing clothes on the decks of the boats stopped to stare, as did children and men and even dogs. Miri heard a rustle of conversation from the water, a couple of shouts in poor English that sounded like "boat ride" and "tour" and "very cheap." Some other words were said in Cantonese, a language she did not understand. Koni apparently did, and he shouted back one long and slightly nasal sentence that made the men grin and the women blush.

Miri and Dean looked at him. Koni shrugged, unconvincingly innocent.

Dean led them to the end of the pier and stopped in front of a boat that squatted in the water like a greasy off-white Styrofoam box. A very lean and handsome man sat on the deck with his legs propped up on a crate. He wore no shirt, which was fine because he had a very nice body, golden from the sun. His black hair was short, his cheekbones high and round, and when he smiled a row of white teeth lit up his face with twinkling charm.

"Dean," said the man. "Long time, no trouble, man."

"Ren," Dean said. "It's good to see you. I'd like you to meet Koni, who I guess you've heard of, and Mirabelle Lee, an old friend of mine. She's part of a case we're working on. Guys, this is Ren Li. Agent extraordinaire."

"Too kind," Ren said, standing up and stretching. He was a tall man, definitely a northerner, though his accent was all American. He threw out a narrow plank and held it steady on his boat while Koni, Miri, and Dean crossed over.

"Did Roland call you?" Dean asked.

"Sure did. He filled me in on the basics." Ren gave Miri a curious look that was surprising in its sweetness. "I understand you've got quite a few problems."

"A few," Miri said dryly.

Ren grinned. "Well, my home is your home. This tub doesn't look like much but it's solid. And it floats."

Koni glanced at Dean. "You and Miri planning on doing your walkabout soon?"

"I thought so," he said, throwing Miri a questioning glance.

She sighed. "Sure. Fine. Let's walk and rumble."

"In an hour," Ren said. "Or at least ten minutes. You guys should rest a little. You look worse than some of the dead things I pulled out of the water this morning."

Miri said nothing. It was not just her ass on the line, and Dean knew his business better than she did. If he said they did not have time to waste, then she would find some way of keeping up. She knew he would do the same for her if their positions were reversed, though the archaeological equivalent probably had fewer potentially lethal consequences.

"I guess we can sit back for half an hour or so," Dean said, pointedly not looking in Miri's direction.

Ren wasted no time. He led Miri down a set of stairs that opened into a surprisingly cool and long corridor lined with doors. He pushed open the last one on the right, revealing a small whitewashed room with a narrow bed, a side table with a sprig of dried flowers on it, and a bottle of water.

"There are towels in the bathroom," he said.

"Thanks," Miri replied. "Are you running a hotel?"

Ren laughed. "Nah. But I do get a lot of visitors, and most of them are sick of traveling."

And then he left her, whistling as he closed the door.

Miri sat on the bed. The room was very quiet, blissfully so. She laid her head down and closed her eyes.

Not much time passed—or maybe a lot—but when she opened her eyes Dean crouched beside her, whispering her name.

"Wha?" she asked, bleary-eyed.

"I'm going out. I wanted to tell you, just in case."

"In case what?" Miri sat up too fast; her head reeled and she clutched at it, trying to keep her brain steady. Dean's hand wrapped gently around her wrist.

"Lie down again. I shouldn't have gotten you up. I'm sorry, Miri."

"I want to go with you. Really, I'm fine."

"No," he said, but she touched his face, which was so very near, and then pressed her lips on his cheek, the corner of his mouth, warmth tumbling low in her stomach as he moved closer, tilting her head, ending the kiss she had started with something deep and hot and wet.

Miri had trouble breathing. "Is it just me or are the kisses better now?"

"They're pretty damn good," Dean said, and he kissed her again and she felt his hands creep up her waist, sidling beneath her shirt, and his fingers felt so good on her stomach, on her ribs, on her—

She gasped. Dean, breathless, said, "Wow. You grew up."

"My breasts got bigger, that's all."

"Yes," he said. "Can I touch them again?"

"Go to hell," she said, but her voice choked with laughter. Dean grinned and then went back to work, gentle and thorough, still leaving her shirt on as he kissed her with his hands, his lips busy on her mouth. It was the most perfect torture of the last twenty years, and Miri whispered, "You're picking up right where you left off. We never did get much further than this."

"A fact that stuns me to this day," Dean muttered. "What were we thinking?"

"No condoms, too young. Which, I would guess, is one-half of the problem we've got now."

Dean buried his face in her neck.

"There, there." Miri patted his back. "If you like, I can touch your throbbing manhood and make it all better."

"Maybe I should handle your weeping flower. Water

it with my hot man-juice. Caress your love grotto with my swinging showerhead."

Miri giggled and lay down. Dean moved with her, laughing hard as he curled around her body. His mouth touched her neck, trailing kisses to her ear. She shivered.

"You're not wearing underwear," Dean said, his fingers dancing on the waistband of her khakis.

"I didn't have time for them, if you remember."

"I do," he said. "And we should really be going. This is very irresponsible."

"Very," she said, and then gasped as he sidled his hand down her stomach, inside her pants, pressing his fingers as far as they would go. His palm was hot on her skin. The tip of his index finger danced against a very sensitive spot. Miri clenched her jaw so tight her teeth ached.

"Undo that button," Dean murmured, and she did as he asked, because really, if the entire world was crazy, she deserved a little insanity of her own.

And Dean, very promptly, gave her some.

The rest of Miri's afternoon was quite pleasant, despite the varied discomforts of Hong Kong's unrelenting heat, unrelenting crowds, and her own unrelenting fear of a sudden and violent death or kidnapping.

She and Dean scoured the city by cab and on foot, walking through neighborhoods that were collections of gray-stained concrete complexes, dripping with humidity and creeping vines. The sidewalks were narrow and, much like Taiwan, filled with businesses that spilled out of the confines of buildings and onto the streets. People pushed, shoved—but in Hong Kong foreigners were not such a novelty that anyone stared at Miri and Dean as they made their way through the ramshackle array of stalls and lanes.

Occasionally, she saw a crow with golden eyes. She tried to imagine it as Koni, and failed.

Late in the afternoon, after a brief stop at a dim sum restaurant where they ordered shrimp dumplings, fried turnip cake, and sticky rice, Dean finally said, "You know, I think I'm getting close."

"Really?" Miri said. "You said that an hour ago. What makes this time different?"

"Just a feeling," he said. "Like when you're nauseated, and then all that bad mojo jacks up a notch and it's time to start looking for a private corner, and then even that gets worse and you just start running and exploding."

"Yeah?" Miri asked, suddenly not enjoying the last taste of sticky rice in her mouth. "I'm guessing you're not at the first stage."

"Right. You could say I'm ripe for a bucket."

Miri settled back in her chair. "You do realize, of course, that the jade could be buried directly beneath us under a ton of concrete and steel."

"Sure."

"And that this has been a wild-goose chase and the jade is totally irretrievable."

"Of course."

Miri sighed. "Where do you want to go?"

It was not until they paid the bill that Miri realized that their restaurant's location had been chosen in the spirit of calculation, and that Dean had a glint in his eye that meant trouble. Which, really, was the same glint he always had, but this time it was more … intense.

She followed Dean back out to the street, leaving air-conditioning and relative quiet for sweat and damp and shouts and honks. Dean, holding her hand, led her around the restaurant and down a narrow lane that was intimately residential, so that Miri felt like a trespasser as she and Dean stepped around women doing their wash in buckets on their stoops, yelling gossip from doorway to doorway; rough tables set out with checkers, surrounded by old men, half naked and withered in the heat, pumping their fists and arguing over the game; running children, running dogs, running carts filled with boxed lunches, and at the end of it all, the small red columns of a tiny temple, its sloped and ridged roof covered in pigeons and metal dragons. Dean smiled.

"You knew this was here."

"I had a feeling," he said. "Following the bread crumbs."

"What if you try that disappearing act you did in Taipei? Follow the bread crumbs straight to the jade?"

Dean hesitated. "I don't know if I can do that again, Miri, and if I can? What if I end up in the middle of a mountain? I don't know how this thing works."

A crow cawed; Miri glanced up and saw Koni perched on an electric wire. At least, she thought it was him. From this distance, it was hard to see the color of his eyes.

Dean did not appear to notice or care. The excitement on his face faded; she saw a different kind of intensity replace it, sharp and careful. It was an interesting transformation; Dean was a harder, more eloquent man than she remembered, a hardness offset by his goofy charm, but still with an edge he had never possessed before he left her. Before that night he killed the man who had shot them.

Of course, twenty years also meant a lot of living. A long time for other things to go wrong. Nor she did think this job, this … Dirk & Steele, despite all its obvious perks, was any walk in the park. Though at least he was using his gifts, and was surrounded by others who, apparently, were just as—or even more—unusual.

But the setup still rubbed her the wrong way, and it

was not just the fact that such an organization actually existed. Miri had a bad feeling about Dirk & Steele. Not the people she had met, but something more, something deeper, an emotion she struggled to name—only that it ran deep, made her uneasy. Not with fear, and not anger.

Distrust.

Miri tasted that word, rolling it around her tongue as she followed Dean to the temple steps, past the threshold into a small courtyard framed by ginko trees. Distrust was an ugly word, but she was in an ugly situation, and while she trusted Dean—and maybe his friends—she took nothing else for granted. Dirk & Steele might be home to all those men, but as an outsider—and as a relatively normal human being with no bias or interest—she had to question it. Recruiting people just to use their powers to do good? Great. But having bunkers in the middle of major metropolitan areas stockpiled with weapons, cash, and fake IDs?

Huh. Interesting.

There were other people within the temple's courtyard, most of them standing or kneeling before the shadowed alcove where a golden Buddha sat amid incense and flowers. An old woman pressed her forehead three times to the earth before the altar, murmuring to herself.

Dean moved slowly to either side of the temple, studying stone and wood and painting, until he stopped, quite suddenly, above a grate located to the side. Miri looked down. All she saw was darkness. It looked like a sewer to her.

"No," Miri said, seeing the expression on Dean's face. "You can't go down there."

"It has a ladder. See?"

"What I see is that you're going to get yourself arrested if you start ripping out grates from the middle of a Buddhist temple and go diving into the sewers. Actually, forget the police. You're going to contract some horrible illness and die."

"I don't think it's a sewer down there, Miri. It doesn't smell."

He crouched and looped his fingers through the grate. Tugged. Miri glanced around the temple. Several people were watching them, but so far, no problems.

And then Dean moved the grate. It made a horrible screeching sound that echoed like the cry of a dying animal. Several women gasped, clutching their chests. Miri felt like doing the same. That, and kicking Dean down the hole.

"You coming?" he asked. He had a small backpack that Ren had thrown together for him, and he pulled out a headlight attached to a colorful elastic band. He put it on his head and switched it on.

"I'm coming," Miri said. "But if anything happens ..."

"Yeah, yeah. Death, pain, destruction. Probably some castration. If it makes you feel better, I'll do everything in my power to keep my manhood safe from the possibility of retaliation."

"Don't bother," Miri said. "I doubt there's much there, anyway."

Dean grinned. "Don't knock the goods before you sample 'em, darlin'. I am a love machine."

"Keep talking," she said, as Dean slid into the hole—which suddenly looked far more ancient than her first impression. He began climbing down.

This is so very stupid, right up there with all the other so very stupid things you've done in the past twenty-four hours. Oh. God.

Apparently, she was not the only other person to think that this was maniacally dumb—several people rushed up to the hole, wringing their hands and talking fast in Cantonese. Miri shook her head, tried to edge a word or two in in Mandarin, but gave up. When she tried to follow Dean, an old man grabbed the back of her shirt. Miri swatted gently at him, trying to be polite, but the man was persistent. Miri was considering more aggressive tactics when a screaming bundle of black feathers descended, pecking and clawing. The man lurched away from her with his hands over his head, crying out for help.

Miri did not waste time. She slid into the hole and down she went, step over hand over step, down the ladder into darkness. Just another big adventure, courtesy of Campbell & Lee, creators of *Wild!Times! Incorporated*, where for a small flat fee, unsuspecting victims might find themselves chased by maniacs, with bonus travel to highly exotic locales—all for the purpose of crawling into black holes to run among rats, sewage, and other unmentionables. Lovely. What a winner.

Dean waited at the bottom, his little headlight bobbing like a star on the end of a fishhook. The last few rungs were gone; he grabbed her waist and helped her down. She expected to step in something wet, but to her surprise, the ground was hard and dry, the air blissfully cool, clean-smelling. Dean dug another light out of his backpack and strapped it around her head.

"Which direction?" Miri asked, suddenly less apprehensive about their underground adventure. Her voice echoed. The tunnel was narrow, pale, and rough-hewn, as though carved by hand. It stretched in two directions, both leading into darkness. Miri heard sounds above; she looked up and saw tiny faces peering down. She wondered if anyone would send the police after them.

Dean grabbed her hand, staring at the path directly ahead. "This way. I think."

"Comforting," she muttered.

They walked carefully. Miri trailed her fingers along the wall, taking impressions of the stone. The ground beneath them was well worn. She did not think the erosion was water-based. Foot traffic, was her guess, though why anyone would be walking down here—and so often as to wear away stone and earth …

"I wonder if this tunnel is on a city map," Miri mused. "It must be."

"Does it matter?"

"I suppose not, but if it has any historical significance—and I would guess it does—then we could find out where exactly it leads, if there are branching tunnels, and who built it and why."

Dean grunted. "Something tells me it's not four thousand years old."

"Definitely not. Which means that if the red jade is down here—"

"It's buried. Or it was put here at a later date."

"That would imply that someone was trying to hide it."

"Yup." He glanced over his shoulder. Miri checked behind them, as well. She did not see anything, but the darkness closed in tight and she suddenly felt like hands were on her neck, crawling up her spine, ready to grab and twist and break. She shivered, rubbing her arms.

Dean's back was turned, but he stopped and looked at her. She did not know what he saw, only that he reached out and wrapped her in a quick tight hug that sent the dark things of her imagination skittering away.

"I forgot," he said. "You don't like the dark."

"I'm fine," Miri protested. "Really."

Really and truly, she was fine when he held her like this and she remembered—so long ago—how he had stood guard against the shadows in her mind. Shadows that sometimes seemed so real she could touch them. Shadows that, on certain occasions, she seemed to remember as having weight and form, presence. As though once upon a time she had rested in darkness, not just in sleep, but as a body alone in a void, and that there, in that place to be forgotten, the oubliette still waited.

They moved on, but Dean placed Miri's hands at his waist and the connection was a comfort as they walked and walked, following the one line of tunnel as it snaked down and up, curving, narrowing until they had to crawl, and still Dean insisted that it was close, that they were almost there, until Miri's feet ached and her body was so tired she was ready to beg for a sit-down, a nap, anything to ease up. She was used to hard digs in difficult locales, but crouching and sifting through layers of dirt used different muscles than hauling ass, and she was out of shape for the long endurance trek.

Indeed, she was just about ready to draw a line in the sand and turn around, when the tunnel abruptly widened. Dean stopped Miri with a finger to her mouth. She held her breath, listening.

Water, running. And beneath that, a muffled sound. Like a groan.

Chapter Thirteen

Dean switched off their headlamps. Darkness swallowed them, so black he could not see his hand in front of his face. He and Miri crept along the path with their palms against the wall, moving slow, trying to be quiet, eavesdropping and hearing nothing but water. Whoever had made that noise was silent now, though Dean smelled incense. A drop of light entered the gloom, enough for him to see Miri moving beside him.

Dean heard a scuffing sound in the tunnel behind. Miri went very still, and he felt her slow exhale, breath moving light against his face. Careful, quiet, he went for his gun. The weight felt good in his hand. It made him focus, instead of dwelling on guilt—guilt for being so hasty and cocky, bringing Miri down into this place without taking the appropriate precautions. Like bringing an army along with him.

But then he thought again of the jade, and felt in his heart a great swelling, almost like music, and a pull that had been at him since touching the artifact in the safe house vault in Taipei. He had managed to ignore it while still in Taiwan—it was hardly more than an afterthought—but ever since touching down in Hong Kong …

Well, he had not expected such a strong reaction, and from his vision perhaps only a memory or two. But not a life, not an experience that was wholly, explicitly painful.

Cut. Broken. Breaking. Watching. Feeling.

The woman and man had committed themselves, submitted willingly to the primitive operation. But with fear. So much fear. Holding that jade in their hands, tasting the stone before placing it in their bodies. Searching it for magic, because it *was* magic. There was no other word for it. Maybe what Dean did was just science, odd wiring—but that glow inside his head when he touched the jade was more than human, more than anything he had ever seen, and it called to him.

It *called.*

Dean shifted sight; Miri transformed into a ray of light, beating back the darkness like the sun. Only, she still left no trail. Dean reached out and found Miri's waist, her hand, and drew her close. His mouth pressed against her cheek, moving up to her ear, and he breathed, "I love you."

She nodded against him, hugging his ribs so tight he lost his ability to breathe. And then her arms dropped away and he heard her move. Metal scraped, a fine hiss. Ren had given her a new knife to replace the one she had lost.

"Do you see anything?" she whispered, and Dean looked up and down the tunnel. He found threads, twisting and bright. Still fresh. He stepped into them and felt stung with familiarity.

Oh, shit, he thought, and considered turning back. But they had come this far, and if not now, then never— and they needed that jade. Might be he didn't know exactly why they needed it, but it was enough that everyone else wanted it—and that somehow, for some reason, he and Miri were both tied up in the mystery of its existence.

"Who's there?" Miri asked him.

"Old friend," he said, and refused to elaborate. He thought it was enough. He felt her go very still, and considered making her stay behind. Not that she would listen to him.

He and Miri pushed ahead, moving swiftly; the sound of running water grew louder, as did other noises: scrapes and shuffles, cloth rubbing. And there, again, a low groan. He clicked the safety off his gun. A low burn entered his heart, a fire in his skin. He was growing accustomed to the sensation. Welcomed it, even, because whatever else had been done to him, that heat, those words, seemed to tell him when danger was near, and that was something to appreciate. Like now. He rubbed his chest.

The tunnel ended. In front of them, a waterfall. On the other side, bodies shimmered inside a room cast in soft candlelight. The smell of incense curled strong through the air. Miri touched his elbow and pointed at deep crevices in the wall beside them. Sunk just within and on each side were metal panels, and on the ground between those panels were track marks, grooves for sliding doors.

Dean hesitated only a moment before pushing through the waterfall. The water was shockingly cold. It formed a shallow artificial creek that led to a large hole in the center of the stone floor where the water poured over the edge. Somewhere distant, Dean imagined splashing, a low roar.

He heard another roar, too, a rumble in his ears that was his heart, his mind, his body rebelling. Across from the hole, across from them, sat a large rosewood chair, elegant and shining. And in that chair, with his feet resting on familiar bodies bound and gagged, lounged Robert.

"I feel like such a king in this place," the man said, idly rubbing the side of his cheek with the barrel of his gun. "It's remarkable, really. It reminds me of the good old days."

Dean sensed movement; he turned too slow. A tall graying man had been standing in an alcove to the side of the waterfall, a man that Dean had sensed only on the periphery while running his scan of the corridor. He pressed a gun against the underside of Miri's chin. She did not struggle or scream—was too smart for that—but Dean saw the knife in her hand angle against the inside of her wrist, pressing tight between her skin and thigh. Waiting.

Dean aimed his gun at Robert's head. It was a clean shot, close range, straight to the eye. The only problem was that it was a worthless opportunity. Dean had already wasted bullets on this man. If he could be killed—and holy crap, he hoped the answer was *yes*— Dean suspected he did not have the know-how or the proper tools. Like a chain saw and a shovel.

"Tell that son of a bitch to get the fuck away from her," Dean said.

"Very eloquent," Robert replied. "But I think we can all agree that making demands on me is virtually useless."

"You won't hurt her," Dean said, and his voice was terrible: low, hard, full of death. Out the corner of his eye he saw the gun held against Miri's neck grind even deeper into her flesh. Her gaze rolled sideways; she looked at Dean, her mouth settled into a hard line.

"No, Dr. Lee," Robert said, as though able to read her intentions as clearly as Dean could. "Please, no acts of heroism. Using that knife will not be necessary. Desmond? Release her."

"But Mr. Locksley—"

"*Desmond.*"

The man let go. Miri slipped away, still palming the knife against her thigh. She stepped backward out of the water, moving close to Dean.

Another man pushed through the waterfall, weapon extended. His thick black beard dripped. Robert said, "Albert, don't shoot."

Albert said nothing. He moved quickly to Desmond, and the two men leaned against the wall, weapons still ready, waiting for instructions.

Dean angled himself so that his back was also against the stone wall, Miri following his lead. Their vantage point gave them a clear view of the room, which was rough and small, compressed around the hole and the chair and the altar behind that chair. Incense smoked gently before a tiny Buddha, around which tall candles burned.

Dean, for the first time since landing in Hong Kong, wished the air was warmer. Only the skin above his heart had any kind of heat. His clothes clung with a chill, and it was a struggle to keep his arms from shaking. He wondered how Miri was faring, but he did not look at her.

Robert stood, stepping over the bodies in front of his chair. Miri gasped, and he knew that she had only just realized that it was Kevin and Ku-Ku lying there, eyes open and staring. If it hadn't been for their somewhat familiar energy trail, Dean might not have recognized them, either. They were filthy, their clothes singed, skin dark with soot. No obvious injuries, though, and given the fire and smoke he had seen around them, that was surprising. Not that he had suffered much injury from Lysander's fire, either.

"I thought they were dead," Miri said, gesturing at the two captives.

Robert stood at the edge of the hole. Silver flashed at his throat. He slowly, carefully, rolled up his green linen sleeves. It was a new shirt—no blood, no tears—exactly the same as the one he had worn only last night. "I had men posted nearby. When the shape-shifter began wreaking havoc, some of my people went in to save as many as they could from the lab. But don't worry, I didn't do it out of the goodness of my heart. I needed someone to question. Especially after the way I was treated by this gentleman's colleagues when they found me in your hotel room."

"Right," Dean said. "They give you some sweet lovin'?"

Robert gave him a hard look. "Not nearly as sweet as you, Mr. Campbell."

"Flatterer. I'm blushing."

"I'm not," Miri said. "I want to know what the hell it's going to take to get you off our backs."

A cold smile touched Robert's mouth. "If you had asked me that question last night, I would have given you the easy answer. The *acceptable* answer. Which is that I am a gun for hire, and therefore I would require both you and the jade to … cease fire. But things have changed."

"What things?" Dean asked, wary.

"My curiosity. Which is why I am contemplating something that is very much against my better interests."

"Suicide?" Miri asked.

His mouth tightened. "Mercy."

"Yeah," Dean said. "You're a regular Gandhi."

"Why, thank you. I always did consider myself an advocate of lofty ideals."

"I think you're scaring me more now than you did before," Miri said. "Can we just get on with it?"

Robert sighed. "My employers offered me a very large sum of money to collect you, Dr. Lee. They did not tell me why. Nor did they explain the significance of the red jade. Normally I would be content with such a situation, but in this case, given the chase, given the … attention … that this particular artifact has drawn, I find myself in the very unusual position of caring more about the *why* than I do the money."

Dean frowned. "Was that a long-winded way of saying you want a truce?"

"I believe that *would* fit the exact definition of what I was attempting to get across."

"Why should we believe you?" Miri asked. "And why bother? You don't need us. We're as clueless as you about what this thing represents. You might as well steal the jade right now and keep it for yourself."

"Clever," Robert said. "But then everyone would be hunting *me*, including my employers, and that is *not* a situation I desire for myself."

"Very selfless," Dean said, and then, "Just who did hire you?"

Robert gave him the most curious look. "I don't think I should say."

"And I don't think I care," Miri said, glancing at Dean. "The two of you can work out your politics later. I want to know why we should trust you not to stab us in the backs."

"Because I stab people in the front," Robert said. "Other than that, I can give you no reassurances. I am not a good man."

Miri narrowed her eyes. She gestured at Kevin and Ku-Ku. "What about those two? Did you hurt them?"

"Would you care if I did?" Robert asked.

"I would care," she said, looking at Kevin as she spoke. The man's eyes rolled around in his head; Dean did not think he would show a similar compassion for Miri, although he had given back the jade. Kevin stared at Dean; he could almost feel his eyes drilling a hole through his shirt to the scar beneath.

Robert seemed to notice. He nudged Kevin with his foot and the man cast him a baleful glare and groaned around his gag.

"They have not been very talkative," Robert said mildly. "I only managed to find this place—which, I must admit, was a complete surprise—because one of their young associates was so terrified, so mistreated, that by the time I found him, he spilled out everything he knew, which had more to do with location than actual motivation. Except for one thing." Robert smiled. "He said the second jade fragment could be found here. Imagine that. More than one artifact."

"And you haven't grabbed it yet?"

"I was waiting for the both of you to arrive, as I knew you would. Eventually. And besides, I was in no hurry. The hiding place itself is apparently … booby-trapped."

"Booby-trapped."

"Yes. My understanding of the matter is that the traps themselves are quite old-fashioned. Which, frankly, I find overdone, but I gather the devices were built some centuries ago by individuals with great imagination, much dedication, and far too much time on their hands."

"Right," Dean said. "My question still stands. Why haven't you gone after it yet? This should be a piece of cake. You can't die."

"But I can become stuck," Robert said. "Trapped."

"Get your men to free you."

Robert said nothing. Dean studied his impassive face, his gaze flickering to the two men in the corner who were pretending not to listen. It occurred to him that Robert, despite his great power, his cool, his control, did not trust the men he was with. Or rather, he trusted them to a point, but not where it counted. Not with his life. He had no real leverage over them, except, presumably, the money he was paying them.

And money was not always enough. Dean and Miri, on the other hand …

"Why would we help you?" Dean asked. "Why go down there and risk our lives?"

"Because you want the jade and you want the truth," Robert said, quiet. "You want those things as much as I do. But if you try to descend without me, I will shoot you, and while you, Mr. Campbell, might be immune to my bullets—*maybe*—Dr. Lee most certainly is not. At least, not if her hospital records are to be believed."

"And shooting *you* would be a waste of time," Miri said. "Though maybe not a total waste."

"So spirited," Robert said. "Oh well. Shall we go?"

Dean looked at Miri, who met his gaze with narrowed eyes. After a moment, though, she nodded.

"Lovely. The men will remain here and keep an eye on things. You can imagine what will happen if either of you returns without me."

"They'll thank us?" Dean asked, thinking, *There's the leverage, there is why he trusts us more than his men. Because we have something to lose.*

"Maybe," Robert said, with a thoughtful glance in their direction. "But fortunately they *are* paid to follow *most* orders."

"And you?"

He smiled. "My dear Mr. Campbell. I follow nothing but my own heart."

Down the rabbit hole. Alice, through the looking glass, crawling through ancient tunnels, marking time beneath glittering cities, surrounded by Cheshire Cats and Mad Hatters, knights and queens, and here … here … darkness.

The water spilled over only one side of the hole, and

thankfully, that was not the side with grooves in the stone for climbing. Miri did not see them until she stepped close with her light shining.

"You have got to be kidding," she muttered, bending down to feel how deep the cuts in the rock were. Not deep at all. Luckily, the intervals were meant for shorter people—no long reaches. At least, not in the part she could see. And if this thing was booby-trapped ...

We're going to die.

She almost said it out loud, but suddenly felt suspicious that words were things, and that by saying them, she would make it happen. So she thought her fear instead, and then buried it quick, because she was not dead yet, and in this, she had no choice but to descend. Perhaps if she argued, the men would leave her behind—though Robert did not strike her as the chivalrous type. But there was Dean to think of, and she could not stand the idea of him leaving him alone with Robert. Dean was of no real value to the other man, not a tradeable commodity like herself.

She could not stand, either, the idea of not knowing. Not after spending twenty years in that twilight state of holding on and letting go, loving and hating and wondering. She had him back. It was a miracle. She refused to let go of that.

Dean went down first. He took a deep breath, gave Miri a look that was probably meant to be reassuring, but only made her stomach hurt, and then swung himself over the edge of the hole and began his slow vertical crawl. Miri stood on the rim, looking down. The height made her dizzy, but she gritted her teeth, lighting the way, trying to see to the bottom. Movement, maybe; water, splashing. She thought about drowning.

Robert glanced at her. "I suspect you hate me."

Miri raised her eyebrows. "I don't hate you. Not really. But you do … concern me. Greatly."

The corner of his mouth curved. "You are not the type to admit fear, are you?"

Miri said nothing. Robert touched his neck. "You are a woman of constant surprises, Dr. Lee."

"Because a fearless woman is so rare?"

This time Robert did smile. "Because you *want* to do what has to be done, no matter the consequences, no matter the horror. And that is a rare courage, Dr. Lee, in both men *and* women."

And then he sat down, swung his legs over the edge of the hole, and began climbing. Miri watched the red crown of his head and glanced at his men in the corner. They stared back. She looked away first and checked out Kevin and Ku-Ku, who still sprawled behind her like large hot dogs. She looked at them, contemplated saying a few words like "I hate your guts" and "Burn in hell, you liars," but figured the message would be lost on them. They couldn't give a rat's ass about how she felt. They had their own problems now.

Miri sat down. She took a deep breath. She hoped she did not fall. Awkward, feeling like all her coordination was fading fast, she edged herself over the mouth of the hole and lowered her legs until her feet felt the first cut in the stone. It was just large enough for her shoes. She scooted down, and found another cut. And another—until her body was all the way in and her fingers dug like a vise in the stone and there was no going back. Only down. Down and down and down. The air passing between her back and the falling water was very cold. Her fingers hurt with the chill, the unusual pressure on them.

Below, Miri heard a loud splash. Dean said her name. Miri did not respond. Too much effort was required.

One foot left the crevice and found another. Her hand followed. Then a foot, then a hand. The rock was slippery. Her breathing rasped loud and her heart pounded like the water below, drowning her ears with sound.

Somewhere distant, another splash. Miri kept her face pressed to the rock. She stopped thinking, just moved. Moved because she had to.

And then, quite suddenly, hands touched her ankles, her waist, and she felt herself pried off the wall and held against a warm body that smelled so good she wanted to cry. But she pulled herself together fast, and gazed up with a shaky smile at Dean, who did not smile, but looked as serious as she had ever seen him.

They stood ankle deep in cold water, which flowed downward along another narrow tunnel, the walls black and sharp. Only one way to walk.

Robert took the lead. He did so silently. If there were booby traps down here, then he was the best person to trip them. She simply did not understand why he was bothering. Yes, it made sense if he wanted the jade, but to have a change of heart? To go from cold to hot, in the space of hours, and all for simple curiosity? There had to be more to it than that. There had to be a better reason.

"So," Miri said, speaking to Robert's back. "You're a mercenary."

"A mercenary," he echoed, with a trace of amusement in his voice. "I suppose one could call me that. Among other things."

"And you can't be killed," Dean said.

"I suppose not. I am almost unique, that way."

"Yeah," Dean said. "I know another man who used to spit bullets. Just like you. *Exactly* like you."

It was a shock for Miri to hear Dean say that. Apparently, Robert thought so, too. He stumbled and turned. His eyes were flat, cold, but his voice, the tremor in it, was not so removed when he said, "You are lying to me."

"No."

"You must be."

"Hey," Dean said.

Robert drew in a slow breath. "In what way could he not die?"

"Every way. He was indestructible."

"Like you, if I remember?" There was a hunger in Robert's gaze when he asked.

"Different circumstances." Dean ran his fingers along Miri's wrist, tapping. Four, and a slow draw on her skin. *Weird,* he said.

Robert looked like he was going to turn away, start walking again, but he hesitated, and in a quiet voice said, "How? How was it done to him?"

"A man cursed him," Dean said, after a brief hesitation. "It's complicated."

That was an understatement. Miri stared, trying to decide if she had really just heard correctly. Curse? Yes, *very* weird.

Robert's jaw tightened. "You said, *used* to spit bullets. He no longer has the gift?"

"He broke the curse," Dean said, and Miri looked from man to man, ignoring for a moment the craziness of what they were saying, studying instead the contrast in their faces: the terrible emotion hidden beneath the surface of Robert's flat expression, revealed only by a tick in his cheek; and Dean, with his cool and calculating gaze, contemplative in a way that was far more remote than Robert.

"What is this?" she asked, finally daring to break the silence between them. "What is it the both of you know?"

Robert smiled, impossibly grim. "Men like me are not born, Dr. Lee. They are made. Made and broken and remade, again and again. And oh, what a tiresome thing that can be."

He gave Dean another hard look, then turned and walked away. Dean watched him, still with that unreadable expression on his face.

"Dean," Miri whispered.

"I'll tell you later," he said. "It really is a long story."

Which was no comfort to her. She wanted to know now. But Dean started walking and Miri followed, sloshing silent and seething through the cold water. Someone had made Robert the way he was? Well, she had already guessed that part, though originally she had contemplated genetic engineering, some kind of government supersoldier à la the *X-Files*. Of course, given everything she had recently seen, maybe magic was the better answer. Magic, the bending of reality: a mysterious and inexplicable quality.

Or not. You don't know what the hell you're talking about.

The floor narrowed. It was difficult to walk. The ground had been worn smooth by the water, but it was still slippery, cold, and Miri clutched the walls on either side, trying to keep her balance as the water suddenly deepened.

And then Robert disappeared.

It happened fast: one blink, then nothing. Dean shone his light down, and there was no break in the path of flowing water, no whirlpool. The walls were solid and slick.

Miri edged close, careful … and her toes met a dip, a drop in the ground. She teetered. Dean grabbed her shirt and hauled her back against him.

"Hole," she said, breathless.

"Uh-huh," he agreed, also unsteady. "But he didn't pop back up."

"Trapped?"

"Wait." Dean crouched, shining his headlight on the

moving water. He pointed and Miri bent close. She saw bubbles.

"Oh no," she said.

Dean hesitated. "Do we really want to save him?"

"We promised," Miri said. "And if he can't die, then being stuck underwater …"

She did not need to finish. Dean stripped off his shirt and tied the end of it around his ankle. He handed the other end to Miri, who wrapped it securely around her wrist. She sat down in the water and braced her feet against the walls.

"Be careful," she said. Dean glanced over his shoulder and grinned.

"If I don't make it back," he said, still smiling, "just think of this moment and let it keep you warm at night."

"Oh, brother," she said, and tapped his backside with her foot. He ducked low, and went into the hole headfirst.

It was a startling sight, seeing him slip under like that—another shift in her perception of reality—but she had no time to marvel because the shirt suddenly yanked so hard she almost went in after him. The pull was incredibly strong; Miri leaned backward, almost lying down in the water, groaning as her arms stretched and stretched. She felt vibrations along the shirt, movement, and then the pressure eased just slightly and a head emerged from the water. Red hair. Robert shot up, gasping, and pulled himself along the shirt until he straddled the ground, the bottom half of his body still underwater.

"Dean!" Miri shouted at him. "Help me!"

Robert heaved himself out and twisted, gathering up the shirt in his hands. He pulled hard, pushing backward into Miri—her legs practically in his ears—and together they hauled and hauled until Miri saw a foot—a beautiful, lovely, foot—and then a leg and a waist and finally, finally, Dean's head popped out and all three of them lay together in an exhausted, soaked, and quivering heap.

Robert coughed, choking up water. Dean did the same. Miri felt like she was going to have a heart attack.

"Well," Robert finally said. "There's one."

"It felt like something was holding on to you both," Miri said.

Dean flopped on his side. "I think we're walking on some kind of shelf. There's more water running beneath us. And it's fast."

"I managed to grab a portion of rock before I was sucked all the way in," Robert said, "but the lower part of my body became trapped by the current. I couldn't pull myself up."

"There must be more of these all over the place," Miri muttered. "Good job, Robert. Glad you're here."

"Oh. Thrilled to oblige."

All of them were soaking wet; Miri was very glad for her light jacket; she glanced down and saw her breasts clinging to the flimsy T-shirt.

Robert stood. Dean grabbed Miri's hand and helped her up.

The hole in the path was not that wide—perhaps as long as a man's shoulders turned sideways—and they were able to step over it without difficulty. They clung to the sides of the tunnel after that, trying to stay only on those parts they could see for certain beneath the water. They passed several more dark spots, places of indeterminate depth.

Robert stayed in the lead, with Miri in the middle and Dean bringing up the rear. It was a reverse of their earlier position, but Dean kept one hand on her waist or shoulder at all times, and she thought it might be his way of reassuring himself that she was safe. It made her feel better, too, having him touching her. She tried to imagine them as children again, recalled sitting in dark corners with her braids swinging and him with some stick or piece of rope in his hand, trying to make a toy. And after movies, or after Miri had read a book and told him all about it—talking and talking about what it would be like to find the ring, the wardrobe, the magic that would lead them into a fantastic adventure away from city streets and grit and gray Philadelphia skies.

Look at us now, she thought. *It took twenty years, but here we are.*

Yes, here they were. She almost laughed. A good laugh, too, and not one tainted by irony. Even now, it seemed as though all she could do was marvel at Dean's presence, think again how remarkable it was, how wondrous. She could feel herself slipping into a kind of acceptance—moments taken for granted— and it was easy, because being with Dean was as comfortable as being with herself, like two peas in a pod. They had always been that way. Inseparable.

And here, now, twenty years of the quiet life were done and gone, and maybe in an hour or a minute she would be dead, rolling away from this existence into another, but right now it was the old days, and she felt like Queen Bonnie to his King Clyde.

The tunnel curved; around the bend, they came to a fork, a three-way split. Water flowed down all three directions. Robert sighed and leaned against the wall.

"Suggestions?" he asked.

Dean said nothing. He closed his eyes and Robert watched. He did not seem particularly surprised by what Dean was doing, and it bothered Miri that the man seemed to know so much about them.

She edged close. "Just how much do you know about us?"

Robert glanced down at her; she thought, perhaps,

there was a glint of surprise in his eye. "I was given files, Dr. Lee. Very detailed files. However, seeing you with Mr. Campbell—your comfort with him—has been somewhat of a surprise. It indicates that you knew each other before last night's events, and while Mr. Campbell's documents indicate a childhood spent near your old neighborhood, I did not make the connection until I saw you both together."

"You didn't know he would be there at the hotel, did you?"

Robert hesitated. "No, I did not."

"But you had done research on him. You knew who he was when you saw him."

He did not answer her. Miri, forgetting all the fear she had felt for this man, all the danger he represented, pressed close. "Tell me," she insisted. "Who gave you the information? And why? What was your next job? Going after him? One of his friends?"

Robert finally looked at her. His eyes, even in the dim light, shone bright and pale and cold. A killing gaze, but Miri held herself steady. She did not falter. A muscle ticked in his cheek—anger, she thought—but his voice was surprisingly gentle as he said, "The files I was given do not matter, Dr. Lee. The moment I entered into a truce with you, I gave up my future contracts with this particular employer. There will be no retaliation, as long as I do not keep for myself what I was supposed to fetch, but I will no longer be trusted. Which is somewhat of a disappointment, though I have lived with worse. Either way, your Mr. Campbell is safe from me." He smiled. "For the most part."

"But that just means someone else will be hired." A deep sickness entered her stomach, twisting.

Robert shrugged. "Perhaps. But I doubt there is anyone out there who is quite as good as me."

"So good you couldn't catch us?"

"My dear woman. The only reason I could not catch you was that I was not allowed to kill you. Had the rules been different …" He held out his hands, the corner of his mouth curling up. Miri swallowed hard. This time, she looked away first.

Dean opened his eyes. Miri did not know if he had heard anything of their conversation, but he gave Robert the hardest, meanest look that she had ever seen on his face, and said, "We need to take the right tunnel."

"Well, then," Robert said, and away he went, hopping from side to side of the water like a skipping monkey. Dean curled his hand around Miri's wrist as she passed him. His gaze was solemn.

"You heard," she said.

"Don't get too comfortable with him. He can't be trusted."

"But if it's true?"

"Then that's something to worry about later. Right now, I just want you to focus on here and now. Staying alive. That's all I care about, Miri. I want you safe."

"Right back at you," she said softly, and kissed him.

They followed the tunnel, which eventually began showing cracks in the walls, tiny fractures that drained off the water until they once again walked on dry land. The path curved up. Miri wondered which part of the city they were under now.

And then the tunnel ended.

"It is just a wall," Robert said, and took a running jump, propelling himself with surprising grace up the almost sheer face. His hands reached the top edge and he hauled himself over. He straddled it and held out a hand. Dean gave Miri a boost and Robert pulled her up. Miri did not go over to the other side. She braced herself, held down her hand alongside Robert, and the two of them together pulled up Dean.

The ground level was higher on the other side; it was

barely a jump to get down from the wall. Miri gazed up and up. She stood in a cavern with a ceiling so high and dark she could not see the top. The light from her headgear did not touch it.

But hanging from the murky darkness, trailing like the long hairs of a giant, was a forest of rope. Thick rope that smelled musty, of mold and decay. She edged close and picked out many different kinds of fibers: hemp, silk, actual hair.

"Dean," she said. "Please don't tell me we have to climb these things."

"I don't think so," he said. "I don't feel any pull in an upward direction."

"I cannot see to the other side," Robert said, trying to peer through the tangle. He stuck his hand in and pulled aside a bundle of the hanging rope. Miri heard an odd tinkling sound, like glass or metal.

And then Dean yanked her back. He grabbed Robert, too, hauling the man off his feet just as a group of glittering objects hit the ground where he had been standing. The three of them scrambled away, Miri half expecting the objects on the ground to leap up and start attacking.

Robert edged close. He crouched, picked something up, and brought it back to Miri and Dean, who aimed their lights at his palm.

It was metal and shaped like a star. The edges were razor sharp and covered in a sticky brown substance.

"Poison," he said. "At least, that is my best guess. I could be wrong."

"Poison," Miri echoed. "And those things come down when the ropes are moved."

"There are a lot of ropes out there," Dean said. "To push through, it's going to be impossible not to move some."

"And we do not have anything with which to protect

our bodies." Robert sighed. "Mr. Campbell, do you know the approximate direction of the jade?"

Dean pointed. It was at an angle to the right of where they stood.

"Very well," Robert said, rolling down his sleeves. "I cannot imagine there is an unlimited amount of these things contained above. I will tear down as many as I can along the path you pointed out. Once that is done, the two of you should be relatively safe to follow."

"You've got a hard-on for pain, don't you?" Dean said.

"What else is there to do? There are no rocks to throw, and even if there were, we could not possibly hope to release them all. Are you willing to risk Dr. Lee's life on that? No. Some things require a personal touch."

Robert threw himself into the tangle. The resulting sound reminded Miri of a church—all those tiny stars, tinkling like bells as they fell through the jungle to the ground. Dean pushed Miri back, away, shielding her with his body as though some random bit of metal and poison would fly out to strike her. She stood on her tip-toes and watched over his shoulder, anyway; the ropes nearest them had stopped moving, but the chimes did not fade in volume and Miri wondered just how far Robert was being forced to travel, and whether he would make it.

And then, like the end of a rainstorm, silence. Dean called out Robert's name, but he did not respond. Miri stirred, uneasy.

"Do you think he's alive?"

"No," Dean said, and walked to the rope. Miri followed close behind.

"Stay here," he said. "Let me go first."

"No," Miri said. "Together, or not at all."

He almost argued with her, but Miri held his gaze,

stubborn, and Dean finally nodded. He grabbed her hand, kissed it, and said, "This is a good life, Miri. Everything else may be crap, but you and me together is a good life. I had forgotten how good."

"I know," she said. "I forgot, too."

He nodded, then drew her in front of him. She felt the heat of his chest press through her clothing, the heat of the glowing word against her shoulder. She felt another kind of heat settle in her own chest, and she touched herself, and wondered.

They tugged on the ropes ahead of them. Nothing fell. They pushed through and it was hard to breathe; her heart pounded loud in her ears and her focus narrowed to the spot directly in front of her, rope and more rope, and only once did she look down—and that was because her foot nudged something hard. It was a skull. So. Someone else had tried to make a go of it. She wondered why.

"You okay?" Dean breathed in her ear.

"Peachy," Miri said. "You?"

"I've got a beautiful woman rubbing up against me. I'm fantastic."

"Sex and danger. Turn-on, huh?"

"Oh, baby." He reached past her to push aside rope. "When we get out of here—"

Miri heard a tinkling sound. Dean shoved them both into a staggering run and at the last moment he knocked her down and she felt him cover her body with his own, wrapping her so tight within himself she lost the ability to breathe. She squeezed her eyes shut. Felt something hit her legs. She thought of Dean above her, and a cry rose up in her throat.

"Dean," she gasped. "Dean!"

"It's okay," he mumbled. "I think I'm okay."

He slowly uncurled from her. They both stood, very

carefully watching for metal near their hands and feet. Miri turned Dean around. There was not a single cut on his back. She looked at the ground around them. They were surrounded by stars. She checked her leg. There was a slight tear in her pants, but the skin was unbroken.

"I wish I knew what happened to me," Dean murmured, almost to himself.

"Do you think someone did this to you?"

Dean shrugged, helpless. He kept close to Miri as they moved on. They did not talk. She did not feel well enough for words. One more scare and she was just going to keel over. Any longer in this jungle of rope—

They stepped free. Ahead of them, another room. On the ground, Robert. He was covered in blood. Death from a thousand cuts.

Miri's knees gave out. She sat down, hard.

Chapter Fourteen

It took some time for Robert to resurrect himself. Miri and Dean sat on the ground against the wall and waited. They did not explore the small room. There was a way out, a tunnel, but Miri felt no interest in going near it. Cowardly, maybe, but this was survival and Robert was more than willing to play bait. Of course, there was the good possibility that Dean was in a similar boat physically, but Miri did not want to begin testing the limits of his abilities. Robert could drop dead, for all she cared. Again and again and again.

Dean startled whistling the theme to *The Twilight Zone* and Robert finally stirred. They did not go to him. They sat and watched his body flop, seize, writhe like a man stabbed by electric cattle prods. It was not very pleasant.

Trapped. She remembered him saying the word, like there was a memory attached, and she wondered what it would be like to never die, if Robert's ability made him immortal.

Miri nudged Dean with her elbow. "You said you know another man like him."

"Hari. A shape-shifter. He married a friend of mine. Before that, he was … cursed."

"Cursed. As in …"

"Magic. Voodoo. Bad mojo."

"Huh," Miri said. "Okay, and … the curse was broken."

"Yes," Dean said, and there was a heaviness to his voice that made her think the story was indeed more complicated than she could possibly imagine. "The curse made Hari immortal. The man who cursed Hari was also immortal. I've got a bad feeling that the same dude who got him got Robert."

"That doesn't make sense."

"Which part?"

"All of it. Because even if you put aside the … the *magic*, it's still weird. Why would someone keep making immortals? Because he liked them? Because he thought he was doing them a favor?"

"Not this guy. He was a sadist."

"Then I'm confused. Which … I'm sure is a huge surprise."

Dean smiled, but only for a moment. Robert sat up. His eyes were open and the cuts were gone—though he was still quite bloody. He looked at Dean. "Do you have water in that bag of yours?"

Dean pulled out a bottle and tossed it to him. Robert drank fast; water trickled down the sides of his mouth. He wiped his face, and blood smeared across his cheeks.

"Do you think this is the last?" he asked. Miri wondered if he was beginning to regret this little excursion.

"No way to tell until we reach the jade," Dean said. "You ready to move?"

Robert gave him a dirty look. It was the closest thing to a normal expression she had seen on his face thus far, and Miri found it comforting. But only a little.

Stumbling, Robert took the lead once more and they moved into the tunnel. Only, this time the walk was short. They entered yet another room, carved precisely into a square, with flat chiseled walls and a flat chiseled ceiling. Directly ahead of them, across the wall, there was a painting.

Their headlamps illuminated only bits and pieces, but Miri saw enough to make her sigh and lean close. Before her, a story: pale winsome figures dressed in flowing robes of white and red, a dance of bodies, among them bearded men in armor, on horseback, running with leopards and white tigers, dragons curling fierce with golden spheres in their claws—and inside white pavilions, yet more women, long black hair flowing like rivers, shadows, upon which butterflies fluttered.

"Lovely," Robert said. "What does it mean?"

"I don't know," Miri said. "But it's reminiscent of works I've seen in northern China. There's an old wall just south of the Mongolian border. The Imperial Postal Service had a station there, and inside are temples with paintings like this. Telling stories."

"The vibrations are strong," Dean said.

"Mr. Campbell," Robert said, quiet. "Is the jade inside or near this room?"

"I think it's on the other side of that painting."

"Ah," Robert said, and pulled out his gun. Miri did not think guns that had been underwater were supposed to work, but she stifled a breathless scream as Dean hauled her backward, away from the painting. Robert pulled the trigger.

The bullet slammed into the wall, gouging a hole in the masterpiece. Miri felt like she was watching Michelangelo's *David* being hacked to dust with a mallet; the *Mona Lisa*, taken to with scissors; the original text of *The Dream of the Red Chamber* burned to a crisp. She wanted to howl.

Robert stepped up to the wall and checked the hole. He poked his hand through. "There is a room on the other side."

Miri wrenched herself away from Dean. "I can't believe you just did that. You … you *ape*."

Robert paused. "Now that is something I have never been called." And then he went back to work pulling down the wall.

"Miri," Dean said.

"Fine. Go. Help him." It made her sick, but if the jade was on the other side, there was no good way to it but through the wall.

While the men worked, she moved to the far end of the painting, examining it. The colors were incredibly bright, the details exquisite, but as she studied the images she noticed something quite odd: in the lower corner there were words. Not Chinese. Not logographs. The same writing as on the jade.

She got down on her hands and knees. She had not studied the words enough to know for certain whether these on the painting were an exact match to any she had yet seen—except for one. She traced it with her fingers. Almost expected it to glow.

"I think I see some kind of wall on the other side," Dean said, and Miri stood up, pacing down the length of the painting, searching for any other script, any symbols that were similar. She noticed only that some of the figures in the painting had unusual coloring, of the kind not usually found in traditional Chinese works of art. Green eyes. Golden eyes. Red eyes. White eyes. All those gazes, staring in one direction: the words in the lower corner. Miri ran back. She imagined, around those words, the faint outline of shoulders.

"Oh my God." She sat back on her heels and looked up, saw another dragon entwined at the top corner of the painting, directly above the words. It had golden eyes. Human eyes. Also not typical. Miri scooted backward for a wide view. There were more dragons in the painting, many animals. Some of the humans had wings.

She felt herself shaking her head, and could not stop. This was not right. This did not fit.

Stone crumbled; Robert broke through. Dean gestured for Miri to come to him, but she did not move. She stared at the painting, her headlight moving from scene to scene.

"This explains everything," Miri said to Dean. "Look, look here at their eyes. Isn't this familiar?"

Dean, frowning, did as she asked. He made a low sound when he saw the dragon, the other creatures, and she pulled him to the corner with the writing. She pulled the jade from her purse and compared the writing on its smooth red surface to the painting. There were some differences, but it was most certainly the same language. Dean closed his eyes.

Robert shouted; they ran to the hole and peered in.

"There is nothing here," he told them, turning around within the darkened interior. "The room is completely empty."

"That's impossible," Dean said.

But they scoured the room and it was true. No clues, either. Just bare walls that were rough-hewn, carved without art or purpose. They curved downward, covering a good portion of the partition they had entered through. She stared at the section of the room that ran directly opposite to where the painting's inscription should be. It was just solid stone; the wall jutted farther than the painting on the other side.

Miri grabbed Dean's hand and pulled him into the outer chamber. Pointing at the inscription, she said, "Knock it out."

Dean did not hesitate. He began hammering on the wall with the butt of his gun. Three strikes and the stone crumbled, more easily than Miri had anticipated. Robert emerged—watched for a moment—and then bent down to help. The three of them scrabbled at the edges of the painting, and though Miri felt guilty for what she was destroying, a new excitement burned through her, a feeling of being close to something great.

This is what you live for, she told herself. *This is in your blood.*

Bones and dust and history—the inviolable truth, sustained by facts and evidence. And if the truth was larger than she thought, if the truth included the fantastic, creatures out of legend, then so be it. The world—her world—was big enough to handle anything.

There was a hole behind that section of painting. A hole leading into a separate chamber running parallel to the other. Robert entered first. The room was larger than it appeared at first glance, spreading far to the right. Miri smelled water. The air was cool, and there was a draft, almost a breeze.

And in the center of the room, surrounded on all sides by moving water, was a stone platform rising above the gentle current. On the stone lay a shriveled body, and in that body …

"Those remains should be dust," Miri said. She glanced at Dean, found his face full of sorrow. Memory, perhaps.

They stopped at the water's edge. Robert said, "Should I fetch it?"

Miri shook her head and stepped over the water to the platform. Her headlight illuminated a shriveled face that nonetheless had a masculine quality to it. He was better preserved than the Yushan mummy. His condition was miraculous. Four thousand years. Buried with a secret below his heart.

She straddled the body and crouched, examining the chest cavity. It did not take long to realize there was something very wrong.

"The jade isn't here," she said.

"What?" Dean leaped onto the platform beside her. "I feel it, Miri. It has to be here."

"It's not," she protested, but the two of them kept poking and prodding until the body fell in on itself. And for a moment, the world disappeared, and Miri heard a voice say, *When the time is right, you must, he will kill you otherwise.* And then the disturbing whisper faded and images took its place, along with a great pressure above her heart as she saw—she saw—

White peaks capping mountains of purple rock, frothing clouds spilling low over ancient trees set high against deep valley walls, a turquoise lake—waters still and quiet over a dragon's back. And past that, farther, *weeping—a woman weeping, endless tears—and deeper still, darkness, the scent of death, the hiss of water striking hot stone, and eyes that glowed golden, shedding light on bones ...*

The vision faded abruptly, and then cut off for good. Miri staggered, and felt hands upon her, Dean whispering her name. She could not see, her eyes refused to focus. Her chest throbbed.

"Miri," Dean said. "Miri, what happened?"

Something impossible. She was not psychic. She did not have visions.

Miri swallowed hard, trying to stand on her own. She ended up braced against Dean's body, his arm tight around her waist. She almost told him the truth, but remembered Robert.

"Nothing," she said. "Just ... light-headed, that's all. The body."

Which would sound ridiculous to anyone who really knew her. Dean managed to smooth out his expression, but she saw the question in his eyes. Even Robert stood back, watching her. He looked ... thoughtful. Miri was not sure it was a good look on him. It bothered her.

Thoughtful and Robert probably meant a great deal of trouble.

Miri and Dean jumped off the platform, leaving behind a body that was nothing more than a loose pile of desiccated parts and dust. It made Miri sick, but she pushed away her guilt, her shame. All of them stared at each other.

"So," Robert said.

"No artifact," Miri said. "The jade isn't here."

"I still say it's impossible," Dean argued. "I felt it. It's been ... pulling me."

"And if it was just the body you felt the connection to?"

"If so, we're shit out luck. I don't know where to go next."

Miri's hair stirred; she felt a cool breeze against her face. "Where is that draft coming from? Do you think there's a way out from here?"

"A way out that isn't a death trap?"

"A way out that does not require retracing our steps?" Robert smiled. "I would be very much in favor of that."

But it was difficult for Miri to leave. She turned and stared at the dusty remains, the face of the man she had destroyed lingering in her memory. How things had changed, that she would so willingly desecrate the ancient dead, and for nothing but a trinket, some treasure.

Grave robber, she called herself. It didn't matter that she had a good reason, that she was doing it to save her life, and maybe others. Money could save lives, too. Stealing for cold hard cash, just like any other thief of the grave, was no different.

"Miri," Dean said. She shivered when he said her name, visions dancing in her mind; that voice, that whispered, *He will kill you otherwise*. She remembered Dean's confession.

He told me I needed to kill you.

The skin between her breasts burned. Miri did not touch herself. She grabbed Dean's hand instead and squeezed. Squeezed so hard he looked at her, frowning, but he said nothing, and Miri eased up after a moment.

They followed the flow of water, which meandered through the chamber in an artificial creek that, had there been more light, might very well have painted a lovely picture. The cavern they found themselves in was very large and Miri again wondered, this time out loud, how such a place could exist directly beneath one of the most urban cities in the world.

"Power," Robert said, as though it was the simplest thing in the world. "Power and money."

"What do you mean?"

"I mean that someone—perhaps those whom Kevin and Miss Ku-Ku work for—once stored the jade in this cavern. I will assume that, because they are so very familiar with this locale … and because of certain facts I obtained from the young gentleman who was so helpful. They are caretakers of this artifact. Protectors, if you will. The jade has been moved, but I doubt for long. Otherwise, the builders of this place would not have gone to such great lengths to watch over it. But to protect something that is stationary, that must *remain* stationary, for whatever reason, requires great amounts of power and wealth. Enough power, anyway, that it would be possible to divert builders and planners and other government officials from particular areas, either through misdirection or bribes."

"You're saying this is yet *another* conspiracy?"

"The entire world is run by conspiracy, Dr. Lee. It is what drives and shapes history."

"And rewrites it."

"Of course. There is no such thing as historical

truth. The only truth is what we live and experience for ourselves: the moment. Once that is past, it is reshaped by our hearts and our minds. It is not raw. It is not honest. It is memory. And memory is changeable. Memory is not trustworthy."

"But we need to rely on something," Miri protested. "History teaches us, history—"

"Is nothing but fairy tales that are treated as truth. You have seen so much in the past twenty-four hours, Dr. Lee. And yet, none of it—none of *this*—will ever be relied upon as a means of understanding the world. Perhaps for you it will, but not anyone else. Learn from history, Dr. Lee? Better, I think, to learn from yourself. That is all the history you need."

Miri wanted to say more—she could tell that Dean had a pithy comment on his tongue—but Robert had the last word.

"Did I just hear a scream?" he asked.

Chapter Fifteen

They ran. The water led them, and they did their best to watch for traps, danger, but the screams were loud, too terrible for caution. It was the sound of men dying. Men being ripped apart. Dean had never heard anything like it in his life.

They moved through the cavern, which narrowed around the water, leaving little room. The ceiling was low, the walls rough and dark. Only the floor was flat, but farther from the center, the altar, its surface became uneven and Miri stumbled. Dean caught her elbow. She was small against his side, warm. Warm like his chest, like the brand above his heart, which cast its own glow, like fire.

Dean shifted his sight, looking for signs of recent passage, and saw nothing, dead air, a world far removed from the living. Only, on the edges, inside his head, he felt a buzz—even a sucking sensation—pulling him in all directions.

Not here, he thought. *It's not originating here.*

But it was close. Almost … on top of him.

The city. I'm feeling the city. All the people above me.

The living world, humming—all those people, so many memories and voices and lives, running together until the music was too much, more static than song. That buzz inside his head.

You never used to be able to do this before.

Yeah, and he hadn't been able to teleport, either. All of which should have been very cool, but the only thing he could think about was how and why. Why now? Why such extremes in his abilities? Was it really all him, or was someone else responsible?

Ahead, light. It was very faint, barely there, but the others saw it and they all pushed hard. Dean heard grinding, the dry hiss of a large body moving over stone. He stumbled, dragging them all to a fast stop.

"It's him," Miri said.

"Him?" Robert murmured.

"A killer, a shape-shifter, the key guy in all this mess. A mind-reader, too." Dean looked at him. "He'll know we're coming, if he doesn't already."

Far ahead, the tunnel ended. Dean saw light. The water flowing past them spilled over a break in the rock. He heard it splash, burble: clean sounds, gentle. No more screams, but the hissing continued, and the light suddenly flared, flickering its reflection against the walls directly in front of them.

He smelled incense.

"We're right back where we started," Miri muttered. "Kevin and Ku-Ku did that on purpose, misdirected us, hoping we would get killed. We went all that way, and all we had to do was—"

Dean held up his hand. Miri's eyes were profoundly grim. Robert's face showed nothing at all.

"We cannot go back," the man said. "The exit is the same. Nor do I wish to … wait him out."

"Ditto," Dean said. "The only way to get away is to move fast and stay out of his direct line of sight. I think that affects his pyrokinesis."

"He's a telepath," Miri said. "It shouldn't affect anything."

"I do not plan on running," Robert said.

"Well, good luck with that. I hope you can grow back your body from ash."

"Burning at the stake is a similar experience, I expect." Robert smiled, grim, and pulled out his gun.

Dean reached for his own weapon. He glanced at Miri, and thought about her last encounter with Lysander, the near miss that had been. He thought about bodies, ash, burning and burning and burning, and himself trapped in flame. While he had survived, and maybe things had changed within him, those were flukes that could be taken away as quickly as they were given, and he could not risk Miri.

Her warm hand curled around his arm. She felt like an extension of his body. He had forgotten what that was like. He had forgotten so much. Robert was right. Memory could not be trusted.

But Miri had that stubborn determined look in her eye, and in his head he could see her twenty-odd years younger, with her hair in braids, giving him that same resolute expression. Ready to fight, ready to watch his back. It killed him. It scared the living shit out of him.

"I wish you weren't here," he said. "I wish it so bad, Miri."

She touched his face. "We take care of each other. And we've come this far, haven't we?"

She made it sound so easy. Dean wished it could be that way. He closed his eyes and said, "Miri. When we get down there, you run. None of this heroic bullshit. I'll be right behind you."

"But only if you're behind me," she said. "I'm not going anywhere without you."

Robert moved close. His green eyes were especially bright; a muscle ticked in his cheek. His red hair suddenly made him look wild, even a little crazy.

"We should do this now," he said.

They crept to the edge of the rock face. Water spilled over into the pool below. The ceiling to the chamber rested several feet lower than the ledge they stood upon, blocking out most of the room. Dean could see the edge of the hole, the water streaming into it.

He also saw a white tail, covered in scales. Blood. He smelled, beneath the incense, ash.

Robert waved at him and pointed down. Beneath them there were indents in the rock face; a narrow decorative jutting, just enough to form a step in the middle of the wall. A hop, skip, and a jump down. Perfect, if they could do it fast, although Lysander could burn things at the speed of thought. That was hard to outrun, and the shape-shifter had to know they were there, what they were planning. Dean just hoped he was in a talkative mood.

He heard smacking sounds, flesh tearing. Miri looked very pale. He tapped her arm, mouthed, *Ready?* She nodded. He thumped his fingers three times against her arm, and she nodded again. She set her jaw, pressed her lips together.

Robert went down first, lean and graceful, swinging and hopping quietly off the ledge's decorative rim like a monkey from a tree. Miri was next; she was not as coordinated, but Dean breathlessly held her and Robert waited with his arms raised. He did not look at the dragon, and Dean gave him credit for that; his entire focus was on Miri. Once she was on the ground, Robert pushed her back against the wall. Dean slid over the edge, grappling for a hold. His feet found the ledge and he jumped, landing light.

He turned, pushing Miri toward the exit behind the waterfall. She moved, but her head turned in the other direction, eyes so wide and horrified that Dean could not help himself. He looked, and there ... there, more terrible things to fill his dreams, more awful visions. The dragon laughed, rolling on his back like a dog on a dead animal, squirming fat and large over Kevin's dismembered body. The archaeologist was little more than a smear in the stone, his torso broken and flattened by Lysander's writhing massive weight. The dragon's silver back rippled red. Ku-Ku sat in a corner, huddled in a ball. She was covered in blood, but did not seem injured.

Miri grabbed Dean's hand. She tugged on it, hard, and Lysander stilled, looking at them upside down like a cat caught in the middle of play.

"Mirabelle Lee," he said. "How soon we meet again. I believe you have something for me. Or ... not. My mate's servants lied to you, didn't they? Told you the jade was here, when in fact it has been taken far away. So the hunt continues. I think I am glad for that."

Robert stepped forward. He held his gun loose in his hand. He aimed it at the dragon and fired.

The bullet exploded in midair. Dean ducked, covering Miri. Robert flinched. Blood rolled down his arm. He tried to fire the gun again but it jammed. Lysander's eyes began to glow.

Robert whirled and looked at Dean.

"Run," he said.

Dean shoved Miri under the waterfall just as Robert's body burst into flame. The man threw back his head, screaming. Dean raised his gun, took aim, and pulled the trigger. His gun worked. The bullet entered Robert's head and he went down fast, limp, still burning.

Lysander began to laugh.

Dean ran.

Night. Downtown in Hong Kong with the flavor of fire in the air and the neon blazing bright over a concrete jungle filled with people and cars. Dean and Miri ran through the light, through the golden ambiance of the city, which glowed and glowed, bathing them in warmth, sinking beneath their skin and holding them tight like they held each other, hand to hand, and they did not stop, no matter the stares, no matter how their lungs and bodies hurt. They did not stop until they reached the sea.

Ren stood on the boat. Koni was with him. They gathered up Dean and Miri, shoving them belowdecks. Ren said, "I'm pushing off now," and then he ran back up and slammed the door behind him. Miri, standing in the hall, leaned hard against the wall and slid to the floor. She covered her face.

"What happened?" Koni asked. "Did you find the jade?"

Miri shook her head. Dean knelt and wrapped his arm over her shoulder. Tugging her against him, he pulled Miri down until she lay in his lap, curled in a ball. Koni quietly backed out of the hall.

"I'm going to move you," Dean murmured after a moment. "Are you ready, Miri?"

She nodded, and Dean slid gently out from under her. Trying not to groan as his back rebelled, he bent and scooped her from the floor. Miri sighed, pressing her face against his neck. Her cheeks were wet.

Dean took her to the room she had slept in earlier that day. He set her on the bed and lay beside her, curling tight, holding her with his legs and arms. He kissed the top of her head and said, "Go to sleep, *bao bei*. Rest your eyes."

"When I close my eyes I see fire. I see dragons and blood. I hear screaming," she said.

"It'll fade."

"No," she replied. "I don't think it will."

But after a time she fell asleep. A little later, so did Dean.

The next time he opened his eyes he was alone in the bed. He sat up, but Miri was not in the room. Panic filled him, even though he knew it was irrational. She was safe, she was surrounded and among friends—

He left the room at a fast walk, his mind reaching out ahead of him, searching for her trail, her thread. He saw nothing and hit the stairs at a run, slamming his way to the top deck, bursting through the door with a shout on his lips.

But he stopped fast, teetering on his toes, swallowing down his voice. Miri sat in a lawn chair with her legs propped up on an ice cooler. She wore a loose silk robe. Her hair was up in a bun. Red paper lanterns hung above her head, casting a warm glow. Her eyes were dark, hollow, but she had a smile on her face and a cup of tea in her hands. Ren and Koni sat around her, easy and relaxed. Dean knew it was an act. Guns might not be visible, but he knew they were there and within easy reach. Koni, no doubt, had his knives.

"Sorry I didn't wake you," Miri said. "But I needed air and you were still out."

"I cooked dumplings," Ren said, with an easy smile and sharp eyes that were anything but relaxed. "You want?"

"Sure." Dean touched Miri's shoulders and sat beside her on the deck. His pants and shirt were still damp from the waterfall; dampness he had left on Miri's bed where he'd fallen asleep. He did not care. Water didn't kill.

He looked, and in front of Miri on a small table was the jade artifact.

"I would really love to smash that thing," he said. Ren handed him a bowl and chopsticks; on the side was a small mix of soy sauce, vinegar, and sesame oil.

"I almost did," Miri said. "Threw it overboard, at any rate."

Koni cleared his throat. "Miri told us what happened."

Dean stuffed a dumpling into his mouth. "I should have seen it coming. Everything else has gone wrong. I feel like I've got a big sign on my back that says 'shoot me now, asshole.' "

"How do you think I feel?" Miri leaned back in her chair.

"Either way," Dean added, "we need to figure out our next move. Fast."

"Fast?" Ren said. "Koni and I will brainstorm, but the two of you are ready to collapse. You need more rest."

"I don't know if I can sleep," Miri said, and it hurt Dean to hear her voice so ragged. He set down his bowl and took her hand, holding it carefully as Ren and Koni looked politely away. Dean pressed his lips to her palm and then turned, trying to get his bearings. Behind him, the glittering city rose like a band of gems against the darkness. Breathtaking. He heard static in his head, felt the push against his body, this time like hunger. He felt the same from his friends, though in a lesser amount. Energy, power. Miri, he could see ... but he could not feel. Like Long Nu or Lysander, she was self-contained, which was new. She had never been like that as a child. Before the accident. He wondered what that meant. There had to be a connection. Everything, he was discovering, had a connection.

"Look," he said, turning Miri so she could see the city. "Look at that shine, sweetheart. It's still a beautiful world."

"Doesn't make it any less frightening."

"And when did fear ever set you back? What would Ni-Ni do at a time like this?"

"Charge on," she said immediately. "Keep straight, walk tall. Beat the crap out of someone with a frying pan."

"I got one of those," Ren said.

Miri cracked a smile. "Maybe I'll borrow it." And she looked at Dean and said, "Do you want to take another reading of the jade now?"

"Tomorrow," he said, suddenly weighed down by a terrible sense of inevitability. Lysander was nearby, as was Robert, and perhaps more of Kevin's men, still working for some unnamed woman who wanted the jade. All of them, trouble. It did not matter if they took the time to plan or sleep, took a day to play and act like fools. The future was here. The future had arrived. It was only waiting to reveal itself—in gun or fire—and nothing they did would be able to stop it.

So rest. Get your strength back. It's going to be the fight of your life and you have to be ready.

Miri did not protest as he took her tea and set it on the cooler. She did not say a word when he put her arms around his neck and picked her up from the chair. It felt good holding her close, being the one man in the world allowed to do so much for her. Even when they were children, Miri had only ever felt safe enough to ask one person for help. One person who was not her grandmother.

Koni and Ren watched. Dean gave them a look, a simple *watch our backs,* and the two men nodded.

He carried Miri downstairs and put her to bed.

* * *

Dean showered in Ren's bathroom, pulled on some sweats, studied himself in the mirror. His eyes were bloodshot, tired. He needed to shave. His chest looked exotic, but a little less so than if part of it had been glowing. The word was dark. All was safe.

He left the bathroom. Hesitated a moment before going to Miri's room. He knocked once, heard her voice, and opened the door. She lay on top of the covers. The robe was on the floor.

"Oh," he said.

"You are planning on sleeping in here tonight, aren't you?" she asked. Dean swallowed hard and shut the door behind him. He walked to the bed, staring at her naked body.

"Um," he said. Miri smiled.

"Take off your pants," she said. He did, and when she looked at him, when her gaze settled on his body and stayed there, it was hotter and sweeter than any touch he had received in the past twenty years.

"Nice," Miri murmured. She reached out and touched him. Light, easy, fingertips brushing, feathering. Dean looked down and watched. Clenched his jaw so tight he thought he was going to break teeth.

"You like that?" she asked, and he heard a note of breathlessness in her voice that made him want to shout. He wrapped his hand around her wrist and sat down on the bed. Kissed her palm. Touched his lips to her fingertips. Breathed a trail up her arm to her shoulder and that lovely delicate collarbone that tasted so damn good he thought he would die. Her throat was hot, her jaw soft; kissing her lips was like sinking into the softest, warmest bed on a cold, cold night, and he could not stop, could not bring himself to come up for air, because every time he came close he thought of fire and blood, and how if this moment would last, if he could make time stop and bend and stretch, the danger would pass away inside some untouchable future, and all that would be left was him, her, now, here, mouth and body, heart and heart.

"This is our first time," Miri said. Dean smiled against her mouth, running his hands around her sholders to draw her close. She leaned back, exposing her throat, and he kissed it, loved it, followed a sweet trail to her breasts. He had never touched them with his mouth, never hardly seen them but once or twice in his life, and it was good to explore, to savor, to practice all the things he had learned on the woman he loved.

He moved lower. Her hands trailed against his back, his neck, his hair, and his own fingers reached down to stroke a path over her leg, which curled, so sweet and hot, over his body. His heart felt good and he told her that, and she laughed, low, and said, "I love you, Dean Campbell. I love you so much."

He kissed her stomach. He kissed her thighs. Her breath caught and he kissed another kind of heat, tasting sweetness as he pushed deeper with his mouth. Miri moaned and the sound rolled and rolled through his stomach, pooling lower, and the more she cried out the harder he got.

He worked at her with his fingers and tongue until she came, calling out his name in a gasp that had her arching off the bed, putting him in a headlock with her legs. He wrestled with her for a moment and lost on purpose. She wanted him on his back. He was happy to oblige, and Miri pinned him with a lazy grin. She slid down his stomach, wet, and he loved the feel of it on his skin. Down she went, down some more, and then her mouth closed over him and it was his turn to beg, his turn to squeeze the covers between his fists, because her tongue was so hot it seared his skin, and the things she did ...

She stopped at the last moment and it was a good thing, though he wanted more and more and more than was possibly healthy for him, and he grabbed her hips, bouncing her, and said, "I hope to God you have some condoms, Miri, or we're going to have a fucking problem."

"Literally," she said, then leaned over—her breasts in his mouth—and pulled open the drawer of the nightstand.

"Ren," she said, holding up several packages.

"My name only," Dean growled, and she squirmed against him until he cried out. Miri laughed, low, and straddled him in the other direction. She rolled on the condom. Dean touched her back, her hair, reached out to touch her deeper. She squirmed again, sliding against him, and it was fun watching her get off on nothing but his hand, that his fingers pumping and twisting could make her move like that, like all she was made of was pleasure. He moved his hand faster and she gasped, jerking against him in an awkward rhythm that was hotter than hell, and he wanted to be inside her, wanted to pin her down and see her face while she felt those things, watch her glow and writhe beneath his body as he moved.

So he did that. He stopped and she grabbed his wrist, which made him laugh and say, "Easy there, tiger," and he sat up, pushed her off him, flipped her over with a twist, and then he was there, resting the tip of himself against her.

"You ready?" he asked, and it felt like the most important question of his life, because this was not just sex—this was history and love and loss and all that time apart. It was Miri beneath him. His best friend in all the world.

She did not answer with words. He saw it in her eyes,

in the way she looked at him, dreamy and lovely, with her lips parted and her skin golden and rosy, and she shifted her hips down, swallowing the very tip of him, and he did the rest, pushing so slow he thought his eyes might burst from the effort. Miri exhaled and he moved, swallowing her next breath with a kiss.

He kissed and moved and rocked and thrust and clutched her close with his hands, cradled tight as he was within her legs, and he watched her face and said her name, and she smiled and laughed and moaned, until he felt her body quicken around him in a shuddering burst that had her jerking in his arms, throwing herself back, and he moved, on a whim, faster and faster, his own pressure building, and Miri kept up—oh God, did she keep up!—until finally he was the one lagging and he flipped over again, this time on his back, losing her for only a moment until she buried him in herself, hard, on top of him, making him cry out, and it wasn't long before she did the same, and finally, finally, Dean let himself go.

And it was really, really good.

He fell asleep for a while, but when he woke up, Miri had her eyes open and was staring at his face.

"Hey," he murmured, still drowsy. His body felt heavy.

"Mrrrow," she said, and raked her nails down his chest. He woke up a little more.

"You wanna go again?" he asked, and she laughed, wrapping a leg around him.

"Later. Maybe sooner rather than later. I want to talk first."

"Oh boy."

She slugged him on the shoulder. "Stop."

"Gee, hitting now. You must be up for a wrestle."

"Dean."

He sighed, smiling, and settled back down on the bed. Miri tucked herself under his arm and said, "It's about what happened tonight. Not with us. Earlier. Underground."

"My afterglow just died. Thanks, Miri."

"Before that," she said sternly. "When I was touching that dead body."

He nodded. "You almost fell."

"I had a vision. Mountains. A lake with a land mass or something that looked like a dragon, hills and forests all around. I think I know that place. I didn't really remember it until just a couple of minutes ago."

"You had sex with me and it inspired you to think of land masses. Again, thank you."

"Can't you be serious about this?"

"I just made some totally righteous love to the woman of my dreams. I think I should be allowed to celebrate."

Miri grinned. "If you liked it that much, the sooner we finish this conversation, the sooner we can start making love all over again."

Dean reached out to the nightstand and pulled out another condom. He reached under the covers. "So talk. I'll be ready in a minute."

Miri burst out laughing. "Get your hand out of there, mister. Put it where I can see it."

"Which 'it' are you referring to?"

"Dean!"

"Okay, okay." He held up his hands. "Talk."

She gave him a look, but he stayed silent, concentrating, and she said, "I can't be entirely sure, but I think the place I saw in my vision is Jiuzhaigou. It's in Sichuan."

"Do you think that's where the jade has been hidden?"

Miri hesitated. "This is going to sound stupid."

"Think about who you're talking to."

A scowl touched her mouth. "It's nothing but a feeling, Dean. A hunch. Maybe more than a hunch. I just … know that's the place. The history of the region lends itself to the idea, too. Did you know that the Baima people believe in devils and demons? They have this ancient 'folk devil dance,' almost six thousand years old, one of the oldest of its kind to still be practiced. They wear masks of animals during the ceremony. There used to be over thirty kinds, but the only ones that remain include phoenix, sculpture—like a stone animal—dragon, tiger, lion, bear … and demon. Another kind of demon. A good kind, I guess."

"Shit," Dean said. "I've been hanging around weirdos for too long. That actually makes sense."

"Shape-shifters, demons, a people who still venerate some ancient balance? Given what we know, I'd say it's a tradition with a basis in absolute reality."

"I trust that. Okay, then. We'll go there."

"I could be wrong."

"Don't start second-guessing yourself. Besides, for all we know you're psychic. After all, everyone who's been chasing us has got some kind of more-than-human powers, and they're not after you just 'cause you're hotter 'n hell."

"And if they were?"

"You'd still be in bed with me."

"Confident."

"We just made love. I could walk on air if I wanted to."

She laughed, and he pulled her close and tight; her body felt like his body, and she rose and fell with his breath, so warm and sweet.

"We wasted so much time," he said.

"We didn't have a choice," she murmured. "All our choice was taken from us. It was a … conspiracy of fate."

"Kind of like finding each other again, after all these years."

Miri pressed her cheek against his chest. "I never saw this coming, Dean. Never, in my wildest dreams. Though I did think of you. Often. Dreamed of you, too."

"I dreamed of you," he said quietly, and kissed the top of her head.

She smiled. "I think I am ready, my love slave. Prepare. We have talked enough."

"Finally." Dean shook his head. "I was fit to burst. All that heavy talk made me hard as a rock."

"I think that was my fault, actually. My hand wandered."

"I wondered who that was. I was getting a little worried."

"You hid it well," she said, and rolled on the condom. She rolled onto her back, too, and stretched her arms over her head. "You are prepared. You may take me now."

He began to kiss her and she said, "No. I really mean it, Dean. Take me."

"Oh." He settled on top of her, sliding in with an ease that shocked him. She really was ready.

But she smiled, wriggling about, and in a high sweet voice said, "Dean? Are you in yet?"

"Oh God. Don't do this to me."

Miri laughed, and slapped his ass. "Go on now, cowboy. Start moving."

"I am," he growled.

She laughed harder, wrapping her legs around his waist, digging her heels into the small of his back. "You are so easy."

"Tell me about it," he muttered. "I only waited thirty-six years before having sex with you."

"You're not done yet," Miri said.

"You better hope not. I haven't done this much in a

long time. I could be a one-shot man, if you get my drift."

"No stamina is the price of old age, Dean. That's okay. I'm all about quality over quantity."

But he managed to provide both, again and again, for the rest of the night.

Chapter Sixteen

In the predawn light of the Hong Kong morning, with Ren's boat moored on the other side of Victoria Harbor on the edge of Kowloon, Miri watched Dean take the jade artifact in his hands and open his mind.

She was, of course, deeply interested in what, if anything, he would find, but she was also recovering from being a well- and hard-loved woman, and it was difficult to focus completely on anything serious when looking at Dean's shirtless body made her want to roll around like a kitten and make funny squeaky noises.

She wore the red silk robe. A breeze stirred her loose hair, warm and humid, but with enough of the nighttime cool to be pleasant on her tingling body. Behind Dean, the distant lights of Hong Kong rose like a crowd of stars, a glittering rainbow against dusky green mountains shrouded in mist. A bit of moon still clung to the sky. It was a lovely morning.

Koni appeared and sat down. He held two cups of tea, and passed her one of them. She sniffed before drinking and inhaled jasmine. Perfect.

"You look relaxed," he said, in a voice that was a little too mild. Miri caught the edge of his grin and blushed.

"Sorry," he said, which he very clearly was not. He drummed his fingers on the arm of his chair, but made no other attempt at conversation.

Dean opened his eyes. "All I see is water. A lake. The bluest lake I've ever seen in my life. There are trees all around it. I can't tell if it's past or present."

"I wonder why you didn't see that before?"

"And why I was pulled to Hong Kong for nothing but a body? That's doesn't make sense. I was just sure the jade was there."

"It could have been recently moved," Miri said. "It wouldn't have been difficult for anyone who knew the layout of the place."

"If it was moved, Kevin and Ku-Ku weren't the ones who did it. If Lysander can read minds, he would have known immediately where the second piece is."

"I don't know the people you're talking about," Koni said, "but don't rule out the possibility that they're good at shielding themselves from telepaths."

"How would a person do that?" Miri asked, remembering her own encounter with the dragon. "How do you protect yourself against someone who can look into your thoughts?"

"It's not easy," Dean said. "I sure as hell can't do it."

"Neither can I," Koni said. "But I just don't think it's wise to rule out the possibility."

"Well, you don't have to worry about Kevin," Miri said. "And Ku-Ku …"

She was probably dead. Miri did not want to think about it, how she had run without even trying to help the girl. All for one, and one for one—no second thoughts; no hesitation. Not that Miri thought Ku-Ku would have done anything different, but Miri had high standards for herself. Standards that had failed miserably when put to the test.

And then, of course, there was Robert …

I thought you didn't care, she told herself, but that was a lie. She cared a little. Robert was dangerous, and Robert was bad—but not all bad. Not entirely.

"So the lake," Dean said. "I feel a pull to the west. Do you still think it's the place you mentioned?"

"Jiuzhaigou," Miri said. "Like you said, it's a start."

Koni grunted. "Beautiful area. I have some cousins there."

"You can have a family reunion," Dean snapped. "Because I get the stinkin' feeling that's where we're headed."

"Cheer up," Miri said. "Just think about how lucky you are to have a life where you can combine natural scenic wonders with unremitting death and destruction, all in one trip."

"She's right," Koni said. "That's a fantastic opportunity."

Dean sighed. Behind them, a door slammed. Ren leaped onto the deck, hair standing straight up, clad in cutoffs and little else. His eyes were bloodshot.

"Rough night?" Koni asked.

Silence. Nothing but the rocking of the boat and the gulls and the faraway moan of barge horns. Miri clutched her tea cup, ignoring the scalding heat against her palm as Ren stared and stared at Dean, then tore away his gaze to look at her. His mouth was nothing but a hard white line.

"What?" she asked, uneasy. "Why are you looking at me like that?"

"Ren," Dean said.

"I'm sorry," he said. "I'm so sorry. It was an accident. I didn't mean to look."

"What are you talking about?" Miri asked. "What the hell does that mean?"

Dean stood. Behind him the sky was turning golden with the dawn, a sheer light softened and pampered by gentle layers of peach and rose and cream. Blue arced, clouds raced; the city took on a different kind of glittering light, perched on the edge of a deepening green; the sea. But all that caught Miri's heart was the man in front of her, with his blond hair bright as his eyes, sharp and hard like the slant of his mouth.

"What did you see?" he asked Ren.

"Your dreams," Ren said. His skin glistened with sweat; muscles flexed beneath his smooth golden skin. "Your dreams are not right, Dean. They're not dreams at all. Miri is the same."

She stood. She had to. There was something is his voice that made her need that steadiness, the illusion of control and grounding that her feet could give her. Moving with the boat, swaying.

My body, my mind, my thoughts—

"Tell me what that means," she said, and Dean edged near, reaching for her hand.

"Memories," Ren said. "In both your heads at night, what you think are dreams. They're *memories*. Extraordinary memories."

Dean stepped forward. "Don't bullshit me. The things I see—"

"Are not what you think they are. They're not just dreams."

There was no way to call him a liar. Miri did not even consider the possibility. There was too much conviction in his gaze. Koni rose from his chair. Golden light streamed from his eyes, flowing down his cheeks like tears; in its path, darkness. Feathers that pressed and faded like fleeting shadows. He looked ready to fight—or take flight.

Magic. So much magic.

"How can you can say these things?" Miri said to Ren. "How can you see our dreams?"

"How can Dean hold a kid's teddy bear and find her halfway around the world? How can Koni turn into a crow?" Ren shook his head. "Each of us is different, Dr. Lee. And based on what I saw, you've got your own secrets, things even you don't know about."

"Then you better tell me," she said. "Right now."

Ren closed his eyes; the rising sun made his skin glow. The air suddenly felt too hot, all the cool of night passing away as humidity crawled across Miri's body. Silk stuck to her back. It was hard to breathe.

"Someone's taken your memories," Ren said. "Someone's buried down both your lives, and whoever did it was so good, the only way you've been able to access anything is through your subconscious."

"No," Dean said. "No. Roland's been in my head, man. He would have found any tampering."

"Not this," Ren said. "I told you, this is good work. The only reason I found it is that I know dreams."

Dean sat down hard, dragging Miri into his lap. She did not protest; his body was too tense. She thought he needed someone to hold, and frankly, she felt the same. She was not entirely sure what Ren was saying; his words were clear, but the meaning was too strange. Tampering? Memories instead of dreams? And just what *had* she been dreaming last night?

Bones. Sand. Chains. Darkness in my mouth, swallowing my heart. Something cold beneath my back, all over my body. Stone. Water. No clothes and somewhere nearby a man on the ground, a man buried in iron.

"Ren," Miri said. "There's no way the dreams I had last night could be memories. No way. I've managed to accept a lot over the past couple of days, but that's too much. I know my life. I *remember* my life."

"So do I," Dean said, but there was a thread of doubt in his voice, and Miri craned around to look at him.

"You think it's true," she said.

Dean hesitated. "I don't know."

Ren threw himself down into the chair Miri had vacated. He held out his hand and Koni gave him his tea. He swallowed it down in one long gulp and then tossed the cup back to the other man. His eyes were still bloodshot, but clear, focused. "Believe me or not, I don't care. But I'll tell you this. If I'm not right, then there's still something strange going on, especially between the two of you. You have the same dreams, man. *You have the same dreams.*"

Miri felt sick to her stomach. Again, she looked at Dean, and found him staring at her.

"There's a circle," he said softly, as though speaking just to her, as though no one else in the world existed but the two of them. And maybe, Miri thought, maybe that was true.

"Sand," she said. "Bones."

"Something holding me down. And nearby a woman, and she's crying. She's crying so hard it makes my heart break. And I have to go to her. I have to help her."

"But there is a darkness," Miri breathed, and her throat hurt, her eyes burned, and she closed her eyes against Dean's changing expression, pressing her forehead against his neck.

You thought there was nothing left to surprise you and that anything else could be accepted, that you could ride out the craziness. But this, now?

She felt Dean's hands push into her hair, fingers warm against her scalp. He pressed his lips to her forehead and said, "So we have the same dreams. You say that it's memory. Dude, the last time Miri and I were together was when we were kids. We got separated at sixteen, and before that? Nothing like this shit happened.

There's no way. We lived in the fucking middle of Philly. No sand. No circles. No people with chains."

"I can't explain it," Ren said. "All I know is that I left my body for a swim last night, and got sucked in hard by your heads. That doesn't happen often, man."

Miri drew in a ragged breath. "I've had this dream for a while now, Dean. It's been more intense lately, but even when I was little, there was always the darkness."

"I remember," he said, and she knew he would, because the shadows had always crept upon her in the night, more oppressive than simple air, and once upon a time she had told him this, confessed, and he had stayed the night, sleeping on the floor beside her bed. Keeping guard while she rested.

"Didn't see anything," Dean had told her the next morning, the grimmest and most hollow-eyed ten-year-old she had ever met. "But don't worry, Miri. I still believe you."

He had always believed her. Trusted her.

"Nothing's changed," Miri said, looking up and staring at the men. "We still need to find the last piece of jade. I think if we do, the rest will fall into place. We'll find how … how we fit into this."

"You think it's related?" Koni asked.

"Can't take anything for granted," Dean said. "Not after everything that's happened."

"But that still doesn't explain how," Ren said. "Or why."

Miri pulled back just far enough to look into Dean's eyes. He matched her gaze, and it was no longer like the old times, but instead something new, something she had never seen before—and she kissed him hard, biting his lip, dragging him with her as she slid off his lap and forced him to stand. And when he was on his feet, his hands hot on her body—so much heat, the world on fire—she broke off the kiss and said, "Let's finish this, Dean. I want to finish this now. I don't want to waste any more time."

Not on this. Not when we have so much more to do with our lives.

And he said, "Yes."

Hong Kong's airspace, much like its economy, operated under different regulations from the rest of Mainland China, which ruled out the use of the private jet. Miri was disappointed by that. She was in a much better mood to appreciate luxury, given the future of violence looming over her head.

They left Ren behind in Hong Kong. He offered to come along—almost insisted—but Dean refused. Too much risk. And besides, there were other ways for him to follow that did not involve the body.

Miri, Koni, and Dean flew into Chengdu early that afternoon on an Air China flight. They had to leave their weapons behind—all their firepower gone, though Miri thought it just as well. Bullets had been useless thus far, and were nothing more than an invitation for someone innocent to get hurt.

Chengdu, besides being the capital of Sichuan Province, was also an industrial city, and it showed. Miri knew for a fact that its main industries covered everything from machinery to chemicals to agriculture, but the sky was thick enough with smog that she thought, perhaps, the production of edible organics had taken second fiddle to other processing industries.

Koni left them almost immediately after they stepped through the airport's massive sliding doors. He tossed a small duffel to Dean, and then, much to Miri's shock, reached down and hugged her.

"I'll be around," he said quietly. "Don't you worry, Miri."

"That's my line," Dean said, but he said it with a

smile, and Koni grabbed his hand and pulled him in, too, crushing her between them both.

And then he let go and without a word or glance, stalked away, tattooed arms swinging, hands clenched into fists.

"That's a first," Dean said. "He usually shits on the windshield as a sign of affection."

"You and your friends," Miri replied, but there was a warmth in her heart as she watched Koni leave, a warmth that she felt for Ren, and whoever else had taken care of Dean, who had given him a home that she could so clearly see meant the world to him. She did not doubt he loved her, but Dirk & Steele had given him something she had not been able to, and that was a mission, a sense of destiny and purpose and focus, and that was a beautiful thing.

Even if she did not entirely trust them.

There was a car waiting, hired by Ren. The driver was a small compact man with smoke pouring out of his nose and mouth. He called himself by an English name: Steven. Miri thought if it had just been her, he would have used a different moniker, something traditional— but Dean was clearly foreign, and so it was a foreign name to make it easy on the "simple" Westerner, Steven gave Dean a box. A gift from Ben. Inside was a gun and holster.

It was a ten-hour drive to Jiuzhaigou, on a narrow winding road through the mountains of northern and central Sichuan. There was a local airport, a way to get to the park faster, but Dean did not want to fly. He wanted to take time, with the jade in hand, and test the lines of energy in his head as they traveled. Make sure they were going in the right direction. Build and strengthen the connection. Perhaps, even, discover more information. Miri hoped he would. She wondered, too, if she should not handle the stone herself, but held herself back. She was afraid of what she would see, of what would happen, and for once, she let that fear guide her.

The mountain road was narrow, but heavily trafficked with tourist buses, compact cars, and the occasional donkey pulling a cart. Steven enjoyed passing the buses while oncoming traffic rushed directly at them—playing games of chicken, which always had one or two cars clinging to the edge of cliff faces, dancing air on brinks of oblivion. Higher and higher they climbed, surrounded by the relics of ancient walls and temples perched on mountaintops—and at the bottom, the wide river, cutting a ribbon through the land. Villages perched precariously; Miri saw fields hacked out of mountainsides, planted with corn and wheat and fruit trees. Only one water source: the river. Women trudged up the steep mountain paths from river to field, yokes on their shoulders. Some children followed, hauling the same burdens, the same weights; tiny girls with rosy cheeks, no older than five or six, bearing it all and staggering.

They traveled through towns, the occasional small city—houses tucked into hills. The bumpy road passed through plateaus, green places of easier living where fields of sunflowers, the largest she had ever seen, pushed and pushed skyward like crowns of gold, and the houses clustered with their roofs shining under glimpses of sun, shining like the river, which still wound and pulsed, diverging into irrigation ditches planted thick with the grain fields. They stopped, once, at a lonely restaurant. The low wooden building had a friendly feel, with plastic tablecloths and a courtyard full of trees. Fresh fruit for sale: local white peaches and nectarines, plums and grapes that had to be peeled before eaten. Koni, though they kept an eye out for him, did not make an appearance.

They stopped at a hotel just before dark, with still another five hours to go. It was a nice place, a little overdone with marble floors and thick creamy pillars, but it was clean and modern and had a restaurant. Nice views, too, of the gloomy green mountains. It advertised itself as run by locals, but while the girls working the front desk were surrounded by Tibetan kitsch, the manager who came out spoke his Mandarin with a distinct Taiwanese accent. Still, it seemed nice enough, and at least it was a place to rest.

Later that night, as Miri lay in Dean's arms, she pressed her cheek against his chest, listening to his heartbeat, and asked, "How do you explain us? How do you explain why we feel the way we do? Still, after all this time?"

It took him a long while to answer. So long, in fact, that at first she thought he was asleep. But then he sighed and pulled her closer.

"It's the kind of thing that's hard to talk about, Miri. But the way I see it, the best way I can say it, is that some people have friends and it doesn't mean much. You hang out, you do stuff, and maybe you think it'll last, but distance tells. A little bit of time, and you stop thinking about that person. They're just a memory, sometimes not even a good one, and after a while you forget everything except a name, and then maybe even that." He stopped, rolling them over so that he propped himself up on his elbow to look into her face. The room was dark, his eyes nothing but shadows, but she felt the gentleness of his touch as he stroked her face, the quiet heat of his skin as he rested his finger against her neck. She touched his hand, holding it, and in a soft voice Dean said, "But sometimes it's different,

Miri. Sometimes you find a friend that gets under your skin so you can't think how you lived without her. You can't imagine a life without this person because it's like losing an arm, and if you do lose that person, it's the same as cutting off a piece of you. You still feel the ghost pains, the echo. You still feel that presence to the point you turn around to look for it, talk to it, but hey, no go, 'cause she's not there. And you think, *fuck*. How am I going to live the rest of my life like this? How in the hell, when the part you need so bad is gone?"

Dean stopped. Miri held her breath. Finally, he said, "When I thought you died, it wasn't like losing a limb. It was like losing a whole fucking body and I was just this ghost, cruising along in the world. It got better. I won't lie to you about that. I didn't stop grieving, but I did remember who I was again. I never fell in love, though."

"That's a long time to not have love."

"I fooled around. Did some stupid shit."

"What kind of shit?" Miri asked, because he stopped so abruptly she had a feeling it was something pretty embarrassing. "Not drugs or anything, right?"

"No," he said, and she heard the scowl in his voice. "It's just … I had a lot of sex. I did it because I thought it would make me feel better—but it just made it worse. I kept thinking about you, which after a while felt pretty sick, because first you were dead, and second, I kept remembering you at sixteen. Which, when you hit a certain age, just seems wrong. So I stopped. Sleeping with women, that is. I just … didn't do it anymore. Which, uh, didn't mean I lost my drive. I was still, um—"

"You don't have to reassure me," Miri said dryly. "I am completely convinced of your manliness."

He grinned, though the smile faded. "Yeah? I put on

a good act. All my friends think that sex is the only thing on my mind."

"Isn't it?"

"Well … yeah. But the point is they got no idea I haven't been with anyone in years."

"Years," Miri said. "How many years?"

"A lot," he said, somewhat warily.

"My God," she said. "You went celibate because of me. You were a total monk."

"A monk with *Playboys*, Cinemax, and nightly dates with the magic fingers. But yeah, I basically kept it private."

"Huh," Miri said. "I don't think I was quite as extreme."

Dean looked mildly uncomfortable. "I don't need to hear this. Really."

"I did think of you the few times I had sex, so I suppose—"

"Miri," Dean interrupted.

"Well, *you* said you slept around. And besides, what I got from those men wasn't any picnic."

Dean grunted. "That almost bothers me more."

"At least you're consistent."

"Hey. I never said I was perfect."

"Ah," she replied. "But you are perfect for me."

He kissed her, and they spent the next half hour wrestling on the bed, making out in random heated spurts that left Miri breathless and tingly.

"Miri," Dean said, during a short break when his hands remained still and his mouth was not busy. "After all this is over, I want to get married. I want to make this permanent."

She smiled. "You realize, don't you, that I would stay with you for the rest of my life, regardless of any marriage contract?"

"I don't care. I want it legal, I want it on paper, I want it to be legitimate and traditional and all that shit. I want the whole fucking world to say, hell yeah, those two are hitched."

"You're so romantic."

"It's only going to get worse from here on out," Dean said, and pulled her in tight for a hard kiss.

Chapter Seventeen

Miri dreamed of darkness that night, a dark that was not a simple and unaffected night, but something heavier, something living that moved with purpose and skill and grave intent. She could not struggle, could not open her mouth to scream, and in her dream the darkness settled upon her chest, peeled back her glowing skin to feed.

She woke up. Stared at the ceiling, trying to calm her heart, to breathe through her nose so she would not disturb Dean. He lay beside her, passed out. Miri, watching his face, carefully edged out from under the covers and walked through the shadows into the bathroom. She closed the door and turned on the light. Did her business, washed her hands. But when she looked at herself in the mirror, she could not move. For a moment it was like looking at a stranger.

And then, even more so—for a brief moment her reflection seemed to waver, the world falling away as her face disappeared in the glass, replaced by another woman with the same eyes, but with different skin and hair. Lips moved—words—and behind her, Miri saw a snowcapped mountain—lights, rippling iridescent.

On her chest, between her breasts, a shadow. A series of words, like the ones on the jade.

Miri blinked—the vision snapped, faded—and suddenly she was in the bathroom again and the world was normal.

No such thing as normal, she thought, still staring at the mirror as a great and terrible dread filled her body, prickling her skin with heat. *Not anymore.* She almost ran from the bathroom, but forced herself to stay put. If she ran now in fear, she knew she would keep running, and now was not the time to chicken out. No matter how weird or unsettling her life was.

Breathe, she told herself, and she did, slow and deep, still looking at the mirror, still focused, body alive with fear, and her vision narrowed on the skin between her breasts. She imagined those words from her vision and for a moment saw them again, so clear she touched herself. The moment she did the words disappeared, but she pressed even harder and imagined lines, a ridge, curving and twisting.

Stupid. Getting caught up. This is nothing, just your imagination. You've been seeing so much crazy stuff for the past couple of days, your mind is running on overdrive.

It made perfect sense, but Miri could not turn away from looking at herself, and she wished suddenly that she could just peel up her skin, tear it apart, because underneath, underneath that layer of flesh—

Miri dug her nails into her body, pressing as hard as she could. Outside the bathroom, she heard movement. Dean called her name. Soft at first, and then louder as he stood outside the bathroom. Miri ignored him, still digging with her nails, raking—so hard she made terrible welts, red marks that seemed like some kind of reminder, hypnotic and strange.

"Miri?" Dean said, voice muffled. "Why won't you answer me?"

She could not answer because she could not speak. The doorknob rattled and Dean entered the bathroom. He did not say anything for a moment—simply stared—and then he was there, pressed up against her body, holding down her hand as she tried to mark herself again.

"No," he breathed. "No, *bao bei*. Stop."

"There's something there," she said, and her voice sounded faraway. "Like what you have. Beneath the skin. I can feel it, Dean."

"Okay," he said, still holding her. "I believe you. But this isn't right. You have to stop. Miri, *listen to me*."

And she listened, and it was like having a veil torn away, or lines cut. She staggered and Dean caught her, cradling her against his body. He carried her back to the bed and laid her down, crawling close. He did not turn on the light, but pressed his warm hand between her breasts.

"It hurts," she murmured.

"Why did you do it?"

Miri shut her eyes. "My reflection in the mirror ... I was different. It was me, Dean, but my face belonged to someone else and there were mountains behind me. Lights. Words on my chest. I could see them so clearly."

Dean said nothing. He pressed his lips against the welts, and wrapped her up tight in his arms and legs until her heart calmed and all around her body, the only thing she could feel was him, holding her, taking care with that gentle ease that was so like him. Heart of gold.

"We are going to get through this," he whispered in her ear. "But you can't scare me like that again. You have to promise me, Miri. Don't hurt yourself."

"I didn't mean to." So surreal, having to say that. She was a rational woman, practical. Not prone to wild fits.

"I know," he said, and then, softer, "I won't live without you again, Miri. I won't do it."

"Dean."

"No. I won't kill myself. It's not like that. But live? Live for any length of time? I wouldn't last long, babe. It would just be me and my shadow, and then just my shadow, and then … zip. Gone. I don't have enough heart left inside me to come back. I lost most of it the first time around, and a man can only pretend to be happy for so long."

Her throat hurt. She turned in his arms and kissed his mouth. Dean let her pull away only far enough to turn her head, and they lay cheek to cheek, sharing breath and heartbeats. Miri remembered a little boy, she remembered a young man, she remembered grief and memory and years of dreams, and she thought, *I'm going to keep this. I'm not going to let go.*

Not ever. But her throat would not work, and she could not find the words to tell him. All she had was her body. Her very willing heart and body.

And that was more than enough.

They entered Jiuzhaigou early the next afternoon, after a ride through grasslands tumbling high among purple ice-capped mountains, stark peaks that inspired such feelings of awe and thrill that for a time, Miri forgot her troubles and could not help but imagine herself a climber, a trekker, another kind of adventurer, braving the wilds in search of archaeological treasures. She had no doubt that some lost civilization, extinct or not, lived in that virgin wilderness; the world was still large enough for mystery. Mysteries of all kinds and shapes and forms. It felt like home.

Nomads had their camps along the road; colorful

striped tents that reminded Miri of the circus, and which dotted the landscape like waving flowers. Cattle grazed. Men roamed on horseback, tall and dark and lean, and Miri thought they looked so handsome dirty, she could not imagine how fantastic they might look if they were clean.

The road curved away from the grassland into lower ground, the Minshan Mountains, within which Jiuzhaigou was tucked deep and away like a jewel of pine and straw grass valleys. Miri caught distant glimpses of it through breaks in the tree line as their car made the slow and curving descent.

"Reminds me of Montana," Dean said.

"Just wait," Miri said, trying to hide her excitement. "Just you wait."

He had to wait quite some time. The road leading to Jiuzhaigou was rather crowded with hotels, and at the monument itself, tour buses and cars packed the extremely large parking lot, which was framed by mountains and wild cloud-covered hills.

"They only let in a certain number of people every day," Miri told him, as they made the trek to the ticket counter. "And technically, you're supposed to be out of the park by five-thirty. No camping, no staying overnight. No wandering away from the marked paths."

"Technically?"

Miri smiled. "Some of the villages inside the park offer rooms. It's hush-hush. The only reason I found out is that Owen knows some of the ladies who live there, and they were more than willing to earn some extra cash. We stay with them, we can sneak out. Do what we have to do. We may not even have to sneak. They know I'm an archaeologist. They think it makes me more qualified to do the wilderness thing on my own."

"Girl power rocks," Dean said, and dodged a light blow to his arm.

The quota for the day had not been met, so Dean and Miri walked through a metal swinging gate to the lines waiting for buses. It did not take all that long to get a ride, and Miri and Dean soon found themselves bumping along a narrow road, carried past ribbons of water that were the colors of pure emerald and turquoise, glittering clear as crystal as the sun peaked occasionally through the pearly clouds.

"This place is beautiful," he said, and then, in a voice only she could hear, "The jade is so close I can practically feel my teeth vibrating."

"Good," she said. "That means my hunch may not be far wrong."

"Though we were wrong last time."

"It was the body," Miri said. "For some reason you had a strong connection with that man."

Twenty minutes later, Miri made them get off the bus at a spot in front of Huohahai, the Sparkling Lake. Around them tourists mingled, taking photos, oohing and aahing over the deep turquoise surface that was a color so rich and pure, it was almost a taste in Miri's mouth: juicy and cool. The lake was quite large, surrounded by pine and wild grass. No one but locals were allowed near its edge, but Miri saw a few intrepid souls trying to creep off the boardwalk.

A low stone wall bordered the road. As Miri and Dean walked up to it, she pointed at the water. "Take a look at the middle of the lake, Dean. You see that yellowish stuff? Tell me what it resembles."

It took him some time, but when he finally made the connection, a small sound escaped him. Miri smiled.

"I see a dragon," he said.

"It's called the Lying Dragon," Miri told him. "It sits in about sixty feet of water, and when the winds come down from the mountain and the lake surface ripples, it looks like its stretching itself. And when the wind is really strong … well, wait."

Several minutes later a powerful breeze swept over them, and though it died quickly, more followed until the surface of the lake whipped up into frenzy—and through the clear water, the dragon appeared to shake its head and wag its tail. It was a powerful illusion, and had Miri not been recently encountering the fantastic, she would have chalked it up to a curiosity of nature, and nothing more.

But things had changed.

"I saw this exact place in my vision," Miri said. "It means something."

"Yes," he said. "I saw this lake, too, but just not with the dragon. The jade is nearby, but I can't tell if it's in the water. I hope to God it's not."

"You may be going for a swim tonight, handsome."

"That water is going to be cold, Miri."

"No pain, no gain."

They took a bus to one of the nine native Tibetan villages inside the park. Tall posts stood near the borders of village and wilderness, red and blue and yellow flags cut like gigantic ribbons, hanging and fluttering from tassels dyed in similar colors. Near the rivers and waterfalls, other lines had been hung with flags, lovely in the sharp and constant breeze. In the water itself, Tibetan prayer wheels turned in the current. It was summer, but the air was still comfortably cool. Miri had to remind herself that they were not so distant from glaciers.

Miri led Dean to a small home selling food: buns and sodas and other snacks. An old woman stood out front, dressed in navy blue robes. Silver dangled from her ears. She had bright clear eyes and a smile to die for, which she used on Miri when she finally noticed her.

It was easy enough to get a room; not many visitors realized local stays were possible, and upstairs in her home the old woman pulled aside a curtain, revealing a relatively clean bed tucked within a small alcove. She gave Dean a sly look, took Miri's money, and then scampered off.

"I just know that lady has a dirty mind," Dean said.

"It can't be as dirty as yours," Miri replied.

They spent the rest of the day exploring, Miri following Dean as he traveled a path of his own making, exploring the vibrations of the jade. They passed along boardwalks that led through marshes and crystalline streams, walked around waters so blue she wanted to fall into them and make her skin the same color. They passed Pearl Shoal, a stream that splashed water about like millions of bouncing silver pearls, and later, Hanging Dagger Spring, which overlooked Swan Lake and resembled a dagger cutting the sky. Waters rushed from the peak, creating a waterfall almost a thousand feet tall.

Occasionally during their walk, Dean's chest burned. He did not have to tell her. She saw him rub himself. She imagined it glowing, soft, out of sight.

"Lysander?" she asked him, feeling the pit of her stomach drop away as she remembered the scene in that chamber: the white body covered in blood, Kevin torn apart, and that pitiless voice that had shaken down her bones like thunder.

"Maybe something else," he said, though he was clearly doubtful. "It doesn't happen around regular people. Not even all shape-shifters. But I felt it with Robert, Lysander, Bai Shen …"

"What do they all have in common?"

"Magic, I assume."

Miri frowned. "Robert had magic done to him. But Lysander? He's a shape-shifter. And yes, he can set people on fire, but …"

"Magic," Dean said again. "Maybe he can do it. Or maybe we're missing out on some other clues, and it's something else entirely. There isn't any good way to find out."

"Not until it's too late," Miri muttered. "I'm scared, Dean. I admit it. I'm terrified."

"I am, too," Dean said quietly, and kissed the top of her head. Miri's skin tingled, but not from his lips. She rubbed her arms and Dean frowned.

"You're cold," he said. "I feel it, too."

There was also a burning sensation in her chest. Pain. *You hurt yourself last night. That's why.*

But it felt different, as though the heat and discomfort were pushing up through her body. She remembered the dead woman with the jade in her chest, and though she did not understand what was happening to her, she felt on a deeper level some kinship, some sense of why the jade had been placed into that spot. The significance was very real.

A crow cawed above their heads. Miri looked up and saw a large black bird winging down. She glimpsed others, very high in the sky, but they kept their distance. Dean held up his hand; the crow settled on it, flapping its wings to balance. Golden eyes glowed.

"I was beginning to wonder," Dean said. "Slow ass. You were probably picking up chicks on the way in."

The crow bit his hand. Dean, swearing, tossed him back up into the sky. Miri laughed, but it was short-lived.

"Come on," she said. "Let's go back to the village and rest. We're going to have a long night."

But when they arrived at the small home, with the mists rolling in and the sun fading into a deeper chill, it was difficult to sleep. There were too many sounds, the bed uncomfortable—and she wanted suddenly to be anywhere but here. Hiding sounded good. Any kind of hiding, as long as it kept her away from craziness. Danger.

She said as much to Dean, and his only reply was "I

love you, Miri." And that, she found, was enough to calm her. She settled into sleep, and chased herself into dreams.

Ren was waiting for them, golden and shining, with a softness to his edges made it seem like she was looking at him through a filter or soft focus lense. His presence was unexpected—as was Dean's, whose body looked much the same, like some cheesy soap opera dreamscape of the Man She Loved. At first Miri thought they were all still awake, but the background was different—more woods, shadows—and she was lucid enough to resign herself to the fact that not even her sleep was sacred anymore.

"This better be good," Dean said.

"I think I found a way to access more of those dreams," Ren said. "I can't fix your memories, but I can help you ride your unconscious all the way down to the root, which might be enough to let you see everything else that's been taken from you."

"And if it's not?" he asked.

"What do we have to lose?" Miri said to him. "And besides, I want to know if what we're really seeing in our heads is the same thing. We'll be doing this together, right?"

"I'll provide the link," Ren said. "You'll have access to each other's dreams at the same time."

He reached for their hands. Dean first, and then Miri. As soon as he touched her, even the dreamworld slipped away, and she felt herself falling and falling. She kept expecting to hit ground, but it never happened; like Alice in that damn rabbit hole, she could see things around her as she moved—or maybe it was the world moving, and she was standing still—but nonetheless there were glimpses of her life, tiny picture shows, and she realized just how good it had really been. So much wonderful in her life, and all the bad that happened was just another stepping stone. She had to believe that. She had to believe she had the rest of her life to make and find more that was good.

Movement stopped, everything lurching like a elevator slamming rock bottom, and as Miri stumbled, all around her the world seemed unchanged—woods, water, mountains—except there was an added weight to the air that was heavy with age, with the still quiet of a place that had never seen human life—and that any life, big or small, was inconsequential under the weight of such endless time.

We forget, Miri thought, remembering all those shards of the past that regularly passed through her hands. *We forget that we are nothing.*

Ren was gone, but Dean stood beside her, holding her hand.

"Which way do we go?" he asked.

Miri turned in a full circle; some distance away, set into the trees, she saw a great darkness. The mouth of a cave. Dread hit her when she saw it, but she tugged on Dean's hand and they set out walking. It should have taken them several minutes to reach the cave, but in seconds—just steps—they were there, craning their necks to look up into a gaping maw that was all rock and shadows, and beyond, inside, nothing but more of the same.

Dean squeezed her hand, and they stepped inside.

Again, it was as though they floated; Miri expected pitfalls, uneven ground, but nothing caught her feet and she traveled with a feeling of exceptional grace and speed, flowing through darkness, through the empty space like a ghost. The only thing that felt truly solid and real was Dean's hand clamped tight around her own, and she focused on that, on his strength, and for a moment thought she touched his gift. She felt energy inside him, a great flickering warmth, and she wondered what it would be to always see that side of people, to have the world stripped away to nothing but energy.

And to be able to use that energy, all that power, as he had done for her.

"I hear something," Dean said, stopping them. Miri listened hard, and sure enough, she caught the sound of a woman weeping. Hoarse sobs. A terrible noise to float from the darkness, and it was accompanied by the clink of chains.

Behind them, Miri heard movement. Dean tugged and they ran, flying, and ahead she saw a pinprick of light, and then closer: a ring of white, like a halo, surrounding a large sandy circle. Nothing else existed beyond the darkness, but within the light, bones covered the ground. Human bones—and some that might not have been human, though the shapes were certainly similar.

Buried in the bones was a man. Miri recognized him. His body was the one she had glimpsed during her vision in the university lab, a lifetime ago. Brown lean body, compact and small. Chains bound his ankles. There was a woman behind him, just out of reach. She was tied, spread-eagled, to a stone platform. She wore a loincloth, though her chest was bare, and on it were words—curling words, red words, hanging like jewels between her breasts. Miri looked into her face, wet with tears, and saw that miserable gaze bear down on the man. The woman said something to him. It sounded like she was begging.

Behind, Miri saw moving light. There was no place to hide. Dean pulled her over to the side and held her tight against a rough rock wall. They watched, breathless, as the light entered the chamber—a light wrapped within a globe of shadow. It passed through the ring, floating, and the man chained to the ground began to shout, trying to stand, beating his fists on the ground. He scattered bone, and reached for one that was pointed, wicked. Not sharpened; it looked like a natural growth of some kind, though Miri could not imagine the animal it belonged to. Tears rolled down his anguished face. His chest began to glow.

The light stopped in front of the woman, and it unwound itself like yarn, flowing down, filling up the air, taking shape—until Miri gazed upon a man. A man of skeletal gauntness, but with a shine and glow to his skin that was like pearls.

His face contorted when he saw the woman. He fought—twisting, trying to turn away with a desperation that seemed to far exceed the threat. He acted as though his life was at stake, and yet, no matter how viciously he writhed, it seemed he was struggling against himself, or merely the air.

But then—a flash, on his body—and Miri looked down and saw rings of dark light around his wrists, cutting close as a second skin. Likes cuffs. Restraints.

He's being held. Someone brought him here against his will.

The other man, the human man, was still screaming, brandishing the long sharp bone. The woman called out to him, but her voice choked; Miri watched as darkness curled like smoke around her face, sinking into her nostrils, through her eyes and mouth.

She stopped crying. She stopped speaking. The whites of her eyes bled away and were replaced by darkness. Miri thought of the dragon's eyes, how the gold had become shadow, a pure black oil, and a terrible dread weighed heavy in her gut, an awful premonition, because she *knew* this, she knew it like it belonged to her, and if this was a memory, if this was not just a dream—

The woman spoke. Miri still could not understand her—but the woman's voice was chilling, deep and quiet and perfectly without emotion, and the man in front of her, the man of light, opened his eyes wide and gazed upon her naked chest, where the words between her breasts suddenly glowed.

He began to read. Miri knew he was reading; his eyes traveled over the words in a descending pattern, and what he spoke was melodic, almost a song. Resistance had died, but his gaze was terrible to look upon, as though he knew something awful was coming, and simply had nothing left with which to fight it.

And then he stopped speaking, and the light of his skin, the light that seemed to have been at the core of him, leeched away in threads and tendrils, rising up through his mouth, leaving a body shriveled, dying—

—and the light entered the woman. She smiled. She laughed. And the man in chains began to howl. He lifted up the bone, raising it like a short spear, and Miri already knew what was going to happen, knew it because she remembered. She felt a pain in her heart, sharp, and listened as the woman—that possessed and black-eyed woman—said a word. The man said another. And he threw the bone.

Miri never saw the impact. She felt it in her heart, and in that moment, the ring and sand, the bones and darkness and death—all disappeared, and Miri opened her eyes and found herself back in their tiny room in the village. No sign of Ren. She guessed waking up had bypassed him completely.

Dean stirred against her. His skin was slick, his breathing rough.

"Jesus Christ," he said, hoarse. "What the fuck? There's no way that's a memory. We never saw that. We couldn't have."

"Maybe we didn't see it," she murmured, rubbing her chest. "But I think we may have lived it."

"Miri."

"What if those aren't memories from this life, Dean? What if they're memories from another?"

Another life, an impossible life, a life that had ended at the hands of another.

He will kill you, whispered a voice inside her head. *He will kill you again because he must. Unless you stop him. Unless you end it first.*

A horrible thought, beyond crazy. Dean would never hurt her. *Never.* And maybe after all these years apart it was too soon to trust, and maybe it was wrong to believe in him with all her heart—but she did. And she knew he felt the same about her.

Dean propped himself up, but whatever he was going to say was cut off by a smell that wafted through the room.

Ash. Smoke. Somewhere near a crow cawed, sharp.

Miri and Dean rolled from the bed and ran.

Chapter Eighteen

The night was cool and the sky held not one cloud. The stars were so bright, so crowded in the sky, it was like having another kind of light to move by, and Dean finally understood how it was in the past, before industry and cities, when people had no choice but to travel at night. Moving by starlight. He had always thought it was bullshit, but here—all around him—a faint glow over the world.

"We need to find the jade before he does," Miri said. "If we put it together first …"

"Then what? We still don't know what this thing does, babe."

"It's power," she said. "And maybe I don't know what to do with power, but I'd rather see us have it than Lysander and that thing in his head."

"Fine, but I still don't know where it is. I can follow a hunch and say it's in the water you showed me, but that doesn't make a guarantee. It's a big lake."

She hesitated. "Could you … jump out there? You

know, with your gift? Just think really hard about the jade, and then will yourself to it?"

A fair question. Dean had been thinking about it all day, trying to talk himself into trying it. Just trying. Now he wished he had. The pressure was on, and he had no room for mistakes. He did not know what would happen if Lysander got the last piece of jade, but presumably he needed both pieces, and that would mean more violence, more risk of harm or death, and he was tired of it. He was sick of running, of being chased.

They made it to the water's edge without seeing anyone, scrambling off the road and down the embankment. Dean crouched, feet sinking into mud. He laid his hand in the water and shifted sight.

The world exploded with light. Everywhere, threads coursing; inside the water, on the shore, in the woman beside him. A hum filled his head, and he reached inside Miri's purse for the jade, holding it tight in his hands. Vision surged, but he shut out the past, focusing instead on the missing link between the stones, the bond that existed where it should not. Inorganic material did not capture energy on its own, not unless the living had been in contact with it. And that always faded quickly. But the power was there, in the jade, and Dean drew on it, trying to follow the same instincts that had allowed him to build that inexplicable bridge to Miri.

Don't push. Just let it come to you. Let that energy flow.

Flow in ways he had never known it could, like actual threads, rivers, waters to be diverted or stitched or bound, and he found himself doing it again, drawing in with his mind bits and pieces of the living world around him, until the light in his inner eye was so bright he felt blind with it.

And then the light stretched, snapped, and he found

another bridge and he placed himself upon it—an act of faith, a leap—and with all his focus centered on the jade, he jumped—

—and promptly began to drown.

The water was crushingly cold and dark, and Dean thrashed, unable to tell which way was up. But then, quite suddenly, he saw light moving beneath him, darting skeins of electric threads. Fish. Many of them—but above, not so much. He took a guess.

It was the right choice. His head burst above water, and he coughed up a lung as he tried to suck air into his abused body. So much for experimentation. The shore was dark; he did not know what direction Miri was in, and he did not dare call out to her.

You were brought to this spot for a reason, he told himself. *The jade is here. You have to find it.*

If he didn't freeze to death first. The water was cold—glacier fed—and he could already feel his limbs stiffening up. He had minutes at best, and nothing more.

Dean forced himself to take a deep breath—focused on his memory of the jade, of light—and shut his eyes, floating upward on his back. It was difficult to relax, but he tried, and after a moment felt a pull directly below him, like there was a string attached to the small of his back, tugging. Dean filled his lungs with air—trying not to cough—and went back under.

This time, he did not need to open his eyes. He felt his way through the water with nothing but his mind, following the pull of the jade. Around him, a pulse—thunder through the water—energy—the living energy of the world, so beautiful he wanted to shout—and he found himself gathering it around him, pulling it into his body like food or drink, until it was suddenly not so difficult to swim or hold his breath.

His hands connected with something soft and tangled—grass, dirt, all kinds of debris—but beneath there was a familiar heat, and he dug in, pouring himself into the effort until he touched something small and smooth and hard.

Dean's fingers closed around the jade. He placed his feet against the surface below and pushed hard. He had been underwater too long; he knew he should be dead—or at the very least feeling the effects of holding his breath—but his body felt strong. Unnatural.

Don't think about it. Just move. Move now and get the hell out of here.

Fast. Dean kicked down his fear and swam, crawling up through the water. The jade felt warm in his hand, a warmth that traveled through his body and rested heavy in his chest. Light cut the darkness—a light emanating from the skin beneath his shirt—and the jade seemed to sing with it inside his head. He felt a pressure in his mouth; a fluttering sensation.

But he knew something was wrong before his head broke the surface; his lungs pricked, a sharp heat entered his gut. He thought of Miri and reached out to her, and though he had no trail to follow, the bridge was still there. He saw fire in his head, a great inferno rising up and up, and inside the blaze a face with its mouth open in a silent scream. Burning down to ash.

Miri.

Chapter Nineteen

Right up until the moment Dean disappeared, there was a part of Miri that did not believe it would happen. That even after everything she had witnessed, that this, at least, would stay the same, and that reality, once torn, would not tear again.

But, of course, she was wrong.

Dean disappeared—displaced air rushing cool over her skin—and the jade artifact hit the ground. Miri stared. And stared. She waved her hand through the spot and felt a chill.

Out on the lake, she heard water splash. A harsh cough. She almost called out to Dean, but kept her mouth shut. Too much noise was dangerous. She picked up the jade and cradled it to her chest. The stone felt hot. She felt hot. Not feverish, exactly, but like there was a fire burning, pulsing, lapping at the insides of her ribs. Her heart picked up speed. She tried to calm it, but all she could think of was that woman chained to the altar, and how she knew that face because it was the

330

same one she had seen in the mirror last night. A
stranger with Miri's eyes.

*Because I am her. That was me on the stone. That was me
eating darkness. That was me, killing with nothing more
than a mark upon my body.*

Miri closed her eyes, sinking to her knees. She
clutched the jade so tight it cut her palms, but the pain
felt good, something she could control—and it was
nothing compared to what others had suffered, all because of this mystery, because of something wholly inexplicable that had taken place in the distant past.

In *her* past.

Wind rushed her body; the chill bit down, but the
heat did not disappear. She smelled ash and smoke,
and thought of blood. She heard the slow rub of scales.
Lysander. Dragon. Here.

Miri did not run. She did not see the point in trying
to hide. If this was going to be the end of it, she did not
want to the leave the world as a coward. And besides,
even if she did try to hightail it in the dark, she would
probably fall down and break her neck. Or at the very
least, end up in the same bad situation as the one approaching her. Only disoriented, exhausted, and probably ready to puke.

Great options. Die terrified, or die terrified and
sweaty.

But the choice was taken from her. She saw a large
white figure detach from the darkness of the woods,
and though her stomach twisted, heat spiking rough in
her gut, she kept her cool, she stayed calm, and she
pretended to have control. Pretended, when for a moment, she thought there was a mistake. The ghostly figure was no dragon, but instead a man. Two legs, two
arms, a very large … naked … torso. All of him, naked.

And then the man's eyes began to glow—golden,
twin points of light within the night—and that was al-

most as unmistakable a mark as his voice, which said her name, deep, and weighed her down—her entire body, heavy, anchored by the presence of her imminent death.

A screech filled the night air; Miri shouted as a small black body rammed into Lysander's face, twisting and clawing and pecking. Miri stumbled forward, intent on helping, but at the last moment one large white hand wrapped around the crow's head and Lysander flung away the bird, throwing him down hard. Koni's small body hit the rocky ground with a wet crack. Miri tried to go to him, but Lysander caught the back of her neck and lifted her off the ground. His thumb dug into her throat; she choked, legs kicking. The jade slipped from her fingers.

Lysander caught it with his other hand. He tossed Miri away and she fell hard on her knees, coughing and gagging. Koni lay very still beside her. She wanted to touch him, drag him close, but Lysander suddenly crouched, body looming like a white boulder made of flesh, and she peered through watery eyes into his wide face, which stretched and stretched, losing all humanity as he shifted into something scaled and feathered and sharp. He held the jade, which looked ridiculously tiny in his claws, and Miri felt her mind reach out to it, felt her thoughts fill with light and words.

"You know where the other half is hidden," Lysander said, and Miri could not stop herself from thinking, *Dean.*

"Dean," whispered the dragon. "Ah, the water."

He stood and Miri scooted back, cutting her hands on rocks. She imagined she heard some distant cry on the wind, some shout in the air, and Lysander smiled. Golden light spilled from his eyes, gold cut with darkness, and he said, "Yes. I think we have played enough."

And Miri burst into flames.

The fire started at her feet, which gave her just enough time—seconds—to think, *This is totally unfair*—and then the heat poured up her body, drenching her, incinerating clothing, scattering all to dust. She opened her mouth to scream, but the only sound was in her own head, and through the roar she heard a voice say, *Do not be afraid, the fire is quick,* and that was just what she was afraid of, because even though she felt no pain, she could feel her skin sloughing away, her body losing definition, and soon she would be a girl without a face, a girl with no mask, a girl made of ash—

And then, quite suddenly, the fire changed. It became something else, something without heat, but bright nonetheless. Energy, maybe. Quivering, pulsing, like the heartbeat of the world was touching her face, and she felt an even greater heat between her breasts, something more terrible than fire.

Miri could breathe again; she could think.

And she could move. Only her arms, but that was difficult enough—like crawling through burning tar. She managed to raise her hands as far as her chest, but that was good enough and all that she wanted. She pressed her fingertips against her skin and imagined lines, words, symbols cut into her flesh, and she threw back her head and screamed.

Only this time there was sound, and as the cry left her throat, another set of hands reached into the fire and she heard her name called—*Dean*—and in her mind she reached for him, pushing outward—

—and the fire disappeared—everything gone—

From light to dark, heat to cold; Miri thrashed, choking. Strong arms pulled her tight against a soaking wet body that was deliciously cool, and Dean said, "Miri, are you hurt? Miri, talk to me."

"Lysander," she said. "Where—"

"I am here," said the dragon. Miri tried to see, but

the switch from shadows to fire had cut away her night vision, and she was almost blind. She shut her eyes and listened instead. She heard water lap the shore, the crunch of rocks, the rough rasp of harsh breathing. Human voices distant and shouting—and somewhere close, an odd rhythmic flapping sound, like wings beating the air.

Dean began to stand; Miri moved with him, staggering. The air was cool on her skin, the rocks sharp beneath her feet. She was completely naked, her clothes burned away into ash.

Miri opened her eyes. Her vision was better; she could see Lysander again, standing near the lake's edge. All vestiges of his humanity were gone; the only skin he wore was dragon, and though she knew the threat, the sight of him towering in shadow and starlight, feathers cutting the night sky against his folded wings, was breathtaking.

This is what legends are made of. Dragons and golden light, magic rocks and fires burning bright. Masks and demons and dances in the night.

And more to come; she could feel it in her chest. Power. Power sleeping, power stirring, power waiting for its moment to rise. Butterflies bursting in her mouth, ready to fly.

"Give me the other half of the jade," Lysander said, and there was something in his voice that seemed off, wrong; a quiver, almost like weakness.

"No," Dean said, and Miri felt him push something smooth and flat into her hands. Its edges were rough. Ready to be made whole.

Dean tapped her wrist. *Run,* he told her. *Run fast.*

But Miri kept her feet planted firmly on the ground, stared past him at the dragon, at the tiny piece of stone cradled in his massive claws, and said, "Tell us why. Tell us what will happen when the jade is put together."

"Miri," Dean hissed, but she was done—*no more, no more*—and if it ended now, fine. She had already been burned alive and survived. Anything else would be nothing.

"Nothing," echoed Lysander softly. "There is no such thing. But now I understand, now the pieces have come together and you will not … You will not prevent me from making the Book—" He stopped, swaying. "The Book … The Book is—" again his voice broke. His tail lashed, cutting the air with a whistle, and his spine curved and curved until he bent over himself. Pain, Miri thought. Weakness.

Or maybe a fight. A struggle for control.

The flapping noise was louder now; a drum in the sky. Dean grabbed Miri by the shoulders and pushed her away from Lysander. She looked up, stumbling, and saw something large block out the stars, moving fast, diving—

Dean shouted, turning Miri and shielding her with his body as the world behind them boomed with the sound of a terrible impact. Screams cut the air—wet snarls, roars, snapping teeth—and Miri turned in Dean's arms, watching in terrified awe as two sinuous bodies writhed from the lakeshore into the water.

Bai Shen, she thought, and remembered the jade. Pulling Dean behind her, she scrambled down to the water's edge, scouring the ground, gambling on the hope that Lysander had dropped it, that the jade was still here to be found. She could barely breathe as she searched; her heart hammered, bursting with each painful beat like it was its last, as though at any moment, *boom,* and she would be gone, gone, gone.

The dragons fought only yards away; water splashed over Miri's body. She smelled blood.

"Got it!" Dean cried, and the relief that swept through Miri made her knees weak. Dean grabbed her hand,

and she let herself be hauled away from the fight. A high keening wail split the air; she turned in time to see both dragons rear from the water, but only one of them—the smaller of the pair—was still struggling, and weakly at that. Miri blamed the fist lodged wrist-deep in his stomach—a fist that turned and wrenched and pulled out something soft and tangled and long.

"God," Miri breathed, as Bai Shen screamed.

"Go," Dean muttered. "Go, Miri!"

She started to, and then stopped, racing back for the pile of feathers still lying limp on the rocks. Koni. She bundled the bird to her chest, her palm cutting open on the edge of the jade in her hand, and ran. Dean was already two steps ahead of her, shouting and waving his arms. She did not understand why at first, but then she caught movement on the ridge above them, and realized that people had come. The villagers, watching silent and slack-jawed.

"Run!" Miri cried at them. "Go, please!"

But they did not, and as Miri neared she saw that some of them carried masks. The air trembled with bells. A few of the women began to dance. Tradition. Welcoming dragons. Chasing devils.

A scream split the air; Miri heard a great splash.

"Don't look," Dean said. "Give me the jade."

Miri handed over her half of the artifact and set Koni down in a patch of grass and rock. Dean sucked in a deep breath, holding the pieces in front of him. He looked at her. She nodded once. Behind them, wings beat against the air. She saw a throbbing glow push against the thin material of Dean's wet T-shirt—

—and he slammed the edges of the jade together.

For a moment the world stopped, everything around Miri gone except for Dean and the jade. But it was fleeting, transparent, and the world returned with a rush and a roar that was as violent as the breath Miri dragged into her lungs, and as tragic as the realization that nothing at all was different.

"Did anything happen?" Dean asked. "Miri?"

"No," she said, shaking.

"Oh, God," Dean said. He bounced the pieces of jade together. "Oh, *God.*"

"This is wrong," Miri protested. "We're missing something."

"No," Dean said. "We're just screwed."

No, Miri thought, as the skin between her breasts began to burn. *No, there's more. There's so much more than just that jade.*

"Miri," Dean whispered. "Miri, you're glowing."

She looked down and gasped. Rising up beneath her skin was light, soft light, gold edged in red. She touched herself and for a moment imagined something more than flesh, more than bone, rising to the surface.

But she had no time for anything more. Dean shouted, reaching beneath his shirt for his gun. Too late, too late—a clawed fist struck his face, knocking him flat on the ground. Miri darted after him, but tripped as a tail knocked out her feet, slamming her face into the rocks. Pain twisted her body; something heavy pushed down on her back and then she was flipped over like a meat pancake. Lysander crouched above her, his breath hot, eyes wild and bright.

"You killed your son," Miri gasped, trying to reach whatever spirit still remained of Bai Shen's father. "You tore a hole in his stomach, you son of a bitch, and you killed him. You killed your baby."

The light in the eyes flickered, but only for a moment; darkness swallowed the dragon's gaze, and he raised his fist. Miri braced herself to be struck, but instead watched as he opened his hand and revealed both pieces of jade.

"Dreams and illusions," he whispered, staring at Miri's glowing body. "I realize now my mistake. Oh, my clever mate. Oh, my love."

And he rammed his claws into Miri's chest.

She screamed. She screamed until her voice broke, until all she could do was endure the terrible pain raking through the front of her body as Lysander used his hand to tear a hole through her flesh. She felt his claws scrape bone, make a dance across her breasts, and then listened as he whispered, "Yes."

Miri struggled to look. At first all she could see was blood—so much blood it was a fight not to pass out. She held on, though, still staring, and beneath the wet mangle of flesh and fluids, she saw the glow, she saw red, she saw … stone.

"No," she gasped.

"I should have known you," Lysander whispered. "I should have recognized you the first time we met. I should have seen that spirit sleeping under your skin."

"What is this?" Miri breathed. "What am I?"

"Treasure, sweet Mirabelle." The dragon leaned close, lips peeling back over his sharp teeth. "Do not be afraid. I will make this quick. All you have to do is tell me yes. Tell me yes, Mirabelle. Tell me yes and we can be together and I will give you power, and together, oh, the things we will do."

"What will we do?" Miri whispered.

"Ah," he said, still smiling. "Ah, Mirabelle. We will open the gate. We will find my brothers. We will remake the world."

We will remake the world, she heard again, though it was not Lysander's voice, but another, older, the woman she had been in another life, and she realized that this was yet another circle, that this promise of power had been made before, and all that had happened from its acceptance was death, and yet more death.

"I don't need you," Miri told Lysander. "I don't need you to give me anything."

"No!" Lysander said, eyes black, teeth sharp. "Take me, Mirabelle. Accept me."

Like hell, she thought.

The dragon leaned close. Darkness seeped down his pale cheeks, curving and floating in the air, light as butterflies in smoke, dancing, dancing toward her face. Bad dreams, bad memories. Miri tried to scramble backward, but the pain was too much and she collapsed. A strong hand caught her shoulder, pinning her down. Claws bit. Miri thought, *I will not be chained, I will not be taken,* but the darkness poured from him and she felt it cover her like a terrible mask, an oily hood.

And then, behind Lysander, she saw movement. Dean. Rising from the ground with blood pouring down his face, stepping right up to the shape-shifter with his hands outstretched. Even as the dragon turned, Dean made an odd gesture with his hands, a pulling motion, and for a moment her vision flickered and she glimpsed energy pouring from the dragon into Dean.

You're too late, she wanted to tell him. *The shadow is gone, inside me.* But all she could do was listen as Lysander groaned. Her vision blurred; she tore her gaze away from Dean, focusing instead on the darkness surrounding her, and she felt it gather, she felt it enter, and she fought for her life.

But she was not strong enough, and it was an odd and terrifying thing, feeling her body succumb to another—a kind of rape, a violation, a horrible certainty that she was going to become nothing but a puppet, a thing, an *it*, some robot to another mind. She could see the strings and they were made of black smoke; she could feel the hands and they were black oil; she could see the face and gaze upon eyes of night.

She fell backward into the oubliette, and she knew

what Lysander must have felt, what so many others had suffered with this creature—falling and falling inside an eternal dark that was effortless and overwhelming and cruel.

Yes, said the shadow. *Yes, you remember.*

Miri did not respond. She did not play the game. Because the alternative was no mystery. She knew what would happen. She had already seen it; been used, in another life, as a tool for death, stealing lives and being stolen, turned into nothing but a receptacle for awful things. Only this time, she felt quite certain that the power this thing wanted was going to be harnessed for something larger and more terrible than murder. She knew it in her heart, she knew it like it was already a part of her, as though the memories and desires of the creature overpowering her mind were leaking into her consciousness.

We will remake the world, she heard. *We will remake the world, and then we will break and bury it.*

No, Miri thought. *No.*

But it was too late, and Miri remembered the woman dying, the woman being killed by the one she loved, and she remembered, too, that Dean had been told to do the same. She understood now. She was ready.

She only hoped that Dean was, too.

Chapter Twenty

Dean realized his mistake a moment too late, but the damage was done. Even as he released Lysander and ran to Miri, he felt her slip away from him. He shifted sight, watched the darkness wrap around her light, and he could not pry it away. No matter how hard he pulled, he could not free her.

Nor could he follow. Dean cradled Miri in his lap, stifling a scream as he gazed down at her torn and bleeding body. Her chest still rose and fell, her pulse was strong; but the area between her breasts was raw, broken.

And … covered in words. Dean leaned close and saw a faint glow beneath the thin layer of blood pooling inside the cavity. A glow emanated from words, words that were inscribed upon …

At first he thought it was bone, but he looked closer and realized that not all that red was from blood. There was a stone there, too. Another stone, much like the pieces of jade discarded at her side.

Holy crap.

"No," groaned a familiar voice. "No, you're waiting too long. You need to end it now."

Dean glanced over his shoulder. Lysander stared, blood trickling from his mouth. He looked more human now than dragon. His eyes were simple, golden—no light, no shadow, nothing sharp. Even his voice sounded different: deeper, softer.

"End it how?" Dean asked.

"With death," said Lysander. "You must kill her before the darkness consumes her body."

"You're out of your mind," Dean said. "I won't kill her."

"You don't know what that thing has planned," Lysander whispered. "You can't begin to imagine what it will do once the Book is made whole."

"Made whole in Miri?"

"Made whole with you. The both of you. The book has two halves. Two stones, two pieces. And once both are awakened …"

"I don't understand," Dean said. "How can I help Miri?"

"You can't. Don't you see? You must kill her, Mr. Campbell. You must kill her before she awakens. You are the only one who can. If you don't, if she binds her side of the book to yours, all the power that is released will be raw, uncontrolled—and he will be there to harness it. He will be the first to claim it, and that is all that matters."

Right. Dean had no idea what Lysander was trying to tell him, nor did he care. What mattered was Miri. Getting her free of the thing wrapped around her spirit.

She stirred in his arms and Lysander made a choking sound, a low weak cry. Dean ignored him, leaning close.

"Miri," he whispered urgently. "Miri, are you there? Can you hear me?"

"I hear you," she said, and opened her eyes. Dean bit back a gasp. Her eyes were black—entirely black, as though all the white had been torn away into shadow and he could find nothing of Miri in that gaze. It terrified him.

"Mr. Campbell!" Lysander shouted, struggling to rise. "Mr. Campbell, do not wait!"

"Oh, wait," Miri said, and even her voice was different—slicker, with a cruel edge. "Wait, my love. Wait a little longer."

Pain slammed into Dean's chest. He cried out, and realized that Miri's hand had crept up under his shirt while he listened to her. Her nails dug into his flesh, ripping at him like he was nothing more than tissue paper.

"Miri!" he gasped, trying to fight her off. "Miri, stop!"

But she only bared her teeth and kept clawing. Dean rolled, trying to dislodge her, but she held on tight and simply moved with him until she was on top. Her blood splashed his face, dripping off the glowing stone hanging between her breasts as she pushed up his shirt and ripped into him. Dean howled.

You know what you need to do. You know what the answer is.

"No," he gasped aloud. No, no, no. Not that, ever. Let the world go to Hell, let her claw out his heart if she had to—he was not going to hurt her. He was not going to lift one hand against her body. He remembered—those dreams, those memories and visions—and once was enough. He was *not* that man.

And Miri was still in there. He knew it. Buried beneath that darkness was her spirit, and his girl was a fighter.

"Bao bei," he said, voice breaking. "Bao bei, listen to me. Remember your grandmother. Remember Ni-Ni.

Remember *me*. I'm not gonna end this, sweetheart. I'm not gonna end this unless you help me. Please, Miri. Please, baby. Help me."

For a moment nothing happened and he was tragically disappointed, but then he reached out for the energies still humming around him, for the golden light of the world, and wrapped himself in it and willed the same for Miri, pouring all his love and all that radiance across the bridge between their sould—that mysterious link, that line that had never existed for all those lost years—until now.

And he crossed the line again, slipping past the darkness, slipping deep into another struggling light. One step. He heard a howl rise around him, felt the immense and suffocating pressure of the spirit cutting into Miri's soul, but he gave it up, ignored it all, and whispered, *Miri. Miri, please.*

You should have killed me, she said, but there was no despair in her voice; only a hard cold practicality that he knew was born entirely from love. *Dean, he's going to use us both.*

Then he can use us, Dean told her fiercely. *He can wipe his ass with the world for all I care.*

Dean—

No, he said. *Help me fight, or don't, but I didn't come here to listen to all the reasons I should hurt you. That's not me, and that's not you. You don't give up, Miri. Ever.*

Ever, she echoed, and he felt her strength gather close and tight. Dean wrapped himself around her soul, pouring light, pouring energy, dragging threads from his body into hers as he pushed and pushed against the darkness. For a moment he thought it would work; he felt the creature loosen its grip, peel back—but then he felt something else, too, and Miri said, *Go. Go back to your body. Hurry, Dean!*

He hurried. Just a thought, and *boom*—crippling pain, blood, distant screams. Good old body. On his right, Lysander's great white hulk lay still, silent, but that was only a glimpse, a distant dazzled recognition, because the night sky whirled around his head, circling and circling, spinning him around the face of a looming woman both unfamiliar and dear. Her chest glowed. He saw black, the edge of a sneer.

"She's mine," said the creature, Miri's mouth twisting around the words. "And so are you."

Dean glanced down at his chest, which was a shocking mirror of the one above him. He could feel its weight and burn. And yet, he could not muster the energy to be surprised or care. So what if there was rock inside his body? So what if he glowed? That was easy compared to the possibility of losing Miri.

Her body lowered itself against him, sliding close. Dean's chest throbbed, his heart pounding as the two stones in their chests hovered only a breath apart. The expression on Miri's face was hungry and sharp—not hers, not *her*—and Dean sucked in a mighty breath.

If she binds her side of the book to yours, he remembered Lysander saying, *all the power that is released will be raw, uncontrolled, and he will be there to harness it. He will be the first to claim it, and that is all that matters.*

First to claim, Dean thought, hearing those words rattle around his skull. *First to claim the power.*

Power that was energy, energy that was lines, lines that he could feel all around him, and that he had only just begun to learn how to use.

And he was still thinking about that when Miri—the creature possessing her—pushed their bodies together and touched the stones inside their chests. The pieces interlocked; he felt them slip into place like pieces in a puzzle and heard a click, a sound that entered his body like a key in a lock, tumblers turning and turning. Opening a door.

Their chests began to glow. From collarbone to solar plexus, their bodies shone with a soft light. Dean felt no pain, nothing at all, but there, right before his eyes, he watched as the flesh around the stones rippled, peeling away, smoothing out under the light soaking through the tops of Miri's breasts, Dean's chest, lapped up by bone and blood, until at the last, all that remained were words—the words that floated on their skin, skin that was stone, floating like butterflies burned red.

And then the power came. Dean felt the swell, a tidal wave from the world—and the darkness reached and reached. But Dean was ready and he took it first, grabbed it up like the thread it was, and he did not hesitate, did not think about the possibilities as he poured it into Miri, a pure clean fire, burning her spirit free of the shadow wrapped around her soul. He heard a scream, and then music, and he felt inside his mouth the flutter of wings. He let them out. He let them sing.

And the light disappeared.

Dean dreamed. He dreamed he stood inside a circle made of sand, only this time the bones were gone and he was not bound. There was no woman sobbing. Just light, just darkness. All very simple.

"So," someone said behind him. "I guess you found another way."

Dean turned. Rictor stood on the edge of the circle, arms folded over his chest.

"I never believed you anyway," Dean said. "I still don't."

"You would have thought differently had you suffered the alternative. You got lucky, Mr. Campbell. That's all."

Dean studied him. "Why did you even bother? Was it

because of that worm thing that possessed Lysander? You all hung up on that because of what happened to you in the Consortium?"

"Partially. They're bad news."

"And your other reason?"

Rictor smiled. "I don't trust you. I don't trust the woman. Together you have a lot of power, but if one of you dies, the problem goes away."

"I don't exactly consider that a good reason for killing the person I love."

"It's good enough for me," Rictor said, moving backward into deeper shadow, slipping away and away, light sliding off his body like water. "And I think you'll find I'm not the only one who feels that way."

He disappeared and the circle vanished.

The next time Dean opened his eyes, it was in a very different place. There was a ceiling above him, for one thing, and he smelled bread and grease and, somewhere distant, heard the sharp clang of pots and pans. Voices, too, speaking an odd curling language that was not quite Chinese.

A gentle weight covered his body. Blankets. He was in a bed. And he realized, after a moment, that he was not alone.

Miri lay beside him. Her eyes were closed, her breathing sure and steady. He shifted his sight, soaking in the golden hum of her spirit, which was wonderfully, blessedly, alone.

Dean rolled onto his side, wincing as his chest burned. He peered down; bandages covered him, some of which were stained red. Dean pulled back the blanket and looked at Miri. She was wrapped up in much the same way. Both of them wore underwear and not much else.

"Miri," Dean whispered, but received no response. Gritting his teeth against the pain, Dean scooted close and placed his ear to her chest, listening to her breathe. Sleeping Beauty. He kissed her, but she did not wake up.

"Come on," he muttered. He needed to hear her voice. He needed to look into her eyes. "Don't do this to me, *bao bei.*"

"Do what?" Miri finally murmured, and cracked open an eye. A bright normal brown eye. Dean coughed down a sob and pressed his lips against her warm shoulder.

"Hey," she murmured. "Hey, is it really over?"

"I don't know," he said. "But God, Miri. Don't do that to me again."

"Okay," she said, hoarse. "I'd hug you, but I think I might pass out."

"We took a beating," he agreed. "But I think we won."

"We're still alive. I guess that counts for something."

"It counts for quite a lot," said a strange voice, speaking from across the room. Dean tried to sit up, but before he could hurt himself too badly, a small pale hand touched his shoulder and pressed him back onto the bed. He looked up and saw golden eyes, black hair cut with silver, and a familiar round face etched with wrinkles.

"You," he said. Long Nu. Dragon woman. Self-proclaimed guardian and leader of the shape-shifters. There was no good reason for her to be here, save one, and suddenly everything made a horrible kind of sense. He was just too tired to be surprised or angry.

"Wendy?" Miri said, and then stopped. "No, it can't be. What are you doing here?

"You know this woman?" Dean asked.

"Yes," Miri said. "And … apparently so do you. Oh, God. This isn't going to be good."

"I'm afraid not," Long Nu said, sitting down on the edge of the bed. "In fact, I can guarantee you might just want to kill me when I'm through speaking."

"I think I want to kill you now," Dean replied. It had been a long time since he had encountered Long Nu. More than a year at least, though he knew she occasionally dropped by the Agency's main office to speak with Roland, one leader to another. Her presence here was just one more sign of Dean's personal apocalypse. He did not know what the old woman was capable of; only, she was dangerous and very powerful. That, and she occasionally ate people. Much like someone else he knew.

"You're Lysander's mate," he realized, feeling the pieces fall together. "You're Bai Shen's mother. You hired Kevin and Ku-Ku to kidnap Miri and Owen, and steal that jade."

"Yes," she said.

Miri made a small sound of protest. "You awful woman," she said. "How could you betray Owen like that? How could you use us?"

"There was too much at stake to leave to chance," Long Nu said coldly. "And I was trying to protect you. If things had gone according to plan, this mess would never have happened."

"You mean the mess of all those people dying? All those people who worked for you?" Dean shook his head. "You knew exactly who was killing your men, and you let it stand. You didn't lift a finger while all those guys were eaten and burned alive. And look at you now. You could care less."

"Assume what you will," the woman said, in a voice so brittle, so cold, Dean's skin puckered up and his mind said *Gotta run, gotta go, gotta get the hell out.*

But he could still see those people dying—feel the heat of the flames—had stood in those flames himself— and he could not abide the idea that anyone with Long Nu's power had known what Lysander was doing— what he was capable of—and not made one single attempt to kill his ass. When Dean thought about all the problems that could have been solved …

"You're a coward," he said.

Long Nu moved. He did not see her move, had no time to shout before she pinned him to the bed. Scales erupted down the length of her throat, gleaming, iridescent. Her back arched, arms extending as muscles flexed long and tight. Dean heard popping sounds— bones cracking—and Long Nu's waist was suddenly longer than her legs, which were not legs at all, but a tail with feathers sprouting along the curving spine. Her skirt rode up. Dean saw green skin.

He felt very small compared to the old woman, a tiny man whose body groaned under the weight of her. Long Nu's shoulders and head were still quite human, but the rest of her rattled long with scales and the click of claws. Dean tried not to look at those claws, but they dug into his arms like a vise.

Miri tried to grab Long Nu around the neck, but the old woman shrugged her off and she collapsed back onto the bed with a painful wheeze. Dean wanted to wheeze right along with her—his chest hurt like hell— but he clenched his jaw and stared into Long Nu's pale wrinkled face, her cheeks flushed with gold, eyes glowing bright as suns, hot as fire. He said, "Stop it. Stop it right now."

"No," she said. "I want you to listen to me. I want you to hear every word I have to say. I want you to look into my eyes and understand what these people meant to me, and how I would have done *anything* keep them safe. Given up my life, if I could have. But I made a promise, Dean Campbell, a very long time ago, *and there are some things I am not allowed to break.*"

He listened. He looked into her blazing inhuman eyes as she spoke, and he believed her. He could not help himself. But he thought, *It still doesn't make it right.*

And as her gaze faltered he felt something move within his heart, a twist, a gathering of golden energy like a spring loosed. Long Nu's hands flew off his body and she fell back with a low cry, hunched within her coiled tail so that only her shoulders and face were visible. Looking at her body, caught in that half-light between animal and woman, was like seeing an image from a dream—a dream too bizarre to come true, and yet, there. There.

"You fight dirty," Dean said. His chest hurt; his entire body tingled.

"You make it very difficult to do anything else," Long Nu said. "Impossible, even."

She uncurled her body and, within moments, under a cloud of gold, was human again. Her blouse was torn, gaping, as was her skirt. Dragon bodies, not meant for human clothing. Long Nu did not seem to notice her nudity. She stared at Dean and Miri, who clutched at each other's hands like lifelines. He wanted to ask Miri how she was doing, but he figured he already knew the answer.

"Will you listen to me?" Long Nu asked them. "Will you listen without fighting?"

"Owen," Miri said. "Tell me about him first."

"Owen is safe. I have been taking personal care of him, Mirabelle. He is very dear to me."

"Just as dear as your husband, right?"

Long Nu's mouth tightened. "I wish things could have been different. And not just for you."

"Where is Lysander?" Dean asked. "Where is he, and how will he pay for his crimes?"

"What makes you think he has to?" Long Nu said. "He was possessed."

"That's too easy," Dean replied. "Too easy, and you know it."

"And I know there are too few of us in the world to

hand him over to your brand of justice. What would it be, Mr. Campbell? A bullet to his head? In cold blood?"

"He killed. And no matter how ... how *guilty* he might feel about that, I know he could have fought back sooner. I saw him try at the lakeshore. I saw him hesitate. If any of his other victims had been given that same hesitation, a chance—"

"Enough," Long Nu said. "Lysander is my responsibility, and no longer your concern."

"And Bai Shen?" Miri asked in a hard voice.

Long Nu's gaze faltered.

"I barely arrived in time to save him. It was foolish of Bai to become involved. I underestimated his resourcefulness."

Dean grunted. "You underestimated how much he loved his father."

"Not particularly," she said. "His father was never very loveable."

Miri frowned. "I want some real answers. I want to know about the jade, about ... About us." She glanced at Dean.

"The jade," Long Nu murmured, and sat back down on the edge of the bed. "Those jade fragments are nothing but aftereffects. They have no real power."

"You're shitting us," Dean said. "I've handled those rocks. There's power in them, Long Nu. And besides, why go to all the trouble of hiding something that does no harm?"

"To draw attention from the real treasure," Long Nu told him. "The jade artifacts do have some power, but that power rests only in their history. They tell a story, you see. The story of two lives, two very tragic people. Everything those individuals were—all that they suffered—rests in those stones. Which, I might add, are not the only one of their kind. There are other sets, even older, scattered throughout the world."

"But the lives you spoke of … you're not referring to the mummies," Miri said. "Those pieces of jade were surgically placed in their chests."

"Yes. That man and woman were mere practitioners of a long tradition, a kind of religion devoted to protecting and celebrating what rests so securely in you both."

"Which is what?"

"A book," Long Nu said quietly. "A very powerful book."

"A book," Dean repeated in a flat voice. "We have books inside of us."

"One book, broken into two pieces. A book made of flesh, a book made originally for only one purpose."

"To kill," Miri murmured, eyes distant. Dean remembered his first vision from the jade artifact, those men speaking of death and dying, of cutting life short for no reason other than just being damned tired. Long Nu glanced at him, a sad smile playing over her mouth.

"Long ago," she said quietly, "there was a man who could not die. He was not the only individual with that gift, but he was the only one of his kind who did not want it. He wished for death, and so he created a spell that would give it to him, and set that spell into a stone. But that … proved difficult to control, and so he broke the stone—and the spell—into two pieces and placed them into a human man and woman. It had a certain poetry, I suppose. What better way to achieve mortality, except through mortals? And what better way to safeguard a powerful spell, than give it to someone untalented, simple?"

"Not simple enough, apparently," Miri said. Long Nu shrugged.

"He had another reason for breaking up the spell. By placing it inside humans, he created a buffer, a way of making sure the power did not … get out of hand.

But despite his … somewhat awkward precautions, he never truly understood the full extent of what he created. In devising the spell, he intended only for it to provide a release. The immense power he summoned could strip away immortality and turn a god into … something else. But power is nothing without focus. And the spell's creator failed to think of what would happen after he died, that by making something that could be used again and again, that it might one day pass into hands with a different vision, another set of priorities."

"So he was powerful and dumb," Dean said. "But how does involve us? Shouldn't the spell have just … died out?"

"Another lack of foresight. By placing the spell inside human beings, the energy was … transformed. Altered by the bodies surrounding it. And that alteration took on a life of its own. The spell … *lived*. The very magic that allowed it to kill also allowed it to create. And it created itself, again and again and again."

"Like reincarnation," Miri said slowly. "But we're not the same people who lived all those years ago."

"But the magic chose you, and the magic imbued you, and the magic became you," Long Nu said. "You are both individuals, both yourselves, except for that one thing, that one transformation, which is not just a spell, but also a collection of memories and history, a repository—much like those jade fragments you found—of all who carried the magic before you."

"Just like a book," Miri said. "A book of … of life."

"Yes. And when you die, and when all that is left is a red stone encased in your brittle chests, the magic will, in time, chose other hosts, other lives, and so it will go on, forever and ever, until there is no more energy left to pull from the world."

Miri sighed. "That's beautiful."

"It's fucked up," Dean argued. "So we're stuck with

this for the rest of our lives? And then when we die, everything that we experienced will just go pouring into someone new? I don't know if I like that."

"I don't think you have a choice," Long Nu said. "Nor do I pity you."

Dean narrowed his eyes. "You might not pity us, but you sure as hell went to a lot of trouble covering all this up. You would have been happier if we had never found this part of ourselves. If we had never found each other."

"Yes," Long Nu admitted. "It would have been safer for us all. What you both carry, what you can do together, makes you too dangerous to live."

"Well, hell," Dean said. "Just shoot us now."

"I would if I could," she said, with such chilling honesty that Dean almost looked for a weapon. Instead, he swallowed hard, and gently squeezed Miri's hand. Her knuckles were white. She looked angry. All those sighs and talks of beauty had gone *bye-bye*.

"You're telling us that we can't be killed," Miri said in a hard voice.

"The magic protects you until your natural deaths, though one of you could always end it early. Your only weaknesses are each other, and that is the way it has always been. Better to keep you whole and safe for anyone who might wish to … use you."

Dean did not care for the implications of that statement. Given the sharp way Miri looked at Long Nu, he thought she didn't like it either. But instead of asking for more, Miri said, "I died once before, Wendy."

"You obviously came back."

"I recently had a bullet bounce off my chest," Dean said. "That didn't happen when I was a kid."

Her smile was frigid. "I suppose some things change."

Some things like fire, Dean thought darkly. *Some things like a hand wrapped around my heart. Care to explain that?*

But Long Nu, if she could hear his thoughts, gave no indication that she wished to explain anything at all—although what she had already told them was enough to account for certain oddities in Dean's life. Like, how he had walked away with a gunshot wound to the chest and lived to talk about it. Managed to even go without a doctor, treating himself with nothing more than a bottle of peroxide and a lot of Band-Aids.

"So we're dangerous," Dean said, staring from Long Nu to the low wooden ceiling, thinking about all the fights he had been in over his life, how things might have turned out differently if he had known the truth. "I want to know why. Is it just power? Is power all that creature inside Lysander wanted?"

"Isn't that enough?" Long Nu asked, grim.

Dean met the old woman's gaze. "Not really, no. And it's not like we can trust you, either."

Long Nu hesitated. "I did what I must. And there is a difference between what is easy and what is right, Mr. Campbell. Think of that before you start condemning me."

Miri shook her head—out of frustration or agreement, Dean could not tell. When she spoke, though, her voice was low and rough. "How long have you known what we are, Wendy? How long have you been manipulating us?"

Again, Long Nu faltered. "Since you were born."

Dean flinched, but before he could say anything, the old woman held up her hand. "Do you think those stones in your chests were always covered in skin? Do you truly think you were born whole and human?"

"Someone would have said something," Dean protested. "There would be pictures, medical reports, a goddamn story in *The National Enquirer!*"

"And our families would have told us the truth," Miri added.

"Mr. Campbell's family, perhaps. *If* they had known."

Dean frowned. "What do you mean, *if*?"

"Your mother was the fortunate recipient of an anonymous donation, one that allowed her to give birth in the luxurious setting of a private hospital. My hospital. It was easy to have my people spirit you away just long enough to effect the change in your body. Before your parents could see you." Long Nu smiled.

"Jesus Christ," Dean said, appalled. "You *are* a bitch."

"Such language. I gave you a normal life. You would have been treated like a freak had I not intervened."

"And me?" Miri asked, before Dean could continue arguing. "You didn't mention my family."

"Because they knew the truth," said Long Nu slowly. "Or rather, your grandmother did, and that was enough. She and I were old friends."

Miri's breath caught and Dean squeezed her hand, watching as a streak of sunlight floated through the open window to touch her face. He saw with perfect clarity the tears rising up in her eyes.

"She lied to me," Miri said, and Dean felt the sting of those words like a slap. He understood what she felt; the idea of Ni-Ni knowing so much, and for all those years—and saying nothing....

"She did not lie," Long Nu said, and for the first time, Dean thought he saw concern cross the old woman's face. "She would have told you the truth if you had asked the right questions. Fortunately, you had no idea what you carried inside you."

"But she knew. About Dean, too."

Long Nu, glancing at him, said, "Yes. We did not know when or how it would happen, only that you would both be drawn together in unmistakable ways."

"Which is why Ni-Ni encouraged my friendship with Dean."

"I did not force her, if that is what concerns you. She

liked the boy enough on her own to take care of him, with or without me."

"What a relief," Dean muttered sarcastically. "I'm glad to know that all the love in my life has been approved by *you*. Speaking of which, that first time we met, up in the mountains after we found Dela and Hari ... you already knew who I was?"

"Yes," Long Nu said. "Though I did not keep track of your life quite as stringently as you might imagine. All I knew was that you were alive and my magic still intact. That is all that mattered to me."

All that mattered. Dean had a bad feeling that there were other manipulations of their lives, both large and small—that perhaps the reason he had been unable to find Miri for all those years had more to do with the old woman in front of him than any random act of nature. It was a difficult idea to stomach, and no matter how many questions he had, he seriously doubted he would ever receive a good answer to any of them.

"You're a mastermind," Dean said. "You've got your finger in everything. Was Robert working for you, too?"

"Robert," Long Nu said slowly, tasting the name. "You mean that man who interrupted the work of my people. Yes, I know of him. And no, he was not working on my behalf."

"He was hired to kidnap me," Miri said. "And the person who paid him knew well in advance what Owen was going to pull out of that mummy, including when and where."

"Kind of like you, huh?" Dean said to Long Nu. "After all, you knew when *our* little buns were gonna pop out of the oven."

The old woman said nothing. Dean glanced at Miri and the two of them shared a long knowing look. Secrets, and yet more secrets. Dean was sick of them.

"Why all the subterfuge?" He asked her. "All of this could have been solved so easily if you had just gotten involved directly."

"Perhaps," Long Nu said. "But my ancestors swore a blood oath to the immortal who created your legacy, a binding contract that has been passed down from one generation to the next for thousands of years. It limits us. It … binds us."

"Boo-hoo," Dean said. "Cry me a river."

Long Nu's mouth tightened. "Fortunately, we have compensated for the loss in other ways."

"With people like Kevin and Ku-Ku," Miri said, as her fingers plucked at the edges of her bandages. Dean noted shadows beneath her eyes. He thought she needed rest. Or at least, some quiet time to lick her wounds.

Long Nu stood. The room seemed very small with her in it; she was not a large woman, but she filled up the space with suffocating intensity. Dean heard footsteps outside, treading lightly up the stairs. Long Nu's eyes flashed gold just as a familiar face peered through the door. Miri let out a sharp breath. Dean grinned.

"Hey," Koni said, giving Long Nu a wary look. "You guys all right?"

"I could ask the same thing about you," Miri said. Her eyes were still far too bright, and the rich tones of her skin were cold, sallow. "I thought you were dead."

Koni shrugged, walking into the room. He stood with his shoulders hunched—at first Dean thought because he had an injury, but his gaze kept flickering back to Long Nu, and Dean wondered if his posture had more to do with trying to stay small, inconspicuous, out of the way of the dragon woman, who watched his movement across the room through narrowed eyes.

But when Koni drew close to the bed and smiled at Miri, his face relaxed, and Dean breathed a little easier.

"I'm a tough bird," Koni told her. "It takes more than a knock on my head to keep me down."

"Good," Miri replied. "Thanks for helping me."

He shrugged. "Sounds like I missed all the exciting parts."

"It was boring," Dean told him.

"Ah. That must be the reason why all the villagers in this valley can't talk about anything else. You guys are legends."

Dean was not at all sure he liked that, but Koni did not appear particularly concerned—and usually he was the careful one.

"So, what's next?" Dean asked Long Nu. "Any more dire predictions? You got other henchman waiting in the wings to drag us away?"

"I believe you and Miri are safe," Long Nu said, eyes distant and thoughtful. "For now."

"Still so ominous," Dean said.

"Still so egnimatic," Miri added.

Long Nu raised her eyebrows. "What you do not realize is that those who came before you had no psychic talent, no ability to reach beyond what they were given. They truly were vessels, and nothing more. But with you and Miri, everything changed. For the first time, there were two vessels who could harness the power, so that when it was released, there was someone there to control it."

"Me," said Dean.

"And the black worm," added Miri.

"Not just him," Long Nu said. "You have a gift, too. You merely haven't opened yourself to it yet."

Miri made no outright denials, which surprised Dean. But then he thought of her brief vision in Hong Kong, of the way she had reacted to holding the jade while in Taiwan, and thought, *Yes. Yes, there might be something to it.*

And he thought of himself, too, of the changes he had experienced in his own gift. He raised his hand and placed his palm, very lightly, on his chest. Beneath the bandages he felt something hard, and imagined words and light and red stone. Red stone that was as much a part of him as his heart.

"Yes," Long Nu said quietly. "Things are different now. *You* are different, Dean Campbell. You can do things that have not been seen from a human in over a thousand years. Do you have any idea what you are? What your potential is?"

Dean hesitated. "I don't know if I like where this is going."

Long Nu's mouth curved. "Then do not go there. For now. Although I do not think you will be able to resist the taste of power."

"And where do I fit in?" Miri asked.

"Wherever you want," Long Nu said. "There is magic in you now. The oldest kind of magic, and it is your birthright. You own it. Your future is your own."

Epilogue

Three weeks later, Miri found herself sitting behind a cluttered desk in her office at Stanford. Just a visit, really. A chance to reacquaint herself with another life—to find out if she even had one. And she did, if she wanted it. Despite the murders, despite the fires, not one person had brought up the possibility of an inquiry, that she might no longer be welcome at the university. In fact, it almost seemed to Miri that nothing had happened at all. Which made her uneasy, but she was willing to go along with it. For a while, anyway.

Besides, she missed the smell of her books, as well as the look and feel of the afternoon sun cutting through the window behind her, bathing the hardwood floors and white walls in good clean light. All of it, familiar and normal.

And surreal.

Her chest ached. Ghost pains, maybe. The wounds Lysander had given her had healed in those first few days as she and Dean rested inside the home of the old Tibetan woman. Miri expected a longer recovery; she remembered every cut, every splash of blood. But she was finally convinced that she could not die. And if she could not die, then it only made sense that she would heal fast, too. Miri idly rubbed the hard spot beneath her blouse. She felt the stone between her breasts—stone where there should be flesh. Its surface felt like skin, complete with nerve endings, blooding running through the words and rock. Organic. The sensation was eerie. Magical.

But she was getting used to it. Much like the realization that she was never going to be able to publish or discuss any of the remarkable discoveries she had made during the course of her adventure. She couldn't even pretend; the bodies that had held the jade pieces were gone, Owen's files were deleted, and all the computers and notes burned in the fire at National Taiwan University. Even the photographs that Owen had sent to the Stanford server were missing.

Wendy, Miri thought sourly. *Or Long Nu. Whatever your name is.* She imagined the old woman holding hands with Owen, who was still in Taiwan, and wanted to gag. Her friend and mentor had no idea what or who Wendy was—nor did he suspect what had really happened during those few days while he remained disoriented and isolated inside a high-rise apartment on the eastern edge of Taipei. Wendy's idea of personal care had been to make sure he did not starve or become injured; not once had she shown her face to Owen. Too many questions, she'd said.

And, of course, she expected Dean and Miri to keep quiet about her involvement. It killed Miri to do so—she had never lied to Owen, not once, but if she told him about Wendy, then she would have to tell him about the jade, and if that, then about herself and Dean and a whole host of other people and truths that were not hers to share. Miri did not care about helping

Wendy—but Dean? Koni? Even herself? She knew Owen—was certain she could trust him—but a promise made was not to be broken; not when secrecy was important to so many.

So. She had to live with lying. She had to live with watching others tell Owen lies. And no matter how it hurt, she had to keep her mouth shut.

For now, Miri told herself. *But not forever.* Not when she was quite certain that it had been Wendy's intervention that had kept Dean from tracking Owen. And if Long Nu could do that with Owen, then it was quite possible the old woman was the reason Miri and Dean had spent twenty years apart.

Unforgivable.

In the hall outside her office she heard footsteps. A light tread. Dean, maybe. He was supposed to pick her up soon.

Only, when her door opened, it was not Dean who greeted her, but Robert. His red hair was tousled, his green eyes a perfect match to his dark emerald shirt. His sleeves were rolled up. Silver flashed at his throat. Miri did not know whether to say hello or scream.

"So," he said. "I've heard things. I sense my job is done."

"You never did your job," Miri said. "Though you certainly suffered enough for it."

"I suppose," he said quietly, still standing in her doorway. Miri stood, too.

"Are you here for a reason?" she asked, uncomfortable. "And if it's a bad reason, don't tell me."

"I wanted to make sure you knew that our truce was still in effect," Robert said. "I am not your enemy."

"Oh," Miri said, not quite sure how to respond. "Thank you, Robert."

"My pleasure." He swayed toward the door, and hesitated. "Tell me, Dr. Lee … what did you find?"

"Too much and not enough." She smiled, though she felt sad. Why? What are *you* looking for?"

He thought for a moment, and something bitter-sweet passed over his face. "Peace, Dr. Lee. Peace would be a most excellent discovery."

It was not the answer she expected, and as he turned to go, Miri stepped around her desk. She said, "Thank you, Robert. Thank you for your help."

The corner of his mouth curved. "Would you like a surprise, Dr. Lee? I think I have one you might appreciate."

Miri hesitated. Robert said, "Look out your window."

Wary, she edged backward and peered through the glass. At first she saw nothing of interest—only students, massing down the wide sidewalks, sitting on grass. But then, directly below, she saw a red convertible, and in the passenger seat a very familiar face gazing up at her window. Pigtails swished.

"Ku-Ku," Miri breathed, and looked at Robert. "How?"

"I am not entirely sure," he said. "She was still in the room when I returned to my senses, and was quite help-ful in the aftermath. A very resourceful girl. I hired her on the spot."

"Huh," Miri said, thinking of Wendy, remembering Ku-Ku in the lab with that gun pressed to her head. "Do you think you can trust her?"

Robert smiled. "Of course not. But then, I don't trust anyone."

"No one at all?" Miri tilted her head. "So cynical. Just how old are you, Robert?"

He threw back his head, laughing quietly. "Dear Dr. Lee. I am older than I wish to be, and that is all I will say on the matter."

Again, Robert turned to go, and again, he stopped.

"I will give you this much," he said slowly. "Robert is not my real name."

So Miri asked, because she knew he wanted her to— and when she did, he smiled until it reached his eyes, softening the hard lines.

"Robin," he said slowly. "My name was Robin."

Miri stared. "But," she began, and Robert shook his head.

"Given enough time, we all change. Some more than others. It is, I am afraid, inevitable."

"Maybe," Miri said, still stunned. "But we have some control over what we change into."

"Spoken with the voice of innocence." Robert's smile slipped. "Yes, Dr. Lee. If it makes you sleep easier at night, you may think that."

He held open the door, but did not leave. Facing away from her, he said, "Let Mr. Campbell take care of you. Pretend, if you must, that you need him. It is the greatest kindness you can give a man in love."

"But I do need him," Miri said. "I love Dean. I've always loved him."

"Then hold on to that," Robert whispered. "Hold tight."

And he left.

Soon after, Dean arrived at the office to pick her up. Dinner first, then a movie. *Indiana Jones,* maybe. Possibly the whole trilogy.

Miri did not tell him about her visitor, but only because Dean didn't give her a chance. He stood in the entrance of her office and pulled her into his arms, hugging her so fierce and tight that, right then, words would have been a sin. Instead, all she could do was hold on, hold on and ride the heat pouring from his body into her own—so easy, like magic, like love.

"You scared yet?" he asked softly. "You scared of forever, Miri?"

"No," she said, and he squeezed her so tight she almost couldn't breathe. But she didn't mind, because it was Dean and they were together, and things were different now. Different inside, different between, different all around.

But good. So good. Just another kind of adventure, hitting the big road to who-knows-where, and she was ready for anything. Anything at all. For a moment she was struck by the fact that she was lucky: She had the kind of peace Robert sought.

"Mirabelle Lee," Dean murmured. "Mira Mira Lee. Will you spend the rest of your life with me?"

"What a bold question," she laughed. "How very cheeky."

"That's right," he said.

Miri kissed his throat.

"I'm waiting," he whispered.

Miri's lips brushed against his jaw, the corner of his mouth.

"Miri," he breathed, and she smiled, rubbing her left hand against his cheek. Gold glittered on her finger.

"I think you know the answer to that question," she said softly. "I think we made it official before we left China."

"No harm in asking again," he said, smiling against her mouth.

She bit her bottom lip, trying not to laugh. "Don't you trust me?"

His smile faded, but not the light in his eyes, a gaze so sweet it took her breath away. "With all my heart, Miri. All my heart, I trust you. Always."

"Dean," she breathed, and he shook his head.

"No more wasting time, Miri. No more. We've wasted enough."

As he kissed her, she felt the jade inside their chests rub through the barrier of cloth. A spark raced; a firework in Miri's throat, exploding around her heart. She winced and touched herself. Dean pulled away, frowning.

"Does it hurt?" he asked, rubbing his own chest. Miri could not answer. She felt those words with their roots in the jade, the jade with its roots inside herself … and deep within, something else growing, something powerful that she could not name. Her mouth felt full; if she opened it, words would come—those butterflies that haunted her—but she was not yet ready to release them, to see and hear what would happen when she did. She knew Dean felt the same about what slept inside his own head. Power, waiting. Power that was theirs, but still unknown, still strange.

One day, maybe. One day, when she was strong enough inside her head, when she knew enough to not fear herself—this inexplicable birthright that terrified so many others—she might just release what was burning now within her body. Let it out to play.

And when she did, she knew she would not be alone, that Dean would be with her, and she with him. Together again at last. Partners in crime, best friends, lovers—in this life and in the next, and ever after, no matter what might come.

Always. Until the end of forever.